"Scuba in the Keys with the proper Merman"

Keys of Illusion

Copyright © 2011

ISBN 978-0-578-09032-0

Cover design by Ginny Fleming

ACKNOWLEDGMENTS

A few people I'd like to thank:

Each and every member of the Southern Indiana Writers Group. Without your voices in my head adamantly whispering (ordering me) with a strong, suggestive "AH-hemmmm...", that I *must* use a comma *there*, but lose it *there* — I'd waste my writing time listening to my "Tinnitus Crickets" and throw all the commas out the window (where they belong, IMHO). Many other fellow artists and writers, numerous, but unaccountable, contributed to this novel. But... seeing as how I'm very, *very* bad with Math... Okay, okay, don't push! — I'll account them already:

Brad R, T Lee H, Dale Y, Joy K, Marian A, Sara D, Dirk G, "Lighthorse Harry Lee/Jimmy C", Kimberly B, Mildred P, Teddi R, Joanna F, Ardis M, Katy F, John L, Carl P, Ralph C, Jeannine B, Glenda M, Bonnie A, Bill B, George & Sam L. — I've watched you all struggle in the fool's game of writing and selfishly used your cuts and bruises as lessons learned. Your success is hard fought, no one knows better than I.

Semper Fi — Faithful Scribes. May your quills never run dry!

Keys of Illusion

by
Ginny Fleming

And to Richard... my love and my muse.

The stranger's blue eyes mesmerized her. He lay helpless and prostrate, a prisoner before his shapely executioner; sweat glistened across his forehead. Correctly reading panic in his eyes, she clutched for a microsecond, overwhelmed by the raw fear she saw. Her resolve faltered ever so slightly. The sword wavered, poised to behead the dark-haired man. She hoped the vacillation was undetectable, too slight for anyone to notice. Hesitation had never before come between Jerri Delaney and the job at hand.

She'd always been proud of her self-control. After all, just because blue-eyed men always seemed to catch her attention, why should *this* man, in particular, warrant a reprieve based solely upon the color of his eyes? *Wasn't she stronger than that? Was she losing her resolve?* As executioner, she knew even a *tiny*

4

shred of sympathy for the victim could prove disastrous for her chosen career. She steeled herself under the hot lights casting a surreal glow over the darkened stage. The man trembled, as if he were a blood sacrifice.

A voice inside her head pleaded the question: *How can I lop off such a handsome head?* In answer to the little voice, her late father's often repeated words echoed in her mind as she prepared to bring the sword down in its final, carefully choreographed, arc: *Men are a dime a dozen, Daughter.* His eyes never failed to crinkle in good humor when he said such things. *So what if their life doesn't always go as planned? They'll be standing in line, eager to step forward and lose their heads for you.* The executioner nearly smiled at the remembered words. After all, her skills with a sword were handed down from her single parent, much like a proud lioness would lay a fresh and bloody kill at the feet of her curious cub.

Gazing into her prey's eyes once more, she steeled herself for the inevitable. The head *would* roll. A dramatic drum tattoo split the silence. Each rat-a-tat-tat reverberated and kept time with the prisoner's heartbeat. Death licked its lips in gleeful anticipation.

Singing its blood-savage whistling song, the katana flew through the air. The sword's falling blade caught the rainbow-hued lights, sending a prism of blazing colors outward into the surrounding darkness like a kaleidoscope. Her prisoner appeared frozen in terror. The colored lights reflected off his eyes and intensified the fear mirrored there. The executioner noted the extreme panic spreading across her victim's face, conquering what little bravado the man possessed. It wouldn't do for the man's heart to explode in his chest. That wouldn't do at all. *Had she taken this too far?*

Responding to years of intense training, the executioner swiftly became one with the man, his dark wavy hair falling to each side of the chopping block. She fancied she 'heard' his thoughts in her mind. She *knew* he saw the sword descend at lightning speed toward his Adam's apple, and she felt his breath catch in his throat. Likewise, Jerri also felt his terror in the realization that he couldn't scream *even if he tried*. Her victim's silent prayer: *Please God...* echoed in her mind.

Simultaneously, the katana met its mark with a satisfying suuuu-whack sound, and horrified gasps, mixed with screams, filled the surrounding darkness as the blood-streaked head rolled off the table, bouncing across the boards. As if on cue, the audience screamed again. The lights went out, the darkness as total, then....

Seconds later, when the stage-lights came up, The Amazing Jerri Delaney stood hand in hand with the shaky-kneed volunteer, both taking a bow to a sold-out crowd of mostly senior citizens vacationing in Gatlinburg, Tennessee.

The silver sequins that made up the illusionist's shorty-tuxedo costume sparkled like diamonds in the bright spotlights, wisps of her short blonde hair peeked out from under a silver sequined top hat. Bowing low, she held the hat to her head with one hand to the crown. Her green eyes sparkled with fulfillment, vying with her shimmering costume, in its bid to razzle-dazzle the excited and satisfied crowd.

Well done, Daughter, she heard her late father's voice in her thoughts. *No one can razzle-dazzle like you, Sweetheart.* Jerri beamed a radiant smile out over the audience, sending her happy thoughts to the heavens, where she imagined her beloved father resided.

The volunteer glanced uneasily at the bloody beheaded prop still rocking in place where it came to rest under the executioner's table. As he rose from his bow, Jerri heard the man say a swiftly whispered thankful prayer for not wetting his pants in front of the applauding audience. He flashed a quivering smile to the diminutive illusionist and dropped her hand to join the audience in their applause.

"Boy!" He crowed, "Wow! Wait until the guys at work hear about *this!*"

Two more bows and the lights again dimmed. Jerri shook her brave volunteer's hand, thanking him for a great performance.

"You were *fabulous!* It looked like you were really frightened!"

"You — you — *you'll never know,*" he stammered. "Everything was *so* real!"

She chuckled, took another bow, and whispered, "*That's* the keys of illusion!" The 'executioner' added a smile in the aside to the man at her side.

A visibly agitated woman sitting in the audience — her mouth set in a frown — helped the still shaky man from the stage. *Must be his wife,* was Jerri's first thought. Smiling at the disapproving woman, she mused, *If SHE'S jealous, I must be doing something right.* Jerri Delaney watched her brave volunteer being led — or more precisely — *dragged* back to his table, watched his table-mates enthusiastically greet him, then she took a final bow before walking off stage.

The satisfied illusionist stepped backstage and made her way to her dressing room, but was interrupted before she'd completely reached her door. Sandy Kersey, the owner of the Mountain Flower Bar, caught up with Jerri before she could turn the doorknob. "*Jerrrrrri!*" the thirty-something woman purred, drawing out the 'rrrs' in her friend's name. "That was super-damn-near-*fantastic!!!* I thought for *sure* you were gonna hack that poor man's head off!!!" As if it were an ocular headband, she'd perched an over-sized pair of tortoiseshell glasses over her mid-length, brassy-red curls. Her large brown eyes twinkled with boisterous glee.

"You were worried for him?" Jerri smiled. She opened the door to her dressing area and both women entered; mirrors covering the walls refracting and multiplying the lights, causing the small room to appear much larger. Removing her sequined top hat, she gently placed it on her dressing table, in a cherub-decorated hatbox, and then took her seat in front of the makeup mirror. Grabbing up tissues and face cream; she took the first step in removing the stage makeup.

The other woman brayed laughter. "More like hopefully excited! I only wish that'd been my ex you had on that table! *And* I wish it'd not been a magical illusion."

"Oh, Sandy — " Jerri chuckled, as she lathered on the white face cream, "you're so wicked! You *don't* really mean that!"

Sandy smiled. "Tell you what — You leave your props out... I'll get that dirty lying scum over here... I'll tell him I've got his alimony check. Once he's on the table — Snicker-Snack!! He won't come back!!"

"You don't *mean* that!"

The older woman grinned evilly. "Try me."

"I know you're joking, 'cause you wouldn't want to clean up the blood." Jerri daubed the cream from her face, stood and crossed the small room, standing before her friend. "Besides," she said, "the man *must* be good for something."

From her seat on the sofa, Sandy glanced up at her shorter friend, and she screwed up her face, mimicking deep thought. "Let me think...." She hesitated a moment. "Naw. I truly believe he's good for nuttin'. Just a pitiful waste of DNA."

Both women collapsed in laughter on the sofa, the older woman's hoots and giggles filling the little dressing room.

Jerri said, "I'm gonna miss you, Sandy."

"Yeah, me too, kid." Sandy wiped tears of laughter from her eyes, and said, "I wish this wasn't your last performance at the Mountain Flower Bar. When I think of all the times you've performed here... what will I *do* without you?"

Jerri hugged her friend. "Can't stay. The gig's up. Quintan Asher, my agent, called me yesterday and said he's booked me into the Outlander Lounge in Key West. Dad had a passion for all things Key West. You remember, Dad and I always planned to headline in the Keys... never got to. But, I'm leaving tonight. I've already made arrangements for my props to be shipped down, and I left time open for a leisurely drive to the Keys — just me and Baby."

"You mean, you'd risk driving that old cartoon car all that way?"

Jerri shrugged. "Baby's got me this far. If I take my time... break up the trip, take it a few hundred miles a day — I'd say, I'll be in Key West in four days. Five, tops." She suddenly leaped up from the sofa, stepped behind a three-paneled dressing screen, and talked over the panel to the Mountain Flower's owner, while donning blue jeans and a candy yellow sweater. "I'll be sunning on the beach with a boat-drink by the weekend," she quipped. "Sandy? You oughtta come too — let Bess manage alone for a few days. That's her title, isn't it? *Assistant* Manager? Well... let her assist!"

"It's tempting. You don't know *how* tempting," Sandy chuckled. "But, right now would be the wrong time to take a break. I've got that big podiatrist convention booked Saturday. Sold out crowd. Mongo The Magician booked for a bunch of foot docs."

"How apropos," the illusionist shook her head, slipping her feet into a pair of bright white sneakers. "A slap-stick idiot performing for a group of doctors with a foot fetish." Jerri sighed. "*That* should be an interesting weekend. Have you ever noticed how Mongo seems to be following me around? He's booked after me at least four times this year. It's enough to make a girl paranoid. It's like having an idiot clown stalking me."

Sandy giggled. "Jerri — you're a nutcase! Mongo speaks very highly of *you,* you know."

"As well he should!" Jerri peeked over the screen and nodded her head. "Any stalker worth his salt *always* talks up his victim. Let's just say, Mongo is one more good reason to run to Key West."

"But... you're driving down in your old beat up car? You think that's wise?"

"Baby ought to do fine. Besides, where's the fun of having a cute `58 Austin-Healey Sprite if I can't drive it? I mean, *Key West...* Sandy?" She left the little shorty-tuxedo folded on a chair behind the screen and stepped out to stand before her friend. "Do you *know* what that means to me?"

The older woman adjusted her trademark tortoiseshell glasses. "Wasting away in Margaritaville with Hemingway's ghost? Being just ninety miles from the haunts of that beefcake Castro? Your next gig? In a lounge that, I'm sure, pays more than

I can?"

"No — I mean, yeah, of course — but, no!" Jerri chuckled. "No. Key West means *much* more than that. It means, I'm finally being taken seriously in the magic world. In the two years since I took over Dad's act, Asher is *finally* booking me in places — like yours but larger — where I'll actually get some respect. Not that *you* don't respect me now! No! I meant the magic community — not *you,* Sandy." She smiled at the thought, and twirled on the toes of her sneakers like a little girl. "Dad would be *so* proud. Asher said the Outlander Lounge actually *asked* for *me* by name! The Amazing Jerri Delaney... not *Jeremy*... not my father — *me!*"

"Congratulations," Sandy said.

Jerri smirked. "That's it? Just simply 'congratulations'?"

"Okay!" The older woman dramatically threw up her hands. "Congratulations, Way To Go, Mazeltov, Lachiem, Top O' The World, Shalom, Skol, Erin Go Bragh — however you want it said. Any way you say it, it *still* means you're leaving. Of course, I wish you the best... but I'll miss you."

"I'll keep in touch."

Sandy scoffed. "*Everyone* says that. Never happens."

Taking her seat beside Sandy on the sofa, Jerri patted the other woman's hand. "Yeah, but I *will.* I'm all alone in the world. My mother's dead, my father's dead, my grandmother's gone."

A moment's silence told Sandy her pensive friend was visiting old memories.

Bringing her mind back to the present, Jerri shook her head, musing to herself, thinking about how she'd been truly alone since her father's death. Glancing at her old friend, Jerri said, "I've got no one but my friends. And sometimes, friends *become* family. I'll be back in a few months for the holidays, because you're family, Sandy. You're *family.*"

"So?" Sandy reached behind the sofa and snatched a tissue from a box on a low shelf. She removed her glasses and dabbed her weepy eyes with the tissue, wailing, "What's that make mah... mah... *meee?* Some weird old aunt? Some distant cousin?"

Jerri grabbed her own tissue to halt the tears welling in her

own eyes. "A sister," she said. "you're like a big sister to me —
and you know it!"

"So... what's... that make Mon... Mon... *Mong-g-g-go?*"
Sandy's hitching sobs threatened to turn into hiccups. "Your bu...
bu... buggy... big... brother?" The first hiccup testified to the
victorious sobs.

Jerri sat back and feigned thoughtfulness. "No... I think
Mongo's more like my strange, touchy-feely Uncle Arthur."

~oOo~

Chapter 1

Four days out of Gatlinburg, Jerri passed the Homestead, Florida road sign. She sang along with one of the golden oldie tapes that always reminded her of her father. Many of the old rock songs were *Jeremy* Delaney's favorites, and she had fond memories of sharing duets, singing sixties and seventies music as the two traveled from venue to venue.

The father-daughter pair had held a special fondness for Jimmy Buffett, and the 'Head-Parrothead's' Margaritaville-brand of party-hardy musical musings. She carried a goodly stash of tapes to fit Baby's old-fashioned cassette player — and Buffett greatly ruled the pack. Now, listening to the happy island crooner, she watched the achingly beautiful scenery pass by, and the miles were filled with joyful memories.

By a slight deepening hue, due to the reflection of the blue-green gulf waters, the sky showed subtle signs the little car was close to leaving the mainland. Jerri reveled in the bright sunshine, sights, sounds and smells in the air. The sun beat down on her sunscreen protected face and her UV sunglasses shielded her eyes from the harmful rays, but still allowed the colors found only in the Keys to come through.

Road signs clued her to the fact she was now on the South Dixie Highway or US-1. Jerri giggled with the memory of her father calling this road 'Useless-1', giving the credit to the locals for the sarcastic name. "Oh, Dad. I miss your silly jokes," she spoke aloud to the open car.

The sky — cloudless, the white sea-birds dipping and

swirling above the gentle waves provided the only break in the horizon's unreal blue richness. Colorful sailboats navigated the waters on both sides of the long, mangrove-lined road, which in reality was a series of bridges linking the smaller Keys, much like a massive connect-the-dots puzzle.

She'd been driving for the better part of an hour — and her mood was electrified. Blues were bluer — reds redder — all one's senses were heightened. It made simply *being* under the deep blue sky a celebration of life.

Jerri knew *this* long stretch of uninhabited mangrove-laden swamp land virtually *teemed* with life. *Just think,* she mused, *a few steps off either side of this road, I could literally step on an alligator's snout... about a nano second before becoming a future handbag's tasty-chewy snack.* She giggled, happy and self-satisfied with her decision to drive to the Keys, alone.

She pushed another favorite cassette into the tape deck, allowing it to loop and repeat. Being a good little Parrothead, and *knowing every word by heart*, she sang along. With Jimmy, life was always one big Parrothead party — and Jerri loved every margarita-minute of it. The salty breeze ruffled her short blond hair. Bright sunshine glinted off her black, over-sized sunglasses as — *in her mind, at least* — she communed with all flip-flop shod, Hawaiian-shirt wearing, margarita-fueled, sunset-loving happy-idiots who dwelt in the lower Keys, if not physically — at least in their fond-hopeful fantasies.

Down shifting around a curve in the road, she noted the little car balking, its engine sputtering and nearly going into an automobile's version of a coughing fit — seemingly not wanting to slow down, as if it had a date waiting in Key West and didn't want to be late. Jerri revved the motor, hoping to placate her beloved Sprite.

Her dilapidated `58 Austin-Healey 'Bug-Eyed Sprite' had seen better days. At one time, the mega-tiny British import was red, but now with its faded paint, the hue suggested the rawness of an ill-healed old wound. With its hood-mounted headlights and its smiley-faced grill giving it the appearance of a grinning bug or

13

super happy frog, she long ago christened her car "Baby". Its engine ran with the tenuous, yet well-worn rhythm of a terminal heart patient in desperate need of a lifesaving transplant, and in Jerri's mind, "Baby" was a live — *precious* — thing; an old friend in a sometimes cold and frightening world. The last gift to pass from her father into her hands, the tiny car was the last connection to the past — and as such, Jerri thought it irreplaceable.

Just at the very moment Jimmy Buffett took his trip to Margaritaville, the car's sputtered grousing and complaining broke Jerri's train of thought, bringing her musings back to the road.

She passed Curry Hammock State Park and knew she was closing in on Marathon, Florida. Soon, a sign at Mile Marker 58, outside of Grassy Key, announced she was coming into the town and Jimmy sang drunkenly to an out-of-focus lady, posing the ancient question: 'Why Don't We Get Drunk?' as the little car drew near a stoplight in Marathon, Florida. The raucous song, which bordered on the obscene, always made Jerri smile, and this time was no exception.

Savoring the satisfied 'Parrothead Smile', she again recalled the good memories of her father and felt the simple joy of being alive. She raised her hand in the air in the open convertible and waved to the heavens. "No more doubts for me!" she trilled. "Daddy — Grandma — Momma! I think I'm gonna make it! Your little girl is gonna to be the next Copperfield! Look out world! The Amazing Jer — "

Suddenly, there was a flash of lavender in her path, the sound of a horrendous loud crash filled the air and Jerri had the fleeting thought she'd been hit by a tank. Baby spun across the intersection and came to rest beneath the First National Bank's carefully landscaped arrangement of three palm trees. Jimmy's question caught on his lips and he called out plaintively: *Screw... Screw... Screw....* Everything went black and Jerri floated away into a soft darkness.

~o0o~

Wet. Heat. Pain. She felt as if a million wasps had slammed into the back of her neck and she'd just gone a round with RuPaul; losing the match in a bitch-slap from the long-nailed, cross-dressing diva. Her face burned. Her forehead stung with wetness. Raising her hand to her forehead, she attempted to wipe away the warm sweat trickling down her face. "I shouldn't fall asleep on the beach," she mumbled. Opening her eyes a mere slit, Jerri glanced at her fingertips. She murmured, "Blood? *Wha...?*"

Abruptly, she came fully awake to find herself staring into the eyes of an old woman wearing a broad-brimmed lavender sun-hat and clutching a teapot-sized Yorkshire Terrier to her bosom. The elderly lady patted Jerri's hand and touched her cheek. "Don't move, sweetheart," she said. "The paramedics will be here soon, and it's vitally important that you don't move. You're going to be all right."

"What happened?" Jerri whispered. "Was I hit by a Mack truck?"

The old woman chuckled sympathetically, "No, no. It wasn't a Mack truck. It was just my Rolls. My driver — *Daniel* — saw you waving and thought you were signaling a turn. He's a basket case, the dear. It's not every day he takes out a toy car."

"My Baby!" Jerri shrieked. "What's happened to my *Baby?*"

"You had a *baby* in the car?" The woman's tone turned totally serious and she craned her neck performing a visual search of the crumpled little car. "I don't see a *car seat* — "

Jerri tried to shake her head, but pain stopped her. "No —

no *baby.* I meant my car! I call *it* Baby."

The old woman patted her hand again. "I'm so sorry, sweetie. It appears Baby... *died.*"

People ran from the bank and from the touristy souvenir shell shop across the street. A small crowd gathered. Everyone, it seemed, deemed it necessary to huddle with the lavender-dressed old woman, as if they were listening to a coach give advice on the 'big play'. Seemingly from nowhere, a news crew arrived, complete with camera and perky female reporter.

Out of the corner of her eye, Jerri watched the redheaded newswoman interview the dowager standing beside her lavender Rolls-Royce. The old lady's hand — the one not encumbered with toy dog — waved animatedly as she described the wreck in dramatic pantomime.

Minutes later, the ambulance arrived, lights flashing, siren blaring. The old woman disengaged herself from the insistent reporter and hurried to meet the paramedics rushing a stretcher to Baby's crumpled side.

"*Be careful with her!!*" she scolded, her tiny dog yapping its opinion, irritated at the rough jostling it received as its mistress nearly ran toward Jerri's car. "I think she hurt her neck!!"

The largest paramedic smiled, reached out and patted the old woman's hand. "Don't you worry none, Miss Marty. We've got everything under control. Things don't look too bad. Why don't you just stand over there beside your car? Better yet, perhaps your chauffeur should make you comfortable *inside* your car. Are you okay? Were you hurt in the wreck? Should we check you out, too?"

"Don't be *ridiculous!!!*" the old woman huffed, hugging her squirmy dog to her bosom. *"This* is the young lady who's been injured!" Demandingly, she pointed at Jerri, and ordered, "Tend to *her!!* Daniel will look after *me.*" A blond man dressed in a lavender chauffeur's uniform gently took her elbow and silently coaxed the senior back to the Rolls Royce.

After a hasty triage assessment, in which the paramedics checked Jerri's blood pressure and other vital signs, applied a temporary bandage to her forehead, swiped a flashlight's beam across her pupils, and asked her to name the President — Jerri resisted the urge to answer: "*Nixon*" — they then gingerly strapped a hard collar to her neck. Apparently satisfied with her answers, the two medical professionals made removing Jerri from Baby's terminal wreckage appear to be choreographed ballet. The burly pair strapped her at three points to a body board, securing Jerri's neck by tape across her forehead, underneath the already swelling and bloody lump.

All the way to Marathon's community medical center, Fisherman's Hospital, Jerri pestered the paramedic riding with her in the back of the ambulance, asking question after question about Baby, while he busied himself monitoring her, until she overheard him say to the driver: "I'm gonna check her pupils again. She keeps yappin' 'bout some nonexistent baby. I'm worried about brain damage."

She sighed, closed her eyes and settled back for the ride.

~o0o~

"Are you sure it's absolutely necessary for me to spend the night in the hospital?" Jerri asked the doctor for the third time, as he took her blood pressure reading. A stiff surgical collar chafed around her chin and a bloody, angry looking, large lump throbbed above her right eye.

Dr. Sims, the attending emergency room physician, who resembled a slightly grown-up Howdy Doody doll, scowled politely, warming the end of the stethoscope between his hands. He placed the little circular nub against her chest and ordered: "Breathe." He listened, in silence, for a count of five. Then he switched the stethoscope to Jerri's back and repeated the command. He shook his head and scowled again. "Hhumph," was his singular comment.

"*Well??*" She snarled, "Am I gonna live? *Ya think?* And *when* can I leave?"

Jerri picked up a faint note of teasing in his words when he said, "What part of 'over night' did you not understand? Miss Delaney, allow us to extend our formal invitation. Won't you join

17

us for an evening of fine dining and posh accommodations? I've already taken the liberty of sending your bags to your room. Please enjoy your stay with us. Here at Fisherman's Hospital, we'll leave the light on for ya!"

"You *do* know I'm a crackerjack escape artist?"

"What? Am I supposed to be impressed?" Dr. Sims chuckled and washed his hands in the corner sink. He donned surgical gloves and moved an instrument tray to Jerri's side. Chuckling again, he said, "Believe me when I tell you, Amazing," he made quick work of applying the dressing on her forehead abrasion, "the *last* thing you want to do is escape from that collar. While the x-rays tell me you have no massive internal damage, you *have* been gifted with a severe case of whiplash, plus a bonus concussion. You're not feeling it now; you're still in shock. But, given a couple of hours, the last thing you're going to want to do is leave the hospital."

"Fine. Whatever you say, Bones," she grumbled and gingerly touched the bandage on her forehead. "If you only knew what that gig in Key West meant to my career... that crazy old bat who hit me took away *more* than my Baby. I'll get even with her. *Her* and her little dog too."

The doctor shook his head, "Your best piece of luck was being hit by Miss Sebastian's driver."

Jerri growled, "Oh, *yeah!* I'm counting my lucky stars."

"As well you should, 'cause," Dr. Sims smirked, "it's official. You've been unofficially adopted by Margaret Sebastian. Or as we affectionately call her: 'Miss Marty'. Since meeting up with Daniel — Miss Marty's driver — your future is secure. You never have to work again, if you so choose. Miss Marty is very generous with her charges. Believe me when I say," he continued, "I've done everything in my power, short of having her committed, to stop her terroristic philanthropy. But, Miss Marty is an invincible force." He paused while washing his hands once more. Drying them on a paper towel, he shook his head and grinned. "Minutes ago in the waiting room, she personally told me to make sure you had anything you wanted. Her exact words were: *Nothing is too good for Jerri Delaney.* Now does that sound like the ravings of a crazy old bat?"

Jerri glared at the doctor. "Yeah — well," she growled. "The old bat's probably afraid I'm gonna to sue her for all she's worth."

"Fat chance," he chuckled. "Miss Marty doesn't know the meaning of the word *fear*. She also doesn't realize just how much she's worth. And she doesn't much care. Money doesn't really matter to her. To Miss Marty, money is only good for helping people. She's different from most other wealthy people — "

"*Riiight*," Jerri interrupted the doctor. "None of the wealthy people *I've* ever heard of tool around in Rolls Royces, being driven by a personal chauffeur," she scoffed. "I'm *sure* she's Mother Teresa of the blue-blooded set."

The doctor laughed, "Actually, *that* analogy isn't too far-fetched. The reason Daniel drives Miss Marty is because he's one of her charges. And because she's in declining health."

"So, I'm supposed to feel all warm and fuzzy about the looney-tunes billionaire who hit me?"

"Warm and fuzzy?" he shook his head again. "No... but, I challenge you to spend two minutes with Miss Marty and keep a smile off your face."

"The Amazing Delaney takes *all* challenges," Jerri huffed. She scowled again and gently rubbed the bandaged lump above her eye.

~o0o~

After having spent a restless, and mostly sleepless, night being awakened every hour as a precaution against the concussion, Jerri opened her eyes to a vision. An elderly angel hovered over the bed; a contagion of soft white curls framing her round face. The bright morning light streaming in through the hospital window haloed around the old woman's head and played around the golden fluff of her Yorkshire Terrier.

Squeezing her eyes shut against the painful stabbing rays of the morning sun, Jerri groaned. She whispered from within her still confused and pain-filled sleepiness, "Have I died? Are... are

19

you an angel?"

Delicate laughter erupted from the elderly woman's lips. "No — oh, no. My dear — I'm no angel!" She touched her nose to the little dog's nose, and chortled, "Basil? Can you *imagine?* She thought *I* was an *angel!*" She turned back to Jerri. "I'm no angel," she said. "I'm just — how did you put it? — *the crazy old bat who hit you?*"

"Miss Mar... Miss *Sebastian,*" Jerri shifted her position trying for a better view of the dog and the woman sitting beside the bed. "You overheard what I said yesterday. What? Were you listening outside the ER door?"

The old woman laughed again, jostled the little dog until he yipped indignantly and Jerri had a brief urge to join her in her merriment. Miss Marty smiled and said, "I didn't have to listen outside the door," she giggled. "Eavesdropping isn't necessary when the hospital is crawling with my spies. Arni simply told me what you called me."

Jerri stiffened. "What's that to this Arni-guy? And who told you *you* could bring that dirty animal in this hospital?" She frowned at the hyperactive Yorkie; he growled back.

"My dear... Arni merely informed me of your opinion of yours truly." She shook her head as if Jerri were talking out of her head. Then, continuing, she said, *"And,* I'll have you know, *Basil* isn't a dirty animal. I'll wager he's bathed more than you yourself... *and* it appears *you* know *your* way around a bar of soap. Besides, dear. *Everybody* here knows *Basil.*"

Jerri looked into Miss Marty's dancing blue eyes, and fought a mighty battle to keep a smile from her own face. *Damn! This crazy old bat's a pixie! A geriatric pixie!*

"Well, well! It certainly *is* wonderful to see for myself you're going to be fine," the old woman quietly laughed. "When Arni told me you weren't seriously hurt, I found it hard to believe him... at first. What with — *after the accident* — you ranting and raving about your *'Baby'*, and — "

"Speaking of Baby," Jerri interrupted Miss Marty. "What did you *do* with Baby's remains?"

The elderly woman sympathetically patted Jerri's hand. "Was Arni wrong? Is it more," she asked, "than a simple case of concussion and whiplash?" She shook her head and continued, "I mean, you're talking about that car as if it was a *living person.*"

"That car — *that car* — was like a member of my family," she murmured. "Baby was the last gift my father gave me before he... she was my *Baby.*"

Miss Marty nodded her head. "I see," she said. "I've had a few *'Babies'* in my time... isn't that right, Basil Rathbone?" She addressed the tiny dog, kissed him, and reached out, patting Jerri's hand. "Feel better, my dear. Baby was taken to a safe place. She'll be given the respect and care in her final hours that *your* Baby deserved."

"Thank you." Jerri's smile was reluctant, but heartfelt. She looked into the old woman's dancing eyes and felt her purposeful icy demeanor melting away. "Thank you, Miss Marty. I may be wrong — *and I may be crazy*, but it sounds like you... *perhaps,* understand a little bit of what Baby meant to me."

The old woman smiled, and nodded her head. "Yes, dear. Now, let's talk about The Amazing Delaney. Arni says you're ready to leave the hospital."

Jerri reached up and touched the lump on her head. She hissed, "Who *is* this *Arni,* and *why* is he talking about me?"

Miss Marty giggled. "Arni Sims is your *doctor,* dear! Didn't he introduce himself yesterday? I swear, that young man is *never* going to find the right girl if he doesn't learn to be more forward."

"Is Arni Sims one of your 'charges'?" Jerri asked, wryly. "Were you and Daniel trying to bag the young doctor a girlfriend?"

A cascading peal of laughter erupted from the old woman. She put her fingers to her lips and rocked back and forth in her chair. "Oh, my dear, dear girl. You are *such* a caution. Bag Arni a girlfriend. What a hoot!" Basil barked and yipped his laughter.

"May be a hoot from the bagger's point of view, but from the baggie's perspective...."

"This old bag-*ger* is taking you home with me."

"Excuse me?"

While she picked up an ornate lavender walking cane and a brightly colored box wrapped with a huge lavender ribbon, Miss Marty allowed Basil to climb across the coverlet into Jerri's arms. "Here," she commanded. "Arni says use the cane for a few days for balance. Open the box and put this on — " She paused while she retrieved Basil from Jerri, and then continued, "We'll be on our way. Daniel's waiting by the entrance. Isn't that right, Basil?"

Jerri unwrapped a lacy lavender-colored gown and matching plush robe. The soft robe bore the monogram letters: "JBD" — Jerri Bonita Delaney. The simple act of opening the package filled the room with the scent of Miss Marty's lavender perfume *What else?* was Jerri's thought. A bag of netting held lavender-hued colorful crystals that rested on fresh flowered sprigs of lavender. The pretty flowers cushioned the bottom of the box.

Jerri began, "I can't wear *this*...."

Miss Marty laughed. "Sure you can," she said. "That's what all the fashionable young ladies are wearing home from the hospital... isn't that so, Basil?" The little dog yipped, turned his face to the girl in the bed, and growled low, sternly warning Jerri she'd be wise to heed his mistress.

"Rocks?" Jerri held up the bagged crystals. "You gave me colored rocks?" *Oh, this is getting really woo-woo here....*

She watched as the old ladies' hand went to the necklace at her throat. The day before, it'd caught Jerri's eye as the dowager had hovered over the scene of the accident. *It's lavender — like everything about this old loony!*

"Not colored rocks, my dear." Miss Marty whispered. "Crystals. Healing crystals. The true purple ones I call my Lavender Magic. They bring the goodness of love to you. Of course the other crystals are good, too — and today, you need them all. For the next few days, I'm surrounding you with... *good vibes*. Anything to facilitate The Amazing Delaney's healing. Deal?"

Whatever floats your boat, Granny, Jerri thought, but

answered: "Yeah... whatever."

The old lady patted Jerri's hand accompanied by a good-natured smile. "Perhaps," Miss Marty said, "tomorrow you'll feel up to picking out a *new* wardrobe."

Jerri's hand went to the hard cervical collar encircling her neck. "I don't think I'll be shopping for awhile."

"Silly girl. I'll arrange for some things to be brought to the house." The old woman laughed again and ruffled Basil's fluffy fur.

"What makes you think I'm coming home with *you?*" Jerri snorted. *What's she on? Nobody's THAT jolly without a little pink or lavender pill!*

The elderly woman ended her chuckles and patted Jerri's hand. "I think," she said, "you're coming home with me simply because you have *nowhere else to go,* my dear."

~o0o~

Chapter 3

The wheelchair ride to the hospital entrance was nearly festive. It seemed every nurse, doctor, or nurse's aide had a greeting for Miss Marty and Basil, and she in turn had a kind word or hug for each person. Jerri wondered if the wheelchair-pushing nurse's aide would *ever* get around to wheeling her through the hospital doors.

Dr. Arni Sims took over for the aide and grabbed the wheelchair's handles. "So," he quipped. "The Amazing Delaney makes good on her vow to escape the hospital. The audience goes wild! The people are awed! How *does* she do it? Must be mirrors."

"Skeptics... you're *all* alike." Jerri snarled, "If you can't *explain* magic, then it must be smoke and mirrors. This escape was accomplished with help from my able assistants," with a flourish of her hand, she motioned toward Miss Marty and her dog. "Observe, how even now, they create the perfect diversion for my magical getaway."

Dr. Sims snickered at the sight of the elderly woman under the lavender sun-hat and her toy-sized pooch, both happily enclosed in the middle of a small crowd of nurses. He shook his head, and quipped, "The last rock-star who came through here didn't cause such a stir. What can I say? We just love the woman to death."

The 'I ♥ Miss Marty' party slowly moved outside, where the smartly-dressed chauffeur, decked out in a sharp, crisp, pale-lavender uniform, waited beside the matching lavender Rolls Royce. He opened the luxury car's door, abruptly turned, shoving his hands under Jerri, lifting the petite magician from the wheelchair.

"Hey!" Jerri cried. "Hey, Chauffeur-Boy! Put me down! I can *walk!*"

"Oh — for heaven sakes, Daniel!" Miss Marty tsked. "The young lady injured her *neck!* Her *legs* work just fine!"

The blond, gray-eyed chauffeur, who looked as if he'd just stepped out of the cover of *Playgirl*, shook his head in a silent apology and gently sat Jerri back into the wheelchair.

"Jerri, dear. Meet Daniel Tiger." Miss Marty chuckled. "The nicest man and the best chauffeur in the Keys."

Jerri took Daniel's offered hand and he helped her into the Rolls. "Tiger...." She queried, "*Daniel Tiger?* Where have I heard that name before... oh, yeah! One of the puppets on Mr. Rodgers' Neighborhood."

"Guilty as charged." Miss Marty smiled. She and Basil climbed into the car beside Jerri. "Daniel is Mr. D. Tiger's namesake. Daniel, dear boy, may I explain your unusual name?"

Daniel touched his fingertips to the brim of his lavender hat, nodded once, smiled and started the car.

Miss Marty turned to Jerri. She murmured, "Buckle up, dear. You've already had one wreck this week. Here's the skinny on Daniel Tiger." The old woman leaned in and whispered, "He's gorgeous, isn't he?" She grinned naughtily and raised her voice again. "Mr. Daniel Tiger was found wandering one of Key West's public beaches. He'd been beaten up something horrible, shot in the head — *If you can believe it!* — and left for dead. The bullet ricocheted around his skull. Thank God, it did little permanent damage; but he had no idea who he was, and hadn't a clue what had happened. But even though Arni says there's nothing wrong with his equipment — *his voice, that is* — Daniel can't talk." She tsked and shook her head. "Never utters a sound. But he's not deaf!

"When Arni introduced us, Mr. Tiger was so kind as to see his way clear to become my houseguest. We had the grandest time, the first week. Found out Daniel enjoys watching Mr.

Rodgers' Neighborhood, just as I do. You know, don't you — Mr. Rogers likes us just the way we are? Anyhow," she continued, "I christened Mr. Tiger and employed him as my chauffeur. And the rest, as they say, is history."

The lavender-dressed elderly woman sat back into the soft leather seat, cuddled Basil and beamed as if she'd told nothing fantastic. Jerri wasn't quite sure *what* her reaction should be. *Imagine! A geriatric pixie with a Fred Rogers fixation!* Finally, she reached out, patted the old woman's hand, and smiled. "That's nice," she said. *How lame. Why didn't I say what I REALLY think? That's CRAZY, you lavender loony!*

Shifting her attention from the daffy billionaire to the back of Daniel Tiger's head, she noticed the good-looking man nodding in affirmation of Miss Marty's sordid confession. Jerri glanced into the rearview mirror and caught Daniel Tiger's gaze. His dark-lashed eyes danced merrily. *I believe that mute Adonis loves this crazy old bat! Have I fallen into the Bermuda Triangle? Is EVERYBODY crazy here?*

She carefully turned and looked out the car's window. *Strange... everything LOOKS normal. Perhaps it's the bump on my head — I mean, when Dorothy fell into The Land of Oz, wasn't SHE the only normal person in a land of loonies?* She pulled herself up in the plush seat, and peered out the window, trying her best to see the pavement.

"What are you doing, dear?" Miss Marty asked. "Don't strain yourself."

Jerri sighed and mumbled, "Just looking for the yellow brick road...."

~o0o~

After a leisurely fifteen-minute drive, the lavender Rolls pulled onto a palm tree-lined driveway that snaked for a quarter mile up to a massive three-story stucco mansion.

At first, Jerri thought the color of the mansion to be off-white, but as the car drew closer, she realized the huge structure was — *!!!SURPRISE!!!* — indeed lavender — very soft *pale* lavender. *Is everything this woman touches lavender? Is she some*

Queen Midas with the magical lavender touch? Look! I think that fountain over there is spouting purple-tinted water! And there's lavender trees dotting the lawn!! Jeez, Louise! Would Prince, with his 'Purple Rain' fixation, love this place, or what?

Daniel pulled the car up to a side entrance and Jerri caught sight of the back of the beautiful estate, and the spacious surrounding compound. She could see the corner of a lanai, and smiled in spite of herself at the thought of a covered pool. Jerri loved the water, loved it so much she'd certified as a scuba diver the previous year. Touching the hard collar again, the thought crossed her mind: *I don't think I'll get in much diving for a while.*

A muscular, sexily-tanned pool-boy carried a bucket of supplies around the corner of the lanai. The young man's fondness of Miss Marty became apparent the very moment he saw the Rolls Royce. He waved as if greeting his best friend. *Maybe this old woman hasn't lost ALL her marbles. At least, she's still got good taste when it comes to her 'Boy-Toys'. Gotta give her credit. If I had the money, I'd surround MYSELF with beefcake, too.*

"That's Cory," Miss Marty startled Jerri. "He's quite the gorgeous boy, too, don't you think?"

Jerri carefully nodded. *No argument from me, you Lavender Looney.*

"Daniel?" Leaving the car, the old woman steadied herself with her chauffeur's outstretched hand. "Would you be a dear boy," she said, "and help Jerri to her suite?" Miss Marty made the command sound like a request.

The chauffeur gently helped Jerri from the car and escorted her into the mansion. As she carefully walked by Daniel Tiger's side, using her lavender cane for support and balance, Jerri leaned in close to the gorgeous blond-haired man, and discreetly sniffed. *Hmmm! Smells as good as he looks! And thank goodness he's not lavender scented!*

Boarding a full-sized elevator, Jerri and the chauffeur rode to the estate's third floor. *Wow! I knew the old woman was rich — but, an ELEVATOR? This is wild!*

She reached her destination, the elevator doors opened and

Daniel led her down a long hallway to the third door on the left.

He opened the door and bowed dramatically, ending the bow with a flourish of his hand. *For a mute, he's certainly expressive. But then, when you look like a young, gray-eyed, Paul Newman, who needs words?*

The hunky chauffeur scribbled a note and handed it to Jerri. She read: THIS IS YOUR SUITE. I HOPE YOU'LL BE VERY COMFORTABLE.

Okay, she thought to herself, *whadda ya wanna bet it's decked out in lavender — Death by Lavender.* But, by the simple act of stepping through the doorway, the room's color scheme surprised Jerri. Although she'd expected *some* purple shade; she found the decor a very fashionable blend of teals, blues and burgundies. *Beautiful! This is beautiful! Maybe it won't be TOO terrible to recuperate in Loonyville.*

Daniel took a small pad from his jacket pocket, scribbled a note, ripped the page from the notebook and handed his message to Jerri.

She read it aloud: "MISS MARTY SAYS REST. I'LL BRING YOUR BAGS SOON."

Carefully seating herself on the teal-plaid couch, Jerri smiled. "Thanks, Daniel. It *is* all right if I call you Daniel? I don't think I can call you Mr. Tiger with a straight face. No offense."

A quick scribble from Daniel: NONE TAKEN. He decorated *this* note with a smiley-face.

Suddenly, Jerri surprised herself by yawning. Covering her mouth, she looked into Daniel's eyes. He winked and scribbled another note.

Remembering her manners, she said, "Forgive me, Daniel. I didn't mean to yawn in your face. I didn't realize I was so," — she read the note — "*tired* — I TOLD MISS MARTY YOU'D BE WASTED — What? *Daniel?* Are you a mind reader? How'd you know that just riding home from the hospital would wipe me out? How'd you know?"

Another quick note read: BEEN THERE. DONE THAT. BOUGHT THE OBLIGATORY T-SHIRT.

Two smiley-faces accompanied this note. Daniel Tiger winked again and smiled.

~o0o~

Chapter 4

Jerri opened her eyes slowly, half expecting to see a lavender scented, white-haired angel hovering over the couch where she'd napped, but this time, she was alone in the room. After pulling herself up to a standing position — no easy task in a hard-collar — she explored the spacious suite.

Opening a door to the left of the sitting room, she discovered a huge bedroom with a queen-sized canopied bed. Teal and burgundy colored the room; the bed piled with a multitude of like-colored pillows. "Nice," Jerri whispered, "*very* nice."

A door beside the bed revealed a massive bathroom; the teal-hued porcelain was embellished with painted flowers and the fixtures gleamed gold. An exquisite fresh flower-filled oriental vase complemented a delicate love seat. Behind the door, a small television mounted into the upper corner across from the spa-sized tub caught Jerri's eye. She slowly stepped into the bathroom and saw her reflection multiplied many times in the mirrors lining the three walls at the end of the room. "This is beautiful," she whispered again. "It's a shame to even run water in such a porcelain Xanadu... but, I'll *try* an' get over it."

She smiled at her mirror image and twisted one of the double washbasin's gold handles. As the warm water ran into the delicate bathroom sink, she spoke to her reflection in the massive mirrors, "Jerri, you're just gonna have'ta bite the bullet and let that little lavender pixie take care of you — *for her sake* — you understand. To refuse her help would be rude." She shook her finger at the mirror, admonishing her own reflection, and continued, "After all, one can't call having a temporary life of luxury forced upon one an *imposition.*" She gave herself a severe glare as a warning to listen closely, and concluded her self-scolding. "Miss Marty Sebastian is more than likely feeling a ton of guilt from wiping out The Amazing Delaney's career *and* Baby with the same steamroller. So, kick back a few days. Let your neck heal, and make a rich and lonely old woman a little bit happier. Can you say '*Paid Vacation*'? *I knew you could.*"

Again, Jerri smiled at her scolding reflection and carefully removed the hard-collar. She freshened up and replaced the brace. "Boy, I'll be glad to get out of *this* torture device," she said. "This particular 'fashion accessory' nightmare must have been designed by the Marquis de Sade." She grabbed the lavender cane, intent upon a cautious exploration of the mansion.

With a curious anticipation, Jerri threw open the bathroom door and walked into the arms of the most beautiful dark-haired man she'd ever seen in her twenty-two years.

~oOo~

"Who ARE you and WHAT are you doing in MY suite?" Jerri pushed herself away from the handsome stranger, though she couldn't help but note the hardness of his chest. "*Two seconds!* I give you *two seconds* to explain yourself," she growled, "before I start screaming my head off! And — and — *I'll simultaneously beat you senseless with my lavender cane!"*

"Whoa! I *heard* you were pretty amazing! What do you do for an encore? Whip little kittens in a burlap bag?" The dark-haired intruder grinned mischievously. "I knocked," he grinned again and continued, "but there was no answer."

Looking up into his face, Jerri noticed his dark-shrouded eyes. They were blue mesmerizing pools — rivaling the delicate color of her favorite blue sponge coral. The man noticed Jerri studying him and grinned again, causing her to lower her gaze in blushing embarrassment.

"You haven't answered my question. *Who are you?"* she repeated, gritting her teeth in a white-hot anger. *"Who are you —* and who told you *you* could invade my privacy? This was *my* private suite, the last I checked! Start talkin' or I start screamin'."

He didn't immediately reply, but gently grasped her arm and led her to the sofa. When he'd settled her comfortably, he grinned again.

Jerri growled, "Hey, Happy-Boy — whadda *you* got to be so happy about? Don't you know how close you came to meetin' your maker?"

"Miss Marty told me you'd be difficult," he chuckled, shook his head and continued, "but, her warning was a few sandwiches short of a picnic."

She snorted. "Woman *herself* is a few sandwiches shy — "

"*That's* where you're wrong," he interrupted, his finger emphatically stabbed into the air under Jerri's nose. "Miss Marty Sebastian is a feast. She's also a good friend of mine."

"I can accept that," Jerri offered in lieu of an apology. "But the burning question *is* — " she hissed, *"who ARE you?"* Her hand wandered of its own volition to her injured neck.

He grinned again and she thought his merriment maddening. *Great! The lunatics in this posh asylum are each more gorgeous than the last!*

"I'm Mark Pendragon." He settled himself on the sofa next to Jerri and she felt the heat of his body radiating the few inches between them. He continued, "I'm Miss Marty's physical therapist. I was told to come to your room and evaluate you."

"Ex-*cuse* me?" she scoffed. "Why would I need evaluating? *I'm* not crazy!"

He chuckled. "*That* remains to be seen," he said, shaking his head. "Miss Marty is one of my clients. I see her five times a week. She had a hip replacement last year, and I'm working to keep her mobile. Anyway, Dr. Sims called and requested a physical evaluation and a course of therapy."

"And, Arni took it upon himself to sic you onto me?"

Pendragon's eyes twinkled with mischief. He quipped, "You make me sound like a bulldog. As far as Arni Sims 'siccing' me on you, that's his *job*. With your type of injury, physical therapy is a must. Ms. Delaney — *you need me* — you need me *bad*."

Her mouth went dry. *What? Can this knockout hunk of dark-haired male beauty read my mind? What I really need is to run my fingers though your hair and gaze into your blue, blue eyes.*

"Let me rephrase that," he grinned. "What I *meant* to say is, in order for your neck to heal properly you must follow a specified regimen of specialized exercises. We won't begin your exercises today. I'm sure you're still bruised and stiff from the accident. But, in the next couple of days we'll start you off slow and gentle." He paused, then continued, "By the end of the week, I'll have you doing stomach crunches, one-armed push-ups — "

"In your dreams, Pendragon — in your *dreams*," Jerri snarled her interruption. "For *your* information, I'm in perfect condition. In my line of work, I have to stay in shape to stay alive. Plus, I'm also a certified open water diver. But *no way* am I going to go through basic training. Not for you — not for *any* army!"

He grinned his maddening grin again. "You remind me of a certain woman I know. Marissa. She, also, has a stubborn streak...." Mark shook his head and dropped his voice to a pensive tone. "Sorry. She's been on my mind lately... a lot."

"And she matters to me — *How?*" Jerri felt a sour jealousy rising from the pit of her stomach, and she wondered, in confusion, the reason for her quick possessive feelings. Why should *she* be jealous of a woman she didn't know? Her natural instinct was to shake the unreasonable emotion from her head, but, before she could complete the negative head movement, her injured neck screamed its indignation. "Ow!" she moaned, and grabbed the hard collar.

"Yes... I can *see* you're going to be difficult," he sighed. "Miss Marty wasn't joking. But *I* was. No stomach crunches, no one-armed push-ups. We'll start off with range of motion exercises in three days. Until then, move slowly and rest every chance you get. I'll bring you a soft collar tomorrow. I'm sure you won't mind exchanging this hard collar for a more friendly version."

"...and just *how* did you know I hated this collar?"

Pendragon chuckled. "What's not to hate? It chafes, binds and irritates," he said. "The only good thing about it is, it's a *great* incentive to heal. Now, take off the robe."

"Again — at risk of repeating myself — ex-*cuse* me?"

"I can't put your hot pack on until you take off the robe." His eyes danced with deviltry, as he explained, "Heat pack treatments don't penetrate thick material too well. Here — put this hospital shift on. You'll be more comfortable in this. I'll wait for you... while you get... *undressed.*"

Jerri fought to keep from blushing, but silently cursed herself, losing the battle. She felt her cheeks burning. *The man's maddening! How can he look so innocent? I think he's enjoying teasing me.* Her eyes met his and she saw laughter there. *Dammit, I KNOW he enjoys it! Fine — give it your best shot, Happy-Boy! I can give as well as get!*

"Okay. I'll go slip into something more... *comfortable,"* she cooed. Winking, she made to get to her feet, but quickly found she was unbalanced without her cane. With a thud, she fell back into the sofa. Jerri groaned and grabbed the hard collar constricting her neck.

He handed her the ornate lavender walking stick, and grinned a slow grin. "Winks carry more meaning with the proper cane," Pendragon conspiratorially whispered.

"Had something in my eye," she murmured. After struggling to her feet again, Jerri knew she was blushing again as she made her way to the bathroom, hospital shift in one hand, lavender cane in the other. *Damn the man! He's exasperating!*

~o0o~

She floated in a warm dream. Christopher Cross' soft music played in the background, and while Christopher sailed, Jerri languished, stretched out on her stomach, baking on a sandy beach. The sun beat down hot on her shoulders and she shifted her position. Her neck screamed in indignation, bringing her out of her mid-afternoon sofa-nap.

"Heat pack's over." Pendragon removed the heavy towel-wrapped thermal strap from her back. Cool air hit Jerri's hot, damp shoulders and she shivered. "Try not to move your neck," he warned. "You're not wearing your hard collar. Now, be still while I give you what you need."

WHAT an EGO! This man doesn't give up! Jerri pushed herself up from the sofa intending to give Mr. Pendragon a hefty piece of her mind. Her neck screamed again and she felt strong, warm-lotioned hands hold her down.

"Neck massage," he said, and she *knew* he was grinning that maddening grin again.

She opened her mouth to protest and he began kneading the back of her neck. The words that were intended to be scathingly upbraiding came out as a weak moan, sounding embarrassing close to a cry of pleasure. "That feels *soooo* good," she breathed, after catching her breath. "My Lord! I can't tell you *how* good —"

"It's meant to feel good," he whispered his interruption in her ear. "*That's* why I do it. Just shut up and enjoy it. By the way," he continued, "you don't have to call me 'Lord'. A simple 'Master of the Universe' will suffice."

Oh, Great Master of the Universe! If I told you to do it to me one more time, would you think I was singing you a love song? Oh, Jeez! Your hands are MAGICAL! She bit her lip, attempting to hold in the groans threatening to escape from deep in her throat.

Pendragon slid his strong hands down her shoulders, squeezing and releasing her back muscles, slowly working his fingers up her neck. Pausing just under her ears, he sensuously massaged her skin in concentric circles. Before she could stop herself, Jerri groaned softly. She felt her cheeks burn again, and she grasped the desperate thought that perhaps Pendragon *hadn't* heard her quiet exclamation of pleasure.

He leaned in close, whispered in her ear, his breath hot and minty. "Feels good, doesn't it? You must be a virgin to the —"

She stiffened, "Ex-*cuse* me? *Why, of all the nerve! Mis-ter* Pendragon, I'll have you know *that* happens to be *none* of your business!"

The physical therapist laughed as he applied gentle pressure to her neck muscles. "If you'd allow me to finish — I was merely making an observation that this must be your first *massage*. Your 'first time', so to speak. You must be a *virgin* to the *fine art* of *massage*. Ms. Delaney? Are you always so touchy?"

Touchy? TOUCHY? Here I am, stretched out half undressed before this gloriously gorgeous man — a man whose masculine beauty causes me to drool — I'm helpless — literally putty in his hands. He makes suggestive remarks about the status of my VIRGINITY — and HE calls ME touchy? Me — TOUCHY? She fumed, squirming on the sofa.

"Boy! Your neck muscles are *really* tight," Pendragon remarked, applying extra pressure. "Do you have a lot of stress in your life? A lot of repressed rage?"

I've got your 'repressed rage' right here, Happy-Boy! But, instead of voicing that angry sentiment, Jerri sighed and silently gave in to his delicious, though maddening, massage.

~o0o~

Before climbing into his car, he folded the small four-by-four's canvas top, stuffed the top under the back seat, and slipped on a pair of black UV sunglasses.

Taking one last look at the lavender house, he found the third floor window, and smiled, thinking he'd caught sight of his new client. Mark Pendragon turned the dark teal-colored Suzuki Samurai onto US-1 toward Key West.

He found the scent of the sea intoxicating and the strong allure of the rippling blanket of water an irresistible force tugging on him as he drove away from Miss Marty's mansion. As the warm, sea-scented breeze whipped through his dark hair, he chuckled, and shook his head.

"Jerri Delaney — " he mused aloud, allowing the ocean breeze to whip his words away. "I'll bet she's one *masterful* magician. She's certainly got fire. Too bad she's so uptight."

Two miles down US-1 took Pendragon to a small key on the Gulf side of the road — an island cove — very little more than white sand and mangrove trees. Hidden by the gnarly trees, an unassuming blue bungalow sat beside a carport. A mermaid

36

stood guard at the front of the short drive — a statue carved from white marble.

He pulled the jeep under the carport and killed the engine. Then, instead of entering the bungalow, he kicked off his loafers and walked to the edge of the small man-made white sand beach at the back of the house.

Many minutes found him falling deep in thought, gazing out across the tranquil water. "Jerri Delaney," he murmured again. Pendragon closed his eyes and inhaled the crisp salty air deep into his lungs. "Jerri," he repeated once more, as if testing the name out on his lips. "Yes... *that* woman certainly reminds me of Marissa. And surely, *she'll* arrive by next week."

A party of seagulls sailed on the breeze, dive-bombing the surf for tiny fish. Near the horizon, a sailboat skirted the water, its multi-colored sails billowed in the breeze. The hot sun heated the sand and cast shadows from palm trees, while a cooling breeze rustled through the sea oats on the small beach.

Shifting his weight, his toes sank into the wet white sand. A small wave broke over his feet, and Pendragon stepped back from the water, as if finding the white foam floating on the surface hot to the touch.

~o0o~

After struggling to her feet and hobbling to the window, Jerri gripped the hospital gown closed in the back and leaned on her cane.

She'd arrived at the window just in time to catch sight of Pendragon. Unconsciously holding her breath, she watched him don his sunglasses and drive away in his toy car. Spying the stunningly handsome man turning out of the long driveway, she saw the breeze catch his hair and a tingling thrill ran through Jerri.

She cursed softly, irritated by the strange attraction the man held over her.

Being a professional entertainer, she'd worked around all kinds of men. Many were attractive; some were flamboyantly stunning. But, *none* — not even *one* of the magic circuit's toothy,

37

polished, Adonis-clones — caused her pulse to quicken, her heart to climb into her throat longing for a peek of perfect, manly beauty. But, *this* man turning his jeep toward Key West... *this man* — was dark-haired, blue-eyed eye-candy, and she deeply resented the attraction she felt for the man.

"I don't need this," Jerri grumbled. "Like Dad always said: *I need a man in my life like a fish needs a bicycle.* What right does *that* man have to be so damn gorgeous? And who does he think he *is* telling me I remind him of another woman — *a stubborn woman,* for pity's sake. Marissa, indeed. *Marissa this — Pendragon."* She traced a crude gesture in the air and angrily stamped the cane on the floor. Then she made her way with cautious steps toward the bathroom, intent upon changing back into her lavender gown and robe.

"I think it's time I gave Miss Marty a polite piece of my mind," she growled, "because *some* of her pretty-boys have a definite attitude." Nodding her head to agree with herself, the neck injury reminded Jerri of her limitations. She put her hand to the brace to calm her screaming ligaments, and allowed the opened-back hospital gown to drop to the floor. Habit caused her to bend, intending to retrieve the gown, but her still protesting neck halted her mid-reach. "I'll leave it there," Jerri said. "The more I pamper my neck, the sooner I'll get rid of Happy-Boy."

Dressing slowly, she murmured, "It's a good day for a walkabout. Better stop by the kitchen and pack supplies for a three day's journey...we all know what happened to the passengers of the ill-fated S.S. Minnow — and this *is* a huge mansion." Her hand on the doorknob, she grinned. "Maybe I'd better drop bread crumbs so I can find my way back." She left the suite and walked into a cane-aided fun-house tour.

~o0o~

Chapter 5

Going from room to room, Jerri discovered the nine suites she'd found so far were all tastefully decorated, as if Miss Marty had hired a whole team of talented interior decorators. Then, the last door at the end of the long hallway opened to an *explosion* of lavenders....

"Bingo," she smiled, peering around the door. "I think I've found the cuckoo's nest." Quickly, but politely backing out of the room, she pointed to the elevator at the end of the hallway, and cried out, in imitation of Captain James T. Kirk: "To boldly go where no *sane* person has gone before!" Carefully cane-stepping her way to the elevator door, which bore a large silver and very ornate "M-L-S" monogram — *Margaret L. Sebastian* — Jerri silently nodded.

Inside the elevator, she pushed the second-floor button and muttered a rambling rant, "Beam me up, Scotty! Or more precisely — beam me down! To mix a few more Sci-Fi metaphors — the silly lavender natives of this planet have had one too many Pan-Galactic-Gargle-Blasters — *and me without my towel.*"

The elevator door opened, and Jerri leaned out into the hallway. "Mr. Spock," she muttered, "send in the red-shirted yeoman. You know... the crewman who always 'bites it' early on? We'll throw *him* to the Lavender Loonies and — " Happy noises down the hall interrupted her silly, sarcastic rambling, and Jerri cane-tapped her way to the source of the pixie-like laughter.

Daniel, Basil and Miss Marty sat together on a lavender-leather sofa. On the nearly wall-sized television; Fred Rogers sent the trolley around the track to the Neighborhood of Make-Believe. Miss Marty clapped her hands, while Daniel beamed, completely enjoying his benefactress' glee. Computers, multiple vending machines — accompanied by art glass bowls filled to the brim with quarters, video games, and old-fashioned pinball machines filled the huge room. A Peter Max-ish mural covered the far wall; its cheerful logo borrowing the chorus line from the famous Bobby McFerrin song: "Don't Worry; Be Happy!"

"Golly, Toto!" Jerri whispered, "I don't think we're in *Kansas* any more."

As if she'd overheard her remark, Miss Marty turned to her incapacitated guest and chirped, "Jerri, dear girl!" The jolly senior patted the sofa between herself and her chauffeur. "Join us! Take a load off and soak in the Tao of Fred. It seems, Lady Elaine Fairchilde is picking on King Friday *again*. Oh, the trouble that snippy little woman causes." The old billionaire tsked, shook her head, kissed her dog, and again patted the sofa.

Daniel made room for Jerri and pantomimed the trolley car taking Fred Rodgers' young viewers into the Neighborhood of Make-Believe.

Jerri glanced from her lavender-dressed hostess to the silent, but expressive chauffeur. *Well... if you can't FLY over the cuckoo's nest,* she thought, *then I suppose the next best thing is join them on the sofa like a good little loony-bird.*

"Room for one more in the Neighborhood?" Jerri smiled at the uniformed Daniel, and watched as he extended his hand to assist her to the couch.

Carefully lowering herself to the cushion and settling in beside the blond Rolls driver, she immediately noted the hardness of his thigh resting against her hip. Jerri grimaced as the warmth radiating through Daniel's formfitting lavender slacks brought a memory of erotic sensation to mind, and she cursed silently, thinking back to Miss Marty's physical therapist's masterful touch, knowing the maddening man had brought long denied desires to the surface. As the familiar puppets interacted on the television show, thoughts of Pendragon mingled with the warmth of Daniel

Tiger's thigh and soon Jerri feared she'd always and forevermore connect "The Neighborhood" with some very un-Fred Rogers-like emotions.

Oh, it's a BEA-U-TIFUL day in the neighborhood, Jerri groaned to herself. *Here I am watching a wonderful, saintly man — whom I admired very much — and all I can think of is the magic in Pendragon's hands and the way he made me feel — And the gorgeous man sitting beside me.... Oh — Forgive me, Saint Fred. I've committed a sacrilege and I'm GONNA BURN IN HELL!*

Lady Elaine Fairchilde tormented the other puppets in the Neighborhood until Trolley returned to Mr. Rogers and his wise summation. As the credits rolled, Jerri sighed and shifted in her seat, still feeling the guilt left over from her thoughts of Pendragon.

Clicking the giant screen to black, Miss Marty chuckled, and quipped, "I'll wager, you think Daniel and I are total loons."

Jerri jerked, jarring her injured neck. She covered up her surprise of the old lady's psychic wondering by grabbing the hard collar and groaning. "No!" she lied. "No, Miss Marty. Total *loons?* I never thought any such thing. Fred Rogers was tops in my book, too."

The old lady shook her head. "Jerri, dear girl. I believe you're missing the point by about a mile and a half. It's not so much the puppets and the Neighborhood... it's Mr. Rodgers' philosophy. The little jewels he shares with his tiny audience are *really* profound, at times. *If* you open your ears *and* your soul to the man's words, you'd be surprised at what the man is saying. At what the man is *really* saying."

"Well — " Jerri screwed up her face, "if I'm reading the man correctly — today, he said — and I'm paraphrasing here, *mind you* — he said sometimes... Lady Elaine Fairchilde can be a little poopy-head. When King Friday XIII wanted to declare a special day for Daniel Striped Tiger, Lady Elaine stepped in and screwed up the works. And all the king wanted to do was to make Daniel Tiger feel a little bit better and — "

"She's got it!" the old lady crowed to her Yorkie and her bemused chauffeur. "By George! I *think* she's got it!"

"Ex-*cuse* me?" Jerri chuckled.

"Don't you see?" Miss Marty beamed. "All King Friday wanted to do was to make Daniel Tiger feel a little bit better. And isn't that *really* all we can do in this life? Make our fellow 'Tigers' feel just a *little* bit better?"

She gazed into the old woman's dancing eyes. "Sure," Jerri began, "I *guess* you could say that, but — "

"No buts about it," Miss Marty interrupted, patting Jerri's knee. "None of us are born onto this Earth as a solitary creature. We're *all* God's children, one way or another, no matter how you address the All-Powerful. More simply put, we're not in this mess alone. Every morning, you should ask yourself: What can I do today to help my fellow 'Tigers'? Now, perhaps you'll say: Miss Marty, that's easy for *you* to say, what with all your millions and billions. And I say: *donkey waffles.* Anyone can help another person in some little way." The lavender-dressed senior paused for her injured guest to digest the synopsis of her unusual life philosophy.

As best as her damaged neck allowed, Jerri swiveled to face the pixieish woman. "So what turned *you* into Florida's version of Mother Teresa?"

Daniel shook his head in mock exasperation, took his notebook from his uniform vest pocket and scribbled a short message before handing it over to Miss Marty.

"That's all right, sweetie," she told the chauffeur. "I know you've heard my story before. *Many* times before. You go ahead and take the car into the body shop. Jerri and I will spend the day getting to know one another better." She chuckled again, and shook her head. "Florida's Mother Teresa, indeed."

Daniel took his leave and Miss Marty stood up, crossed the room and inserted coins into a juice machine. "How about some liquid Vitamin 'C'?" The old woman poised her finger over the choice buttons. "I warn you: This is going to be a long story. You'll need all the 'C' you can get."

42

"Ruby grapefruit juice, if you have it," Jerri said. She chuckled at the image of the old lady standing at the colorful metal and plastic box. "You get your juice from a *vending machine?*"

"Think of it as a healthy, good for you, piggy bank," Miss Marty said, poking the buttons and retrieving two juices.

"Of course," Jerri murmured, taking the offered grapefruit juice. "Naturally. Living in this grand mansion, you *would* keep your juice in a *vending machine.*"

The scent of lavender wafted off Miss Marty as she again took her seat beside Jerri. "I purchase the juice outright and send the change I save to the local food bank." She popped the top on an orange juice can and continued, "What can I say? I *enjoy* punching the buttons and it creates a job market for Paul down at Murphy's Vending. And in the end, it feeds a lot of people. See? You can help your fellow 'Tigers' and have fun at the same time."

Jerri smiled and took a sip of her grapefruit juice. She searched the older woman's face for any sign of senility, hoping to explain away Miss Marty's strange ravings, but all she found was sincerity. Quietly chuckling, Jerri mentally threw up her hands. *I give up — if she's nuts, she'd only be better with a little salt.* She grinned at the senior sitting beside her and quipped: "You know? *Somehow* it fits. Now... you were going to fill me in on your reasons for following the Tao of Fred?"

"Let's just say," the old woman began, "I've seen the evil *and* the good in people. If good people don't keep vigilant, evil prevails. Helping people is just my way of evening out the odds."

"So, you've always been easy?"

Miss Marty smiled and shook her head. She chuckled softly, *"Easy?* Oh — my Eddie would have laughed at *that.*"

"Eddie? Your son?"

A cloud crossed over the old lady's face and she lowered her voice. "No... I never had... children," she said. A moment's silence hung in the air between the two women.

"But," Jerri murmured, "didn't you once tell me you'd had a lot of babies in your lifetime?"

Miss Marty sighed and smiled sadly. "I meant... I could understand how you could grow close to an inanimate object like *your* Baby. No. Eddie wasn't my son. Eddie was my — "

"Señorita Marty," the maid interrupted. "Señor Grüber is to see you. He says is muy-muy urgent. I show him in now? Sí?"

"Dolf?" The old lady stood and smoothed her lacy lavender dress. "Yes! Yes, Conchita. By all means! Show him in!" The maid left and Miss Marty turned to Jerri again. *"Every* meeting is an *urgent* meeting to Dolf. But, the man's so handsome, I really don't mind."

The tall blond man's machine-gun delivery began immediately as he crossed the threshold. "Miss Marty — " he blurted, "so good to see you this fine morning. Listen — we need to go over a few items in your portfolio. I've *got* to get word back to the Wentworth Foundation by three o'clock. May we go into your office? ...oh... Oh! I'm sorry!" He paused, as if he just realized his client wasn't alone in the room. "You were having a visit with this lovely young lady, and I just barged right in!" He offered his hand to Jerri. "Allow me to apologize for my atrocious manners and introduce myself, properly," he said. *"I'm* Dolf Grüber."

"Jerri, this exuberant ball of kinetic energy is my accountant," Miss Marty giggled. "Dolf, this is The Amazing Delaney — Magician and Escape Artist Extraordinaire!"

"Pleased to meet you, Miss Delaney." He brought Jerri's hand to his lips with a gallant gesture causing a quick blush to rush to her cheeks.

The man's model-gorgeous, just like Pendragon, only on the other end of the coloring spectrum. Grüber was as blond as the physical therapist was dark. His gold-flecked green eyes hinted at an Irish-Gaelic heritage. Well-manicured fingers and blinding white teeth testified to a self-assurance that translated to an appealing personality. Jerri sensed the man was well aware of his good looks, but carried enough poise not to appear overly vain.

Her mouth went dry and she swallowed, trying to rid her

throat of the tiny green amphibian snuggled in the 100% cotton sock.

"Jer... Jerri, please," she stammered. *Is it my concussion? Is it the water down here? Is there a checkpoint in Miami that bans ordinary looking men from the Keys? This man is a demigod! If I stay here much longer — someone's gonna have to hose me down!*

"Jerri." Grüber's smile was disarming. "*So* pleased to meet you. I'd heard rumors a beautiful magician was recuperating on the grounds. What happened? Did one of your smoke and flash mirror tricks prove too solid?"

Jerri smirked with a good-natured chuckle. "Nothing so exciting. A lavender Rolls Royce wanted to be in the same spot as my car. Big car bites; little car buys the farm."

"I see," he laughed. "Well, at least you weren't seriously injured. And there's another bonus point."

"Which is?"

"Lavender is *truly* your color." He laughed once more, and Jerri was totally charmed. "It brings out the fire in your eyes."

She blushed again and giggled. "My, my. Your Irish is showing, Mr. Grüber. It's clear *you've* been kissing the Blarney Stone."

"If I've leprechaun in my blood," he quipped, "it's news to my German-speaking father. We Grübers are *strictly* Teutonic. *Our* genetic brew *isn't* watered down."

The thought flashed through Jerri's mind: *Surely, he doesn't mean it quite like THAT... Besides... GREEN eyes? I'd say something other than hops got into the "brew".*

Miss Marty interrupted, "Dolf? Let's go into the office and take care of this. It's too pretty a day to spend a lot of time on business. Will you excuse us, Jerri, dear?"

"Surely." Jerri got to her feet. "I'll just take a walk outside and get some sun. It's time I took in some of the local sights."

Grüber took her hand again and kissed it gently. "Hopefully," he said, "when you've recovered, you'll allow me to show you the Keys. When do you next see the doctor?"

"I'm hoping he'll spring me from this mousetrap in about two weeks."

"Then the minute you're released from that neck brace, we'll do Key West, you and I. We've got a date for your first Freedom-Friday — deal?" He flashed his too-cute dimples and grinned.

"That's not necessary — really... I...."

"*Necessary?* You make it sound as if taking you out would be a chore," he laughed. "Believe me when I say, when I take you to the Outlander Lounge it will be *anything* but a chore."

"The Outlander?" Jerri paused at the doorway. "Starting this weekend, I was supposed to headline at the Outlander. According to my agent, when he called to tell them I was laid-up, they were bummed big time. They'd booked "The Amazing Delaney — Escape Artist Extraordinaire". But it looks like the only thing I'm going to escape is this Chinese puzzle of a hard collar — that is, if I'm a good girl and do everything my whip-cracking trainer tells me."

"Trainer?" He shook his head in confusion.

"That's Jerri's sarcastic way of describing her physical therapist," the old lady smiled. "Mark Pendragon's just one of the hardships of recovery. Right, Jerri?"

"*Riiight...*" Jerri turned and headed toward the elevator, waving her farewell over her shoulder. As she walked, she ranted, hissing as she took Pendragon's name in vain. "Hardship is a *great* description of Pendragon. I'd be surprised if his *middle name* isn't Hardship. Famine and Pestilence are probably his siblings. Man ought'a have a Hazardous-Zone sign hung around his neck. Better yet, the man ought'a be hung by the throat, *dangling* from a Hazardous-Zone sign...." All the while, she continued her muttered grousing, boarding the elevator for the first floor.

~o0o~

Chapter 6

Daniel found Jerri strolling — *with lavender cane* — around the pool. He mimed a genial 'hello' and scribbled a quick note informing her of a late lunch served in the formal dining room, then the chauffeur offered his arm in an expressive sweep.

Jerri quipped, "Aren't you supposed to show me to a pumpkin-carriage pulled by a team of tuxedoed mice?" She laced her arm through his. Daniel grinned and touched the end of Jerri's nose in a 'you're-so-funny' gesture.

"And while you've 'got my nose'," Jerri teased, "may I ask a personal question?"

Daniel's quick notation was his reply: FIRE AWAY.

"First, I've gotta confess... I was snooping around. I musta' peeked in over four hundred and seventy-five sitting rooms."

Daniel scribbled: AREN'T YOU EXAGGERATING JUST A TAD??

She chuckled. "Okay. You're right. Just a tad." The two paused outside the rear door and Jerri continued, "Anyhow — I poked my head into a very masculine sitting room that had some marvelous Native American artifacts and a curio cabinet lit up like a Christmas tree. *All the marbles!* I just gotta know — are they yours?"

The hunky chauffeur smiled and once again scribbled in his notepad: YES. GUILTY AS CHARGED. THE MARBLES <u>ARE</u> MINE. MISS MARTY THOUGHT A HOBBY WOULD AID IN MY RECOVERY. IT'S FRUSTRATING NOT BEING ABLE TO TALK. SO, I READ AND MANAGE MY MARBLE COLLECTION.

After she'd read Daniel's note, Jerri looked up into his face. "Yes. It must be hard dealing with... what do they call it?"

Another note: APHASIA.

Jerri nodded her head. "Aphasia. That must be hard."

IT'S ROUGH SOMETIMES. BUT MISS MARTY "RESCUED" ME. AND DR. SIMS HELPS ME OVER THE ROUGH SPOTS. YOU KNOW WHAT THEY SAY — I GET BY WITH A LIL' HELP FROM MY FRIENDS.

"The gospel according to Lennon and McCartney."

YUP. I'D BE HAPPY TO SHOW YOU MY COLLECTION ANY EVENING. BUT NOW — YOUR PUMPKIN CARRIAGE AWAITS.

He punctuated the last of the note with a smiley-face.

"Oh, pooh!" Jerri patted Daniel's lavender-clad sleeve and accompanied him into the mansion. She whispered, "And me without my glass slippers...."

~o0o~

She found the formal dining table set with fine china, finger sandwiches and tea biscuits at the ready. Daniel showed Jerri to her seat between the pool-boy and a plumpish lavender-uniformed woman, and then seated himself on the other side of a prim-looking young woman in a — *lavender* — power-suit. Suddenly, Miss Marty pushed through the kitchen doors carrying a tray laden with a delicate English bone-china tea set.

"Tea-time!" Miss Marty trilled, placing the hot teapot in front of the young magician. She paused and indicated Jerri with a turn of her hand. "*This,* my dear family, is The Amazing Delaney. Known to her friends as Jerri. I'm afraid I've had a hand in sidelining Amazing. Her professional costume isn't usually a robe and hard collar. But, no matter *how* she came to us — welcome, Jerri."

Jerri's eyes flew around the table. *Oh-Oh! Must'a fallen down the rabbit hole! I wonder when the perpetually late White Rabbit'll hop up to the table. If this Lavender Loony starts yelling "Off with her head!!" — I'm SOOO outta here! Well, Alice — one sip makes you bigger, and one sip makes you small.* Jerri smiled, as the elderly lady seated herself at the head of the table and then nodded in her direction. *I think she's expecting me to speak....*

"Thank you, Miss Marty." Always the entertainer, Jerri launched into a treacle-dripping mini-speech. "While I'm not *thrilled* to make my appearance in this *torture device*." She touched the hard collar and winced for effect. The others giggled politely, and she continued, "You've made me feel at home while I recover, and I thank you for that. You're *more* than a gracious hostess."

"Now that we've performed the English/American tea-ceremony according to Miss Manners," Miss Marty paused while her 'family', once again, politely giggled, exchanging knowing glances. "Now, it's time to get down to business."

"Business?" Jerri murmured. "This is a *business* meeting? Perhaps I shouldn't be here — I wouldn't want to intrude."

"Nonsense," Miss Marty smiled and reached across the table to pat Jerri's hand. "This is *'family* business'. And for the moment, dear heart, consider yourself adopted."

Jerri couldn't help but smile, thinking: *I give up! I surrender to the Lavender-Loonies!*

As if Miss Marty picked up on her shock and bewilderment, the old lady winked at her while pouring Jerri a cup of dark tea. "Sugar or honey, dear?" she offered. "Or, perhaps you prefer milk? I've heard that's how they take their tea in Europe. Can you imagine?"

Jerri spooned a dollop of honey into her fragrant tea. "No — that's hard to imagine," she murmured. *Sugar in my coffee — honey in my tea — what's all these crazy questions you're askin' me? Man, this bunch is loonier than a three-dog night!!*

Miss Marty giggled and served the others in turn. "Let me introduce my little family. Jerri, you've already met Daniel. And this is Conchita — our Professional Domestic Engineer. More *crass* people might title her our *maid.*"

"Estoy satisfecho encontrarle Srta. Conchita. I'm very pleased to meet you."

Conchita smiled and nodded. "Your español is very good,

Jerri."

Jerri grinned. "High school and college. But I'm rusty — need practice. Perhaps I can impose upon you, Conchita? A Spanish word every now and then?"

"No hay problema."

"Who'd like to begin today?" The old lady glanced around the table.

The pool-boy raised his hand and said, "Miss Marty? I've received my rooming assignments. I'll be driving up to Miami next week to meet my roommate and find out what books and things I'll need to start out. I can hardly wait!"

"And, Jerri, this fine young man is Cory, my adopted — *legally* adopted — son. Cory's entering the University of Miami this coming semester to study Oceanography." She turned to her young charge and whispered, "When you check in to your dorm, I'll feel like I'm losing my little boy... you've been with us for ten years, you know?"

"You'll never lose me," Cory said, obviously choked up himself. "I'll be back home most weekends and holidays. Besides, how could I leave my mom? Miss Marty — I can't begin to thank you enough. I owe you my life. After my parents died, you stepped up and — "

"Now, now. You don't owe me *anything*, Cory," she stopped him with a wave of her hand. "I saw a boy who needed a family, and I just happened to have a family who needed a boy."

Cory blew a kiss toward his lavender-dressed mother.

Miss Marty freshened Cory's tea, giggled and continued, nodding to the young lady to her right. "This is my lovely secretary, Phyllis — in charge of keeping this house running smoothly."

The twenty-something woman nodded at Jerri, as her elderly employer refilled the silent woman's teacup. With her ram-rod straight posture, her hands neatly folded in her lap, Jerri thought the woman strongly resembled a mannequin.

The prim secretary cleared her throat. "*Miss* Sebastian...." When she spoke from behind her huge tortoiseshell glasses, Jerri at first thought the woman mimicked her boss' unique voice; but it took her only seconds to realize this was the woman's usual manner of speaking. Not a hair stirred on the secretary's head; it was pulled back into a severe bun, and seemed to strain at her temples. "*Miss* Sebastian!" The stiffly-dressed woman continued, "...that *matter* I mentioned yesterday on the phone? About — "

"Now, now — Phyllis. This is *family* business time," Miss Marty scolded her interruption. "This is *not* the time for business-business. Tell me," she deftly changed the subject, "any news from your sister?"

Phyllis blushed, betraying her composure. She hesitantly answered, "The last... I heard... Sharon is doing very well in that drug rehab program you arranged for her. I truly believe, she would have died if you hadn't sent her to that clinic in Arizona."

"Fine! Wonderful, dear!" Miss Marty beamed. "Be sure to tell Sharon when she completes the program there'll be a job waiting. I spoke to a television producer friend in Atlanta. He's expecting Sharon to send a tape in. He's always looking for fresh news-anchors. That's what Sharon did in Texas, right?"

"Right... but, do you think...?"

"She can handle it?" Miss Marty finished her secretary's thought. "We can only hope, dear heart. One can only reach out a helping hand. One can't *force* the drowning person to grab hold."

Phyllis nodded her head. "True," she whispered. "But, sometimes it's so *hard* to watch someone you love destroy their life. And so hard to stand by and do nothing."

"Your *family* knows when you supposedly stand by and do nothing, it's the hardest thing in the world to do," the old lady offered. "*And* — we realize you had to let Sharon hit bottom before she truly accepted help. We're all in your corner, dear."

"Thank you, Miss Seb... thank you, Miss Marty." A tiny tear snaked its way down Phyllis' perfect cheek. She whispered an additional grateful thank-you to her boss.

The tea party continued, with further discussions about the trivial and monumental things that affect any family, and suddenly Jerri found herself aglow with a happy melancholy.

Haunting memories bombarded her of family ties she'd missed since her father's untimely death. The confusing emotions of warmth and sadness caused quick tears to well up. She daubed the corner of her lavender napkin to her eyes, hoping she hid the tears discreetly.

"Jerri, dear," Miss Marty asked, taking her third tea-biscuit from the delicate china plate, "is something wrong?"

"Wrong?" Jerri hiccuped. "Nothing — nothing's... *wrong.*"

Getting to her feet, Miss Marty walked around the table to Jerri's side. "Nonsense. How thoughtless of me. This is your first day out of the hospital, and I've let you overdo. Mark and Arni will have my hide. But, maybe they won't have to know if we get you to your room to rest. Daniel? Be a dear and bring my wheelchair from the closet." She patted Jerri on the shoulder. "Mark had me out of this wheelchair in six weeks — but I keep it around for bad days."

Daniel pushed the wheelchair near Jerri and helped her settle in before wheeling her to the elevator. Monogrammed doors opened, Daniel deftly moved the wheelchair to the back of the elevator and spun Jerri around to face the 'family'. She raised her hand to wave farewell and was shocked when Cory, Conchita, Phyllis *and* Miss Marty crowded into the elevator around her and her mute escort. *What's with the Walton's-Mountain-Togetherness-Seminar? Good Lord, John-Boy! I can put my own self to bed.*

After the whole family shared the elevator to the third floor, everyone disembarked to Jerri's bedroom. They stood beside her bed while Daniel took her robe and settled her under the down comforter. Miss Marty held Basil as the little dog squirmed to be allowed to leap into Jerri's arms. The bedside gathering's festive atmosphere, and Basil's fruitless squirming, brought to Jerri's mind the sentimental after-tornado scene from 'Oz'. *Auntie Em — Auntie Em! ToTo's foaming at the mouth!!* She looked to Daniel and sighed to herself, *Scarecrow — I'll miss you most of all.*

"Now, you get a good night's rest, dear," Miss Marty fussed, handing Jerri her pain-pills and a glass of water. "I'm sure Mark will be here early tomorrow to begin your exercises. Take it from me; before he's done with you, you'll be calling him 'Marky de Sade'. Some of the exercises he'll force on you have sadomasochism written all over `em." The old lady pulled the comforter up to Jerri's chin and leaned down and whispered, "But, he's so gorgeous I'm sure you'll forget *all* about the pain."

"Gorgeous, huh?" Jerri grumbled. "I hadn't noticed."

Miss Marty giggled. "I think I'll have to arrange an eye examination for you while you're visiting us. Try and get some sleep, dear."

After saying their separate 'good-byes' — *Don't cry, Tin man. You'll rust — and we don't have your oil can!* — the 'family' took their leave, and Jerri sighed again, sinking back into the plush bed.

She reached over, tuned in soft music on a bedside radio and muttered, "There's no place like home... there's *no* place like home." She yawned in spite of herself. "Must be more worn-out than I thought." Shifting uncomfortably in the hard collar, she murmured, "At least, tomorrow, I'll be rid of *this* tool of the devil."

One more sigh, and Jerri closed her eyes, trying to will herself to sleep. The soft music filled her thoughts with pleasing images, and just before she drifted off, Mark Pendragon entered the door of her subconscious, staking his claim upon her dreams. She sank into a warm night under the soft comforter, dreaming of the dark-haired man with the coral-blue eyes. Her soft sighs of appreciation went unheard as she mumbled and groaned in her sleep.

~o0o~

Chapter 7

"Are you gonna sleep the whole day through? *Jeez, Delaney!* Do ya think Miss Marty is *running a resort spa here?"*

Jerri jerked awake, sending pain shooting down her neck. At the side of her bed stood Mark Pendragon, his hands on his hips, his face stern and hard. He was decked out in an all-white shirt and shorts that set off his dark good looks and accentuated his tan.

Her breath involuntarily caught in her throat and she attempted to cover-up her automatic reaction to the gorgeous physical therapist by clutching the comforter to her chin and grabbing the bedside clock. Trying her best to yell, but quickly losing the momentum needed to give her voice the added venom wished for, the words came out in an anemic croak. "*Sleeping the day through?* Why... it can't be any later than 9 a.m. — " she glanced at the clock, " — half past *FIVE? Pendragon?* Are you *insane?* Don't you know the only thing you get from rising with the birds is *worms?"*

"Good golly, woman — you're such a wimp."

"*Wimp?* Did you just call me a *wimp?"* Jerri tried to leap from the bed, but only succeeded in flailing under the comforter like a dying fish.

"That's some kind of amazing, Delaney." Pendragon shook his head and grabbed her hand to help pull her to her feet. He joked, "Can't wait to catch your magic act. If your escape techniques are as effective as this... then you must put on *quite* a show."

She snarled, "*Oh, yeah?"* Pendragon's strength pulled her

tantalizingly close to his chest, and she couldn't help but breathe in his brisk scent. To cover up the fact her senses were now standing at full attention, she snarled again: "*Oh, yeah? Well... well... well — bite me — Happy-Boy!!!*"

He playfully furrowed his brow and wagged a finger under her nose. "Watch your language, Amazing. And just *what other* bad habits did you pick up when you took your magic act on the Gutterpalooza Tour?"

"Do you think," she growled, "you can come in *here* and harass me so *early* in the morning?" Jerri steamed. She glanced at her hand and noticed Pendragon still held it captive, close to his chest. Yanking her hand free — while ignoring a tiny voice wheedling inside her head: *Noooo! I don't wanna leave!!!* — she sneered, "So, what are you doing, hovering over my bed at this *ungodly* hour?"

"My job," he laughed, flashing his usual maddening grin. "Which would be a little bit easier if you'd answer the door when I pound on it. Now take these exercise duds and change for me."

"*Never,*" she hissed, snatching the lavender stretch coordinates and lavender sports shoes from Pendragon. "I'll not change for *you*, I'll not change for *any* man! But — it just so happens I *feel* like getting dressed, right now."

She turned, stalked to the bathroom, catching his stifled snickers as she passed. Once inside the bathroom, she sagged against the door. "That man is *Satan in white shorts*," Jerri muttered.

The little traitor inside her head whispered lasciviously: *Wonder what he's like UNDER the white sho —*

Jerri hissingly interrupted her own thoughts, "Shut up!!! Will you just *shut up?*" She doffed her gown, donned the swimsuit halter-top, pulled the sweatshirt over her head and stepped into the bikini bottoms, before completing her ensemble with matching sweat pants. Lifting one foot at a time, she was able to slide the lavender socks over her feet. She dropped the shoes on the floor in front of her feet and held the hard collar steady trying to see her targeted shoes. By backing up a few feet,

Jerri gingerly located the sneakers and managed to slide her toes in, one foot at a time.

"What I wouldn't give for Velcro," she muttered, and left the bathroom. She found Pendragon sitting on her bed, his well-tanned legs spread tantalizingly apart. "So, make yourself useful, Happy-Boy. *Tie my shoes*," Jerri ordered, slapping her foot on the edge of the bed between the physical therapist's legs.

The gorgeous dark-haired man disdainfully glanced down at the lavender shoe, inches from his crotch. "Your wish, my Queen," he deadpanned, "is my command. Would Madame care for a peeled grape?" He tied the shoe with a flourish, slapping the back of her calf to call for the other foot. This one, Jerri swiftly and deliberately placed *closer* to his crotch. He muttered, "Target practice?" Nevertheless, Pendragon tied Jerri's other shoe. "Better luck next time, Wilhelmina Tell."

She grinned until Pendragon's gaze raised from her shoe. In the microseconds it took for the man's dark-lashed eyes to meet hers, Jerri's expression turned sullen.

"Where's the torture chamber?" she asked. "Down in the dungeon?"

"How'd you guess?" he quipped. Pendragon jumped to his feet. "Come on! Let's not waste any time! Let's get you on the rack! And after lunch, we'll try out the Iron Maiden!"

"Miss Marty *told* me your true name was '*Marky' de Sade*," she growled, following the physical therapist out of the bedroom, "and I'm beginning to doubt she was kidding."

Pendragon wrung his hands in exaggerated anticipation. He gushed, "Now that you know my secret there's no reason to hold back! I say we break out the whips and chains early! Jeez — I love it!!" They came to the elevator and he pushed the down button.

When the elevator arrived, Jerri stepped in first, pivoted, pushed the first floor button and shoved the physical therapist away from the elevator door.

"Hey!!" he cried out, stumbled backwards, and fell to the carpeted floor with a bouncing thud.

As the door slid shut, she quipped: "See ya around, Happy-Boy!" Jerri smiled, closed her eyes and hummed a few bars of Queen's "Another One Bites The Dust" while she waited for the elevator to arrive on the first floor. The door slid open. Her eyes still smugly closed, she took the first step out of the elevator, walking directly into a muscle-firm, brick wall.

Jerri's inner-child sang out, *Déjà vu!* She sensed, rather than saw, that Pendragon's muscle-solid arms were crossed at his chest. Still, holding her eyes closed, Jerri relied on her searching hands to file their reports after running their reconnaissance mission up the physical therapist's folded arms. She cautiously peeked out of her left eye, and caught him scowling sternly down at her roving hands. *Mercy! He's even more gorgeous when he's angry!* She blurted out, "*How* did you get here so fast?" *Good one, Jerri! Why don't you just bend down and kiss his — like I COULD bend down even if I wanted to....*

"You're not the only magician around," he said.

"Yes... but *how?*"

Taking her arm, he led her down the hallway, grinning wickedly as he whispered in her ear, "I'll take my secrets to my grave."

"A simple 'I'm not gonna tell ya' will suffice," she pouted.

He opened the door to the exercise room, filled with many pieces of exercise equipment and related paraphernalia. A massage table sat in front of the floor-to-ceiling wall of windows. Picking up a soft foam collar, he turned and shoved it at Jerri. "Your irascible antics have put us behind schedule. Just for that, you owe me ten extra push-ups and twenty more leg-lifts."

"*Irascible?*" Jerri scowled, "Pendragon? What century were *you* born in?"

He stifled a grin and made to help her remove the hard collar. "*I* was born in a time when men were men and women knew their — "

"Place?" She finished the physical therapist's thought, stopping his hand at the plastic collar's Velcro stays.

As he carefully removed her hard-collar, he released his

wicked grin, whispering with exaggeration, " — *own minds*." He was equally as gentle wrapping the new *soft* foam collar around her neck. "Now," he said, "let's get to work. Drop down and give me five."

Flashing him a defiant scowl, Jerri bent to drop to the floor.

Grabbing her elbow, Mark chuckled. "Okay! Okay! You win. I can't let you do that. We'll start out nice and easy."

"But... I heard," she quipped, "*you* always use the 'Ike and Tina Turner Method'."

He shook his head in confusion. "'Ike and Tina Turner Method'?"

"You know — " she smirked, " — they never do nuthin' nice and easy — they always do it nice... and *rough*."

Mark's laughter filled the room and Jerri felt amazement at the surprising thrill shooting through her heart. She fought hard to restrain her own giggles; to keep from joining in the maddening man's laughter. The feeling vexed her. *Why does he affect me this way? Jeez, I believe I'd break out in goose bumps listening to him read his grocery list. I don't need this. A man is the last thing I need in my life. You know — the fish and the bicycle thing? Maybe that high-priced lavender steamroller, that temporarily flattened my career, knocked something haywire in my head.*

"Let's start with range of motion exercises," Pendragon interrupted her thoughts, leading her in front of a full length mirror. "You stand here, roll and shrug your shoulders in an exaggerated manner, and then do this — "

While he demonstrated the movements; Jerri sent a silent stern warning to the little traitor in her head: *I don't wanna hear a PEEP outta you, if ya know what's good for ya. Sure, I admit this is a fairly good-looking man stretching his muscles in front of me... well... at least, he's not bad to look at. Okay, okay — so he's the most gorgeous man I've ever seen... I admit it. Looking at him makes my heart skip a beat — but then, a couple'a cups of strong coffee has the same effect — and I can give up coffee!*

" — and after you do fifteen of those, I want ten of these motions." Pendragon ran through a short regimen of exercises, designed to test Jerri's range of motion and to stretch and strengthen her upper body muscles, "Give me all that, and I'll be a happy man."

Extremely proud of herself she'd barely reacted to his 'happy man' comment, Jerri mimicked him, spending fifteen minutes working muscles that griped, complained and finally *screamed* for the torture to end. "I'm finished," she sighed, collapsing onto a straight-back chair. "So, Marky de Sade. What's the next punishment you've got on the list? Cat-O-Nine tails?"

"Nope."

"Thumb screws?"

"Don't think so."

"Okay. Outta guesses here...."

"The tank."

"Excuse me?" She narrowed her eyes, suspiciously.

"Time for your after-exercise hydro-treatment. I call it 'de Sade's Water-Torture Deluxe'. In diver terms — let's get wet!" He led her to a large oval metal tub. Dipping his finger in the steaming water, he turned to her, nodded, and said, "Okay... looks like we're ready. Get out of your sweats and climb in."

"And what if I say no? You gonna throw me in?"

"No, no *need* to throw you in. No skin off my nose," he grinned, "if you want your muscles to ache all night long."

"All right," Jerri growled, trying her best to sound put out. Hoping not to groan from the muscle pain, she slipped the sweatshirt over her head and stepped out of the sweat pants, kicking them across the floor. "So, let's get wet." Offering his hand to assist her into the therapy tub, she watched Pendragon watching *her* as she climbed the steps and stuck a toe in the water. "*It's scalding!*" Jerri yelped. "Pendragon... whadda you tryin' to do? *Poach me?*"

"Wimp."

"Insufferable man." She stuck her toe in again, gritted her teeth and suffered the pain, forcing herself to endure the temperature of the water. Slowly lowering her body into the tub, she loudly drew her breath in over her teeth with a tortured hiss.

He asked, "How's *that* make you feel?"

She cautiously sank back against the headrest, "Wellll...."

"Don't you mean 'good'?"

"No... I was *trying* to say," Jerri groaned, "it makes me feel like a lobster — *Wellllll-done.*"

~o0o~

Chapter 8

"You've come a long way in the last two weeks," Arni Sims said, washing his hands in the therapy room's sink. "Mark's program works wonders."

"Oh, Pendragon's a little wonder worker. Yes, indeedy," Jerri quipped, speaking from behind a changing screen. She pulled her blouse into place over her shorts, fluffed her blonde hair and stepped out from behind the screen.

Dr. Sims smiled. "I see he's put *you* through the ringer."

She dramatically collapsed into a chair in front of the amused physician. "Really? What," she asked, "would make you think that?" She imitated a panting dog.

"I dunno," Sims chuckled, "maybe because your tongue's dragging on the floor? Come on now, he hasn't been *that* rough, has he?" Sims picked up her well-used cervical collar, turning it over and over in his hands.

"Pendragon rough?" she scoffed. "Pish-Posh. Put it out of your mind. Just because that man's temper makes a grumpy drill sergeant look like a cloistered monk under a vow of silence? Just because that man's exercise program makes Arnold Schwarzenegger's Terminator look like Pee-Wee Herman? Pshaw! *Naw* — I wouldn't say he's rough! *He's insane!* He's like a rabid cookie-selling Girl Scout run amok!"

Dr. Sims laughed, tossing the neck collar into the trash. "I've *never* heard Mark Pendragon described as a *Girl Scout*. Women usually use words like 'hunk' and 'stud-muffin' when they talk about the man. But then, you did tell me you were a master escape artist. I guess you've managed to escape from Mark's fatal charm."

"*Fatal charm?*" she huffed. "That man's charm wouldn't be fatal even if taken with a glass of rattlesnake venom."

"Uh-Huh. If you say so." The red-haired man nodded, gathering his medical instruments into his leather bag. "And I'll make a note to get your eyes examined."

Jerri hissed under her breath, "Why does *everybody* want me to get my eyes examined?" Aloud, she grumbled, "I'll ignore that remark." She touched her bare neck, and asked, "Why did you throw my neck collar away?"

He smiled. "You can thank Mr. Girl Scout/Stud-Muffin for that. He's hastened your recovery. Keep this new soft collar around in case you need it, but I think if you take it easy for awhile you'll be able to resume normal activities, soon."

She brightened. "Normal activity? Like diving?"

"Are you talking sky diving, pearl diving, diving for cover or scuba diving?"

She scoffed, "No — I'm talking industrial deep sea diving. What do *you* think? Scuba, of course. It's one of the main reasons I requested my agent book me in the Keys. I've looked forward to diving here for weeks — since the booking was confirmed."

"Well, I think you should put it off a while longer."

"You mean I can't be in the water?"

Sims shook his head, and replied, "No, I never said that. Jump in the water. Get wet. Go swimming. Go snorkeling. The exercise will do you good. Just use some common sense. Okay?"

Jerri set her jaw defiantly. "Do I *look* like I lack common sense?"

The doctor chuckled. "*That* — I'm not going to answer."

Jerri scowled.

"Take two aspirin, and call me in the morning," the doctor said, carrying his medical bag out of the therapy room. He chuckled, "Oh, and by the way, very soon, you'll be playing the violin like Jack Benny. Which is funny, really, because you couldn't play before, right?" He chuckled again and shook his head. "I've always wanted to say those things."

"Well," Jerri scowled again, her teasing eyes giving her away. "Aren't you the Groucho Marx of the medical profession?" She playfully glared at the red-haired, freckled-face man, as he removed his glasses. *He has lovely eyes, she thought, feeling almost amazed to be noticing her physician's features. They're warm and friendly. Brown, with flecks of green. He may not be a Key West Adonis; but he's got beautiful eyes just the same. Jeez, just another gorgeous island man.*

"Now, just because I've released you from the collar," Sims wagged his finger at Jerri, dragging her attention away from his eyes. "I don't want you thinking you can run willy-nilly around here."

"*Willy-Nilly?*" Jerri scoffed. "Can you *be* any more juvenile?"

Sims fixed her with a stern glare. "You've had a serious accident," he admonished her, "and you're still not completely healed. So, take it easy, understand?"

She hid her crossed fingers behind her, and smiled. "I promise."

"Good," the doctor nodded. "I like it when my patients behave."

Pendragon walked into the foyer just as Arni Sims turned to leave. Jerri stood behind the doctor, bidding him farewell. "Well, Doc," the dark-haired physical therapist grinned. "How's our little escape artist?"

"Healing *magically,* because of you," Arni quipped, his hand on the mansion's front door. "You know, don't you, I'm one of your biggest fans?"

Jerri steamed, "Well, *I'm* not. And I'm also not *anybody's* little escape artist."

"Bit touchy, aren't we?" Sims smirked, walking out the door.

As the door closed behind the young doctor, Mark Pendragon turned to his healing client and sighed, adopting an affected voice and swishing in a limp-wristed manner. "*Men —* they can be such... such *pigs!* I swear, how do you women put up with those... those *men!*"

"You're not funny, you know," she grumbled. "Besides, you do that limp-wristed act a little too well." She flashed a quick grin to show him she was teasing. "So, do you want to know what Dr. Sims told me, or not?"

He set his hands on his hips and grinned. "Okay. Like the diaper-rashed Chihuahua said: I'll bite. What did the Key's version of Doogey Howser have to say?"

"He said I should get out more. He said — " She looked into his nearly cobalt eyes, hoping by facing the man head on, he'd not notice her unique slant on the truth, " — He said I should get more *exercise.*"

"Exercise?"

"Yeah..." She tossed her hand in a matter-of-fact fashion. "Exercise. Like walking, tennis... *scuba diving.*"

"Scuba diving? You *sure* Arni said you could get wet?"

"Of course he said I could get wet. Would I lie to you?" Holding two fingers crossed behind her back, Jerri fought to keep from grinning.

"I didn't say *that...*" he hedged.

She stuck out her bottom lip in a pout. "You can ask Arni yourself if you want. I'm just telling you what the man said: 'Resume normal activity... jump in the water... the exercise will do you good.' Any more questions?"

"No... no," he rubbed his chin, "no more questions. Actually... on the other hand... yeah. I've just got *one* other question." The maddening man set his dark hooded eyes on hers, silently waiting for her to speak.

Ten seconds passed, before Jerri broke eye contact. "Okay, okay. What do you want to know?" She held her breath, thinking Pendragon was just the kind of man to phone Arni Sims and catch her in a bald-faced lie.

"When do you want to go diving?" he grinned. "How's this evening?"

Caught off guard, she stuttered, "*You'd ta...ta...take me?*" Composing herself, she spoke again, "I mean; you'll take me diving? *Really?*"

He grinned again. "Really. We'll borrow Miss Marty's boat. You want to get some gear together and we'll head out in about an hour?"

"Can't."

"Wait a minute," he growled, "you badger me into taking you diving, then you say you can't go? What gives?"

Sheepishly, she murmured, "I can't go *now* because I have a date."

"You have a *date?*"

She huffed, "You make it sound like I couldn't get a date without selling raffle tickets and tying a pork chop around my neck!! I'll have you know, Mr. Pendragon, there are *still* some gallant men who'd give a mercy date to the Elephant Girl."

He laughed. "Good golly — Sims is right. You *are* touchy today. I wasn't passing judgment on your personal life, I only meant — "

Jerri sneered her interruption, "You only *meant* The Amazing Delaney would have to bind and shackle a man to get a date. I *know* what you meant."

Hanging his head in mock sorrow, the dark-haired man stuck his bottom lip out and batted his eyes. "Give a pig a break? Okay? I swear, I never meant any such thing. I'm sure there's a whole *army* of men out there just aching to go out with you."

"*Oh?* So, now you're calling me a *tramp?*"

He threw up his hands in exasperation, lamenting, "I give up! Talking to you is like being straight man to Don Rickles. Let's start again, shall we? Fine. So, Jerri — you say you're going on a date? Why, yes; Mark... I am," he answered for her, turning back and forth as if switching roles in a one-man play. "How nice. Yes, Mark... I do think it is. Thank you so much for taking an interest. No prob, Jerri! Who's the lucky fella? Anyone I know? Why, no. I don't think you know — "

"Dolf Grüber," she interrupted his duel monologue. The physical therapist's eyes flew open, his lips parted and Jerri prepared herself for a smart aleck comment about Grüber.

Pendragon nodded his head and rubbed his chin. "Dolf Grüber, huh? Miss Marty's accountant? Yeah... I've seen him around."

"What?" she growled. "Does Grüber pass muster with you, or are you going to warn me I've got a date with the Ted Bundy of the Keys?" She glared her anger, sending mental daggers directly into Pendragon's eyes.

A strange expression crossed his face. "Nothing... so... dramatic," he snarled, grabbing the door handle. "If you'd allow me to get a word in edgewise, I was just going to say: *Have a nice time. And I hope you enjoy your evening out.*" He clinched his teeth and nearly hissed, "You *deserve* it; you've worked hard to heal! See you tomorrow! *Okay?*"

"Okay!!"

"*Fine?*"

"Fine!!"

"Well — okay!! *Fine!!!*" He stalked out the door, but not without making sure she overheard his parting comment. "Jeez, Delaney — *that's just like a woman!*"

Leaning against the other side of the closed door, Jerri's mouth fell open in shock and she muttered to herself, "Of all the nerve!! *Insufferable man!* Just wait until I — "

"Señorita Jerri?" the maid interrupted from the great room. "Is anything wrong? I thought I heard voices."

Jerri shook her head, "Don't worry about it, Conchita. It was just Mr. Pendragon leaving. He has a bad case of P.M.S."

"P.M.S.? Señor Pendragon? I... I don't understand." Conchita shook her head in confusion.

Jerri turned and stalked down the hallway. "Yeah — " she quipped. "Pompous Male Silliness. It affects all men his age," she continued her grumbling into the elevator. "It's a wonder they even *allow* men to be President. The White House is practically infested with male P.M.S. Why, I wouldn't be surprised, if someday the President hits the wrong silly button, blows up some silly-freakin' desert and swears — " The elevator door closed on her ranting and the rest of Jerri's impromptu tirade was lost to the maid.

"Gringas!" Conchita sighed. "Muy, muy loca!"

~o0o~

Chapter 9

Leaving the Purple Plantation, the very anger that caused his eyes to sparkle, fueled an unconscious 'need for speed', and he drove his jeep a little too fast. Then, as if thinking better of it, he deliberately slowed his speed driving through the small town; he knew the local police weren't kidding about the posted speed limit.

"That *woman!!*" He hissed, "That *obstinate...* that *stubborn... that pigheaded woman!!*" Pendragon steamed and stewed all the way out of Marathon. "You'd think her main purpose in life is to vex me! Well, Delaney, *amazing or not,* you're not going to get away with driving *me* insane! I don't care if you date Grüber! I don't care if you date the *Pillsbury Doughboy!* What do I care *who* you date?"

He growled at Jerri as if she were in the jeep along side of him, instead of back at the mansion.

"I'm not jealous, either. Don't get the idea I am," he grumbled. The closeness of his home slightly eased his seething anger and he sighed, shaking his head with the memory of Jerri and the perplexing emotions she left in her wake. It seemed, just the sight of her made a thrill pass through his chest and caused him to catch his breath. *And yet, sometimes... when the little magician opens her mouth... let's just say... wars have begun with friendlier words.*

There was only one other woman who could affect him in the same manner; another woman whose wit and lightening-quick verbal sparing could bring him to peaks of joy and just as easily to the needle-sharp sting of boiling anger.

Pulling into his drive, the jeep's tires threw gravel and sand in its wake. Leaving the little teal 4 X 4, the angry man slammed the door hard, ran out onto his tiny private beach, stopped at the surf's edge, looked out over the water, put his head back and screamed one word: *"Marissa!!!"*

~o0o~

Standing in front of his lighted curio cabinet, Daniel rolled a sparkly two-inch cobalt-blue marble in his hands. He thought back to the day Miss Marty had presented the beautiful glass ball to him, wrapped up in festive paper, a lavender bow on the small box. He remembered desperately wanting to thank the jovial old lady, audibly, but the very reason he couldn't convey his appreciation was the very reason for the marble collecting. His muteness.

He lovingly brought the cold glass orb to his cheek, closed his eyes and was rewarded with a non-physical jolt. An immediate flashing image exploded in his brain. A beach. Shadows. Angry voices. Pain. Fear. Silence. These images and emotions, powerful in their intensity, frightened him to his knees, and he wept silently, the marble clutched to his chest.

~o0o~

Jerri smiled with pride at her reflection in the mirror.

Since I've been more than diligent with my exercises the last two weeks, Arni Sims was persuaded to grant my early escape from the cervical collar. Sweet!

"Pendragon *did* do magic with my neck," she murmured, looking in the mirror, and fussing with her hair. "Not that I'd admit it to *him*. That insufferable man might think my healing was all his doing. He might get the big head, and I can't let *that* happen."

Touching her fingertips to her neck, she found it felt strange not to have the cumbersome foam adornment fastened under her ears. She picked up a silver and diamond solitaire necklace; her usual jewelry selection. Looking at it thoughtfully, Jerri decided, *Tonight, the tiny diamond seems understated.* Instead, she chose a delicate heart-shaped amethyst and diamond necklace set in

69

silver, and matching earrings, both borrowed from Miss Marty. The purple multi-gem necklace matched her light lavender, backless, scarf-hemmed dress. The neckline dipped nearly to the waist; dangerously low in the front. Twirling, she smiled, watching the filmy material settle into place around her legs. Checking her reflection in the mirror for the third time, a knock on the door startled Jerri from her last minute grooming.

"Señorita Jerri?" Conchita called through the bathroom door, "El señor Grüber está abajo. Puedo ser yo de cualquier ayuda?"

"No, Conchita," she called, "I've got it covered. I would appreciate it, though, if you'd tell Mr. Grüber I'll be right down."

"Sí, Señorita Jerri."

She felt butterflies in her stomach much like she always felt before walking out on stage for a performance. Another knock at the door tore her attention away from the mirror.

"Conchita! I'll be downstairs in a few minutes!"

The knock came again; this time to the beat of 'Shave And A Haircut — Two Bits'. Jerri furrowed her brow. *Conchita wouldn't be so insistent.* She opened the bathroom door to find Daniel Tiger waiting, notebook in hand.

Whistling low, communicating his wordless, but obvious, appreciation of Jerri's appearance, he tore off a pre-written message from the pad and handed it to her.

JERRI — PLEASE FORGIVE ME FOR BUTTING IN; I SHOULD PROBABLY MIND MY OWN BUSINESS. BUT, AS A FRIEND (AND I HOPE YOU CONSIDER US FRIENDS) I FEEL I JUST HAVE TO TELL YOU ABOUT MY FEELINGS. (OVER)

Reading this, Jerri's eyes flew open. *What is this?* The chauffeur leaned against the doorjamb, an ambiguous expression on his face. She flipped the paper over to read the rest of the message.

WHILE IT MIGHT NOT BE ANY OF MY BUSINESS, I'VE GOT TO TELL YOU HOW I FEEL ABOUT GRÜBER. I DON'T KNOW WHY, BUT I DON'T TRUST THE MAN. HE

FRIGHTENS ME. NO REASON. I JUST HAVE A <u>REALLY</u> BAD FEELING ABOUT THE GUY. <u>PLEASE, BE CAREFUL</u>. I WISH I COULD TELL YOU MORE. BY THE WAY, I HAVEN'T SHARED MY BAD VIBES WITH MISS MARTY. THE DEAR LADY'S NEVER MET A STRANGER. TAKE CARE, <u>PLEASE</u> — DANIEL.

Jerri blinked back her surprise. "Daniel... I don't know what to say. You must feel really strong about this, or you wouldn't have given me this note. What can I say? Mr. Grüber invited me out for the evening, and... I'm going."

A look of dismay crossed Daniel's face.

She didn't need his words to interpret his thoughts. "Don't worry, I'll be careful. As far as I know, Dolf Grüber's intentions are honorable. And if they're not, don't worry about me. I've had defense training. I may look small, but I pack a powerful punch."

Daniel grinned and mimed a boxer backing away in defeat. He wagged a finger under Jerri's nose and tapped the note in her hand. Dramatically miming being strangled, stabbed, and shot, he ended his one man show by pounding his chest, indicating his feelings came from his heart. Then, he "walked" two fingers in the air, pointed at her and gave a "no way" sweep of his arm.

"I get the message," she said, "you *really* think I shouldn't go out with Grüber." She handed over his note, and shook her head. "I *do* appreciate your concern, Daniel... *I do*. But, since you haven't got anything to back up your feelings, I'm gonna go. Okay?"

The chauffeur threw up his hands, stepped back, and made an expressive sweeping motion, as if to say "I give up! If you won't listen to me, then go ahead." He mimed tipping his hat, before leaving her room.

"How perfectly odd," she mused aloud — but only when she was sure Daniel was out of earshot. *"So...* Daniel Striped Tiger has bad vibes about my date for the evening. I'll wager, King Friday XIII and Queen Sara Saturday probably feel the same way about Grüber. Perhaps I should ask Henrietta Pussycat, 'X' the Owl, or Cornflake S. Pecially for *their* opinions." She sighed.

"More than likely, Lady Elaine Fairchilde is the only one who'd give me a thumb's up on the man. And we all know what a poopyhead *she* can be." She threw up her hands and sighed again. "Oh, Mr. Rogers? *What* should I do?"

Taking one more look in the mirror, she flicked a stubborn errant curl out of her eyes, pronounced her reflected image as perfect as it was ever going to be, and left the room for the elevator.

~o0o~

Chapter 10

The elevator delivered Jerri to the second floor, where she hurried to meet Dolf Grüber. Pausing outside the doorway, she found her date sitting on the playroom sofa beside Miss Marty. Jerri silently watched her night's companion and her hostess wage what seemed to be a mighty war. From the cries of victory and loss, it appeared the accountant, and his client, were engaged in a heated battle. Miss Marty nearly bounced with excitement, wielding the video game's wireless remote control. She crowed her complete victory over the handsome man who'd just, at that moment, lost his head to her bloody sword.

"I told you, Dolf," the jolly senior laughed. "The most important rule of 'Swift Sword Warriors' is *always* watch your back. To paraphrase Rudyard Kipling: 'If you can keep your head when all around you others are losing theirs... then you'll win the game, my son.' Words to live by." She threw her hand back and released an evil cackle; then sweetly smiled. The effect was like watching Cruella Deville don a nun's habit.

The blond formal-dressed man scowled. "I can't believe a gentle, sweet lady like you would take such glee in a bloody decapitation. But, next time — mark my word, Miss Marty — *your head's mine.*"

"Oh, Dolf," she laughed again. "Don't you know it's *only* a game? Didn't your parents teach you to be a gracious loser?"

The briefest display of anger flashed across his eyes, but in the next instant, there were no traces of temper showing on his handsome face. "That goes without saying," Dolf chuckled. "My parents taught me a great deal, each in their own way, but they never taught me to watch out for sweet ladies who want to take my head. M'lady — I concede to your superior pirate skills." He stood and bowed low to his employer.

Miss Marty giggled. "Ninja, Dolf," she smiled, and said, "I'm a better *ninja* than you. You *do* know it's only a game? Right? I'd never harm a hair on your head. Not in real life, anyway." The old lady suddenly noticed Jerri standing outside the door. "Dolf, I believe we have an audience. Jerri? You can come in now — "

"Yeah, please come in," Dolf interrupted. "The bloodletting is over. I'm nothing but a bloody, headless corpse."

Jerri giggled and stepped across the threshold. "Well, you look very handsome for a bloody corpse. Do I need to fetch a first-aid kit?"

"Yes, please..." he groaned, grabbing his neck. "I think I need a tourniquet to hold my head on."

"Please, Dolf," Jerri smiled. "If I used a *tourniquet* to hold your head on, I'm afraid it'd be the death of you. Don't you think a little bandage will do?"

"What a wimp," Miss Marty scoffed. "One little beheading and the man's crying for a bandage." She turned off the large screen television and got to her feet. "To quote the People of the Village: Mucho-Macho-Man. You have *got* to be a Macho Man."

"I believe you mean the *Village People,*" Jerri hugged the old woman. "Not the People of the Village. And I also believe, the headless corpse and I will be leaving now. Please don't wait up for us. I'm sure we'll be in quite late."

"Count on that," Dolf agreed. "And may I say, right at this moment, I'm in the company of the two most gorgeous and sexy women in the Keys."

"Mister Grüber," Miss Marty gently cuffed his shoulder, "you are so full of it. It's a wonder your nose isn't two feet long."

Jerri shook her head. "I don't know about that... I think his nose is just fine. Furthermore, I think he's right about one thing. You're a doll!" She leaned in and kissed the old woman's lavender-scented cheek. "Thank you for the dress and jewelry. I feel like a fairy princess in this dress!" Jerri twirled, sending the dress' lavender scarf edges out, causing the chiffon tips to appear they were flower petals. Her close-cut blonde hair contrasted with the tan she'd obtained since her arrival in the Keys.

"Well, Sweetie," Miss Marty cooed, caressing the amethyst and silver necklace dangling from her own lace-trimmed neck, "you look like a princess. A lovely lavender princess. I hope you have a wonderful time with Dolf." She turned to the blond gentleman standing beside the doorway. "And you, young man. I've never seen you looking so genteel. You're very dapper in your off-white linen suit. Very Miami Vice, don't you think, Jerri? — Wait a moment! I've *got* to have a photo!!" She hurried from the room.

"Where'd she go?" Dolf asked.

Jerri giggled. "I'll bet she ran to get her camera. I feel like this is my high school prom."

Dolf smiled and said, "Jerri, I wish I'd *had* such a lovely date for the prom. I didn't go to mine. My family moved three times my senior year."

"That's one thing we have in common, then," Jerri returned his smile. "Difference is, my dad and I were *always* on the move. I was home-schooled. No prom for me."

Miss Marty breezed back into the room, bringing her camera and her familiar lavender scent. "Now, let me get a few snapshots of you two dearies. Jerri? Why don't you and Dolf pose over there by the fireplace? Okay?" The old woman hustled the couple across the room, nearly forcing them to pose in front of the unlit dark wood fireplace. "Oh, you look like you just stepped off the pages of a fashion magazine!" She snapped photo after photo.

"Jerri?" Dolf asked, fidgeting the tiniest bit, "Don't you think it's time we were leaving?" He looked from Jerri to Miss Marty and back again. "The show starts in a little over four hours, and I don't want to set a land speed record getting there. I had hoped to give you a leisurely driving tour of Key West while the sun was still up. Thought we'd park on a side street and stroll down to Mallory Square. Watch the sun go down the 'down-island way'."

Jerri chuckled. "I've heard it's the law in Key West to watch the sun go down on Mallory Square. After all, that's the last view of the sun on US shore. Right?"

"There's some debate about *that*," Miss Marty retorted. "Remember California? And don't forget Hawaii. But, no matter the argument, it'd be a crime to miss the sunset on Mallory Square. So, you two dears better run along. Be sure to catch the street performers — and say 'Hi' to Dominique's Magic Cats." The grandmotherly senior hustled them toward the elevator. "And have fun! Especially you, Dolf. You're *much* too serious, you know. Loosen up! Learn to have fun! After all, your date for the night *is* a lavender princess!"

"Yes, Ma'am." Dolf feigned shyness as he boarded the elevator with Jerri. As the elevator's door closed, leaving Miss Marty on the second floor, the accountant turned to his date. "Guess I've got *my* orders," he sighed. "Gotta have fun. Bummer. And here, I was planning *such* a boring night." He hung his head dejectedly.

"Oh, buck up, lil' buckaroo!" Jerri joined him in the teasing. "I'm sure we can tone it down a notch or two. Make you a deal. I'll keep an eye on you, making sure you don't have too much fun, and you keep an eye on me." The elevator opened its doors on the first floor. Jerri stepped out and headed toward the entranceway.

"I gotta say — I think I've got the better job." Dolf whistled. "I doubt I'll be able to take my eyes off you all night."

"Dolf?"

"Yes?"

"Take care you don't trip over that Pinocchio nose."

~o0o~

Parked in front of the mansion, the classic Jaguar XKE greeting the two took Jerri's breath away. She exclaimed, "Wow! What a beautiful car!! Forgive me if I drool."

"Thank you, M'lady," Grüber replied. He opened the passenger door of the low to the ground sleek black convertible and helped Jerri into the black leather seat. "I've gotta admit, I'm attached to this bad boy." He shut Jerri's door and hurried around to the driver's side.

Waiting for her date to settle himself behind the wheel, Jerri patted the dash. "It reminds me of my Bab... *my* car. The car I lost in the wreck. I had a vintage Austin Healey Sprite. It wasn't big. Wasn't powerful. But, it was *tons* of fun." Her expression grew wistful.

Dolf patted her hand. "Don't look so sad. I'm sure everything will turn out fine. Besides, this is our evening for *fun,*" he soothed. "Sad memories not allowed tonight. My suggestion is, we make some new happy memories. You up for that?"

"Of course. You're right," she said. "This night is for laughs only. No fears. No tears."

He smiled. "Sounds like a plan," Dolf said. "Miss Marty slipped me this before you came into the game room. Worried about your hair, I guess." He handed Jerri a lavender scarf.

"That's *so* like her."

They both donned their sunglasses, and Dolf turned the ignition key to a satisfying roar. Laughing, he took a right turn out of the complex. The long, sexy and dark car cruised toward Key West at an effortless speed.

~o0o~

Jerri and her date failed to notice the lone figure in the third floor window watching while they drove away in Grüber's Jaguar. It also escaped their eyes when the man looking out the window, balled his fist in a confused and wordless rage.

~o0o~

Chapter 11

They were forty-five minutes on the road, driving southwest on US 1 in the sleek, long-nosed classic car, when the blond man turned to his date. "It's time we said our prayers," he solemnly said. "You know, don't you, no one gets into the lower Keys without saying the Buffett Prayer?"

"Buffett Prayer?"

"Yeah. Since it's your first visit, I'll help you," he offered.

"How perfectly... *kind* of you."

Dolf grinned toward his date. "Da nada, Jerri. Here's the way the Buffett Prayer goes — though you *do* realize it's usually said after a wild night of Bacchanalian revelry in worship to the Porcelain God? Okay! Here goes: 'Lord — forgive us and protect us. We been drinkin' beer for breakfast.'" He ended the prayer with a straight face, until the laughter won out. Jerri joined her date's chuckles with her own.

Suddenly, Dolf pointed at a mile marker. "Look!" he said. "One mile to Key West. Our adventure begins!"

~o0o~

"We're entering Key West on North Roosevelt Boulevard." Jerri's date affected a staged tour-guide voice and indicated the right-hand turnoff as US 1 continued around the northeast side of Key West. "You'll find most of your larger motels in this area," he said. "It's close to the airport."

"I thought Key West was supposed to be rustic. You know," Jerri quipped, "scenic tourist trap, and all that." Grüber laughed, and Jerri felt the corners of her mouth turn up, joining Dolf in his good humor.

"Sure, it's rustic," he said. "Old Town Key West is wonderfully rustic. Kinda flashy. A little slimy. Very unique. You'll love it. But, for the most part, you'll love it another time. I'm afraid if we're going to make our reservation, we'll have to forego the *complete* Conch Tour. We'll just take a slow rambling drive close to Mallory Square. Not to worry. I'll show you the rest of the sights this weekend. I'll take you on a leisurely walking tour. Point out the special things about this crazy, wonderful town."

The car continued around the southeast side of Key West, driving toward Old Town. Soon, North Roosevelt Boulevard became Truman Avenue and Grüber took a right turn onto Frances Street.

"Is this a quickie tour of Key West or are the banditos on our tail?"

Grüber laughed again. "Sorry," he smiled at Jerri, "I forgot you don't know your way around Key West. I'm just taking a short-cut to Mallory Square."

Soon, Frances Street skirted the east side of Old Key West Cemetery. From the car's viewpoint, she could tell some of the gravestones were very old; it was a very picturesque cemetery. "You know?" Jerri said, "I've heard rumors people are *dying* to get in there."

Giving her a momentarily quizzical look, Grüber snorted, *"What?"*

"Sorry." Jerri grinned. "Quirky superstition of mine. Can't pass a cemetery without saying it. Kinda like whistlin' — "

" — past the graveyard?" Grüber finished for her.

"Yeah." She smiled in his direction.

Grüber smiled back. "My mother was like that. Most people thought she was a bit kooky. But, I remember her as having a wonderful sense of humor. Not like my father. That man never saw anything funny in his whole wretched life."

"I'm sorry." Jerri shook her head in sympathy, and said, "It sounds as if you didn't get along with your father."

This time, his laughter was tinged with bitterness. *"That's* an

79

understatement. I won't ruin our evening by talking about that bast — " he let the word die on his tongue. "He's not even worth the words to explain him." The car reached the far edge of the old cemetery, and Grüber's thoughts seemed to have taken a detour into the past.

"He's still alive?"

"I wouldn't know, really. But, I doubt it." Grüber turned left off of Frances Street onto Angela Street and drove down the north side of the cemetery. He shook his head at the memories, and for one moment, Jerri thought he might spit when he continued. "The last I heard, he was living with his fourth wife somewhere in Texas. One day I received a telegram from the poor woman — *Dad's unfortunate fourth wife*.... Her name was the only one on it. Figured he'd finally gone where *so many* had told the bastard to go. I really didn't care enough to check it out. I chucked it, unopened, into the 'circular file'." He set his jaw in a stern expression, as if attempting to drive his father from his thoughts.

Jerri silently placed her hand over Grüber's resting on the gearshift. The comfort of her hand over his seemed to quench his inner smoldering emotions. She watched him swallow the last of his remembered anger before he turned to her.

"Hey — " he said, "let's not let my old man come out with us tonight." He smiled. "What do you say we change the subject? The Outlander is near the end of Angela Street. Just past the next two corners. It's still early. We'll drive past it, so you can see it — then we'll head on down to Mallory Square to watch the sunset."

Continuing down toward the Outlander Lounge, Dolf quipped, "Right now, we're on arguably the most famous street in Key West."

She sat up straighter in her seat. "Duval Street?" she asked. "Isn't Sloppy Joe's on Duval Street? I've *always* wanted to have a drink at Sloppy Joe's." Jerri stole a glance up the street. Even though they were still over three blocks away, it appeared to Jerri, a celebration was in progress. *I've heard every night's a party in Key West,* she thought to herself. She grinned at Grüber. "That's where Hemingway used to hang — right?"

"Hemingway, right. At least some say. And if you're a good girl... or I should say, if I'm a good *boy,* maybe we'll finish the night at Sloppy Joe's." The classic British sports car continued the drive north on Duval Street. They soon passed Sloppy Joe's and Jerri turned her head toward the famous bar and gazed longingly at Hemingway's haunt like a child looking in a toy store window.

Grüber turned the corner, and the long-nosed car pulled onto Angela Street. They neared the end of the block and he called out, "There it is! Bet you've never seen anything like it... on second thought, perhaps you have, being a professional entertainer."

"Not from *this* side of the velvet rope...."

~o0o~

Chapter 12

Grüber parked the car close to the corner of South and Whitehead. Pausing in front of Key West's Southernmost Point landmark, the two watched the sun loll over the western horizon, bathing the bouy's right side in golden light. Just offshore, a small squadron of pelicans dive-bombed the water, snatching their evening meal from the sun-kissed gentle waves. Salt-tinged breezes ruffled Jerri's hair as she ran her fingertips over the huge red, yellow and black bullet-shaped, land-bound marker.

"The Conch Republic." She read aloud, "Ninety miles to Cuba... Southernmost Point Continental U.S.A...." Then she smiled and touched the last line's painted letters. "Home of the Sunset." The amusement on her face testified to her complete joy playing the rubbernecking tourist.

Calling its outrage at another seagull's successful theft of its dinner, an angry white-winged bird hovered in a warm thermocline, above the lapping surf a few feet from the marker. Suddenly, seemingly thinking better of the situation, the seagull dove headfirst at the water, apparently spying a fresher-looking morsel.

"You know, Jerri," Grüber teased, "we *could* hop down off this low wall, skinny dip in that inviting warm water, and be just that much closer to Cuba. This very spot where we stand is farther south anyone *can* be — and still be on American soil." He pointed out over the azure water and said, "Just think. About ninety miles... that way... is a completely different culture. Ahh... banana daiquiris... sultry breezes through rustling palm fronds...

good Cuban cigars...."

"Waxing nostalgic, are we?"

Jerri's date laughed, removed his phone from his jacket pocket, flipped it open and pointed the camera. "I've just got to grab a memory of the most perfect day I've ever spent in Key West, alongside the most perfect lady." He captured Jerri's image.

From behind their backs, they heard a boisterous and cheery greeting — "G'Day, mate!" — and someone grabbed the cell phone camera from Grüber's hand. Miss Marty's accountant reacted immediately, much to the heftier man's surprise.

Before the guy could spit out a further explanation of the cellphone-jacking, Grüber swung around, unleashing a lightening fast blaze of pure anger, virtually dancing on the balls of his feet, both fists balled tight, his face beet red. He seemed micro-seconds from pummeling the cellphone snatcher. While a flabbergasted Jerri watched Grüber's instantaneous reaction, her mind whispered warnings, but again the Australian seized her attention.

Seeing Grüber's swift wrath, the hulking man verbally backpedaled. His strange words spilled over each other, as he grinned and babbled. "Holy Dooley! Don't spit the dummy, Jocko! Ain't I just not the full quid? Like I got kangaroos loose in the top paddock... well, you can call me a right Ozzie yobbo. What say you join yer little Sheila in yer snap!"

Jerri suddenly jabbed her finger in the air. "Ah-ha! I think I actually caught that last part! ...*I'm* a Sheila — *right?*"

"...oh. You're saying you'll take a shot of both me *and* my lady?" Grüber smiled. Sunlight gleamed off his radiant teeth.

Searching his now calm face, Jerri wondered at Grüber's white hot fury she'd witnessed mere moments before. *Whoa! If I'd not seen it with my own eyes... Did I just see what I think I saw? And what DID I see, anyway —*

"Yes, that's certainly nice of you," Grüber interrupted her frantic thoughts, his goodwill clearly beaming from his eyes. "Jerri, my dear? Let's stand in front of the marker so this nice gentleman can take our picture."

How can someone be so charming and calm, one second,

and have murder in his eyes the next? Jerri took position alongside Grüber in front of the landmark and posed while the Austrailian tourist snapped a few photos. Seagulls swooped and fluttered around the historic attraction and the gentle breeze rustled her scarf-hemmed skirt.

She glanced at her date, noting his sparkling green eyes. *I swear — if I hadn't seen it — I'd have never believed this gorgeous... gentleman... could be so... so... Jekyll and Hyde. All this guy wanted to do was take our picture. I'd say overreaction is not the word!* Again, she glanced at the man by her side and imperceptibly shook her head. *Well, like my Daddy always taught me — look for the truth behind the illusion. Perhaps he's nervous? Maybe this guy just caught him off-guard? Ahh... well. No matter. I'm not gonna let someone else's bad mood ruin my first day in Key West.*

"Cooeey! That's a right bonzer! Glad we could hammer that nut out!" Returning the camera phone, the man from Oz walked away, leaving them with a souvenir photo of their Key West date. A distant ship broke the pleasant calm with its blaring, deep-throated klaxon, while tiny waves broke against the seawall.

"Dolf, wasn't that the nicest thing anyone's ever done for you?" Jerri waved to the obliging man, the couple turned and set out on the walk to Mallory Square, the historic waterfront. Strolling with Grüber hand in hand, alongside the other people heading toward the dock, Jerri thought back to her date's explosive anger and the possibly disturbing questions she now had about this accountant she knew only through Miss Marty. She shook her head and chuckled ruefully.

"Share the joke," Grüber gently nudged her. "What's so funny?"

Oh-oh... now's not the time to bring up his anger management issues... She thought quickly. "Not so much funny, as sweet — and charming. I absolutely *love* listening to other accents and dialects, don't you? And that Aussie-guy *was* very nice, wasn't he?" She watched his face for clues to his former anger, all the while swinging her date's hand in a 'puppy-love' manner.

"So... interesting. Accents get your kangaroos jumpin', do they?"

She laughed out loud.

Affecting a fakely smooth French accent, Grüber launched into a silly tour of Key West's side streets. He continued his role of tour-guide, down the many blocks from the Southernmost Point marker, until they stepped onto the bricked common that skirted the dock. Gesturing broadly and using much exaggeration, he pointed out the sites to an enthralled Jerri.

"On our left are a goodly select-*shune* of five-star gourmet establish-*monts*. Better known to the Key West up-*pair* crust as Down-Island Fine *Quiz-Zine* — " he gave Jerri a goofy grin and continued, "or what *some* of *zee* — *low-airh* class — might term: Le' Mallory Square *Fooood* Carts."

Jerri giggled at the man being his silly best just for her. *Perhaps I overreacted to Dolf's... overreacting.* "The aroma *is* very tempting. Didn't realize I was so hungry...."

"Ahhh... Qu'est-ce que c'est? Vous ne me croyez pas? Would you like something to... how you say... *eat?* Le French Fry? Crappie Su-*sie?*"

Jerri giggled, once more. "Are you trying to say: Crepe Suzette?"

Chuckling his best Maurice Chevalier impersonation, Grüber scoffed, "But of course! Les Crepe Suzette!" Seeing Jerri desolve into more giggles, he scoffed, pseudo-offended. "Sacré bleu! Pepé Le Pew! Mon oncle a une boîte verte de crayon!"

"...and *why* should I *care* if your uncle has a green pencil box? Eh... Pepé?"

"Ma petite fleur... once more, you chortle!" Again, Grüber channeled Maurice Chevalier. He gently took her hand in his and raised it to his lips. "Ahhh... mon cher," he growled in his pseudo-French accent while kissing her fingertips. "La preuve — allow me to prove it to *yoooo*! Might I tempt Madame with a Chaud de Chien? ...eh... Pooo-*dle* Très Chaud?"

"Are you offering me a hotdog, Monsieur?"

Jerri's date hung his head. "...eh. Le'Busted," he grinned sheepishly.

"You had me at food," Jerri giggled once more. "I'm ravenous — I don't think I'll last until dinner. One with just a little mustard, please? Wouldn't want to muss this dress."

Grinning, Dolf stepped up to the vendor underneath the multicolored umbrella. "Mon bon homme — Deux Le'Poodle Très Chaud. Monsieur — avec seulement votre meilleur moutarde pour ma dame et moi." He turned back to Jerri and smiled the puffed up smile of a man who'd gallently ordered for his lady.

"That'll be two most excellent `dogs comin' up, with only my best mustard — for you and your girl, Mac!" the teenaged vendor laughed. "Boy — that's some bad high school French-mojo you got goin' on there!" He slapped two hotdogs to steamed buns and handed them over.

Dolf leaned in and whispered to his date, "Le'Busted... *again.*"

Perhaps I was mistaken about how he overreacted awhile ago... perhaps I imagined... exaggerated it when he... he's being a perfect gentleman, now. She accepted the offered hotdog.

They took their snacks to the wooden railing and gazed out over the water, facing the coming sunset. The nightly flotilla of schooners, sloops and simple sailboats gathered in loose single files, readying for their sunset parade.

Jerri glanced around, noticing the various street performers setting up their stages. At the far end of the pier, in the shadow of a gleaming-white cruise ship, she spied a girl dressed in old-fashioned clothes.

Pale paint completely covered her face and hands. In fact, every surface of the young woman's body coated in white — including her ankle-length period costume and the pedestal she stood on. She gleamed in the bright sunlight. As Jerri watched, the girl struck a pose and held it.

"Look at that," Jerri said. "That girl looks just like a statue!"

Dolf turned and quipped, "Congratulations, Jerri! You've just spotted your first Mallory Square street performer!"

She finished the last of her hotdog and smiled. "Oh, yeah? What? Do I win a prize?" Counting off the other festive acts, she glanced around at the people already gathering in small clusters. "Over there — there's a high-wire act — there's a dog walking the wire! And there's two teenaged jugglers!" Jerri exicitedly twirled to her right, and pointed at the man setting up what looked to be a minature lion tamer's set. "Ooh! What do you think *he's* up to?"

Dolf smiled. "That's a Mallory Square National Treasure. That's Dominique's Circus Cats. Dominique LeFort trains cats he rescues from shelters. And the remarkable thing is, the performing kitties *really* seem to have a good time — they seem to be enjoying themselves."

Jerri noticed Dolf's tender expression as he spoke of the Key West cats, and she silently berated herself for her earlier doubts.

"Lucky thing, for us," he continued, "Dominique is here most every evening. Let's move closer and enjoy the show, okay?"

Yes... perhaps I misjudged him... perhaps he's just having a bad day....

For the next twenty minutes, while the wind-worshipping sailboats continued their romp in front of the dock, they watched the trained felines walk tightropes, jump through flaming hoops, and perform other tricks that mere cats couldn't manage. By the end of the show, Jerri and her date were laughing and applauding with the rest of the small audience.

"That was *amazing!*" Jerri marveled. "That man and his cats are a true joy!" She looked around at the other carnival-like attractions. "I feel like a kid in a candystore!" she trilled. "You wouldn't believe how much I'm enjoying this! What's next?"

"Your wish, my sweet-toothed princess, is my command!" He bowed low before her.

Jerri lightly cuffed Dolf's arm. "Oh, you...." Then, glancing across the stone-paved commons, she noticed a brightly-hued tent, the door flaps tied back with huge blue ribbons. An exotically-turbaned young woman dressed in colorful flowing clothes sat across a table from a male customer, a middle-aged tourist dressed in white Bermuda shorts and garish Hawiian shirt. The woman shuffled a deck of cards that she placed one by one on the table in front of the man. "*That!*" Jerri crowed, "*I want that!!!*" She excitedly grabbed her date's hand, pulling him across to the bricked common, not stopping until they'd reached the small cabana. The sign proclaimed: "Madame Serena — Knows All. Readings: $20."

"Oh, come on — " Dolf scoffed. "A psychic?" He lowered his voice and said, "You don't really *believe* in this, do you?" Rolling his eyes, he grinned, then added a quick wink.

Cuffing his arm again, Jerri laughed. "It's just for fun, Dolf — just for fun. Come on — I've *always* wanted to do this!" She pulled him to the tent's doorway.

The crowded Square fairly bustled with sunset celebrators; a few people passed by, sipping on boatdrinks. Grüber appeared to glance around at the milling tourists, as if he were guiltily searching out familiar faces. Apparently finding none, he slowly nodded his head. "Of course, Jerri," he murmured. "Tonight is *your* night. One psychic on me!" He pulled his wallet from his back pocket.

"Put your money back." She laughed, and said, "I'm a big girl — I can pick up the tab on my own psychic. Come on! That guy's already got his reading!" The two watched as the tourist left his session before Jerri pulled Grüber across the tent's threshold and they stepped into Madam Serena's presence. The tent's vibrant interior blossomed with the comforting fragrance of Patchouli and Sandlewood candles. The many-hued scarves composing the tent walls, waved in the slight salty breeze and puffed, rustled and danced at the sides of the small enclosure.

"Please." The psychic motioned to two chairs on the other side of the table. "Make yourselves comfortable and we'll begin."

~o0o~

Chapter 13

"From zero to twenty-one, please give me a number from your heart."

From my heart? What? ...okaaay... strange, but whatever floats your boat, Tarot-Lady. "Eh... seventeen?"

Removing a card from the deck, Madam Serena placed it in front of Jerri. "You've chosen the Star as your significant card — this card will represent you in this reading," she smiled, and spoke with a slight accent. "As I place the seventeenth card, the Star, notice it shows a lovely naked woman — completely at peace with her nakedness... her nakedness *to the world*. Unlike her determined sister — Temperance — *this* lady neither controls nor conserves water... or the course of life. Indeed she *is* at peace, unshamefully drinking life, unreservedly emptying her water pitchers, having total faith they *will* be filled again. That is why her message is one of replenishment and faith. As she holds out the comforting promise that we *can* eventually find peace of mind. The Star also reminds us to open our heart and release our fears and doubt, for we must... if we, too, wish to... drink life."

Jerri gave an embarrassed giggle and looked to Dolf. "Eh... naked? This card represents me... *naked?*"

"That's merely symbolic." The psychic shook her head, mumbling, "The only word people ever hear is naked...." She added a chuckle to Jerri's own laughter. "Nakedness — not *nudity*, you understand — is a reoccurrence of a symbolic theme in Tarot. You do realize, don't you, how nakedness is not necessarily nudity? Innocent nakedness is a giving of one's self to the universal 'I Am' — offering yourself to the Greatness that is, can and shall be. Do not think of this nakedness as sexual."

"Okay... I'll do my best...." Jerri blushed and lowered her eyes.

Picking up the remainder of the deck, the woman lightly shuffled the cards. "For this reading, I'm using the twenty-one major arcana only — not the complete seventy-eight — some would say I'm not dealing with a full deck." She winked, filling them in on the joke. "Actually, it's what we call a short reading." Shuffling the cards a moment more, she laid them in a single stack in front of Jerri. "Please be so kind as to cut the cards into three or four small stacks — and while you do this, silently ask questions... questions that have lately filled your mind." She relaxed back into her seat, and briefly closed her eyes, as if she were gathering mental strength for the coming task.

Noting the psychic apparently at rest, Jerri hesitated a moment, then split the deck four ways. As she slowly rearranged the cards, she mused on immediate problems and ones she'd brought forward with her from her past, as per Madam Serena's instructions. *I've been alone for so long....* Stacking the four piles together in no particular order, she asked herself: *What would Daddy have done, suddenly confronted with the invincible force known as Miss Marty Sebastian? All these new people... this new family in my life... what... HOW would Daddy have reacted? Daddy — WHAT would you have done? Join them? Run? Surrender or flee?* Her hand lingered over the single stack of cards, her attention drawn back to the lady across the table. And as Jerri watched, Madam Serena opened her eyes and took the cards from her.

"And now... the questions asked... are answers revealed." The psychic quipped, "Eeiney-Meiney Chili-Beaney — "

" — the spirits... are about... to speak?" Dolf scoffed an interruption and then, apparently hoping Madam Serena would overhear, he loudly whispered in his date's ear. "Jerri — let's get outta here. This is — "

"Bogus?" She patted his arm. "It's all in fun, remember?"

...okaaay... a little controlling are we? Well... that's not gonna fly!

With a barely disguised reluctance, he finally nodded his head and took Jerri's hand in a comforting grip. Flashing a hesitant smile at the psychic, he murmured, "Go on."

The medium smirked at Grüber. "Sorry. Just a little joke." She gently placed a card over Jerri's significator card. "I see much... change... in your future."

Jerri glanced at her date, just in time to gauge his reaction to the psychic's clichéd opening. Picking up on Dolf's swiftly rolling eyes, she watched him telegraphing a silent 'told ya so' her way. Jerri murmured to Madam Serena, "Interesting."

"This card — the Fool — "

Jerri quickly interjected, "I'm a *fool?* I'm confused. I thought I was the star...." She fussed with her scarf-fringed dress, smoothing it over her knees. *I've been accused of acting a fool before, but never by a psychic!*

Madam Serena chuckled. "No, my dear. You *are* the Star. This one merely represents you in relation to your question. The Fool tells us you are at a crossroads. Whichever path you choose will determine the course of the rest of your life. Will you choose wisely? Perhaps not. The Fool encourages us to throw caution to the wind, take the path less taken — when in doubt, follow your heart — prepare to meet all challenges head-on." The pretty dark-eyed woman touched Jerri's hand. "Do you see? Again, let me remind you, with each card, review your silent question in your mind. Ask yourself, what does the Fool tell me?"

...hhmmmm... I suppose... the Fool wants me to... wants me to... to finally make up my mind. — but make up my mind about what? Jerri nodded her head and wanly smiled, looking back to the exotically-dressed tarot reader.

"Good. Let's continue." The psychic horizontally crossed the Fool card with another. "Now we see the Tower card... it's a disturbing one. Card sixteen isn't welcomed by those who dislike change, as it speaks of having plans disrupted — experiencing a crash, so to speak — "

Jerri gasped an interruption. *A crash?* Her mind flew back

to the cataclysmic meeting with Miss Marty Sebastian. *...when I lost Baby to the auto accident in Marathon...* my *career... my Baby....*

Madam Serena continued, as if not noticing her client's reaction to the word 'crash'. "It represents a sudden, dramatic upheaval or reversal in fortune. While usually change is gradual, giving us time to adapt, sometimes it's quick and explosive. ...and *this* is the dramatic action of the Tower. You see, sometimes, sudden crises are life's way of telling you to wake up. Are you too full of pride? Expect a blow to your ego. Are you holding back your anger? Expect the dam to burst. Are you stuck in a rut? Expect a surprise." The woman looked to Jerri, now seemingly gauging her client's reaction to her words. "*How* you respond to the Tower's change makes all the difference in how uncomfortable the experience will be. You should recognize that the disruption occurred because it was *needed*. A necessary evil? Perhaps... *embracing* the change is too much to ask, but try to find the positive in it. In fact, being forced in a new direction, you may feel tremendous release. Perhaps you'll have a burst of insight about your situation and reach a new level of understanding about it. That is the opportunity given to us by the Tower."

Jerri's thoughts momentarily turned pensive. "I see," she murmured. *So... I should look upon having my budding career taken from me, and losing Baby as... an opportunity? Okaaay....*

"We christen the fourth card, placed in position directly under the first three, the Wheel of Fortune."

When her first thought, seeing the decorative card and its title, was of Vanna White and Pat Sajak, Jerri nearly giggled. She looked into Madam Serena's face and caught a wink.

"No... it's not that pretty pair on television and you don't have to buy a vowel. Yet."

Now, Jerri giggled.

The tarot reader continued, saying, "The Wheel of Fortune is one of the few major arcana without a human figure as a focal point," she pointed at the tarot card represented by a huge golden wheel. "This card often indicates a realization that strikes with great force." She paused and seemed to watch Jerri.

...that strikes with great force? A realization? Jerri murmured, "I'm not sure I'm following."

Madam Serena patted her client's hand. "Okay. Think of it this way... let's say you've been struggling with a problem or tough situation. The Wheel of Fortune can signal that you will find the answer if you just stand back and view everything from a larger perspective. Indeed, the Wheel often brings wheel-like actions... changes in direction... repeating cycles and rapid movement. With the Wheel's energy around you, you will feel life speed up, and you find yourself caught in a cyclone that may deposit you anywhere. Round and round and round you go, and where you stop... *nobody knows.*"

"So... I'm caught up in a *cyclone?*"

"Perhaps," the psychic said. "Can you relate? Can you relate to the Wheel?"

Jerri simply nodded her head.

The fifth card landed parallel to the first three cards, but to the left and above the fourth card. "The Emperor," the woman stated. "He is a powerful man. In this position, he speaks of the past. Your past or the past as it relates to your questions. I'm seeing many confusing things around you... a bunny rabbit... a magician's rabbit — like one would pull from a hat... a bicycle — no... no — " She chuckled, and shook her head.

"Now, this is *really* strange... a fish? A fish... *riding* a bicycle?" Again, she shook her head before she continued.

"The Emperor, is the powerful masculine influence of your life... the rule maker, the authority figure of your conscious. This card usually represents structure, order and regulation, for while he *can* represent an encounter with authority or the assumption of power and control, as the regulator, he is often associated with legal matters, disciplinary actions, and officialdom in all its forms. But, he can also stand for an individual father or archetypal father in his role as guide, protector and provider. All your life, you've felt safe in the comfort of the rules set out by the Emperor. Comfortably safe... still... you should remember... rules were meant to be... *broken.* Does this card speak to you?"

Jerri nodded. "I think so," she said. *No need to even wonder who this could be... a man of order and authority? Hellooo, Daddy!*

"Let's continue." The next card placed into the vertical top of the Celtic Cross pattern was the Empress. In her musical voice, she said, "A woman has entered your life. A powerful woman. It is *she* who brings the change."

Miss Marty? Jerri's immediate thought was of the dowager who'd knocked the Amazing Delaney off the magic circuit.

"Do you connect with this card?"

"Perhaps...." *...well, I'd certainly say Miss Marty's a powerful woman...*

"This card — in the position of your present — the Empress...." Madam Serena launched into the sixth card's story," — she reigns over the bounty of nature and rhythms of the Earth. She is the Mother. The Empress lavishes generous abundance of all kinds — a vast cornucopia of delights — especially those of the senses, like food, pleasure, beauty. She gives us material reward, of course, but it's almost as if — *to her* — monetary wealth is inconsequential. If you're fortunate enough to have the Empress in your present, you are truly blessed, for she reminds you to keep your feet firmly planted in... *and on...* the Earth. From the other cards and the postitions they take, I can see you've been alone for so long. You are lonely. But, might I suggest — in your darkest moment — that moment when you feel most *alone* — just... *look around.* See this beautiful lady and know. Love is all around you... *still.* Do you know the Empress in your own life?"

A warm feeling washed over Jerri and she spoke softly, "Yes... yes I do. I know her."

"Good," said Madam Serena. "Cherish her."

"I will... always. Pinky swear." Jerri caught Dolf's silent nod. *Yes. He knows the Empress, too.*

"Now for the eighth card — the one which stands for your self-image. You've drawn the Magician."

Jerri giggled, closed her eyes and shook her head.

94

Madam Serena asked, "Something is funny?" Her long dark hair framed her face, and she blinked her heavily made-up eyes.

"No... no. Nothing really. Please — go on."

"Surely... as I've said, the eighth card is the Magician... but when I told you that your *self-image* was this card, I meant that, although the Magician *is* thought of as a *masculine* figure — the virile aspect of the Universal 'Ki' — the symbolic representation of the asian life-force — it only complicates things to think of the Magician as a male," she chuckled. "To simplify, think of him as a unisex entity. He... or *she* is the ultimate achiever, having the power to tap universal forces, using them for creative purposes. At times, his abilities appear magical because his will helps him achieve what *seem to be* miracles. From the moment I laid the card down on the table, I've felt a strong connection with this card to you. It's as if *you* are the Magician, *you* are the... miracle worker. Strange...."

Once again, Jerri giggled and for the first time, Dolf joined her in her humor. She turned to him and said, "Funny, isn't it?"

He smiled. "A little." Chuckling once more, he grasped her hand and gallantly kissed her fingertips.

Silently sharing the moment with her charming companion, Jerri pulled his hand to her lips and returned the fingertip kiss. *I think... maybe... under all that compressed... energy — he's really a sweetheart.*

"Did I miss something?" Madam Serena asked. "Why would you think the Magician funny?" She looked from Jerri to her date, frowned and shook her head. "The Magician is many things, but I've never found him particularly *funny*."

Jerri shook her head and laughed again, harder this time. "You just said the Magician stood for my self-image."

"Yes," the tarot reader nodded and said, "in *this* position, it does. Why would that be funny?"

Turning to Dolf, Jerri giggled again, feeling herself close to a 'giggling fit'. She touched her fingertips to her lips. "Should I...?"

"Oh, go on. No harm...."

She nodded and returned her attention to the now bemused psychic. "It's just that... you see... *I* am the magician. That's who I *am — that's* what I do."

Now it was Madam Serena's turn to giggle. "How apropos is that! It only goes to prove, the Universe *truly* has a sense of humor. Even before your laughter, I felt a strong connection with this card to you. I'm constantly amazed with the fall of the cards!"

Jerri murmured, "Amazing!"

"Yes," quipped Dolf. "*Amazing...* Delaney."

Jerri lightly cuffed his shoulder. Playfully, the grinning man cried out an exaggerated "Ow."

"To get back to the Magician's relation to you — try to think of him as the masculine force in everyone. And just as Mother nurtures, Father encourages... and draws greatness from perhaps where only fear resided. You — *as the Magician* — should not ignore your fear. Instead, embrace it. From the cards, I understand this is very important for you. You should always remember — if you truly wish to conquer — first embrace."

Dolf leaned in and whispered, "Well, *that's* clear as mud."

Practically glaring her displeasure, Madam Serena interrupted Dolf's sarcasm. "Concerning your *environment* — all that is around you — the ninth card you draw is Death."

"*Death???*" Jerri and Dolf joined their voices.

Steepling her fingers, the tarot reader pursed her lips and paused her words. Wearily, with an escaping rush of breath, as if she'd made this little disclaimer often, she launched into the card's defense. "Initially frightening — much feared, at first — this card — *Death* — is often at the very heart of our nightmares... but the truly enlightened would say, needlessly so." She touched her finger to the card. "With his gaunt demeanor and his stark accouterments — notice the austere white flower decorating his staff — Death is a formidable figure. But much like the powerful white horse he rides in on, above all else, Death is also a *noble* figure. This card rarely has anything to do with physical death... rather... card number thirteen often represents an important ending... an initiation of great changes. It usually signals the end of an era; as in the moment a door closes. There may be sadness and reluctance, but one also finds relief and a welcome sense of completion. With everything and everybody, Death *is* inevitable, and sometimes there are events that are inescapable as well. When these 'brickwall' moments occur, the best approach is to ride your fate, like Death rides his white horse, and see where it takes you. Sometimes... if we're fortunate... we win the — how would you say — *Rodeo*? So... you see where the Death card is not so bad after all?"

"Yes." *But, that doesn't mean rushing out to close doors on all my Rodeos. ...does it?*

"And... does this card whisper to your soul?"

"...eh. Whisper to my soul? Not yet. But I'll try my best to listen more closely. Okay?"

"Deal." Madam Serena smirked. "Let's move on. This next card speaks of your hopes and fears — or more precisely, it speaks of the safety you run to when you find yourself overwhelmed... overwhelmed — *with life*." She placed the card in the tenth position, in an upward stack from the eighth card, to the right of the Celtic Cross. "Ahhh... the High Priestess. She is the guardian of your unconscious — where your mind flees to automatically — your first thought, so to speak. Most times you don't even remember 'going there'. Though she is so much more, think of the the High Priestess as the first female who nurtured you — "

Jerri's thoughts flew to her grandmother, and when she caught the psychic's smile, she realized her memories must have shown in her face.

"You've known the High Priestess." Madam Serena stated this as a fact, not a question.

"Yes, ma'am." She found it strange not wanting to leave the comforting memory of her dear grandmother. *Ahhh... Granny — you're always the one I run to — even though you've been gone for so long.*

Again, the tarot reader touched Jerri's hand. "Just know," she spoke quietly, "she's with you always. Your High Priestess sends me these words for you... *for you alone:* 'Idle hands... idle hands'. Now, *I* don't know what those words mean to you — *but she does.*"

Jerri gasped and tears filled her eyes. "Granny Tyler." She whispered, "Miss you much." Wiping the hot tears dry, she noticed Dolf squirming, clearly uncomfortable. She gave his hand a reassuring squeeze.

The woman smiled. "Yes. I can see that you speak to her daily. Just so you know, she appreciates it. Now back to your reading. The High Priestess in the tenth location — your hopes and fears — she oversees them. This is a fortunate card to fall in this position, for her wisdom is great, and her love for us is boundless, and she is the guardian of the unconscious. She sits in front of the thin veil of unawareness which is all that separates us from our inner landscape.

"Just like a woman wise in her years, she always poses a challenge for you to go deeper — to look beyond the obvious — to search out the obscure answer — to remember the unlimited possibilities you hold within yourself. Sometimes she believes in you when you've lost the belief in yourself. She also asks you to recall the vastness of your potential, telling you it's not always necessary to *act* to achieve your goals — that sometimes our dreams can be realized through a peace-filled stillness. For, as always, the first and last words she leaves with you is the simple message the great 'I AM' wants *all* of us to remember: 'Be still and *know* that I am God'. The High Priestess contains within herself the secrets of these realms." The psychic paused, again, and reached out, brushing Jerri's fingertips with her own. "No need to tell me," she whispered, "I *know* you hear her voice. Take comfort that she guides you through your hopes and fears."

Granny Tyler — you once told me you'd always be with me... and I feel safe whenever I remember your words... safe when I know you're near me. While I'm in your arms — even if it's only spiritually — nothing — nothing can hurt me. Sending her beloved grandmother a psychic hug, Jerri swallowed the lump in her throat and murmured, "I do."

Madam Serena sighed and said, "The last card in the reading. The eleventh position. The card that speaks of the 'Great Outcome'. You ready for this?" She turned over the Lovers card, placing it in the top corner to the right of the Celtic Cross, completing the pattern's shape with a supporting column. The colorful card showed a man and a woman in a glorious embrace, standing in a calm sea, underneath the shimmering starlight, dolphins dancing on the far golden horizon.

"Ahhh... the Lovers... the easiest one to translate," she smiled. "See how they delight in their own private world? See how they are complete within each other? He, the warrior, lifts her up, freeing her from the perils of the water, giving her all his strength, in her time of need. She, a golden goddess, turns her face to the light. Perhaps... *because* of his sacrificed strength, she revels — indeed, unabashedly *celebrates* — in the loving goodness that is her lover.

The Lovers represent both sex *and* love. The urge for union, both spiritual and physical, is a powerful force, and in its highest incarnation takes us beyond ourselves. This card doesn't *necessarily* concern itself with the carnal version of sex — it can, of course — but, more to the point it refers to a relationship based on *deep* love — the strongest force of all. For you see, this relationship may not *be* sexual, although it often is or *could* be... in the future. Do you have the essence of this card in you life?"

Jerri's eyes flew open wide as she thought of Dolf. *Do I have that in my life — and I haven't seen it yet?* Surreptitiously, she peeked over at the man by her side, and noticed his right eyebrow twitch, in a barely detectible 'body-language salute'. *Is it... could it be... Dolf???*

Madam Serena spoke softly, her words musical, given her accent, "Do you *have* this in your life? If not now... the cards urge you to search it out. Remember... *all* the potential... *lovers...* in your life."

Another 'lover'? Not Dolf? Jerri fought the urge to shake her head at the mental image that lightening-flashed into her wondering mind: *Pendragon??? Oh... My... G —*

The psychic chuckled, observing her client's sudden, subtle and silent burst of insight. "As I've said... Consider *all* the possibilities. Our time is now at an end. If you please...." She held out her hand, palm up, awaiting payment.

"Jerri," Dolf removed his wallet and said, "let me get this. Allowing me to be here during your reading has brought me so much... so much... *insight* — I'll never look at life — *and death* — the same way again." He laid a twenty in Madam Serena's hand.

She closed her fist around the bill and murmured in response to Dolf's last words, "I'm sure." The tarot reader rose, and swept her arm toward the tent's entrance. "Thank you, gentle lady, for coming into my life." She watched Jerri leave the tent before she again spoke, "...and thank *you*, sir." She lightly touched Dolf's arm. "You have been... a most *promising* pupil. Hopefully, the wisdom of the cards will lead you... *back to the path.*"

Dolf hesitated, his foot on the tent's threshold. "What?"

"God-Speed, good sir," Madam Serena purred her farewell. "But — before you take your leave, might I reveal the words the cards spoke for *you?*"

"Me?"

"Yes. Sometimes messages bleed through, meant for others than the one whose touch the cards have felt. Are you open to the message?"

He paused, his hand gently resting on the tent flap. "Message? ...I guess so."

Madam Serena reached out, grasping Dolf's jacket sleeve. "Someone... someone on the otherside of the veil, wants desperately to tell you... they want you to know — these words. Sorry. I don't speak this language — my pronunciation may be off, and I really *don't* know the meaning...."

"...okaaay...."

"Eines Tages verbinden Sie mich in der Hölle."

The blond man's eyes flew open wide, and he roughly gripped the shocked psychic's shoulders. Realizing he was close to violence, Dolf suddenly rushed from the tent. A few stumbling steps, and he joined Jerri in the still bright sunshine. Pacing beside her, his breath came in short, angry puffs.

Jerri noticed Dolf's short-breathed agitation. "What's wrong? What's ruffled *your* feathers?"

He fisted both hands on his hips and cast his gaze out over the blue water, where the sun was readying itself for its nightly performance. "Stupid psychic. Bunch of crap cards."

"*Dolf?* I said — what's *wrong?* What did she say?" Jerri spun him to face her.

For a brief moment, it appeared the man would hold his silence — keep the reason behind his ire to himself. When he finally spoke, the hurt he held inside was obvious. "Eines Tages verbinden Sie mich in der Hölle." Dolf hissed the words.

She was silent for a beat of three. Then, softly, she said, "Sorry. I didn't study German. Got no clue what you just said. Sounded nice enough, though."

He smiled, ruefully. "Those were the last words my father ever spoke to me. As I was heading out the door, fresh from another one of his 'fatherly' beatings."

"Okay... what? Give it up."

"Someday, you'll join me in Hell."

Jerri was dumbstruck.

Dolf continued, "Stupid psychic said she'd — she'd — *received* those words from the otherside — for me — *they were left for me!!!*"

Jerri looked back at the little tent. Another couple sat in their chairs. "Calm down," Jerri whispered. *Why don't I just say 'there-there' while I'm at it? Focus!* "

"She was mistaken. She got lucky. She just grabbed those words out of the air...."

Knowing her mind simply and frantically reached out for *any* comforting words she could provide, didn't leave *Jerri* with any comfort.

He surprised her with his calm reply. "Yeah... you're right," he said, while she noticed his eyes crinkled in his usual good humor. "And it *was* just a lark, right? Just for fun. A Key West novelty. Best to forget it. Like I said on the drive down, dear old Dad's not coming out with us tonight."

Wow! Those mental little pink pills work fast!

"Hey — the night is young and so are we — least *you* are. Let's catch a few street shows before we head off to the Outlander. You game?" Dolf's sudden good nature belied his mood mere seconds ago. He took Jerri's arm and they walked out onto the wide wooden dock.

Okaaaay... may I doo-doo now? Her inner child sang the Twilight Zone's ominous opening music — *Doo-doo-doo-doo doo-doo-doo-doo....*

Many of the street performers were only now setting up for their nightly tips-driven shows. In the distance, at the far end of the pier, the white-dressed statue stood on a pedestal, her long painted dress failing to rustle in the breeze. As they walked the pier, mingling among other rubbernecking tourists, Jerri stole glances at the white-statue girl. *There's something mildly disturbing about that girl. She's not quite what she appears... ...like Dolf?*

They strolled out into the growing crowd, and Jerri noticed the diversity of people gathering to watch the sun go down. Every nationality represented, she walked by the mostly white-dressed tourists, picking up words in many different languages.

A colorful sari-clad young woman strolled past. As she passed Jerri, they both exchanged smiles and nods. Two different women from vastly different cultures, but united for one late afternoon. Bound in silent friendship in appreciation of the setting sun.

Grüber bought two margaritas from a street vendor. Once more, they stepped up to the wooden railing and peered over into the water, sipping their boat drinks through straws.

Jerri dropped her Key lime into the salt-rimmed drink and swirled it with her straw. The setting sun like a beacon, sending its last rays skimming over the water toward them, was as bright as a spotlight thrown on an encore. A rippling of silence played throughout the crowd. All eyes focused on the imminent sunset.

"They say," Grüber whispered in Jerri's ear, "if you stand at the railing at Mallory Square and make a wish just at the moment when the sun goes down, your wish *has* to come true."

"Okay," Jerri said, "I wish that we'll — "

"Don't say it outloud!" he frantically interrupted. "*It might not come true!*"

" — meet again in Key West," Jerri finished. "Sorry. You didn't catch me in time. Besides. I'm sure *that* wish will come true."

As the sun-worshipping crowd cheered and applauded one more glorious sunset — just another day in Paradise — Grüber kissed her forehead and smiled.

Jerri noticed how the light from the dying rays of the setting sun caused his green eyes to sparkle, and she silently mused, *Jeez, he's 'Greek god' beautiful... think if I paint him white and put him on a pedestal he'd bring in some spare change?*

"Most definitely," he smiled, and for a swift moment, Jerri thought he'd answered her unspoken thoughts.

Dolf took her hand in his and continued, "Definitely. I'm absolutely sure we'll come back to Key West. The Gulf waters *will* bring us together again."

As the last words left her date's mouth, Jerri shivered.

Wrapping her arms around her bare shoulders, she turned her back to the water and leaned against the railing, sudden and strangely moody thoughts clouding her mind.

"Cold?" Grüber asked.

Jerri smiled, trying to keep her chattering teeth still. "Just a little. It's a bit nippy. Must be the night air coming off the water. I'll be okay." She kept her back turned to the water.

"Here," he said. "Take my jacket." He removed his light sports coat and draped it around Jerri's shoulders. "We'll go back to the car. It's not too early to get to the Outlander. Show starts in a little over an hour, anyway."

"Thanks," she said, "I didn't realize going 'bare-backed' on a Key West evening could get chilly. Maybe I should have worn a long sleeved, high necked, schoolmarm's dress."

He chuckled. "Bite your tongue. You're beautiful. I envy my sports coat, right now. It gets to hold you in its arms."

Jerri shivered again, though she didn't quite know why.

~o0o~

Chapter 14

In the gathering darkness of the evening, the colorful lights from the little shops and restaurants they passed on the drive back to Angela Street sparkled like a festive Christmas tree. Flip-flop shod locals pedaled three-wheeled bikes in the street, sharing the street with Bermuda-shorted, pedestrian-tourists.

The Carnival atmosphere was subdued, seemingly waiting for the Key West nightlife to commence. For her, every person strolling the festive street was eye-candy, and the journey to The Outlander was too short. She felt she could have lingered on Duval Street for hours.

He pulled the car into the Outlander Lounge's front round-a-bout. Six feet tall marquees flanking the outside doors showed a life-sized 'Amazing Jerri Delaney', but a slashing ribbon hung across each poster, bearing one word: 'Cancelled'. At the bottom of each marquee, an LCD panel scrolled a declaration: "SURPRISE REPLACEMENT!!!"

"Look." Jerri pointed out the marquees. "Looks like I'm still searching for clues at the scene of the crime, and those posters might well have police tape over them. The death of the Amazing Jerri Delaney's career. You know? They say she *really* could put on a show. Razzle-Dazzle with the best of `em — sigh."

He grabbed up her hand and gently kissed her fingertips. "Cut it out, Amazing. Stop it or you'll make me cry." Grüber stuck out his bottom lip in a humorous pout. "Remember your vow? No tears tonight. That's Buffett's Law."

"You just made that up."

His face erupted in dimples. "Okay... but is it working?"

Jerri couldn't help joining in her date's joking. "As all us Parrotheads in good standing say: 'Fins Up!'" She patted his hand. "No tears tonight, my fellow Parrothead, no tears." A smartly uniformed valet appeared at the driver's door, as another valet opened Jerri's door, offering his hand to assist her from the car. She smoothed her dress, giving a last look at her posters. "Fins up, Jerri," she whispered to herself, "Fins up."

Waiting for Grüber to come around the car to meet her, Jerri murmured, "Wow. Valet service. This is *so* neat." She turned to watch the valet drive away with the shiny black Jaguar.

Taking her hand, Grüber smiled and leaned in to share a confidence. "Yeah. The first time I came here, I was blown away too. Shall we go in now?"

Jerri hoped the huge smile on her face didn't give her away. "In a second. I want to savor the moment. It's just that… I'm *always* the headliner, never the patron. Kinda like, always the bridesmaid; never the bride. You know?" Twirling on the tips of her toes, her smile threatened to split her face. She attempted to drink in every light, every sparkle that made up the Outlander Lounge.

"Sure," he nodded and smiled. "We'll walk slow."

Jerri squeezed his hand. "Thanks for indulging my quirkiness. I promise I won't do this the whole night through."

"M'lady," he whispered in her ear, "the night belongs only to *you.*"

~o0o~

"This is a fabulous double chocolate mousse! The raspberry coulis takes the chocolate to heights I'd not thought possible. It almost rivals the main-course, doesn't it? Boy! What the Outlander does with raspberries... I'll wager you've never had roast duck with fresh raspberry sauce like that before."

Jerri touched her napkin to her mouth before answering her dinner date. She laughed and said, "I never bet against a sure thing, Mr. Grüber. The truth is, I've never even had roasted duck before in my life and I — "

A piano player coaxed quiet music from a Baby Grand near

the stage, setting the mood for a pleasant evening. "Wait a moment!" he chuckled his interruption. "Why am I 'Mr. Grüber' again? I thought we settled all of that formal stuff before we left Marathon."

Jerri smiled. "Sorry. It's a habit. My grandmother taught me to formally address people, until they offer their first name. She was a stickler for good manners. ...I miss her very much." She quickly focused her attention on her banana daiquiri to head off any rogue tears.

A waiter swept past bearing martinis for a table to their right. "You forget, Amazing Delaney, I *did* offer my first name," he sipped at his fruit-laced drink, and flashed a grin.

When he smiled, dimples decorated his cheeks, causing Jerri to swoon inwardly. She quipped, "So you did...."

"Let's see your amazing powers of prestidigitation at work! Quick — Amazing! Can you pull my first name out of your rabbit hat?" He grinned another dimpled smile.

"Hhhhummm... could it be...? Oh, I dunno... *Dolf?*"

"And the masterful Lady Magician astounds yet another sold-out crowd!" With his humorous words, she again noticed the man's fair good looks.

It's as if Grüber's the sun to Pendragon's moon, she thought, *any way you cut it, they're both heavenly bodies. It's not fair! Why did God bestow all the heart-stopping beauty on the peacocks? Why did He forget the peahens?*

He cleared his throat and Jerri realized she'd allowed her mind to take a hunk vacation. "I'm sorry," she apologized, "did I go away for a moment? Seems I do that a lot lately."

"That's all right. You're more than entitled to veg out every once in a while. After all, your body's been through a trauma. Are you ready for dessert?" he offered, signaling the waiter to their table. "They serve the most delicious Key Lime pie in the Outlander."

"Are you trying to tempt me?" She giggled. "Or is someone paying you to fatten me up to wipe me off the magic circuit all together?"

Grüber smiled. "I doubt one little slice of Key Lime pie would destroy your career." To the waiter he said, "Bring us two slices of your wonderful Key Lime pie. And two more banana daiquiris." Turning back to Jerri he said, "the show's set to start in a minute. It'll be a treat to watch a magic show in the company of a professional magician. You can tell me how all the tricks — "

"No can do, Dolf." She added a chuckle to her interruption. "Those are *professional* Magician's Guild secrets. I took a vow of secrecy."

"So you're not going to tell me? Even just a teeny secret?"

She shook her head while the waiter delivered the pie and drinks to the table. Leaning toward her charming dinner companion, she whispered in a mock conspiratorial tone, "If I told you, I'd have to kill you." Jerri grinned and sipped the daiquiri, inwardly marveling at the banana-flavored delicacy. She watched Grüber enjoying his daiquiri and took a selfish moment to simply enjoy her date for the evening. Her eyes roamed his face, so fair and good-humored. *At this minute, I'd have never guessed that just over an hour ago this man's body held fiery rage. He looks so relaxed....*

The soft music playing in the background changed to a cheer of trumpets as the lighting dimmed and the stage curtains parted. *At last! The show's about to begin and this'll be the first time in years I'm on THIS side of the curtain.* With that thought, her emotions conflicted. On one hand, it was exciting to be sitting in the audience. On the other... it wasn't *her* the trumpets welcomed. Jerri took a bite of pie, silently pronounced it good, and looked up in time to see an emcee sprint onto the stage, a remote microphone in his hand.

"Ladies and Gentlemen!" The crowd was animated, clapping, whistling, and joking among themselves. The emcee raised his hands, 'patting down' the audience. "The Outlander Lounge is pleased to welcome you here tonight. Although our headliner was supposed to be The Amazing Delaney, we're sorry to say she has been forced to cancel." The audience reacted with moans and groans.

Jerri smiled.

"But, we've asked another wonderful magician to fill in tonight." The cheerful emcee continued. "He's been knockin' `em dead, night after night for the last three weeks."

The audience reacted with cheers and whistles.

Jerri frowned.

"In fact," the emcee went on, "Mongo the Magnificent has made *such* a killing here at The Outlander — "

Hearing Mongo's name, Jerri shook her head in shock, while the tuxedoed man continued his lame comedy introduction.

" — He's made *such* a killing, it's rumored O.J.'s haunting him. Wants Mongo to try on a pair of gloves!" A sound effects technician sitting in the sound and lighting booth gave the emcee a rim shot, and the audience exploded in applause. Jerri groaned.

"Come on, Jerri." Grüber chuckled, joining the audience in their glee. "Be a good sport. Your accident's not *Mongo's* fault. Mongo wasn't anywhere around when you had your accident."

She closed her eyes and hung her head. "*What are the odds? Will his stalking never end?*" Jerri opened her eyes, raised her head, and hissed at her date, "*You don't understand...* Mongo's a *clown.*"

Grüber laughed once more. "Isn't that being a sore loser?"

"No," she groaned. "I mean, Mongo's *really* a clown. His act is a farce of the magic profession. Sure, the man's funny. But, so's a rubber chicken." Humiliated, she covered her face, and groaned. "They've replaced me with a *clown!* A touchy-feely stalking *clown!!*"

~o0o~

A far-off storm sent its threatening rumbles over the water in an unanswered challenge. Lightening zigzagged across the distant black sky; like a quilt maker frantically stitching fiery thunderbolts into a storm-fringed crazy-quilt design. The sea air nearly vibrated with static electricity.

A cordless phone to his ear, Pendragon listened to the voice mail demand he leave a message at the beep. The female voice coming through the phone line brought tears to his eyes. The

109

machine beeped — he spoke into the phone, "Call me. *Please, call me. I'm worried about you."

Losing track of time, he sat in the darkness on the white sand of his backyard beach, the Gulf water climbing the shore in teasing little waves. A mournful owl called out in the distance, its sad song bringing shivers not brought by the cooling breeze. The woman named Marissa was on his mind. He could think of nothing else. She was long overdue and not answering her phone. Her name echoed in his mind, as he sent his worried thoughts out across the dark water. "Marissa," he whispered.

~o0o~

Chapter 15

Grüber laughed long and hard along with the rest of the audience, leaving Jerri the sole disgruntled spectator in a room of snickers and chortles. Men looked to their wives and dates, sharing the gift of slap-stick comedy. Mongo the Magnificent stood center stage, dressed in a comically over-sized black tuxedo, yellow goo dripping from his head.

Jerri winced.

She'd seen the clown-magician juggle eggs *so* many times before. When the live white dove appeared from one of the eggs falling upon Mongo's Stooge-like, chili-bowl haircut, she likewise failed to join the rest of the audience in their gasps of approval. Jerri groaned, "Please... get a new act. Better yet, get a life." The curtain came down on Mongo's allegedly failed juggling attempt.

Ignoring Jerri's grousing, Grüber spoke over his eager applause. "That man's cleaning bills must be *enormous!!*" He cheered a 'fingers-in-the-mouth-whistle' and applauded once more. "Imagine! Performing *that* act over and over again!" As the curtains parted for yet another encore, he turned his laughter toward the stage and the clown-magician taking what seemed his last bow.

"Yes," Jerri growled. "Imagine." As Mongo's egg-splattered shoes disappeared behind the ruby-red curtain, Jerri glanced around the lounge at the still applauding audience. From near the stage, a flash of diamonds caught her eye, the stage lights sparkled off of red hair.

A woman applauded wildly, the light catching the many

sparkling jewels adorning her hands. The diamond-draped lady loudly cheered Mongo's encore, as the curtain rose once again. Two more applauded bows and the curtain fell for the final time. The woman turned slightly in her seat, joining her dinner companion in an animated hand-gestured discussion, which seemed to center on Mongo's performance. Jerri's eyes widened at the sight of the dramatic hand-talker's tortoiseshell glasses, and she slowly rose from her seat.

"Excuse me, Dolf." She touched her date's hand. "I've spotted someone I absolutely *must* speak with. Please excuse me for a few moments?" She wound her way around the many tables dotting the lounge until she approached the side of the diamond-clad Mongo fan wearing the distinctive eyewear. Jerri addressed the two women sitting center stage. "Is this a private clown critique, or can anyone get in on the vote?"

The hand gesturer gasped happily. "*Jerrrrrrrrrrri!!!*" she squealed. "You're the last person I expected to see tonight!!! Mongo said... well, he said... He said Asher said you'd been abducted by *aaaliens!*"

Jerri nodded her head. "As usual, Mongo's half right. I *was* involved in a little fender-bender on my way down-island. No aliens... unless you count Mongo."

"You had a wreck?" Sandy gasped, "Oh, no! Mongo didn't mention *that*....Why didn't you call me? — Oh, never mind about that — Mongo *said* they feared brain damage...." Her diamond decorated hands flew to her face. "Were there any casualties?"

Dramatically hanging her head, Jerri nodded. "Yeah... one casualty. Baby died."

Sandy's dinner companion moaned in sympathy, her soft blonde hair tumbling in waves around her shoulders. "How *horrible!*" Profound distress showed in her eyes as she whispered to Jerri, "You lost your *child* in the wreck?"

To the concerned woman's shock, Sandy batted at her table companion's hand and giggled. "No, no. Baby was her *car.*" She turned her attention back to Jerri with a feigned look of grief. "Not that Baby's death is anything to joke about! Lord knows, you *loved* that car! At least, it appears *you* weren't hurt... much. Thank God!!"

"No. Not much," Jerri sarcastically agreed. "Just knocked me off stage is all. And it seems the Outlander didn't waste any time replacing me with that clown Mongo. Some people, ya know?"

Sandy coughed, cleared her throat, and murmured, "Jerri, I'd like to introduce Alyce Cummings. The *owner-manager* of the Outlander Lounge? Alyce — *this* lovely girl with her foot shoved firmly in her mouth is my oldest friend and best headliner, Jerri Delaney. The *Amazing* Jerri Delaney."

Jerri felt a hot blush cover her face and she stammered as she shook the bemused woman's hand. "Uh... uh... uh... pleased to finally meet you, Ms. Cummings. Sorry about that crack. I suffered brain damage in the wreck." *How I wish the floor would just open up and swallow me whole! Way to go, Moron. Like I always say: If you can't wow the people with your magic, at least open your mouth and show them what a complete idiot you are!*

"*That's* why you look so familiar. Your pretty picture is posted at our door... Nonsense, Jerri," Alyce laughed. "When we heard about your accident we had to scramble to fill your slot. I made a few calls and Mongo showed up like magic... no pun intended."

Nodding her head, Jerri sighed. "Yes, I'm sure he did. The way that clown follows me around, you'd think he has a high-powered tracking device attached to my butt."

"And what a cute little butt it is!! Nyuck-Nyuck-Nyuck!" The familiar 'Curly Howard' sound-alike voice 'nyucked', and she turned to face her stalker.

"Hello, Mongo," Jerri sighed again. "Fancy meeting you here." She noticed he'd wiped the egg from his hair, taken time for a quick fresh up and changed into a better fitting, non-clown-tuxedo. Jerri growled, "Couldn't you wait until my body's cold *before* you swoop in like a vulture?"

Mongo brayed laughter. "Oh, Jerri-My-Dear! *That delicious figure of yours?* One thing it's *never* gonna be is *cold!* I swear, three days after you're six foot under, your bod's still gonna be *hot!!!*" He made a charade about licking his index finger, jutting his hip to the side, touching his wet finger to his hip and 'hissing' steam. "*You're smokin'!!* Come on!" he grinned. "Give us a kiss!" He pulled her into a friendly embrace, smacking her cheek loudly.

"*Hey!!!* Hey!!! *Hey?*" Jerri protested, wriggling from the comic magician's arms. "Don't wrinkle the goods, Mongo!"

"*I should say not!!*" Grüber complained in a good-natured manner, gently pulling Jerri away from Mongo. Stabbing the air with his index finger, he announced in a stage voice, "I say, Sir! Kindly unhand my date!"

Jerri giggled in spite of her irritation, relieved Dolf had followed from their table. "Everyone? My date for the evening — Dolf Grüber. Gentlemen, gentlemen...." she quipped. "Please don't fight over *me!* I'm not worthy!"

Using broad exaggerated strokes, Mongo brushed invisible crumbs from Jerri's lavender dress, all the while protesting, "Oh! No-no-no! Jerri-My-Love, for just one blissful moment in your arms, I'd climb the highest mountain! For just one honey-sweet kiss, I'd swim the deepest ocean! And if I can persuade this gentleman to join me out back for a round of fisticuffs, we'll settle this sordid love triangle once and for all! *I'll moider da bum!!*" With both his fists held high, he leaned in close to Grüber, glaring at the blond-haired man with a comical anger.

"Down, Boy." Sandy motioned toward the outrageous comedian, her diamonds sparkling in the air. "Calm down or we'll have you put to sleep."

Jerri's attention was drawn to the outsized marquise-shaped diamond Sandy sported on her left ring finger. *When did Sandy add that Godzilla-Stone? Man, THAT bauble's big enough to choke a horse!*

Noticing her friend staring at her huge ring, Sandy grinned and chuckled. "Jerri... I think," she sighed, "it's time I introduced you to the special man in my life." She beamed, her brown eyes sparkling behind her tortoiseshell glasses. "Meet my fiancé, Mongo the Magnificent. Mongo? Meet Jerri — your soon-to-be almost-a-sister-in-law."

"*Whaaaa?!*" Jerri spluttered.

"Sis!!" Mongo held out his arms to Jerri, grabbed both her hands and plopped his right leg in her grasp in an animated Marx Brothers' shtick. The clown crowed, "Give us a kiss!!" Then he made 'kissy' noises in her direction.

Surprised horror shot through Jerri's mind, but she managed to control her shock as she dropped Mongo's leg to the floor. "How... how... how *wonderful* for you. How wonderful for you both," she murmured after finding her voice. "Sandy? You, me and Alyce. Women's Room. Now." She reached out and patted Mongo's cheek twice. The first pat was gentle, the last pat, more forceful. "Mongo... *I swear.*" She made herself smile and forced the words over her lips, "You'd *better* be a prince under all that frog or Sandy *better* be playing a big joke on me." Then she grabbed Sandy's hand and practically dragged the flustered woman to the powder room; a perplexed Alyce on their heels.

~o0o~

Chapter 16

"What, in the name of Erica Kane, do you think you're up to?"

"Well... if I have to spell it out for you, then I didn't do too good a job on that birds and bees talk we had a little while back." The older woman checked her makeup in the huge mirror. "You see, Jerri. Sometimes when a man and a woman love each other in a very *special* way, they oftentimes — "

Jerri exploded her interruption: *"Cut the crap, Sandy!!* That's *Mongo* we're talking about! And your... your... your *life!!*" Alyce looked from one woman to the other, wondering at the tiny magician's anger.

"Yes, dear." Sandy smiled. "It's *my* life. And I choose to live it with *Mongo.*"

Jerri fumed. "Couldn't I just find you a gorilla? I'm *sure* he'd be more of a man."

Sandy smiled again. "Jerri, Jerri," she sighed, "you've never given yourself much of a chance to know — to really *know* Mongo. He's really a darling man. I probably shouldn't be telling you this... but, all things being equal, Mongo is *tremendously* more *equal* than other men."

Catching the playful inflection in Sandy's voice, Jerri realized the other woman was again talking about sexual matters. "Firstly... let me just say: *EUUWWGH!* Secondly... *gag me, Sandy!*" Jerri groused, feeling her anger mounting. She imagined steam seeping from her ears.

"Give it up, my friend," Sandy smiled. "Come over to the Darkside," she cooed. "You've got until next December to get to know my Sweetie-Pie. I can't get married without my best pal at my side." Seeing Jerri sulking, the older woman reached out and took her hand. "Be happy for me, Jerri. Believe it. *Mongo* makes me happy. *Mongo* makes me *VERY happy*. Some day I hope you find someone to make you just as happy." Sandy looked plaintively at her best friend.

"There ain't no such animal." Jerri pouted, then glanced at Sandy, feeling her heart melt with sweet memories of their years of friendship. Reluctantly, she allowed her pout to disappear. She took her friend's hand and murmured, "If you swear he's the one... *really-really-really* swear. Then I'll *try* to be happy for you." Dropping Sandy's hand, she quipped, "Just don't tell me you're planning any little Mongos. I don't think I could take that. Not yet."

Alyce piped up from her perch on the women's room sofa. "Does this mean we're all friends again?" The nightclub owner looked expectantly from one woman to the other.

Out of the corner of her eye, Jerri glanced sheepishly at Sandy. "I suppose it'll take more than my best friend marrying a clown for me to throw her away." She noticed an impish glint behind her friend's tortoiseshell glasses.

Sandy smiled. "Delaney? Why don't just admit you're jealous? You've always wanted Mongo for yourself. That's been clear to me for years."

"I've got two pearls of wisdom to leave with you, Sandy," Jerri sighed. "First, I want to wish you all the happiness you've brought me throughout the years. Second," her voice dropped to a whisper, "as far as me wanting Mongo for myself...." Her demeanor swiftly turned menacing, and she hissed, "*Bite me!!*"

Huffing her anger, she flung the door wide open, storming out of the Outlander's ladies' room. "Save me from trying to talk sense into Sandy's thick head!" She ranted, "Honestly! How can she even *pretend* she's gonna marry that clown, Mon — "

Suddenly, she collided with the source of her anger. The force of the impact threw Jerri to the floor and she bounced backwards, landing against the wall. The clown magician fell to his knees beside her. His nervous hands, seemingly so in need of a task, reached out to smooth Jerri's hair as if hair smoothing was the first-aid of choice for having been bounced off a wall. Worry and concern etched his comical face while he did his best to assess the damages to the petite blonde before him.

"Jerri!" He exclaimed, "Are you hurt? I didn't mean to run you over like that! And after your accident and all!! Speak to me!! *Speak to me!!*" His hands became two insistent mosquitoes intent upon a Kamikaze mission. They swooped and parried above their adversary's head, fleetingly touching down upon Jerri's disheveled coiffeur before again taking to the air in a continuance of their flight plan.

Jerri batted his well-meaning hands away from her blonde hair. "Mongo... *I swear!!*" She hissed. "No matter where I go... there... you... *are!!*" The chiffon scarves making up the skirt of her dress had ridden up high on her thigh, and she pushed them down to a more respectable position, taking care to rearrange her jewelry. Her last thought was her neck. Fearful fingers flew to the spot last occupied by a cervical collar, but a few moments gentle prodding proved no pain.

"Lucky you," Jerri growled at the concerned clown. "Looks like my rear end took most of the fall. No major damage done." Suddenly, her physical well-being took a back seat to her anger, and she snapped at Mongo. "Hey! You washed-up wizard — you magic-less wonder — you magnificent twit! What were you doing hovering around the ladies' room door, anyhow? Looking for a date?" She ended her tirade by glaring up at the forlorn clown magician.

He offered his hand, but instead of accepting the assistance, Jerri turned Mongo's hand palm-up. "Just looking for the joy buzzer," she growled, before she reluctantly allowed the clown to pull her to her feet. "A girl can't be too careful nowadays." She smoothed her dress and glared at him again.

A look of pure anguish crossed Mongo's face and he hung his head. Jerri momentarily regretted her harsh words, but by the time the clown had raised his eyes to hers, she'd taken care to remove any signs of regret from her face. "You *do* understand? I'd hate to be forced to break your arm," She hissed. "Good thing you forgot the joy buzzer."

"I'd never, never do that to *you,* dear heart," Mongo murmured. "I save stuff like that for the mundanes. And in my book, you, Jerri-Dear, will never... *never* be considered mundane. I think — "

"Save it for the gullible, Mongo," Jerri interrupted, and scowled. "Like *Sandy,* it appears." Turning on her heels, she dismissed the sorrowful clown, stalked through the crowd and returned to her table, where Jerri found her date paying the dinner check.

"Are you all right?" Grüber asked, as the waiter returned his card with the receipt. Now that the curtain had come down on the main attraction, people trickled out of the Outlander. "Everything's okay with your friend Sandy's wedding plans?"

Jerri snorted. "Not if you count the fact that next December my very best friend in the world vows she's marrying the man who's been stalking me. Following behind every gig I do." She growled, "In fact...." She glanced back toward the ladies' room. "Now he's even following me to the ladies' room. Pervert clown. But, you know the worst thing about it?" Tears threatened. One errant tear made good on its threat and trickled down her cheek, leaving a glistening trail of sorrow in its path.

"No, what?"

"I *want* Sandy to be happy." Jerri groaned, swiping the rogue tear with the back of her hand. "But, this Mongo-thing's coming between us. I can't believe she's really marrying *him! Mongo* — of all people. He's been like an albatross around my neck ever since my dad died. He's like a caffeine-deprived, PMS-ridden, bad-hair day in a week full of rainy Mondays."

"Whoa," he breathed. Dolf suddenly rose from his seat. "Would you excuse me?" He didn't wait for an answer. As he wove in and out of departing patrons, Jerri watched her date make his way toward Sandy's table.

Jerri observed her dinner companion speak to her oldest

119

friend, but she couldn't make out his words across the room. Dolf further peaked Jerri's suspicion, when he placed his hand on her friend's shoulder, spoke, and Sandy suddenly glanced her way, grinned, waggling her hand in Jerri's direction. Mongo joined his fiancé, waving at Jerri, his tongue stuck out the side of his mouth. Though confused, Jerri waved back. The next minute brought Sandy to Jerri's table; flanked by Dolf and a strangely shy Mongo.

"*Jerrrrri!*" Sandy crowed in her very familiar manner. "That was a wonderful idea that you sent Dolf over to our table to give me! We'd — Mongo and I — would *love* to go to Sloppy Joe's with you!"

Mongo beamed and hugged Sandy. "I think it's great," he gushed, "you wanting to toast our wedding. You're the best, Jerri. *Simply the best.*"

Jerri's eyes flew open wide and she nearly sputtered, "Gr... great! Let's... let's get outta here. Okay?" She looked from her friend's expressively diamond-flashing flighty hands, to Mongo's eager eyes to Dolf's smiling face. "Okay, then," Jerri simply nodded her head, overcoming the urge to shake her head and throw up her hands. "Sloppy Joe's it is," she said. She grabbed her rhinestone purse and led the group to the doors.

~o0o~

Walking the length of Duval Street toward their well-lit destination, Sloppy Joe's Bar on the corner of Duval and Greene streets, Jerri strolled arm in arm with Sandy. Even though her thoughts kept returning to the strange — but happy — clown following behind her, said clown walking alongside her own date, Jerri felt good in the warm closeness of her oldest friend in the world. Her senses were hyper-tuned and she marveled at the sounds and smells of the old town.

A quick shower had left the sidewalk wet and glistening under the street lamps, the air smelled rain-fresh, and hints of jasmine hung on the breeze. Festive Calypso music wafted out through the open doors of a small bistro on the right side of Duval Street. As if it were a shy voyeur, a nearly full moon peeked over the concealment of a shower cloud sailing the blue-black night

120

sky. Tropical birds called out from their nests in palm trees and on various rooftops.

They'd nearly passed a yellow two-story house when a couple in the upstairs apartment diverted their attention. A man and a woman aired their dirty laundry, and their angry voices escaped the sea mist green Jalousie windows. Jerri thought the argument sounded petty, and turned to Sandy with an upraised eyebrow, as if to say: *Some people, you know?*

Sandy laughed, and the two continued their walk. Mongo and Dolf brought up the rear, their own friendly laughter peppering the air. The bickering couple overhead suddenly picked up the volume of their quarrel, and as one, the four people walking on the sidewalk below turned their attention to the second floor windows of the old Conch-style house.

"Gee-Crips, Mabel!" the male voice sharply declared. "Why don't'cha keep it down!! Yer screamin' so loud I'll bet they'll hear y'all the way down at the Southernmost Point!!"

This bit of drama was followed by 'Mabel' appearing at the window, throwing back the shutters and bellowing with a raspy voice at the top of her lungs: "Hey, everyone!! Toot Magraw is a boozy do-nuthin'! Do ya hear me, Old Town? *I said,* he's a no-good — " Her whiskey-rough voice hesitated as she suddenly noticed she had an audience for her vocal tirade. "Oh, hello," the woman with brassy red hair, makeup to match, and a dangling cigarette, coughed out a greeting.

Her self-rolled cigarette sent up a trail of blue-gray smoke into her right eye, which drooped a quarter inch lower than her left. She lowered her volume as she addressed the four strangers peering up at her from the sidewalk. "Don't mind us. Me an' Toot just airin' it out a bit. Y'all know how *that* is. Yer first time in Key West?"

Jerri surprised herself by nodding at the strange woman. The brassy redhead cackled laughter. "Well, welcome! Goin' to Joe's? Well, course yer goin' to Joe's. I tell ya what.... Tell 'em Mabel an' Toot sent'cha. They'll treat'cha right, don't'cha think they won't!"

121

"Much appreciated, Mabel!" Mongo called to the woman hanging over the windowsill. "You've got a lovely town, here. You ever get to the Outlander?" He waited for Mabel's response and was rewarded by a surprisingly silent, equally surprisingly negative shake of her head. "Well, tell'em Mongo sent *you*. Remember that name. Mongo. Mongo the Magnificent. Two seats, on the house. Tomorrow night. I'll leave word with the House. Whadda ya say? You an' me? We gotta date?"

The crude woman, who moments before plotted character assassination, intent upon the ruin of Toot Magraw's social reputation, visibly melted, as if the 'Charm Fairy' benevolently touched a magic wand upon her disheveled brassy curls. "You, sir, are a true gentleman," she nearly cooed, the thirty-odd years of smoke and whiskey causing her voice to crack and break with the sentiment. "You tell yer lady there, what a special man she has."

Sandy hugged Mongo, stood on tiptoe, kissed his five o'clock shadow-dappled cheek and quipped, "You're preachin' to the choir, Mabel. Preachin' to the choir."

Mongo beamed, waved farewell to his newest fan, and continued his swaggering walk to Sloppy Joe's, bringing Sandy, Jerri and Dolf along with him.

Walking away from Mabel and Toot's downtown 'Love Shack', Jerri stole a glance at her nemesis strolling arm in arm with her best friend. She pondered: *Perhaps there's something there... maybe Sandy knows a different Mongo than I do... could it be I've figured him all wrong? Nah... I'm not ready to believe THAT yet.*

Dismissing the nearly contrite thought with a silent shake of her head, she smiled at Dolf and took his offered hand. The four crossed the street, bringing their small group one block closer to Sloppy Joe's.

The closer they got to the bar Hemingway made famous, the more tiny shops and cafés Jerri noticed dotting the way. The friends slowed their walk as they came to a tiny jewelry shop. Gold, silver, diamonds and other precious stones rested on a royal blue swatch of velvet in an artistic window display. Jerri and Sandy held back at the same time, each one captivated by the sparkly treasures. Dolf and Mongo waited two steps behind their ladies. Both the men exchanged silent smiles as if relaying the message: *It's their night, also. Why hurry?*

Spying a particularly glittery silver bracelet, Jerri whistled low, as she gazed into the jewelry shop window. "Wow," she breathed. "Silver. The *only* jewelry I wear *is* silver. No gold for me! That silver bracelet's gorgeous! I'd sure love it if Santa would bring me *that* little bauble."

Sandy nudged her and coyly indicated Dolf over her shoulder. "Perhaps if you're a good girl," she teasingly whispered, "or better yet, a *bad* girl... if you know what I mean."

Jerri hissed and cuffed her friend's shoulder none too gently. "*Sandy!!*" Then she angrily whispered, "Hush!! *What's gotten into you, anyway?* Do you have sex on the brain?"

Sandy affected a hurt expression and rubbed her shoulder, though Jerri's halfhearted blow hadn't injured her. "Ow!!!" she protested. "You play too rough! I was only trying to help you figure out how to get something you want." The puppy dog eyes she turned up to her younger friend caused Jerri to grin in spite of her irritation.

"You're pure evil, Sandy." Jerri whispered, "*I* know it and *you* know it. And I wouldn't be surprised if *Mongo* doesn't know it."

Sandy grinned and whispered in her friend's ear, "Why do you think we're getting hitched?"

Mongo turned to Dolf and grinned. "Don't you love it when women talk about you behind your back and make you feel like a piece of meat?"

Dolf rolled his eyes; Jerri couldn't tell if he agreed with the clown or not, but his bemused expression gave clue he was thoroughly enjoying himself.

"Well... I'm here to tell ya... *my* sweet baby can talk about me whenever and however she wants." Mongo smiled at Sandy, and continued, "'Cause I know when she's talkin' 'bout her

Mongo, she'll be talkin' grade 'A' Prime."

Sandy gave her fiancé a quick kiss on the mouth, laced her arm in his and pulled him toward the famous bar. "Mongo, my Silly Sirloin — let me tell *you*," Sandy said. "When I think of you, you make me *sizzle!*" She beamed up at the man with the Moe Howard haircut; bald-faced affection plastered all over her face.

"Dolf? Please tell me there's an unstable fault line running through Key West." Jerri dramatically slapped her hand to her forehead and groaned. "What I wouldn't give if the earth would just open up and swallow me whole!!"

He took her hand in his, and with his other hand, pointed at Mongo and Sandy continuing their journey to the famous bar. He said, "I think it's sweet. They seem devoted to each other. Mongo's not so bad, you know. If you'd just allow yourself to get to know him, he's — "

Jerri hissed an interruption, careful to keep her voice at a whisper, "*Get to know him?!* You and Sandy are *both* crazy!! And Mongo is *freakin' nuts!!* I tell you, he's been stalking me for years! If I book in the Windy City, he books there to follow me up. I swear — if I took a booking in Hell — Mongo would follow me *there,* too."

Dolf laughed and his laughter drug Jerri out of her 'Mongo-induced funk'. As she joined her handsome date in his laughter, she looked around the glistening wet street and berated herself. *Really, Jerri. Maybe you need to lighten up on the clown. After all, Sandy seems to like him... yeah, well. Sandy seems to like Jerry Springer, too, but I don't think I'd like to see her marry HIM either.* She shook her head and said aloud, "But, I guess that just proves it could be worse."

"What could be worse than what?" Dolf inquired, "Did I miss something?"

Jerri sighed. "No," she shook her head, and said, "I'm only trying to bully myself into accepting Mongo."

"And how's the battle going?"

"I dunno," she groaned. "I can be a pretty mean bully... and then again... I'm awfully hardheaded. Tell you what, I'll let you know who wins the battle next December." She watched Sandy and Mongo cross Caroline Street a half a block ahead. The clown and his ladylove were now a block's walk from Hemingway's hang, and they turned and waved to their straggling friends.

Dolf asked, "Didn't you say something about the *wedding* being in December?"

Jerri returned Sandy's wave. "Yeah." She shook her head. "Wedding's in December. Unless I can talk her down from the clown."

"Take my advice," he said, "and watch the clown closely. *Really* watch him. I'll bet you'll see a tiny bit of what Sandy sees in her 'Silly Sirloin'. Sandy and Mongo are meant to be together like carrots and peas. All I am saying... is give peas a chance." He glanced at Jerri to see if she was going to let his bad pun pass unnoticed.

Jerri giggled. "*How perfectly lame.* I thought you were going to ask me if I carrot-all."

They both laughed and crossed Caroline Street. Sandy and Mongo waited for them outside of Sloppy Joe's. The famous bar was lit up like a carnival attraction. Red and green neon outlined the outside of the building, with the bar's name spelled out in four foot tall red neon over the top facade. Loud rock and roll music escaped through the open Jalousie doors, and bright light streamed out of the tiny Sloppy Joe's Bar gift shop at the right. Jerri thought it sounded like a pretty good party going on inside the bar.

Sandy trilled, "Let's go into the gift shop first — what say??" She grabbed Jerri's arm and practically dragged her over the threshold of the bar-connected store. Once inside, she whispered to her exasperated friend, "Did you point out the bracelet you want for Christmas? No? Well... perhaps you can pick out something in here."

"*Sandy.*" Jerri spat out her friend's name in a warning. "*If* I want something, I'm a big girl, with big girl money! I'll buy it *myself.*"

125

"Okay, okay," Sandy nodded her head and whispered. "I just wanted to get you away for a second. Whadda ya think? *Is Dolf the one?*"

Jerri sneered. "The one? *The one?* The one *what???*"

"You *know*... the house in the suburbs, two car garage, dog, cat, 2.5 kids? You know — *the one?* What I want to know is: *Is Dolf your Mongo?*"

Jerri pretended to ponder the question for a second. "Sandy?" she smiled. "I can honestly say... Dolf Grüber, with all his gorgeous good looks and his old world charm, will never... *ever...* measure up to Mongo."

A strange expression crossed Sandy's face. "Yeah... well, don't let *that* stop you."

Dolf and Mongo followed their dates into the tiny shop. "Whoa, Sandy!" Mongo crowed, "Look!" He pointed up at the tee-shirts hanging high on the wall, "You can wear Hemingway on your chest!"

"Sure," smiled Sandy, "As if. Like I want a white-haired, American Icon of a boozer-writer on my boo — "

"Sandy! Remember," Jerri interrupted her fun-loving friend, "we're in mixed company!"

"I was gonna say *body,*" Sandy held her hands up in front of herself, defensively. "I wasn't gonna say boobs! *Honest!!*"

Jerri rolled her eyes while Mongo purchased four tee-shirts and four souvenir Sloppy Joe's ball caps. "If you wanna talk about 'honest' — Sandy — " she hissed, "let's talk about how you've *honestly* lost your *freakin' mind!*" Jerri noticed her date approach the cash register.

Dolf turned around and motioned for the group to continue into the bar. "Go find us a table," he suggested.

Mongo took Jerri by the shoulders and gently turned her toward the connecting door into the bar. "Let the man have his privacy, my dear. *Every* man deserves a little privacy."

Sandy smirked.

Rolling her eyes again, Jerri allowed Sandy and her goofy fiancé to lead her into the bar. "I know, I know," she said. "'Lord, forgive us and protect us. We been drinkin' beer for breakfast'."

"What's she talkin' about?" Mongo asked Sandy.

Sandy smirked again, and whispered, "I dunno. If you ask me, the girl's mashugga..."

~o0o~

Sloppy Joe's was dark and loud. Jerri noticed smokers seated at the tables close by, but the large tropical fans swirling overhead made it comfortable, keeping the air fresh. One of the two open Jalousie doors were behind them to their backs, which also helped the cigarette smoke problem. They'd taken a table just inside the door by the gift shop. The tables in the bar were tall and circular; barstools ringed each one.

Their table was next to the bar and if Jerri peered over the various hued liqueur bottles in the middle of the 'open island' bar, she could see the stage at the back wall. A huge banner proclaimed: Faust and Lewis, with 'Picklehead Music' beneath the comedy singers' names. Their music was loud and funny, and Jerri couldn't stop grinning as she tried to take it all in.

Suspended over the cash register, pointing toward the doors, a wooden airplane propeller, all of seven feet long, gleamed with its much-polished golden wood surface. Directly beneath the propeller, sat a tall and dark wooden cat statue, a large brass bell around its neck. Jerri noticed that every time a bartender would ring the bell, a round of drinks had been bought for the bar.

The waitress stopped by the table. She practically yelled to be heard over the noisy music: "Would you like to order now?"

The clown swirled his right index finger and held up four fingers on his left hand, indicating a missing person to his side. Mongo mimed and shouted: "A round of Hurricanes!"

Dolf appeared behind Jerri. "Make one of those Hurricanes a soda. I'm a designated driver." The waitress smiled, made a note on her pad and left to hand the order to the bartender; while Dolf grabbed the barstool between Jerri and Mongo.

Sandy laughed. "I thought we'd ditched you outside, Dolf."

"Can't get away from me that easy," he spoke loudly to be heard over the bar noise, "just made a detour in the gift shop." He handed a large package to Jerri.

"What's this?" she asked, as the waitress brought their drinks. Three were tall colorful, fruited boat drinks, while Dolf's was served in a clear plastic cup with Hemingway's picture — Sloppy Joe's logo — and the words: 'Still the Best Party in Town' beneath it. Jerri asked again, shaking the plastic sack likewise bearing Hemingway's face on the side, "What's this?"

Taking a sip of his soda, Dolf smiled. "Just a little something for you. Go ahead. Open the bag."

She peered down into the plastic package. "It's a Sloppy Joe's jacket!!" Jerri proclaimed, removing it from the sack. "But... but, I can't accept *this!*" She turned the jacket around in her hands. Like on the plastic cup, and gift sack, the jacket's back bore a painted photo of Sloppy Joe's bar. Between their title and word logo, the front pocket area proclaimed the same logo without the picture; the jacket's body denim, the sleeves a dark tan canvas material. Jerri shook her head and repeated, "I *can't* accept this."

Dolf laughed and patted her hand. "I'm afraid you must, Jerri. No returns. And I bought it in a small size. It won't fit Mongo, or me. And as for Sandy? Well, I think it clashes with her red hair. Yep... think you're stuck with it."

Jerri protested again, "But... I *can't* accept this!"

Mongo reached over the table and placed his large hand over Jerri's. "Sweet Potato... Let someone do something nice for *you* for a change. We're not *all* bad men, you know."

Sure! YOU can talk... Psycho-Clown Stalker, Jerri groused to herself.

"Mongo's right, Jerri," Sandy weighed in with her opinion. "Go ahead. Let Dolf be the nice guy. You know you're outnumbered." The brassy redhead laughed and took a sip from her tall drink.

Jerri shook her head. "I give up," she moaned, "you guys win. I'll accept the jacket and say 'thank-you'. Thank-*you*, Dolf. This is a very nice present. Every time I wear it, I'll think of you." She slipped it on, nodding her head at the comfortable fit.

Dolf took another sip of his soda. "That's the idea. Now, you can never forget me."

Inexplicably, even in the warmth of the new jacket, Jerri shivered again.

~o0o~

The black Jaguar XKE pulled up in front of the lavender mansion. The driver left his side of the car and came to the passenger side, opening the door for Jerri. He offered his hand in an old-fashioned manner. *I thought men like this existed only in fairy tales,* she mused, as she took his hand and stepped out of the car. *What a welcome change from Pendragon's uncouth manners.*

Still holding her hand, he whispered close to her ear, "I hope you've enjoyed our night out in Key West." Dolf Grüber smiled, kissing Jerri's hand. "For me, it's been enchanting."

Jerri smiled. "I would like to say its been magical, but with Mongo doing his rubber chicken magic act."

"I'm beginning to agree with Sandy," he chuckled, teasingly touching the tip of her nose. "It appears to *me,* you're a little bit *too* concerned with her fiancé. You're a little — "

Jerri huffed an interruption, "*Don't even go there!!*" She feigned indignation, placing her hands on her hips. "The *only* thing I'm concerned about is my best friend's choice of fiancés!! He's an insult to professional magicians everywhere! In fact, he's an insult to clowns! The only thing he's good for is stalking me... and he does a wham-bang job of *that!!* He couldn't perform a professional magic act if his life depended on it!"

"I beg to differ with you, there," Grüber said. "Remember — I spoke with Mongo while you and Sandy were walking together. He's a superbly trained magician. He really knows his craft. As far as his performance, you were the only one not laughing." A teasing smile played on his lips, as he continued,

130

"The audience loved him."

She scowled, "Two-bit audience for a two-bit magician. They'd go for anything with a cape and a wand. They give new meaning to the word: *Easy*. I still can't believe my best friend's gonna *marry* that clown."

He chuckled and shook his head. "Jerri, Jerri, Jerri," he said, "I think you're going to find you're all wrong about Mongo. He's really quite a guy."

She gave an exaggerated pout. "So says you," Jerri groused. "I think if it were possible, you'd nominate Mongo for sainthood."

"I believe he'd have to be dead for that...."

Jerri grinned; her eyes twinkled. She chuckled. "Now... *that's* a thought!"

"Jerri!" He shook his finger in her face in a mock scolding. "You don't mean that."

He walked her to the mansion's door and they stood under the stars. A distant rumble hinted at a coming storm. Following the earlier brief shower, the absence of clouds belied the chance of rain. The glow from the nearly full moon kissed the green-eyed man's blond hair. He whispered, "I really *did* have a wonderful time tonight. And I, for one, think your friends are great. Both Sandy *and* the clown she's marrying."

He tipped her chin up, gazed into Jerri's eyes, and captivated her with his charms.

His eyes, she silently mused, *his eyes are like glowing emeralds! Is he going to kiss me? Should I let him?* She held her breath, momentarily losing herself in the deep green of Dolf's eyes. Suddenly, her mouth went dry and she felt a quiver rise from the pit of her stomach.

"Jerri," he breathed her name. "You're enchanting... simply... *enchanting*." Lifting her hand to his lips, he brushed a kiss across the tips of her fingers, gently pulling her closer to him. Grüber tickled her cheek with a chaste kiss, again gazing into her eyes. "You're enchanting and the night was truly magical. *Really* — I don't know *when* I've ever had a better time. I feel like I've found two close friends in Sandy and Mongo... well... make that

131

three close friends... *you!* And, I *do* so hope you think of me as a friend, Jerri. Hopefully, this night is the first of many, many more to come." Again, he kissed her cheek.

His warm breath wafted across her ear, and Jerri shivered, while a pleasant tingle made its journey all the distance to her fingertips. She smiled. "Yes... the night *was* magical. No pun intended!" Gently brushing her knuckles over his jawline, she added in a whisper, "Many, many, *many* more nights to come... if dreams do *indeed* come true."

"For you, Princess," he smiled, "I'd sail to the ends of the Earth, just to bring back one little dream, lock it in a tiny box and give it to you to keep forever... *along with my heart.*"

She felt tears coming to her eyes, bit the inside of her lip, and warded them off. *This man... this wonderful, genteel man. A blond angel with a poet's soul. No one ever told me men like Dolf Grüber existed.* Once again, she gazed into his eyes. The moment lingered, and the very air around them seemed electrified. Jerri wondered, *Am I looking into the eyes of my future?*

Dolf broke the moment by softly speaking her name. "Jerri... Jerri." He shook his head, sadly. "I wish this night never had to end... but it's nearly midnight, my car turns back into a pumpkin in a few minutes and I have an early morning... eh... eh... *appointment* at the dock. Besides, I promised Miss Marty I wouldn't keep you out too late."

Smiling, Jerri nodded. "She worries," she said. "You know how it is. She mothers *everyone* around here." She nodded her head toward the mansion. "I think it's kind of sweet, actually. It's been a long time since anybody's mothered me."

He chuckled in agreement. "Miss Marty Sebastian is one special lady, all right," he nodded his head. "I always look forward to my business visits with her. I never know what surprises wait for me at the Purple Plantation. One day it's celebrating the maid's birthday, the next day it might be board games. Last month was the first time I've played Candyland since I was in Kindergarten. Life is never boring when you're friends with Miss Marty." His eyes sparkled and Jerri thought she could see true affection for her motherly benefactress in the accountant's face.

"I'm beginning to feel the same way about the woman, myself," she smiled, and murmured, "and you're right. It's late, and Miss Marty will worry. I should go in. Thank you, again, Dolf. Thank you for a wonderful evening."

"Forgive my foolish heart," he murmured. This time, he slowly pulled her to him, gently taking her into his arms. "One kiss, Jerri. I beg just one kiss, pure and sweet, before we bid good-night to the moon and stars." Closing his eyes, he brought his lips to hers and gently kissed Jerri, his lips parted ever-so-slightly.

Jerri's eyes flew open wide in shock, but the unexpected kiss, with its perfect lip-caress, quickly won her over, and she closed her eyes, lost in the moment. *Silver... tastes like silver. ...now, just where did THAT thought come from?*

Grüber ended the kiss — seemingly with a great reluctance. He touched his own lips and smiled before kissing her hand for the last time. Opening the front door for Jerri, he nodded charmingly, smiled again, and spoke one soft word: "M'lady...."

Jerri fought a mighty battle not to melt in a puddle from her date's gallantry, her hand resting on the door latch. "I suppose I *will* say good-night, now," she said. "I, too, have an early appointment tomorrow, for physical therapy."

"Mark Pendragon runs a tight ship, or so I've heard." Grüber shook his head in sympathy. "Miss Marty had a cute nickname for him... what was it?"

"Marky de Sade," she smiled. "Yes, she told me. And let me tell you, it suits the man. He's not happy until his tortures have you screaming in pain. And I think he likes it!"

Dolf Grüber shook his head again and made sympathetic sounds. "I can't *imagine* a man who'd enjoy torturing a delicate creature like yourself."

Smiling up at the tall blond man, Jerri replied, "Sir, you're a true gentleman. It's refreshing to find men, such as yourself, still exist."

"Stop — please, stop!" he chuckled. "If you insist upon singing my praises, I'll have to leave you here at the door. If I stay any longer, you'll nominate *me* for sainthood. So, I'll say good-night, now."

"Good-night." She stood on tiptoe, kissed him on the cheek, walked into the foyer, turned and closed the door. Leaning back against the closed door, she sighed. *Wow! Good looks and old world manners, too. He's so unlike Pendragon. THIS man is cultured and suave; so totally together.* She thought, *Are the women in The Keys blind? Why hasn't some smart girl snatched up Dolf Grüber by now?* Her leering little inside voice greedily supplied an answer: *So what if other females overlook this gorgeous sprig of Edelweiss? I'll pick him any day!*

"Oh, hush," she scolded her inner voice of insanity. "In your present state of mind you'd think Bozo the Clown would look good. Or — horrors — *Mongo* the Clown. Get a grip!"

Conchita stepped into the foyer wearing a long lavender nightgown and carrying a tray laden with a pitcher of milk, candy, and a plate full of home-baked cookies. "Señorita Jerri?" she asked. "Interrumpí yo?" The maid looked around the entranceway. "Oí yo las voces?"

"No, Conchita," Jerri sighed. "You didn't interrupt anything... and you didn't hear voices. Don't tell anyone, but I was talking to myself."

"Ahh!" the woman said. "Los hombres pueden hacer que a una mujer, no?"

Jerri laughed and quipped, "Tell it, Sister! Men *can* do that to a woman. It's my opinion, men are the sole reason we women talk to ourselves."

"Sígame... Follow me." Conchita winked, indicating the cookies.

"Conchita? For a hot chocolate chip cookie I'd follow you *anywhere*."

~o0o~

Chapter 18

"Jerri, dear," Miss Marty crowed as she held Basil on her lap, "you do have the look of a woman in great need of chocolate." She dunked her cookie in her glass of milk. The little dog begged for a bite of cookie, but the old lady lured Basil's attention away from the chocolate using a healthy doggy treat. With an eye-crinkling smile, she offered Jerri a cookie from the heaping plate, saying, "Have a little piece of heaven; what we common people call chocolate chip."

Jerri kicked off her high-heels, took her place between Conchita and Phyllis, and got comfortable, cross-legged on the floor. She bit a cookie, and paused while chewing, then swallowed. Taking a sip of milk to clear her mouth, she spoke, "Is it written all over my face?"

The old lady giggled, "I'm afraid so, dear. Since we 'ran into each other', so to speak, you've seemed to be suffering from a *horrible* chocolate deficiency. Would you like to tell us about it? Conchita, Phyllis and I are all great listeners. Besides, for the moment, it's just us girls."

Jerri looked around at the three older ladies sitting on the floor beside her, gathered in a half-circle in front of the big-screen television. *If I didn't know better,* she mused to herself, *I'd swear none of them is older than fifteen.* After a swift decision to join them, she said, "This looks like a slumber party. But, you'all are wearing your pajamas and I feel a little over dressed."

"Nonsense," Phyllis offered, touching Jerri's arm in a just-us-girls manner. "You look lovely. You've *got* to tell us *everything* about your date with *Mr. Grüber."* She sighed the man's name. "Is he as *dream-mee* as he seems?" The secretary drew the word *dreamy* out as if she were pulling saltwater taffy.

This Phyllis is NOTHING like the daytime-business-Phyllis, Jerri thought. *I think Miss Marty has been busy working her lavender magic on someone.*

The old woman chortled. "Oh, my! Phyllis, I believe you've been reading those romance novels again, haven't you? You do realize, they're almost as addictive as chocolate? And taken together, they're nearly lethal!"

"You're one to talk." Phyllis snorted, and said, "Miss Marty, I have it on good authority you've picked out tonight's movie. And it's a hunk movie if ever there was one." She pointed at her boss accusingly and quipped, "I dare you to tell me *one* movie we've watched during our girl's night that didn't have Brad Pitt, Hugh Jackman, Harrison Ford, or Tom Cruise. If I didn't know any better, I'd think you were a dirty-minded high school girl."

Miss Marty giggled, pointed to herself and said with complete and utter innocence, "Moi?"

Phyllis turned to Jerri and snickered. "Would you believe this is the *third time* we've watched this movie?" The bemused secretary aimed the remote at the large screen and clicked the buttons. The music and opening credits of Tom Cruise's 'Jerry McGuire' filled the room, and Jerri burst out laughing. The other three women joined in the joke and soon they were tossing M&M's at each other like giggling teenagers.

Jerri leaned back against the sofa and smiled. *The more I'm around Miss Marty Sebastian, the more I like her,* she mused to herself. *Who cares if she's a few petals short of a pansy? I like her!* Grabbing a cookie from the plate, she trilled, "You know? You had me at chocolate!" Munching the tasty cookie, she hurried to catch up with the other chocolate deficient women sitting cross-legged on the floor around her.

...and the chocolate worked its magic.

~o0o~

"Delaney!! Just because you've lost the collar doesn't mean

you're on vacation. Wake up! It's exercise time!"

Jerri sat up straight in bed and protectively grabbed her collarless neck. She opened bleary eyes and glared at the grinning physical therapist. Sleepily, she clutched her unbuttoned nightshirt closed and growled, "Pendragon!! What in the world are you doing in my room? Am I going to have to ask Miss Marty to *spray for pests?"*

"If you'd set an alarm clock and not sleep like a corpse," he said, "then I wouldn't have to pound on your door. Jeez, I thought I'd wake the whole house."

Again, she glared at him and snarled, "Go away! I didn't get to sleep until late. I was — "

"Likely story," he interrupted, picking up the filmy lavender scarf dress thrown across a bedside chair, beside a jacket bearing the name and logo: 'Sloppy Joe's'. "Is *this* why you're a slugabed this morning?" He shook the dress at her and scowled, "I see you weren't encumbered by *too* many clothes on your date. He must have drug you to every bar in town. Were you out with Grüber *all night long?"*

She narrowed her eyes and hissed at the dark-haired man, *"If* that were any of *your* business, I *might* tell you. But, since it's *not...."*

"Oh, but it *is* my business." He smiled tauntingly. "Because, you're still my client and as your *therapist* I must have knowledge of your daily activities if I'm to perform my job in a *professional* manner."

She snarled, "Do you chant that mantra in the mirror every morning? And furthermore, do you realize the *sun's not even up yet?* For your information, I was the guest of honor at one of Miss Marty's 'Girls Only' nights and I didn't get to sleep until after three A.M. We O.D.'d on chocolate chip cookies. I have a chocolate hangover. It's a girl thing. *You wouldn't understand.* So have a heart, whadda ya say? Couple of more hours sleep?" Not waiting for his answer, she pulled the comforter over her head.

Growling, he ripped the bedcovers from the bed. "No you don't — Delaney! I said *exercise* and we're sticking to the schedule! *Now, get out of that bed, or I'll drag you out myself!*"

Jerri glared lividly at the gorgeous man; his dark-lashed eyes launched daggers back at her. His deep blue weapons hit their target like scud missiles on a mission of destruction. Swallowing hard, she hissed, "You wouldn't *dare!*"

He scowled, "Oh, *wouldn't I?*" Setting his jaw in determination, Pendragon swiftly slid his hands under her legs and shoulders and swept her up from the bed into his muscled arms.

Although she kicked and squirmed, batting at his rock hard chest, he held her closer with each ineffectual blow of her fists. Every pummel she rained on Pendragon brought ripples of sexual electricity, every erotic nerve in her body tingled with excitement. Her physical reactions to the shock and surprise of being held prisoner by the sexy therapist's arms literally took her breath away.

With his face inches from Jerri's, his hot and minty breath brushing across her lips, he carefully enunciated each word, as if speaking to a child, "Get... this... straight... woman. You *are* going to go into that bathroom, and you *are* going to get into your therapy clothes, and I'm *not* going to hear another peep out of you. NOT... ONE... *PEEP!! Is that clear?*" As Pendragon set her down gently beside the bathroom door, he allowed her body to slowly slide down his rippling abdominal muscles.

Holding her tightly to his body, her toes dangled inches above the floor. Through his shirt, she relished the heat of his chest against her, imagining what his bare skin would feel like next to her own. As he released his hold on Jerri, she slid lower down his body, registering the sensation of each firm muscle in turn. Just as her toes touched the floor, she realized certain muscles mere inches away from her touch were growing harder by the second. Her breath caught in her throat, and her eyes flew open wide.

Still, he held her close. Their eyes met, and she thought she might drown in his cobalt pools, unfathomable in their murky depths. For the fleeting seconds of their connection, she lost herself completely; their closeness like a drug, lulling her, beckoning her, to a promised euphoria. An undeniable magnetism was building between them, she knew it, but was at a loss to deny it. Her whole being seemed to be filled with desire. Mesmerized by his intense gaze, she wondered at the emotions held prisoner behind his dark lashes. *Was that DESIRE she saw mirrored in his face?*

"I'm sorry," Pendragon nearly whispered. "I... I didn't mean... I didn't mean to...."

Again, his smoldering eyes met Jerri's, and he paused, running his tongue over his lips as if they'd suddenly gone dry.

With a ragged sigh, he gently pushed her away, urging her toward the bathroom. "Please, get dressed," he mumbled. "I'll meet you downstairs."

Quietly closing the bathroom door, Jerri leaned against the inside of the doorway, her breathing heavy.

A single tear born of frustration trailed down her cheek and she mournfully whispered: "Peep."

~o0o~

Chapter 19

Minutes later, she found Pendragon adjusting the weights on the multipurpose, dual-weighted home gym, preparing the exercise station for butterfly arm resistance pushes. His back turned to her, and down on one knee, the view afforded her an opportunity to marvel at his powerful muscles flexing across his wide shoulders as he lifted the graduated weights, loading the rubber padded rectangles onto the back of the gym. *You're gonna have to get your mind off that insufferable man's muscles,* Jerri scolded herself, *going mushy every time he flexes those puppies... Well, it's just not a wise career move.*

She cleared her throat to let him know she stood behind him. When he turned to her, she caught the faintest glimmer of desire in his eyes, and she momentarily clutched. *It's one thing to appreciate his dark beauty... and live... but what will I do if he's attracted to ME, also? I'm not ready for this... I've never needed a man before, and I don't need one now.* Jerri set her jaw and nodded her head in agreement with her now silent inner voice. "I see you're readying the rack," she quipped in lieu of a greeting. "Looking for a torture victim?"

For only a moment, the faint glimmer of desire flared, burning like a bright candle in his eyes. The moment passed, and Pendragon's dark lashes again hooded his emotions, hiding his burning need long enough for the man to gather his composure. "I've thought about it." He raked his hand through his dark locks, shook his head and murmured, "*Boy*, have I thought about it." He lowered his smoldering eyes, and continued, "And I must apologize for my behavior." He spoke quietly. "I had no right to barge into your room and drag you out of bed like a barbarian. I'm sorry. It'll never happen again." He stood from his task, inches away from Jerri, waiting for her to accept or reject his apology.

Even from the short distance between them, she imagined she felt his body heat. Jerri's greedy inner voice groaned with desire for the man standing before her: *It'll never happen again? Never again? But... but... but, I ache for your touch! How will I go on? How will I even draw breath? The precious moments spent in your embrace were bliss. To never feel that passion again? I'll die!!* Hoping to hide her inner turmoil, she tossed her hand in the air, dismissing the incident as meaningless. Trying not to meet the eyes of the gorgeous man awaiting her forgiveness, she snapped: "You say it'll never happen again? See that it doesn't."

"Will you let me make it up to you?" he asked, patting the weight bench's padded seat.

She scoffed, setting her hands on her hips in a characteristic display of her quick stubbornness. "You're gonna make it up to me by making me scream? Tell me, de Sade? Are you for real?"

His laughter filled the room and Jerri fought hard to keep a smile off her face. Her traitorous little voice sang out, again, *That man's humor is infectious! Dark blue eyes, beautiful black wavy hair, tanned muscled body that just doesn't quit! All that and a sense of humor too. I could listen to his laughter forever and--*

She raised her voice interrupting the little man-hungry nightingale that resided in her head, "*Well, count me out!!* No way *I'm* gonna — " She suddenly realized Pendragon was listening to her apparently one-sided dressing down and she mentally reached for a save. "No way I'm gonna... gonna... gonna let you tell *me* what to do! *Today,* I want to start on *that* back resistance machine, first. Then *perhaps* I'll come back to *this* one." *Lame, Jerri. Very lame. Now the man won't just think you're talking to yourself — he'll think you're talking to an idiot!*

Pendragon laughed again. "Fine! Start with whatever machine you want. I only wanted to know if I could make it up to you for losing my temper. How about I take you diving later this afternoon?"

She gushed, "*Diving?* You're taking me *diving* this afternoon? You mean it? *You really mean it?*" She caught herself almost clapping her hands in glee. *Whoa! Reel it in, Jerri! Pendragon's gonna think you're a trained seal! Perhaps you can balance a ball on your nose while you clap your flippers!*

When she allowed herself to speak, it was in a composed voice. "That would be nice." Hoping she'd calmed herself in time, she purposely looked away from the gorgeous man, desperately attempting to cover up her excited emotions.

Wiping his hands on a towel, he flashed his maddening smile. "May I take that response to mean *perhaps* you'd like to go diving today?" He motioned for her to mount up on the back resistance machine, and waited for her to straddle the seat, positioning herself for the exercise. Checking her hand holds on the equipment, he took a seat across from Jerri, monitoring her exercise session.

"Run through your regimen and when you finish, you go round up your gear and I'll go ready Miss Marty's boat." He closed his eyes, tipped his chair backwards against the wall, balancing it on the two back legs, resting his arms behind his head. "It's been awhile since I've spent the day on the water," he said. "It'll be fun to get out. Take my mind off Marissa."

Jerri snapped to attention hearing Pendragon mention the mysterious Marissa. *Marissa, Marissa, Marissa,* Jerri silently steamed, counting her exercise repetitions like a drill cadence. *4-Marissa, 5-Marissa, 6-Marissa... so, he's obsessed with this exotic creature... 10-Marissa, 11-Marissa, 12-Marissa... from the sound of it, he thinks she's perfection on a stick... 16-Marissa, 17-Marissa, 18-Marissa... to hear him tell it, Marissa's God's Gift to men... 22-Marissa, 23-Marissa, 24-Marissa... MARISSA — Aaarrugh!*

~o0o~

Taking up a position behind the little boat's captain's seat, Jerri fought to keep her mind on the upcoming dive as her attention kept snapping back to Mark's dark tan and his stylish

142

burgundy swim trunks. *Gad, I think the man could make a burlap bag look stunning... wrapped around his hips and — JUST SHUT UP!!!* She commanded her leering 'inner child', *Just shut the hell up! Jeez! Hose yourself down, while you're at it!*

He sat at the Little Lavender's helm and headed Miss Marty's skiff away from the boat dock, turning the wheel toward the Gulf side of the island. Allowing the boat to cruise slowly until it cleared the mile marker-buoy, he offered, "I've heard there's some interesting coral heads on this side."

She removed her gear from her dive-bag and asked offhandedly, "You know a lot of divers down here?" *Good one, Jerri. Jeez, why don't you ask him his sign while you're at it? Yeah, Right... do you come here often? If I say you have a beautiful body would you hold it against me? Pleasssse....*

Mark glanced back over his shoulder, watching her unload her mask, fins, gloves, weight belt and buoyancy control jacket. The weight belt was made up of beanbags filled with lead shot, designed to compensate her body's natural tendency to float. The buoyancy control jacket, or B.C., anchored her air tank to her back. Divers filled the B.C. with tank air for floating on the surface. The B.C. deflated, the weight of the tank, added to the compensating weight belt, allowed the diver to sink through the water.

Pendragon's silent answer to Jerri's question was a maddening smirk.

"Come on, Marky de Sade," she teased, "answer the question: Do you know a lot of divers down here?" The sunlight glittered off Jerri's mirrored lavender bikini; twinkling like a bright Christmas ornament.

Finally, he shook his head and smirked, as he said, "Only a few."

"A few?" She dripped the defog liquid onto the faceplate of her dive mask, and used her fingers to wipe the solution across the glass. "*What?* You don't know many people? Or you don't hangout with divers?"

He grinned wickedly, and quipped, "I know the ones who

come back."

" — *ones who come back?*" She narrowed her eyes. "Oh... I get it. That's your idea of a joke. A bad joke — but a joke, nonetheless." She snugged the B.C. strap around the dive tank. "Well, Pendragon. You know *this* diver, and I assure you, I *always* come back."

He grinned again. "I once had a cat like that. No matter what I did... he *always* came back." He sighed dramatically, and said, "Delaney... *you* remind me of my cat. Hold on!"

Luckily, she grabbed hold of the captain's chair to brace herself, as he shoved the accelerator shifter down, just as he ended his non sequitur. The front of the boat reared up as the outboard roared to life. They thundered over the deep-blue Gulf, the bow of the Little Lavender sending a fine spray over them in its wake. Ten minutes found the two nearly a mile from shore; Jerri looked back over her shoulder, noticing she could no longer see the Purple Plantation's dock.

Running full throttle, the boat covered the distance in twenty minutes more, and land was completely out of sight. As the little craft skipped over the water, Jerri peered over the side of the boat. Below the surface, she saw many underwater dark shaped outcroppings scattered around the white sand bottom. "Corals, and sponges, and sea grass — *Oh, my!* It's a good day to dive!" Jerri yelled to be heard above the roar of the boat motor.

"What?" Mark yelled over his shoulder, keeping his attention focused on piloting the boat. "You say it's a good day to *die?* Delaney, you told me you're a certified diver. So, what's all this whining about *dying?*"

She grinned and lightly knocked her fist on his head. "Dive, de Sade! I said: Dive!! Dive!! Dive!!"

"What?" he yelled. "*Dive-Dive-Dive?* You think I gotta submarine here?"

She yelled louder, closer to his ear. "You're impossible, Pendragon! You know that? I think you've — " she raised her voice even as he dropped the throttle, decelerated and switched the motor off. " — heard every word I've said." Jerri ended her high-volume tirade close enough for Pendragon's hair to brush across her lips. The erotic sensation of his dark wavy hair tickling her lips caused her to pause and take a step back, her fingertips held to her mouth as if she were trying to contain even the tiniest touch from this gorgeous man.

Jerri hissed, berating herself for having such a reaction to a simple sensation. *Why do I let him get to me? So he's not butt-ugly! So he doesn't scare little children! So he's the best looking example of masculine beauty I've EVER seen! So... okay! Okay! I give up!*

After dropping the anchor over the side, Pendragon turned to Jerri. "You, who are about to dive," he said, "we salute you!" He mockingly flipped her a smart salute, grabbed up her B.C., attached the regulator connections, ran the dive computer though a pre-dive test and inflated the jacket before easing the buoyancy control device into the water. He then tethered the dive equipment to the side of the boat.

"Wait just a minute, Happy-Boy!" She snapped, "Where do *you* get off running *my* equipment through its dive check? That's *my* job!! And further more, I have to put on my B.C. *before* I make my giant stride! And then I'll — "

"And *then* you'll put your equipment on in the water," he interrupted. "Or you *won't* dive. Take it or leave it. You wanted to dive; I brought you out here. So — you'll dive. *My way.* Your neck is still too fragile for a giant stride. I don't want you to put unnecessary stress on your neck and back by jumping in the water with the weight of your equipment."

Jerri defiantly set her hands on her hips. "Fine. We'll do it your way. Where's *your* equipment? You *are* going to dive with me, aren't you?"

"Nope."

"Aw, come on," she wheedled. "Be a sport. I'll let you be the leader. Any way you want. Suit up! Whadda ya say, huh?"

"No can do, Delaney," he chuckled. "*Nothing* you can say will make me get in that water."

"You won't get wet, huh?" She smirked, buckling her

weight belt around her waist. "What's a`matta? Scared?" She took her teasing farther, "Afraid you'll melt? Fear of tuna? Chicken of the Sea?"

"No." He shook his head, chuckled again and said, "Afraid I'll drown. I can't swim a lick."

She gave him a skeptical look. "*You… don't… swim?* You mean, you live in the Florida Keys and you can't *swim?*"

He laughed again. "Don't look so surprised," he said. "I hear there are people living in Aspen who don't ski." He handed her a dive knife and waited until she strapped it above her ankle. "Ease yourself over the side, and I'll hand you your fins."

"I don't usually dive alone," she protested. "It's not really a smart thing to do. I was taught your buddy was your most valuable safety aid; plus, I thought *you'd* be going down *with* me."

"You'll be okay, Delaney. Just don't stray too far." He waited while Jerri lowered herself over the side of the boat. "Keep the boat and the dive line in sight," he said, "limit your down time, and I'll time you from the surface."

"Fine. If this is the only way I'll get to dive," she sighed. "I've looked forward to this for so long; no way I'm gonna pass *this* up. Just a quick, easy dive, then back to the boat." Sliding into her B.C., she snapped the catches, lay back in the water, pointed her feet toward Pendragon and waited while he slipped her fins over each foot in turn. Then she politely asked, "Hand my camera over, please?"

Pendragon lowered the waterproofed video camera into the water; Jerri attached it to her wrist with a lanyard noose. He then dropped the dive line over the side, watched the red and white bobbing dive flag unfurl, as Jerri adjusted her mask. The red flag, with its diagonal white stripe was a legal safety warning, indicating a diver under the surface. She fitted the regulator into her mouth and took a practice breath.

"Everything check out?" he asked.

"Roger! Copy that," Jerri quipped, patting the top of her head in the 'everything's okay' diver signal. She grinned, "See you in thirty."

Deflating her B.C., she squeezed all the air from the lavender polyester jacket, turned head over heels, pointed her feet in the air, and descended slowly. Clearing her ears by pinching her nose closed and gently blowing until her eardrums equalized and popped, she traveled down the guideline. Her breathing was slow and even. Jerri watched her air bubbles dance through the sparkling beams of sunlight on their way to the surface and checked her dive computer. It recorded all the pertinent information of the dive: depth, length of time down, remaining air. She felt the high price of the tiny electronic gadget well worth it; as the most important dive rule she'd learned was: Safety First.

Ordinarily, I wouldn't go in without a dive buddy, but I'm not going any deeper than eighty feet, she reasoned, *and Mark's staying on the surface. If I run into trouble, which isn't likely, he'll call on the ship-to-shore radio and get help. It's almost as good as having another diver at my side,* she tried to convince herself. *Really. It'll be okay.*

The computer read seventy-six feet by the time she reached the sandy bottom. Looking up, she saw the boat keel's dark outline and the dive line running down from the surface. She checked her start time and looked around, spying a coral head off to the right. Kicking off, Jerri glided through the bath-warm crystal-clear water, relying on her fins alone to carry her to the teeming underwater community.

This whole massive structure was a live thing; even the bits and pieces of long dead coral still provided haven for colorful creatures. She passed the dive light's beam over the reef, the light brightening and intensifying each color to its full potential. *Every surface is a myriad of color,* Jerri mused to herself, *it couldn't hold more vibrant shades if an artist had painted each sea-creature with a many-hued pallet.*

The first thing Jerri did, after reaching the outcropping of marine life, was to check for fire coral. The whitish plant-like creature caused burns if touched or brushed against. A couple of moments search satisfied her, and she hovered in the water, her fins inches above the sand. Removing an aerosol can from her

B.C. pocket, she squeezed a yellow line of sticky cheese onto her gloved finger and held it out for the fish. A small school of red-orange and white-banded clown fish took the first challenge, darting in and out, nibbling on the spreadable delicacy. An amber jack got curious, shoving in and crowding out the clowns. Jerri stifled giggles. *Don't get greedy, Guys! There's enough for everyone!*

The swirling fish schooling around the sponges and corals vied with each other in their rainbow-like beauty. The small colorful acrobats swirled in and out among the sea firs, anemones, and sea fans, performing an underwater circus. She watched as a teal-blue parrot fish and his dinner companion, a yellow-striped trigger fish, bit off tiny chunks of coral, while a brown crab — his eyes on prongs giving his 'face' a cartoon appearance — dined on an unhappily-dead fish's head. Two prickly-spined sea urchins stilt walked in a slow race to see which one would reach a green rock, covered with their algae dinner.

She grabbed up the tethered underwater video camera floating by her side, and began filming. A school of glasseyes, small pinkish fish with large black eyes, circled the coral much like mosquitoes around a campfire, their graceful swimming patterns rivaling a modern dancer. Jerri checked her gauges and glanced upward, getting a bearing on the Little Lavender where Mark waited on the surface. Satisfied, she returned her attention to the aquatic menagerie before her, and the pleasant task of capturing their image on film.

Next, she spied a scorpion fish, recognizing it from the spines along its dorsal fin. It would inject powerful poison if stepped on or touched. A jackknife swam past her, resembling a half-open pocketknife, hence the source of its name. A small school of elongated silver fish, commonly known as snook, glided past Jerri's shoulder. The snook looked somewhat like long-snouted barracuda with black stripes. *I hear seafood connoisseurs prize them. Word is, they're delicious. I'll remember to look for them on the menu.* Interrupting her thoughts by skittering into view, a scrawled filefish, looking like someone had doodled a pattern on his elongated body, appeared to be sticking out his tongue. Jerri chuckled at his very comical face.

A delicate sea-fan held a Basket Starfish, appearing to be an entangled mass of roots and branches. Jerri wished for a few traditional starfish, but knew such a sighting would be rare; regular five-armed sea stars were now usually found in the Bahamas, having been mostly 'fished out' of the Gulf for touristy collectables. Crawling across the sandy floor beside the coral head, a fat sea cucumber made its way from one busy community to another.

Suddenly, a matched pair of French Angel fish swam around the coral head. The glittery black fish-couple, with silver glinting off their scales, feathery fins making them appear as otherworldly ballerinas, stood about two feet from top to bottom. Jerri remembered that these large angels mated for life, and she knew they probably made their home around this reef. Their ethereal beauty was indescribable, and it caused her to momentarily hold her breath. But, just as soon as the air bubbles stopped their dance from her regulator, she realized she'd broken a cardinal law.

Holding one's breath on scuba is a mortal sin... and Jerri knew this. Constant breath holding could cause injury or even death. Jerri taught herself early on to use the absence of bubbles for a visual reminder to breathe evenly; she wasn't a reckless diver. Her renewed breathing sent a bevy of bubbles racing giddily to the surface.

Like a many-limbed contortionist, a small octopus, the size of a grown house cat, slid around the reef, constricting and expanding its arms in its flowing method of travel. Flowing colors migrated throughout the chameleon-like octopus' body, mimicking the coral surfaces it skated over. It purposely refused to approach Jerri, being a shy creature.

Turning to her left, she noticed a neighboring reef. Estimating it to be about thirty feet away, she saw what looked like a statue dropped on its side, stretched across the corals. While she couldn't be sure from this distance, it appeared to be a bronze mermaid statue. She pointed the video camera in the direction of the green-tinged figure, hit the zoom button and captured a telescopic close-up, causing the illusion the mermaid statue was less than ten feet away. *Perhaps it's been dropped over the side of a centuries-gone, treasure-laden galleon,* she mused, *or maybe it's even a figurehead from an ancient ship. I think I'll go over and take a look.*

Quickly referring to her computer, she read eighteen minutes had passed since entering the water. *The dive's more than half over; my air's getting low... jeez, where does the time go? Only twelve minutes left... Guess that statue will have to wait for the next dive. Maybe I better cut this first time down a little short. After all, I haven't done this for awhile.* Then she laughed to herself, *I'll bet Pendragon is getting worried. High and dry, all alone on that big, big boat.*

Saying a silent farewell to the circus-like schools of fish, Jerri kicked off from the sandy bottom, meaning to make a slow ascent. She'd gained a three feet climb, when she felt a tug on her right fin. Looking down, she pulled on her leg and found it tethered with a jumbled and nearly invisible fishing line wrapped a number of times in a tangled knot. Fishing debris, snagged on living reefs, was an environmental hazard. Besides being a danger to divers, it ensnared innocent wildlife such as sea turtles and dolphins, holding them under water until they drowned in the very water that gave them life.

Sending a cascade of air bubbles from her regulator, powered by a few mumbled curses, Jerri sank to the bottom with the intentions of untangling her leg from the snarled mess of nylon line. Drawing her dive knife from its leg holster, she started in on the Gordian knot, holding her captive on the ocean floor. Cutting the monofilament line would take time — she *knew* this. Her B.C. obstructed her vision, she couldn't see her ankles easily, and it would be difficult to cut through the wadded nylon line, strand by strand with a dull dive knife. Locating and separating a strand, Jerri sawed with the knife, conquering the knot piece by piece.

Consumed by the task at hand, she failed to notice the strands of line entwined around her dive tank. She checked her air again, noting the six hundred pounds of pressure left. She'd never run out of air before, but remembered her instructor saying at five hundred pounds the regulator signals would ding like a bell and the dwindling air would prove harder to pull out of the tank. Resolving not to panic, Jerri returned her attention to the task at hand. *If I can hack through this tangled mess, I'll be on the boat and Pendragon won't have to know anything about this... I'm sure if he caught wind of my stupidity, I'd never hear the end of it.*

Five long minutes of cutting and pulling on nylon lines ate up the tank air. When she realized she was having difficulty pulling in air and could feel/hear the regulator 'dinging', she grabbed up the computer. *Good Lord! I've only got four hundred pounds of pressure left! Calm down! You've just got to calm down! If you panic now, you'll suck up your air, and then... I don't wanna think about it.*

Not wanting to dwell on the inevitable, she returned her attention to the knotted nylon string, again hacking and cutting at the line binding her leg. Suddenly, the schooling fish scattered. Still trying to slice through the line, Jerri looked up just as a large bull shark glided leisurely around the coral head. *Ohhmahgod!! I've got to get out of here! Just stay calm! Maybe he'll go away.*

She cut frantically at her bindings. *Come on! Come on! This is no time for theatrics! That shark is not going to beg for an encore! This is a one shot deal if I ever saw one!* Glancing up at the shark every few seconds, she could feel her heart pounding in her chest.

The shark swam past; a bare three feet from her, heading east, gliding in a wide circle, swinging around for yet another tentative reconnaissance sweep. Just as she cut the last nylon strings free from her leg, her left hand encountered a large fishhook and she felt it slice through her thin glove and into her finger.

Feeling the pain of the cut, she fumbled the knife. It slipped from her hand; cart wheeled through the water, and came to rest just out of her reach. *Gotta get outta here!!* She screamed to herself, *Feets don't fail me now! Come on!! Make like Flipper!! Let's go!!*

She pushed off, making a run for the surface, but with each kick, something pulled her back. *Damn! I'm still stuck on something!!* She tugged at the hidden fishing line holding her to the sandy bottom.

Blood oozed, clouding and tinting the surrounding water a reddish-pink. The shark's path led him inches closer this time, his nearly leisurely glide making smaller circles with every sweep. Jerri tore off her gloves and clamped her other hand around her finger, vainly attempting to stanch the blood flow.

She looked up longingly at the boat's silhouette, wishing she were with the gorgeous dark-haired man now; dry, safe and sound in his arms. *Maybe Pendragon will notice I'm down too long and call for rescue... yeah, right! And maybe Mack the Knife, here, will put dinner on hold 'til they get here.*

The shark circled again, this time bumping into her arm. She reached out, warding it away, unwillingly running her hand alone its side. Its skin felt unfishlike, rough and sandpapery. Looking desperately at the dive knife resting just out of her reach, she thought back to class discussions about shark-defense.

Jerri resolved when the blood-aroused shark circled again... *I'm gonna give it the only weapon I have left! A hard fist to the snout!*

~o0o~

Chapter 20

Mark leaned over the side of the boat, trying to catch any sight of Jerri. He ran his hands through his thick dark hair, absentmindedly pulling at it in his frustration. Pacing up and down the length of the boat, he muttered aloud, "What'll I do? I *can't* get wet."

Taking his sunglasses off, he again leaned over the boat as if this might give him a better view through the crystal-clear water. "By my count, Jerri's been down *much* too long; at least fifteen minutes past the time she promised to be back on board."

"I was a *fool* to let her dive alone," he muttered, again. "I should have made her wait and dive with a group. If *anything* happens to her...." He let his words die out to a shake of his head.

He suddenly straightened, tugged at his dark red swim trunks, and slid them off his untanned hips. Mark finished his worrisome thought in an agonized whisper, "If she's in trouble, I'll never forgive myself." Dropping the shorts to the boat's floor, the man who'd earlier told The Amazing Delaney he was afraid of the water, grabbed a small air cylinder, wrapping its tether cord around his arm, and dove headfirst into the warm, salty Gulf waters.

~o0o~

The shark circled again. By the angle of its approach, Jerri could tell this would probably be its last sweep. As she balled up her fist, she steeled herself, hoping to put every ounce of her power behind the punch.

The shark closed in. She realized as the regulator's 'dinging' grew louder, the pulling breaths coming from the mouthpiece were now shallow and sparse. She didn't have need to look at the computer to know her air was almost gone. The shark was a mere six feet away when everything darkened in Jerri's field of vision. Bright flashing lights and dark shadow-clouds warred in front of her eyes. As the shadows gradually won the battle over the lights, her balled fist relaxed and she sunk to the ocean's floor. Before the darkness took over completely, she glimpsed a huge blue-green fish 'closing in' on the shark. *That's funny,* she thought, sinking into the warm darkness, *I didn't know ANY fish would chase sharks....*

The last thing she saw before fainting from lack of air, left her in confusion.

~o0o~

"Jerri — Just lie still," the voice said. "I've got to tend to this cut. It's not deep, but you're bleeding all over everything."

Bright light... must be 'The Tunnel'... voice... calling me... Daddy? Daddy, is that you? She peeped out through slitted eyes. *...angel? Are there dark-haired blue-eyed angels in Heaven? ...wait a minute!!! Maybe I'm NOT in Heaven!*

"I had a *devil* of a time pulling you into the boat," the voice spoke up again. "You're a dead weight when you're wet."

She shielded her eyes from the Florida sunshine, then opened them wider and sighed. "Mar... *Pendragon!* What happened? How did I...?"

He kneeled beside her on the boat's sofa bench, finishing the task of dressing her shallow finger wound. "I told you, Delaney. You floated to the surface, I fished you out. Thought about throwing you back, but then I thought... *naw!* If I just catch a few more, I'll have enough for a decent dinner." Pendragon hid his concern as he stowed the first aid kit under the pilot's seat.

She shuddered at his use of the word 'dinner'.

Mark smirked. "What's wrong? Did I say something?"

She shuddered once more. "I'll never think of dinner in the same light again," she said. "You see... once you've been on the *other* side of the table...." She shook her head, looked down at her

154

right hand, seeing the tether-lanyard encircling her wrist. Surprised it'd survived her adventure, Jerri removed her underwater camera and placed it on the bench seat in front of her. She rubbed her wrist and muttered, "Being on the menu is *so* not a good thing."

"Delaney — you're making even less sense than usual," he chuckled. "Did you hit your head when you got that little boo-boo?"

She hung her head, and groaned. "No... I've got a confession to make."

"Do I look like a priest to you?" He snorted. "I like women too much to be caught dead as a priest."

"*Caught dead?* Boy, you're not making this any easier," she grumbled, pulling herself up into a sitting position. "I cut my finger hacking away at fishing line."

"And? *Why* were you playing around with fishing line?"

"I was cutting the fishing line from around my leg."

"I'm not acquainted with *that* strange diver's ritual." His eyes danced with teasing merriment.

She sat up straight, put her hands to her hips and huffed. "I'm *trying* to tell you something serious! *I was almost killed down there!* I couldn't get away from the fishing line, and a big ugly shark decided I might be a tasty-chewy... *I thought I was trapped!* And... I could swear... just before I blacked out, I saw something impossible. Something that just... couldn't... *be.*"

A strange expression crossed his face. He quickly recovered and quipped, "Good thing you're an escape artist, then. Isn't it? Before you blacked out, you must've unsnapped your B.C., dropped your weight belt and floated up to the surface. I found your B.C. about 50 feet away, floating on top of the water. What a great trick for your act! Looks like you pulled off one neat little grand finale. Boy, Amazing! You're *really* dedicated to your craft."

Her eyes sent daggers at the maddening man kneeling before her. *What right does he have to look so scrumptious while he's picking on me? I was almost KILLED!!!* She glared at the man again.

"Has anyone ever told you," he smiled, his most mischievous smile, "that you're *beautiful* when you're furious?"

This swift turn in the conversation took her by surprise. A quick blush climbed her cheeks, and she blurted out, "*What?*"

He grinned again, reaching out, gently tipping her chin up. "If anyone ever told you you're beautiful when you're angry," he moved in closer, grazing her lips with his, "they were *lying through their teeth.*"

She spat venom and punched him in the chest, hurting her injured hand in the process. He tumbled back on the boat's floor, laughing at her sudden anger. Jerri pulled her feet onto the bench and hugged her legs to her chest, burying her face between her knees. Her shoulders hitched with silent sobs.

"...Delaney?" He crawled toward her on his hands and knees. "*Jerri* — don't cry! I didn't mean it... I was only kidding... *don't cry!*"

She raised her head and beamed at Pendragon. "Did anyone ever tell *you* that you're *gorgeous* when you're gullible?"

His expression told Jerri she'd hit her mark. "Touché." He chuckled. "How about we call a truce?" He held out his hand in a gesture of reconciliation.

Dubiously, she shook hands with the gorgeous man, expecting any second he'd pull her off balance or zap her with a joy-buzzer. "Truce," she said, warily lowering her guard. "What say we head back to shore. I want to put as much distance as I can between me and the Underwater Gourmet, down there."

Mark grinned at her and quipped, "What's a matter, Delaney? Fear of Tuna? Chicken of the Sea?"

~oOo~

Mark guided the small skiff up to the dock. On the shore, a five-foot tall wooden lighthouse model bore the words: 'The Quay'.

Jerri waited until Mark secured the boat before climbing out onto the dock. The sun was setting in a glorious display of red, purple and lavenders. "Jeez, this looks like a sunset ordered up by

156

Miss Marty," she said, admiring the sky. "That woman's so rich, even God takes her decorating advice."

"Looks like we missed dinner," he sighed. "How about I show you this wonderful little seafood bar in Marathon. The Kon-Tiki Bar." He indicated the small building in front of them. "Serves the best red snapper around."

"Sounds good," she nodded her head. "But I think I'll pass on the snapper. `Think this calls for a big thick shark steak. Kinda hair of the dog, don't ya think?"

~o0o~

"How's your shark?"

Jerri touched her mouth with her paper napkin, and sighed. "Wonderful. Tasty chewy. Let me tell ya, it's much better to be on *this* end of the fork." They dined beside the dock. The darkness had gathered and millions of stars took their place on a mammoth ink-black placemat in the heavens. A pelican contentedly snoozed on a large rock, at the water's edge.

Mark sipped his margarita, and settled back in his patio chair, sitting outside the Kon-Tiki Bar at an open patio dining area. The Gulf waters lapped at the coral rocks just feet from their table. When he spoke, he seemed subdued. "You scared me to death out there."

She looked at him as if she'd just seen him for the first time. She whispered, "Really?"

"Really," he said. "Standing on the boat waiting... and waiting... and *waiting.* And then when you floated to the surface... *and you were bleeding.* I tell you, my heart about stopped."

"You should have seen it from *my* angle," she shivered. "When my air ran out, the shark came right at me. And right before everything faded away... I could've *sworn* a huge sparkling fish... at least, at first, I *thought* it was a fish. You see, I was winking out — going down for the count — when this huge fish grabbed that shark and sunk its teeth into its back... I saw it. At least, I *think* I saw it."

"That's kinda farfetched, isn't it?" He grinned at her.

"No... *that's* not the farfetched part," she shook her head. "I

157

could've *sworn* that big fish *was half man.*"

A strange expression crossed his face, and Mark twirled the stem of his margarita glass between his hands. "Heh. Sounds like a big fish story to me." He glanced into her eyes, as if gauging her reaction to his disbelief.

"I'm just telling you what I *thought* I saw." Jerri drained her iced-tea and motioned through the window to the waitress for a refill. "I know it must have been a rare shallow-water narc-induced hallucination, or something like that. I *must've* been narced, with a good dose of near-death panic thrown in. You know, divers can get too much nitrogen in their blood. It leads to nitrogen narcosis. Hallucinations, you know. Hell... I was so out of it, I think I saw Elvis." She laughed uneasily and shook her head. "But it was just a wild hallucination... *had* to be."

He stifled a sigh of relief and another mischievous grin played across his face. "Are you in the habit of telling tall tales, little girl?"

"No... notice I didn't say I saw *Elvis* in a *U.F.O.*" She chuckled, and quipped, "I simply saw a man-fish coming to my rescue."

"Merman."

"Excuse me?"

Mark tipped the margarita to his lips. "Not man-fish. *Merman,*" he said. "Like a mermaid, but a man. Taken from the Old English word: 'mere', meaning lake or pond. So, it's literally: 'man of the lake'. Actually, I think triton *might* be the proper archaic term."

The waitress filled Jerri's tea glass. She thanked the young woman and turned back to her dinner companion. "So. How do *you* come to know about mermaids and tritons?"

"Hobby of mine," he replied. "I hold a minor in Ancient Mythology."

"Jeez, Pendragon. And here I had you pegged for a Himbo."

He paused, the margarita glass inches from his lips. He dryly asked, "*Himbo?*"

"I take it you've never heard the proper archaic term," she

smiled. "No matter. Any man with a degree in Ancient Mythology is automatically disqualified. You, Sir, are no Himbo."

"May I take that as a complement?"

Jerri giggled. "By all means. You see, 'Himbo' is the male equivalent of Bimbo. You know... all looks; no brains?" She giggled again, then grew serious. "By any chance, did you study ancient *art?*"

"Such as?"

She twirled the ice in her tea. "Since you already think I'm crazy, guess I might as well tell you."

"What?" He grinned. "Was Mona Lisa bummin' around with Elvis and the merman?"

Jerri's chuckles held a tinge of hesitation. "No, silly," she said. "But, I did see something interesting down there... looked like some kind of statue or something. I was too far away to tell for sure." Her expression turned pensive, and she absentmindedly touched the bandage on her finger, as she remembered the bronze mermaid sculpture, fallen on the coral head.

"Statue?"

The waitress stopped at the table with more tea, but this time, Jerri covered her glass and shook her head. To Mark, she answered, "Yeah, at least from a distance it *looked* like a statue. I think it was a bronze mermaid sculpture."

Pendragon jerked to attention. He blurted out the word: "*Mermaid?*" Glancing at Jerri, he cleared his throat. "Uhh... you say it looked like a *mermaid,* huh? More hallucinations?"

She glanced around at the other tables as if the Kon-Tiki's other diners might be eavesdroppers. Turning back to Mark, she shook her head and said, "No. I'm *sure* this was real. I saw it before I ran low on air. I think it was life-sized. And it must be bronze, because it looked green — at least at a distance. Bronze turns green in seawater, you know. I'll bet it's valuable. Either monetarily or historically. I think I got it on my underwater digital."

She reached into her shoulder bag and removed her camera.

With the push of a button, underwater images came into view. She keyed past video of the colorful fish on the coral head, finally pausing at one spot, the scene darker than the rest. "See? What's that look like to you?" Jerri passed the camera to Pendragon.

He studied the paused video for many seconds. "Interesting." As he spoke he reached out a fingertip, pausing barely above the murky picture. "It *does* look like a mermaid... a mermaid statue that is. ...I wish I'd've seen it."

"Do you think you could find the spot again?"

He shook his head at her. "You mean you'd dive *again?* After the close call you had?"

"Can't let the shark win, can I?" Jerri laughed and returned the camera to her purse. "Well? Do you think you could find the spot again? I'll get better videos, at least."

Bringing his hand up to his face, he stroked his chin, seemingly lost in thought. Many moments passed in silence, until Jerri thought she'd have to reintroduce herself to the gorgeous dark-haired man sitting across the table. Then just as she opened her mouth to release a wisecrack, a waitress dropped a tray of plates and shook Mark out of his reverie.

He jerked in surprise, and looked over his shoulder for the clattering sound. As if all thoughts of the statue had escaped his mind, he turned back to Jerri, chuckled and said, "I don't know why I do that. I used to hate it when I dropped trays and every eye in the place focused on me."

"You used to wait tables?"

He took a sip of his drink and nodded. "That's how I put myself through college. And yourself?"

"I was Daddy's little girl," Jerri smiled. "While there wasn't a lot of money, Dad made sure I didn't have to work in college. But, I did my share on summer breaks. First I was gopher, then roadie, then assistant. Dad made me do the 'scut' work before he bestowed his wizard's cap and wand." The last words brought back memories, and she felt a lump in her throat and a threat of tears. She spoke to keep from crying, "The last summer before he died... we toured as Amazing Delaney and Daughter. It was the *best* time of my life."

Mark reached out and brushed her fingertips, sending a thrill through her body with the simple friendly touch. "Sounds to me like your dad was a great man."

She murmured, "Yes... he was." Catching a rogue tear before it completed its journey down her cheek, she felt a blush coming on, cleared her throat, and reluctantly pulled her hand from his reach. With exaggerated cheerfulness, she teased, "Listen, here! You never answered my question."

Mark smiled, his dark-hooded eyes joining in on his good humor. "Which question was that? I'll warn you now; it's no use grilling me on whether I prefer boxers or briefs. That's my secret and I'll take it to my grave."

Jerri giggled in spite of herself.

"Your coffin is going to be mighty crowded with all those secrets you insist upon taking to your grave," she smirked. "Besides, I wasn't asking about your choice of undies. I just wanted to know if you can find the same group of coral heads, tomorrow."

Again, a strange expression crossed his face. Dark-lashed eyes hid his warring emotions, and he reached out, flicking chunks of salt off the rim of his glass. After seconds of silence, he mumbled, "Maybe. I'm not the best sailor in the world... *but we'll give it a good try.*"

~o0o~

"If you want to dive tomorrow, I suggest you turn in early."

"A simple: 'See you early in the morning' will do," Jerri quipped, after they'd walked from the Purple Plantation's dock, around the pool area to the mansion's front entrance. As they reached Pendragon's car, she leaned in close to the dark-haired man and smiled. "Pendragon, will you buy a clue? We've long passed the Millennium. Don't you know it's not 'PC' to tell a woman what to do?"

He grinned, a wicked gleam in his eyes. "It may not be 'PC', Delaney; but it's still so much fun being a chauvinist." The tropical full moon peeked through the few clouds in the sky, glazing the tips of his dark locks, giving him the illusion he wore silver in his hair. He laughed and settled behind the wheel of his small jeep.

"For a man who can't swim, you sure like to jump in over your head. Talk about a wimp!" She turned with a teasing huff, and headed for the mansion's front door. Ringing the bell, she waited for Conchita, and heard Pendragon's laughter as he drove away. The maid answered the door, and Jerri smiled to herself, thinking of her maddening — *but sexy!!* the eager little traitor in her head gleefully interjected — dinner companion.

Conchita greeted her. "Señorita Jerri? La tarde era buena, sí?"

She hugged the woman in the lavender maid's uniform and smiled. "Thank you, Conchita! The evening *was* good — *YES!* The night was *so* beautiful, the shark steak was superb, and — "

" — Y Señor Pendragon," the older woman giggled. "El es muy, muy atractiva, no?"

Jerri pulled back, a shocked look on her face. "Sexy, huh? Oh, yeah?" She mumbled, "I hadn't noticed. *Ya really think so?*"

~oOo~

Chapter 21

He drove through the moonlight enjoying the balmy night air, thinking about the feisty lady recuperating at Miss Marty's. *I think Jerri Delaney might be the most independent woman I've ever met,* he mused to himself, *and that frustrating independent streak is very sexy. Very sexy, indeed.*

Turning into his driveway, Pendragon shook his head, as memories of the day on the water and the late dinner ran through his thoughts. "So, she says she hallucinated a man-fish who saved her from the big-bad shark," he whispered, parking under the carport. "Hallucinations. How lucky can you get?" Gazing up at the star-filled sky, he shook his head and sighed. "Hallucinating a *merman* is one thing... I think she's *convinced* herself she was seeing things, but, she said there was a mermaid *statue* down there. And that video *does* look interesting." He walked out onto his small beach, pulled his shirt over his head, kicked off his shoes, and again stepped out of his swim trunks, leaving his clothes piled in a heap on the sand. *"I've gotta check this out."*

Wading out into the still warm, foam-tipped water, his legs took on a light greenish color rising under the skin as if the moon-kissed surf reflected its cast. Stepping further over the sandy beach until the seawater lapped at the top of his greenish thighs, the dark-haired man leaped headfirst into the surf.

His bare hips took on a teal hue as he disappeared beneath the swells and moments later, a luxurious fishtail rose above the waves, unfurling in a glorious display of sparkling beauty. It slapped the water with a resounding report, sending a salty spray flying toward the shore.

~o0o~

Sweat beaded the forehead of the sleeping man and he rolled onto his side, clutching a pillow as if he clutched a lifeline. His lips moved, giving the appearance he conversed with someone, while his eyes darted side to side underneath closed eyelids.

In his dreams, he was on a beach, illuminated by a quarter moon. Shadows lent a sinister quality to the night and gave rise to a dreadful fear that he was not alone. The fear pumped adrenaline into his veins and caused his heart to pound inside of his chest, the sound echoing in his ears.

He cried out against the pain and fear, but his cries went unheard.

~o0o~

Jerri was lost in a delicious dream. A standing-room-only audience reveled at her every move on stage. In her heart, she knew she'd never performed better. The black rhinestones making up her top hat and tuxedo-style shorty outfit sparkled and glittered, sending flashes of light out into the crowd. She glanced around, searching each smiling face, looking for the one man she could share her happiness with — her father.

In her dream, Jeremy Delaney wasn't dead. In her dream, she wasn't alone. She knew she only had to perform the *Dance of the Seven Deadly Swords* to make her father reveal himself. She coaxed a male volunteer up on stage, and encased him snugly in a tall bamboo-sided magic box. The first sword pushed into the six-foot tall Chinese decorated box of illusion. She assured herself, if all went right, her father would step out of his hiding place and proclaim his daughter his rightful heir and publicly bestow his title upon his successor. If only she could carry off the trick.

She'd had this dream many times in the last six months. Each time, just as the last sword stabbed through the pre-designated holes, magically exiting out the other side, her eyes searched the audience. Usually the roar of the jubilant crowd died in her ears as she swam up out of a deep sleep. But this time, she

164

shoved the last sword home, indicated the speared Chinese magic prop with a flourish, and for a grand finale — removed the swords and opened the box to reveal the unharmed male volunteer.

Glancing into the box of illusion, she offered her hand to the man inside, and stared into the darkest blue eyes she'd ever seen. Mark Pendragon extended his hand. Jerri was consumed with a strange feeling that all she had to do was take the dark-haired man's hand, accept him into her life, and her father was sure to appear to give his blessing.

The applause filled her ears just like the wrenching indecision filled her heart and paralyzed her hand. *Should I... could I... give myself to this man; give up my LIFE to this man? Daddy? What should I do?* she moaned in her sleep. *You taught me to be an escape artist, but you didn't teach me how to escape this maddening man.*

"*Delaney?*"

She looked again at the gorgeous man in the illusion box. He was grinning, but silent.

"*Delaney?* Wake up! Jeez, Woman. I think you could sleep through the *Apocalypse.*"

Jerri peeked out through bleary eyes. Sure enough, Pendragon hovered beside her bed, his face inches from hers. "*Pendragon?* Are you auditioning for head cuckoo in this big cuckoo clock? Do we *always* have to do this at dawn?" She grabbed the clock off the night-stand. "*2:30 in the morning?* Are you *CRAZY?*"

Mumbling, "Maybe" more to himself than the woman in the bed, he absentmindedly ran his hand through his dark hair and sighed to the ceiling. "But, I didn't know what else to do. I need you."

Am I still dreaming? Did I just hear this man... this gorgeous hunk of blue-eyed perfection... did I just hear this man say he needed ME? She shook her head, trying to clear the wreckage of her dream-soaked brain.

He gripped her shoulder and whispered, "*Hurry!* There's not much time left! *We've got to get your gear and hurry out to the reef!*"

"What's going on?" She hissed, grabbing her robe. "You're in my room in the *middle of the night!* Pendragon? Is this your idea of a *jo* — ?" The stricken look on his face caused her to cease mid-rant. "This *isn't* a joke, is it?" She murmured, "Something's wrong. Tell me. *Tell me how I can help.*"

"I need your lock picks!"

Jerri giggled in spite of herself. "Ya know, Happy-Boy? I've gotta tell ya... I've often fantasized about a dashing man begging for my attention. But, I've never *once* dreamed said dashing man would *lust* after my lock picks."

"Hurry, Delaney," he begged, "there's no time to lose. *Quick!* Get dressed and let's get on the boat... *hurry — please?*"

~o0o~

In his mind, dark images swirled. Angry voices seemed to lash out in all directions, causing him to cringe in fear. Individual words were jumbled into a mish-mash of sounds and disruption.

"What'cha gonna...."

"Ya dirty double-crossin'...."

"Don't let him do that! Get `im!!"

He was inexplicably on a beach — which beach, he didn't know — details were selective and fleeting. A quarter moon failed to distinguish shapes from the sand, merely throwing deep shadows, adding to the menace and dread building in the man's thudding heart. All he felt was pain, every muscle in his body hurt. His face was covered in his own blood, his only thoughts, fear and the desperate need to escape.

His eyes searched the deserted beach for something to use as a weapon against his attackers or a police officer to save him. He found neither.

Now the images settled into menacing shapes, men with their hands raised against him. Voices promising violence. He screamed aloud to the darkened room, "*Don't!*" And his voice sounded distant to his ears. *And strangely foreign.*

The man who usually donned a lavender chauffeur's

166

uniform, tossed and turned in a restless sweat-soaked bed, crying out helplessly against his assailants.

~o0o~

Jerri yelled to be heard over the boat's motor. "Okay, Pendragon! *Now* are you going to tell me why you dragged me out of bed in the middle of the night? And why you barely waited while I left that note... *and* why you barely waited until I stepped in the boat to fire this baby up. *Just tell me!* What's so urgent we had to come out here *now?*"

"Marissa."

"What?" She yelled. "I don't think I heard you. It sounded like you said: *Marissa.* Tell me... what's *God's Gift to Men* got to do with *my* lock picks?"

Glancing at her with a confused expression, he powered down the boat and idled in a circle, checking the satellite navigation device before shutting down the boat's engine. "Suit up," he said, "*we don't have any time to lose.*"

After dropping the guideline over the side, Pendragon reached for Jerri's B.C. and tank, frantically readying her equipment for the dive. He secured two large dive lights to the lavender jacket, attaching them to carabiners. Although the moon was full, the natural light wouldn't reach down to the coral head. "I'm sending you with *two* lights," he said, rushing his words. "You probably need all the light you can get. This might get tricky. Ready? *Jump in.*"

"Not until you explain yourself," she huffed, crossing her arms at chest level. "You want me to get wet? You better start talkin', buddy."

The full moon sailed high in the sky; the sun would chase it away in a scant few hours. A momentary silence hung in the salt-tinged air around the pair on the small boat. Her frustration growing, waiting for Pendragon's explanation, she rolled her head on her shoulders, attempting to disperse her shoulder tension. Then, she saw the boat floating to the south of the Little Lavender.

The outline of the larger craft stood out, barely perceivable

167

against the still dark pre-dawn sky. Huge nets, held out at a 45° angle, gave it the illusion it possessed wings. More moments passed before it registered to Jerri she was looking at a distant shrimp boat anchored about a quarter mile away. Shrimpers were a common sight, she knew this, just as she also knew working boats would usually trawl for shrimp during the day and sit still in the water at night, their crew sleeping. But, this boat showed more activity than was usual for a shrimper in early morning darkness; the silvery moonlight showed movement on the deck.

From their position on the Little Lavender, Pendragon and Jerri both observed shadowed figures lowering an inflated Zodiac boat over the side, and a low droning from the still dark southern sky brought animated pointing gestures from the shrimpers. The Zodiac's crew grew noticeably excited as the low-pitched sound grew louder. Very soon, the droning could be identified as a medium-sized airplane which, flying low and at a slow speed, gradually closed the distance to the shrimp boat. The closer it got to the shrimper, the clearer it was that the airplane was an old double-prop cargo plane.

"Do you see that?" Mark whispered.

Jerri nodded. "Yeah... curious.... but... what's that got to do with — " Suddenly, the lone figure left on the shrimper's deck pointed in their direction and raised what appeared to be a phone or radio to his ear. She barely had time to murmur: "What's *that* guy doing?" before the approaching plane sluggishly waggled its wings and made a wide left banking and 'swooping' dip, flying over the shrimper; the breeze from the props rustling the nets and the shrimper crew's clothing. The low-flying aircraft abruptly changed its course, roughly switching from north to south. "I'll say it again — *curious*."

"I'd say — curious is not the word... Something's up." The man at Jerri's side raked his fingers through his dark curls and peered through the moonlight at the distant water craft.

"Ahem... Focus? Eh — your full attention, here? All eyes center on *me!*" Jerri crossed her arms across her chest and tapped her foot on the Little Lavender's tiny deck. "Give me one — just *one,* mind you — really, *really* good reason for me to get wet — huh, DeSade? Can you do that?"

Once more, he glanced in the direction of the shrimp boat, a worried look on his face. He shook his head, and Jerri wondered if he meant the gesture one of exasperation for her or the mysterious boat. Pendragon sighed, rubbing his eyes, seeming to wrestle with a weighty decision. "You're right, of course," he sighed again. "I can't expect you to risk your life without telling you the truth."

"The truth?"

"The truth is, Marissa is down there, chained to the coral head."

Jerri shook her head in disbelief. "What would *that* woman be doing diving out here in the *middle of the night?* She's — "

"She's not diving," he murmured an interruption.

She shook her head again. "If she's not *diving,* then she's run out of air a long time ago. And if she's not on *scuba,* then you want me to go after a *corpse.* Let me tell ya', I skipped Corpse Recovery class. On purpose, I might add!"

"Delaney," he hissed with exasperation. "You're not making this easy. I know you're not going to believe me, but here goes. *Marissa is a mermaid.*"

Jerri threw her head back and laughed. "Okay, okay. I give up. This is a good one. But, did you really think it was necessary to bring me all the way out here for your puny little joke?"

"Jerri." He took her hand in his and gazed into her eyes, his words spilling out in a rush, "Please believe me when I tell you, *this is no joke.* I've never been more serious in my life. Marissa is a mermaid, and she's down there... *and she needs our help.*"

"But-but-but... mermaids are — " she sputtered, "mermaids are — mermaids... are?"

"*Not real?*" He finished her thought. "The stuff dreams are made of? Right now, I can't debate the existence of mermaids with you. So, to save time — *this* will have to do for my argument." He suddenly shoved his swim trunks down over his hips, standing before Jerri, completely and unselfconsciously

169

nude, moonlight bathing his firm body with a shimmering silver light.

~oOo~

The images of the beach became clearer as the bedside clock flashed the fleeting minutes of the restless night. Even with the pain and fear, names floated to the surface of his tortured memory. He heard the sharp report of a gun, saw the flash from the gun barrel, felt the impact at the side of his head and relived his 'death' at the hands of his attackers. The dream ended abruptly and the sweat-soaked man sat up on the side of his bed in his Southwestern-decorated suite, eyes wide open, whispering one word: "Him...."

~oOo~

Even in her shock, Jerri's traitorous little inside voice sang its greedy praises of the beautiful naked man standing in front of her: *Ahh! Sweet mystery of life! At last I've found thee!*

She managed to swallow the massive lump suddenly lodged in her throat while silently berating the stupid little idiot trilling gleefully in her head. *Can you BE more cliché? Jeez, you'd think you'd never seen a naked man before!*

Not like this!! Goodness gracious!! He's built like... He's built like —

Never you mind WHAT he's built like! she practically screamed to herself. Trying her best not to allow her eyes the freedom to wander below the waist of the gorgeous dark-haired man, she found she was reduced to sputtering again. "But-but-but-but...."

Mark snapped. "You *do* realize you sound like a child's toy boat when you do that? Before you get the wrong idea — " he moved to the back of the boat and swung his legs over the side, dangling his toes in the sea, " — watch what happens."

She cleared her throat, and again tried to speak. "Watch... watch what *happens?* What? *What* happens?"

The greenish tint appeared first under his toes, and swiftly climbed past his knees, upward over his legs, darkening in the silver moonlight as it traveled up his thighs, until it reached his

170

mid-abdomen. The crocheted green solidified more tightly under his navel, modestly covering his maleness. The green tinge formed delicate scales on his legs, weaving the sparkling oval-shaped plates like a talented spider. The teal and sea-green pattern traveled up his thighs, deepening as it climbed over his sculpted hips, spreading until it reached just below his waist. The variegated greens and blues mixed and knitted into a Jacquard pattern of scales covering his strong legs which melded together, ending in a huge glorious fishtail.

She staggered backward and fell onto the sofa bench, her mouth opening and closing like a beached carp. Her mind told her she'd just seen... *A naked, dark-haired, totally gorgeous man transform himself into a fish right before her eyes — at least from the waist down!* Being a skilled Master Illusionist, she *knew* eyes were meant to be deceived, but she'd been taught by the best to see beyond the surface, to look for the '*truth to the trick*'.

Jerri turned her attention back to Pendragon who sat, impatiently slapping his feathery tail on the top of the rolling water. Her mouth opened again, and she tried to form intelligent words: "How-How-How-How?" She waved her hands in the air toward the merman bathed in the silver moonlight, sparkly scales glittering as they rippled over his legs.

"I take it by your stuttering impression of the Lone Ranger's best friend," Mark quipped, "that you *now* believe in mermaids?" He sighed. "Like I said, *I just... don't... have... the time*. Marissa's in danger. Grab your gear. *We're going down.*"

Cradling her head in her arms, Jerri moaned, trying to reason with herself. "That's it! I've officially gone over the rainbow! I've lingered too long in La-La Land. I'm nuts! I'm crazy! I'm a certified lunatic! An overgrown goldfish is sitting in front of me, telling me we're going down, and *I THINK I'VE GONE STONE COLD INSANE!!!*"

After hurriedly dropping the dive flag over the side, Mark pushed off from the low platform and slipped into the water. He quickly swam to the right side of the boat, reached over the rail and grabbed her B.C. and tank.

Dragging the dive equipment into the water beside him, he impatiently pointed at Jerri. *"Are you quite finished, now?* Good. Grab your lock picks," he ordered, "get the rest of your gear and get in the water. *We're losing time here.* Marissa's chained with heavy iron shackles — they're binding her to the coral, for God's sake and she can't get any oxygen. She's going to drown if you don't *hurry and pick the locks."*

"It was you... It was *you* down there. *You* saved me from the shark," she murmured, leaning over the boat, gazing into his blue eyes.

He anxiously whispered, "Jerri! There's no *time!"*

Jerri shook her head, and threw her hands in the air. "Okay! *Fine!* Good enough! Flipper says dive; *I guess we dive!"* Sitting on the back of the boat, she fitted the fins to her feet, pulled the dive mask over her head, leaving it to dangle around her neck. She snatched up her lock picks, stuffing the small leather pouch inside her halter-top and eased herself off the platform into the warm moonlight-kissed water. Dog-paddling around to where Mark held her B.C., she handed off her escape tools to the merman while she slipped into the lavender jacket.

"Since you're being such a good sport about this," he grinned in unconcealed relief, "I'll let that 'Flipper' remark pass."

"You're a prince. Just answer two questions before we go down," she demanded, grasping his arm to hold her position beside him. "First... am I still dreaming? And second... didn't you tell me you couldn't swim? In fact, you said you couldn't swim a lick, if I remember correctly."

He handed her the escape equipment, and pinched her arm.

"Ow!" she yelped. "Ow! *That hurt!"*

"That answers your first question," he flashed his devilish smile. "As for your second question, I think that's a *gimme."*

She rubbed her arm and asked, "A gimme?"

Pendragon leaned in and kissed Jerri. His lips lingered, savoring the taste of her, the salty seawater mingling between her trembling lips and his hungry mouth. "Yeah," he traced her cheek and whispered, "General Information Mode. G-I-M-me. It's a

172

gimme, *cause I lied.* Actually... *I swim like a fish."* He smiled once more and backed away. Diving head first into the water, his large feathery tail shot up through the water, unfurling before slapping the surface with a sharp whip-cracking report.

Jerri lingered beside the boat, bobbing on the surface. Her fingers hovered over her lips like delicate hummingbirds reluctant to light on hallowed ground. Her mouth tingled and she could still taste him on her lips. She smiled at the memory and stored it away for future daydreams.

She stowed the bag containing the lock picks in her B.C. pocket and popped the regulator in her mouth. Pulling the mask over her face, she checked the time on her dive computer. Next, she switched a dive light on, hung one from the B.C., and wrapped the cord of the other light around her wrist. Finally satisfied her equipment was in order, she pointed her release air hose toward the full moon, squeezed the air from her B.C. and dove head first into the water.

Pointing her fins to the sky, she followed the merman to the bottom. The dive light's glow haloed around her, giving the illusion she was enclosed in a huge bubble of light. The dust mite-sized sea creatures reflecting the flashlight's shine, intermingled with the air bubbles, dancing and swirling as if welcoming the diver into their exotic world. *This is only my second night dive; I remember being terrified on the first one. I clutched my dive buddy's hand all the time we were down. A lot of teasing waited for me that night back on the dive boat,* Jerri shook her head at the memory. *Strange... I don't feel afraid. I guess when you've almost been shark bait, and been kissed by a merman all in the same day, something as trivial as a night dive is a piece of cake,* she thought, playing the light toward the bottom, hoping to catch sight of Pendragon.

By the time she'd reached the thirty-foot depth, his full feathery tail flipped and snapped in front of her. The vibrant colors of his scales, so vivid in the moonlight were muted and grayed at this depth, until the dive light flashed across his tail. The flashlight's illumination returned the full glory and hues to the teal and greens of his lower body. Twirling and undulating like a dolphin guide, he led her down to the reef.

Five feet farther, Jerri thought she caught first sight of the coral. She trailed the dive light across the reef, the gray colors returning to the rainbow shades, until the color-revealing light touched on the mermaid statue. *No, no!* She thought, *NOT a statue! A living woman! But, her skin has a green tinge to it.* She kicked harder, suddenly understanding Mark's urgency: *Her skin has a green tinge, because she's slowly drowning!*

She reached the mermaid and with a quick shot of air into her B.C., made herself weightless, hovering above the lovely lady whose body ended in an incredible fishtail. The mermaid's hair reached her waist — deep burnished red, long, flowing in curls and tendrils down her shoulders. It covered her chest, almost, but not quite hiding her full breasts. Patches of skin peeped through the auburn curtain, enough to let Jerri know the lady was topless.

~oOo~

Chapter 22

"You guys make sure *who ever* is in that boat sitting over the site aren't getting too nibby." Standing in the shadows, a mysterious man barked orders by the dim light shining on the shrimp boat's deck.

Two divers dressed in black wet suits bobbed in the water alongside the boat, a matched pair of underwater personal propulsion units — underwater scooters — floated beside them, their electric motors designed for silent running over the sea floor. "No problem, Boss," one of the speargun-armed men laughed. "You can count on us." They silently disappeared down into the dark water.

The shrimp boat, with the mysterious man at the helm, took up anchor and moved closer to the smaller boat. The remaining deckhands went about their chores in silence, while in the shadowy darkness, the evil smile on the man's face went unseen by his diligent crew as he patted the handgun stuffed in his waistband.

~oOo~

She glanced at Pendragon as he swam to her side and they both hovered over the unconscious mermaid. He unhooked the extra dive light from her B.C., switched it on, and placed it above her head, nestling it in a four foot tall, bright orange, umbrella coral. Taking the other dive light from Jerri's wrist, he positioned it on a sponge-covered rock, aiming the beam at the mermaid's wrists.

Marissa hasn't got much time! — Jerri heard/felt his voice

175

inside her head — *I'm counting on you. Jerri, pick the locks!* Pendragon's words competed with the sound of her breathing, crowding out the gurgling noise of the air bubbles coming from the side of her regulator. She watched in amazement as tiny slits on the side of his neck, beneath and behind his ears, flared angrily.

Closing her eyes, she knocked the palm of her hand against the side of her head trying to clear the voice from her mind. Then opening her eyes, she looked at the merman.

Mark reached out and gripped her chin, turning her face to his. *Yes, Jerri! It's me. I'm talking to you now. My people have used telepathy for centuries. Don't be frightened. You'll get used to it.*

Her eyes flew open wide and she thought, *Telepathy! I can hear EVERYTHING he thinks at me! ...does that mean HE can hear MY thoughts, also?*

His quick laughter filled her head and she felt herself blush. *Jerri — don't worry about it, now. I only use it underwater. Your thoughts are safe on the surface.*

He turned his attention to the unconscious mermaid stretched over the reef. Touching the nearly nude lady's shackled hand, he quickly switched his attention to her face, and lifted her eyelids, each in turn. Her dark blue eyes were unresponsive.

My people can't survive for long if we're held in one place for an extended period of time, he thought at Jerri, *we're a little like sharks in that respect.* Mark moved the mermaid's long hair away from her ears, gently touching her neck. *See? Those tiny gills below her ears? They're hardly moving. She's drowning, Jerri. Help her... help Marissa. I can't break the chains, and I don't know how to open the locks. I need you, Jerri. I need you to save my Marissa. Please... save my Marissa.*

Even though she was nearly fifty feet down in the water, Jerri could see the pleading in the merman's dark eyes. *YOUR Marissa?* she thought, her eyes revealing more of her true emotions than she wanted. She retrieved her escape tools from her B.C. pocket, and sneered while sending a psychic message in

176

Pendragon's direction. *So, tell me... just how long has she been 'your Marissa'?*

His expression was one of confusion. *What does that have to do with anything? She's been my Marissa for as long as I remember. You've got to save* — Mark's attention was suddenly drawn away from Jerri. Twin dive lights glowed from the west, growing stronger second by second. *Visitors! This doesn't look good. I knew that shrimper was bad news. Do your magic! Free Marissa! Get her to the surface. I'll go see what these guys want. Listen to me! No matter what you see, stay with Marissa. Get her to the surface. I'm counting on you* — *Amazing.* With one mighty flip of his tail, Pendragon swam away from the two women, leaving Jerri to her task.

As the merman rushed through the water toward the lights, Jerri removed the tiny tools from the leather pouch. Shedding her gloves, she stuck them in a B.C. pocket and started in on the locks binding Marissa's wrists. Sticking two picks into the first keyhole, she closed her eyes; having mastered the technique in darkness at her father's feet. She twisted the metal picks, moving one clockwise, the other counterclockwise and smiled to herself, feeling the resistance of the tumblers. Hearing her own child-voice — a memory speaking from her past — she smiled. *This one's easy, Daddy!*

Don't get cocky, Jerri, her father's words came back to her as if he were by her side. *You know you can ace a thousand locks and there's always the last one waiting for you at the end of the line. The one that won't trip. Always remember, you are the Warrior; the lock is the Dragon. Get smug and the Dragon wins. Don't get smug, Little One.*

No, Daddy, she spoke to her father's memory, *I promise. I won't get smug. I'll never let the Dragon win.*

She felt the tumblers give way, and the right hand shackle fell from Marissa's wrist, dropping to the ocean floor. *Piece of cake,* she smiled to herself. *Now, if the next one goes so easy...* Opening her eyes, Jerri glanced around, hoping to catch sight of Pendragon, but she could see only shadowy figures thrashing on the perimeter of her light sources. She thought into the dark water: *Mark! Be careful!*

I'll... be fine... Jerri, she heard Pendragon's faint words in her mind. *Don't wait for me. Release Marissa... and get her to safety — GO!*

Marissa's free arm hung limp, dangling from the reef, nearly touching the sandy bottom. Jerri knew time was running out for the beautiful mermaid, and she had to fight a powerful urge to rush through unlocking the other manacle. But she knew if she hurried, she'd fumble and this might well be the Dragon; that last lock her father always warned her awaited the smug. Taking a few deep breaths, she said a silent prayer, closed her eyes and attacked the second lock.

~o0o~

"Daniel? What in the world is so important that you had to wake me up in the middle of the night?" Miss Marty asked the pajama-dressed mute chauffeur standing outside her bedroom door. "Couldn't this wait for the morning?"

He shoved a handwritten note at his benefactress, while she rubbed the sleep from her eyes. Mimicking peering through a pair of glasses, Daniel stepped past his motherly boss into her room, stalking up to her nightstand. He grabbed up her lavender-framed glasses and shoved them at her, with an uncharacteristic abruptness that shocked the old woman.

"Okay, okay. I get the idea. You want me to read this," she said. Donning her reading glasses, she took the note to her bedroom desk. Daniel followed close on her heels, peering over her shoulder while she switched on the desk lamp to peruse his note. She read aloud, "Let's see... 'MISS MARTY — PLEASE PLEASE CALL ARNI SIMS — TELL HIM I'M HAVING FLASHBACKS!' Oh, my — Daniel!"

She looked up from the note, a question in her eyes. Daniel thumped his chest and made a circle with his thumb and forefinger indicating he was physically 'okay'. "Sure, Sweetie, I'll call Arni — but don't you think this could wait for the morning?" Seeing the fierce determination in her young friend's face, the old lady nodded and returned to his written message. She read the note aloud, as Daniel insistently pounded an accompaniment on her desk — "'I'VE GOT TO TALK TO HIM NOW! <u>RIGHT NOW</u>!'"

"Daniel... you're in such a state!" She fretted over her silent friend, taking him in her arms for a motherly hug. "Of course, I'll call Arni. Dear boy, sit down! Sit down over here on my sofa, and I'll call Arni right now!"

The frantic chauffeur allowed the old lady to guide him to the sofa. Settling herself beside him, she grabbed up the phone, and speed-dialed the doctor. Daniel removed his notepad from his pajama shirt pocket and scratched out a note at a feverish pace. He jumped to his feet and paced, ripping his hand through his hair.

"Hello? Arni?" Miss Marty spoke into the phone, even as Daniel forced another note into her hand. This one read: JERRI!! HURRY!! WE'VE GOT TO SAVE JERRI!! SHE'S ON THE BOAT WITH PENDRAGON — BUT EVEN *HE* CAN'T KEEP HER SAFE! The frantic man waved another note above his head. The phone still to her ear, the elderly woman got to her feet and danced on tiptoes, attempting to snatch the pink Post-It note from his hand. Finally, she hissed, "Daniel — quit jumping around and give me that sticky note!" The phone squawked in her other hand. "Arni? Wait a minute...." To her chauffeur, she ordered, "Hand over the *other* note, young man." Like a scolded youngster, he complied.

She stuck the pink note on top of the mute man's hastily scrawled message. "Hurry.... Save Jerri...." She reread the two notes and glanced back at her chauffeur. "Where'd you find *this* little pink sticky note?" In a demanding voice, Miss Marty shoved the papers under Daniel's nose. The phone squawked again. "Arni? *I said wait a minute!* I can't deal with the two of you at the same time!"

Daniel hurriedly scribbled diagonally across his original note, and returned it to his grandmotherly employer.

"In Jerri's room? You found this in *Jerri's room?*"

He nodded while a look of pure horror crossed Miss Marty's face. "Arni?" Her voice was shrill as she commanded into the receiver, "Come quick! *Right this instant!* It's an emergency! No, it's not *me,* Arni. *It's Daniel.* He's all upset about something. Says he's having flashbacks and made me call you — he wants to see you *now.*" She looked at Daniel. "*Yes, right now!*" She paused again. "Okay... *good!* See you in a few minutes." Miss Marty hung up the phone and took the chauffeur into her arms as if he were a little boy, rocking the grown man while his body quivered and shook with fear.

"It'll be all right, baby," she cooed, stroking Daniel's blond hair. "Arni will be here soon, and we'll get to the bottom of this. Don't you worry, sweetheart." Then, almost as an afterthought, she murmured, "Oh, Jerri... what have you gotten yourself into?"

~o0o~

The second lock proved to be more stubborn than the first, and Jerri cursed into her regulator as she twirled the picks once again. Already, she'd carefully ran through the steps twice, knowing each maneuver well enough to perform them in her sleep. Still, the lock refused to give.

Looking to the west, fear stabbed through her when she realized Pendragon was nowhere in sight. *What am I gonna do?* She moaned, twirling the lock picks again, *This lock must be jammed. It's not giving! And what's happened to Pendragon? OH, I NEED HELP! I need help in a BAD way!* A rush of bubbles from her regulator reminded her to monitor her breathing, and she warned herself to calm down. *It won't help Marissa if I run out of air down here,* she thought. *Come on, Amazing! You can do it! There ain't a lock made that you can't crack! Yeah, right* — she answered her inner cheerleader — *and I'm Wonder Woman.*

Returning her attention to the stubborn lock still holding the mermaid captive, she again seated the twin picks through the keyhole, hoping this time her aim was true. Like she had a pair of miniature chopsticks in her grip, Jerri situated the two metal probes against what she hoped were the rusted tumblers. She closed her eyes and imagined her father by her side. *Daddy, this*

180

is a tough one, she whispered to herself. *Please guide my hand.*

Keeping her eyes closed, as she was taught, she suddenly felt a calmness enter her body and Jerri knew she'd received the answer to one of her prayers. The soothing sensation of a warm hand settled over her own. She smiled and thought to herself, *Daddy! You're here!*

Her eyes still closed, she carefully twisted the picks. Halfway through a counterclockwise swirl, she encountered a resistance. Knowing if she recklessly pressed the old tumblers and forced what age and rust held still and stiff, the picks would slide off their purchase and she'd miss the window of slippage.

With every old lock, when the tumblers went unmoved for too long, the metal would nearly meld together. The chance of the tumblers shattering from metal fatigue also increased with age and non use.

She pressed against the frozen metal, using what she hoped was just the right degree of force. The creak of old metal unwilling giving way to the picks 'sounded' through her fingertips, and she felt the resistant tumblers yielding to her will.

The final shackle snapped open, and the metal cuff binding the unconscious mermaid to the coral dropped to the sandy bottom. Marissa's hand fell listlessly at her side, while Jerri returned the lock picks to her B.C. pocket. From the left hand pocket, she grabbed a rolled-up bag and a coil of nylon rope.

Passing the rope twice under Marissa's knees and shoulders, she fashioned a crude sling, which she attached to the straps of the vinyl sack. Jerri looked around the darkness untouched by her dive lights, her eyes searching for Pendragon. *I've got to get Marissa to the surface,* she told herself. *I can't wait for Pendragon to come back.* She untethered her regulator octopus — the auxiliary air supply — and filled the lift bag with air. The yellow sack took the air like a balloon, and soon the large air-filled pouch lifted the mermaid from her coral jail cell.

Marissa's arms dangled from the rope sling, and her feathery fishtail pointed listlessly toward the sand. The mermaid's limp body rose slowly through the dark water, and Jerri kicked off, keeping pace with the lift bag's gradual ascent. Ten feet closer to the surface, a faint voice sounded in Jerri's mind: *Mark... Mark... help me....*

Jerri looked at the unconscious woman, sprawled in the lift bag's straps. A hopeful thought came to her mind: *Perhaps Marissa can read my thoughts, like Pendragon can.*

Marissa! Jerri thought, forcefully: *Marissa! Hold on. I'm gonna get you to the surface and —*

Mark... Mark, where are you? Mark... help me... Marissa's mutterings came to Jerri's worried mind.

She picked up the mermaid's telepathic interruptions and frowned at the unconscious woman. *Jeez, you and Pendragon need to get together to sing this stupid duet,* she groused to herself. *After all... both of you seem to be stuck on the same sickeningly sappy note.*

Checking their ascension rate, she glanced up at the surface and realized in her haste she'd left both dive lights on the bottom. *Damn it! In the dark again,* she grumbled. *There's nothing like living a mushroom's life. You're always kept in the dark, and you're constantly covered in donkey waffles. But, on the upside — people think you're ONE FUN GUY! Boy, I MUST be scared if I'm telling myself lame lounge-lizard jokes.*

Rising a few feet farther, they were soon enveloped in total darkness. By the sense of touch alone, Jerri injected a little more air into the lift bag, and hastened their rise to the top. As the two women broke the surface, the full-moon bathed the gentle rolling waves in a muted spotlight, its glow spread out in a wide reflected streak dancing on top of the water into the eastern horizon.

Spitting the regulator out, Jerri cradled the mermaid in a rescue position. She turned the unconscious woman away from her, laced her right arm underneath Marissa's right arm, and then grasping her chin, Jerri lightly pressed the back of the mermaid's head to her chest, the woman's back against the B.C.

All at once, Marissa took a great ragged breath, coughing and gagging. Jerri smoothed the mermaid's hair away from her face, noting the tiny gills flaring behind her ears, hungrily

182

dragging in the night air. Still, Marissa's eyes remained closed. But, within moments, she moaned softly, giving hint she was still alive.

"Good," Jerri whispered, "at least you're able to breathe. Hold on, Marissa. We're halfway home." They floated together in the water, yielding to the will of the current. "Where's the boat? Where's the Little Lavender??" Jerri worried aloud to an unresponsive Marissa, "Pendragon anchored it around here somewhere...." Suddenly, a spotlight sliced through the darkness. Jerri shielded her eyes as the blinding beam of bright light slowly swept over the water. Figuring the merman was searching for them, she waved toward the piercing beam, and cried out, "Over here! Pen... Mark! *Mark! We're over here!"*

The sweeping spotlight centered over the two women and a strange man's voice called out through the darkness: "Ahoy! You in the water! We're coming about! Hang on!"

~o0o~

Dr. Sims left Daniel Tiger's bedroom, shaking his head. He took the elevator to the first floor, and found Miss Marty waiting in the kitchen, mixing oversized cups of steaming cocoa.

"Arni? Is Daniel okay?" the old lady asked, offering the young doctor a mug of hot chocolate. "He was really frantic. You *know* — don't you — *I* wouldn't have called in the middle of the night if *this* would've kept 'til morning? I'm worried about the boy." She paused to sip her cocoa. "Frankly, Arni... I believe if you hadn't ran right over... well... I don't know *how* I could have stopped him from beating your door down." She shook her head and sighed. "Tell me the truth, Arni. *Is he all right?* Is he having some kind of breakdown or something? Tell me! Tell me, *please!*"

The red-haired doctor set his hot chocolate on the counter and patted his favorite patient's hand. "You can put your mind to rest, Miss Marty. Daniel's not having a breakdown. In fact, this is a good thing," he smiled. "I'd hoped Daniel would arrive at this point on his own; and he did. This is big. This is very big. And it's happening so fast."

"*You're babbling!*" She scolded the man, shaking her finger under his nose. "Now, take a deep breath and talk some sense. *You hear me, young man?*"

Arni Sims grinned and threw his hands up defensively. "Yes, ma'am!" He laughed as his grin widened. "I hear you loud and clear. Mr. Daniel Tiger isn't suffering a *breakdown*. His agitation is normal, for *someone regaining his memory.*"

Miss Marty brightened as her hands excitedly flew to her face. "Oh, Arni! *You don't mean it!* Daniel is regaining his *memory?* How *wonderful!*"

"Yeah," he nodded his head, "it *is* wonderful. And a little frightening... for Daniel. His memory isn't coming back all at once, but in bits and pieces. He told me, in notes, he's had flashes of the night he was left on the beach. He remembers fighting for his life, being shot and in the end, being hit on the head, knocked unconscious. The next thing he remembers is waking up, half in, half out of the water. Some children found him wandering the beach, bloody and disoriented. He says he remembers wanting to talk to them, but finding the words just wouldn't come. Try as he might, he couldn't utter a sound. At the time, I suspected his muteness resulted from head trauma. You know? The gunshot wound. And it was anybody's guess when or *if* he'd get his speech back."

"And *has* he regained his voice?"

Sims frowned and shook his head. "Yes and no." He hesitated as he said, "Daniel... is... *speaking* again. But... the words are coming back slowly. At this point, his voice is weak, seeing as how he's not talked for about two years. He's only spoken a couple of words. So far, he's only said names."

"Names?"

He drank the last of his cocoa, and smiled. "Yeah, names," he said. "He's said your name a couple of times. My name. His name. *Daniel,* that is. He still can't come up with his *real* name. But, mostly, he's fixated on Jerri. And Dolf Grüber. Daniel seems to think Jerri's in danger — from Grüber, no less. Says Jerri and *Pendragon* are *both* in danger from Grüber. Says Pendragon took Jerri out on The Little Lavender, and they're boating in Grüber's waters."

Miss Marty gasped, bringing her fingertips to her lips. "*Oh, my!* He tried to warn me about Jerri's safety," she murmured. "He was *frantic* about Dolf Grüber; but I put it off on a case of jealousy. He said nothing to me about Pendragon; I thought he just had Jerri on his mind. Since she's become my house-guest,

I've caught Daniel sneaking peeks at Jerri. I have to admit; it wasn't too much of a leap to guess my sweet-natured chauffeur was smitten by the pretty magician. So, I didn't pay it much mind when he raised a ruckus about Grüber dating Miss Delaney."

"Daniel caused a scene when Grüber took Jerri out?" He took a sip from his mug.

The old lady chuckled and poured herself another half cupful of hot chocolate. "Oh, not that you would have noticed, Arni," she said. "He tried his best to keep his fears from me, but there's not much goes on around here I don't know about. *You know that*." She made to drink the cocoa, but Dr. Sims put his hand over hers.

"*I also know* you must be over your caffeine limit for the day," he quipped, taking the lavender mug from his elderly patient. Tipping the cup over the sink, he dumped the offending chocolate and smiled. "At this rate, you'll *never* get to sleep — "

"Mi — Mi — Miss — *Miss Marty!*" Daniel interrupted at the kitchen doorway. Fully dressed in his lavender uniform, the chauffeur held his hat in his hands, fidgeting with the brim as if he could barely contain himself. He spoke haltingly, "Miss — Marty... Jerri... da — da — *DANGER!*" He struggled with the words like a miner digging for diamonds. Frustration showed on his face as he blurted out, "Jerri-danger-in!" He threw up his hands and growled at the ceiling. "Words... *words-speak-not.* What? Don't see — " Daniel turned to face the doctor, pleading in his eyes. "*Don't... know!* Wrong? *What?*"

"Calm down, Daniel," Arni soothed, taking a penlight from his jacket pocket. He swept the slender beam across the frantic chauffeur's eyes and patted his shoulder. "This is *normal.* Remember, I told you that first day you woke up after being found on the beach — you suffered from aphasia. Apparently, the beating and the gunshot wound left you with brain injuries. Fortunately, you've healed and it looks like you're going to recover your speech. But, *you'll have to give it time.* You can't expect to get it all back in one night. Rome wasn't built in a day. *And you won't build a vocabulary over night.*"

His fists balled tightly, Daniel howled, "*Aaaugghh!!!* Time-no! Time-not! Time! *Time!*"

"We understand that," the old woman stroked the frantic man's face, and cooed to him as if he were a six foot tall colicky child. "Really, Daniel. We *do* understand. Time is urgent. *We get it.* But, dear-heart, you're just going to have to humor us awhile longer. Write out your thoughts. *I'll listen to your lovely voice at a later time.*" She smiled up at the man who towered over her by a two head span.

The kitchen was filled with the comforting mixture of lavender and chocolate; scents the chauffeur had come to associate with his eccentric, but jovial benefactress. "Miss-Marty-help. Fright. Frightened-so-frightened... *frightened-Jerri-help!!!*" The young blond man folded himself into the old lady's arms and sobbed.

Patting Daniel's heaving wide shoulders, she looked up at the concerned doctor. She asked, "*What should I do?* This is *so* unlike Daniel. Something must be *seriously* wrong."

Dr. Sims shook his head. "I would expect *some* agitation from a person in Daniel's situation. Coming out of aphasia is never an easy process; but I think you're right. Something must be wrong." He handed the sobbing man a pencil and notepad, urging him to write down the information his brain was refusing to give his mouth. "Go on, Daniel. We're listening. Tell us what to do."

The chauffeur dried his tears on his lavender sleeve, took the pad and scribbled out note after note. "Here... phone... here-phone-help." Daniel said, shoving the first note at his doctor friend.

Arni Sims read the hastily scribbled note: 'CALL D.E.A. PASSWORDS: WELCOME TO THE NEIGHBORHOOD' were the only words on the scrap of paper.

~o0o~

Again, the voice called through the darkness. "Ahoy, there! Heads up! I'm throwing out a life preserver! We'll pull you in! Are you injured?"

A white flotation circle sailed from the boat, trailing a rope, landing in the water to the left side of Marissa. "No injuries!" Jerri yelled back, still shielding her eyes from the bright light. She maneuvered the mermaid over to the floating ring and again yelled at the boat. "We're not hurt, but, I've got an unconscious... uh... *woman* here! She needs medical attention!"

Grabbing the lifesaver, she looped her right arm through the middle of the ring, while holding the mermaid close to her body with the other. The boat's crew quickly took up the slack in the rope, and they made short work of pulling Jerri and her mythical passenger nearer the boat.

Just HOW am I gonna explain Marissa? Jerri thought. *WHAT am I gonna say? Hi, guys! I'm the Amazing Delaney, and this is my new assistant. Why, yes — how observant of you! She IS a mermaid! I used to work with the Easter Bunny, but I got tired of sweeping up the little black pebbles.*

"Pass this sling under her arms," a burly man called down from the boat rail, as two other crewmen joined him. "We'll pull *her* up first, then we'll bring *you* up."

"Okay," Jerri replied, catching the canvas sling and working it over Marissa's shoulders. Snugging the wide strap under the mermaid's bare breasts, she tugged on the rope and called up to the waiting men, "We're ready! But, there's one thing you should maybe know, first — " She released Marissa from her grasp, and the men pulled the unconscious mermaid halfway out of the water. Her hips cleared the surface and her scales sparkled in the glare of the spotlight. "Don't be surprised by anything unusual," Jerri hurriedly blurted out, watching the men lift Marissa over the boat rail. "I promise, I can explain everything! *Just don't freak out on me, okay?*"

Before disappearing from Jerri's sight, the crew lowered the mermaid's body over the railing, onto the deck. She listened to their quiet bantering, wondering at the calmness in their muffled words. "Hey! Don't worry about me," she mumbled to herself. "I'll just float here in the water." Jerri smiled, waiting for the inevitable explosion. "Any minute now," she chuckled. "It's gonna hit the fan that you've caught an *actual-factual mermaid.*"

Grumbling out her frustrations, she snarled, "Remember, guys! *You were warned.* All's fair in love and fishin'."

Suddenly, the canvas sling sailed over the boat rail and socked Jerri in the head. She quipped, "I'm *so* glad you didn't forget about me!" Rubbing her head before slipping the harness under her arms, she groused, "I mean, at least you're not letting a little thing like snagging a *mermaid* stop you from pulling *me* up *too.*"

The water lapped against the side of the boat as the men hauled Jerri aboard, still dressed in her dive gear. Clearing the rail, she noted Marissa sprawled in the middle of the deck, her glistening tail quivering in the pale moonlight. She heard the mermaid's soft moans and hoped — *while simultaneously dreading* — the unconscious woman's growing restlessness meant Marissa was coming around.

Her color IS improving, Jerri thought as she slipped out of the canvas harness, *Marissa's looking more normal. Ha! Like I know what's normal for a mermaid.* She unsnapped her B.C. and lowered her jacket and tank to the deck, all the while studying the faces of the crew gathered around the nearly nude mermaid.

Collapsing on a bench, Jerri watched as the three men milled about the back of the boat, winding up the harness rope and halfheartedly mopping up the water dripping from the mermaid's scales.

Something about the bustling crewmen disturbed her, but Jerri shook her head with weariness, passing off the unease she felt about the men who'd plucked her from the gulf waters. "Guys? I tried to tell you," she began, speaking breathlessly, "there *was* something unusual in the water with me. Now, the first thing you gotta do is *don't panic!* You see — "

"Well, Benny?" One of the men interrupted Jerri's frantic explanations. "Just *what* are we gonna do *now? Put'er back?*"

What? Jerri grew quiet and still, not moving as the man's words sunk in. *THAT'S what wrong with this picture! These dorks aren't shocked they CAUGHT a mermaid — cause this isn't the FIRST TIME they've caught her!!!*

189

The frustrated crewman yelled at his partners. "Benny? Paco? *Are you guys even listening to me?*" He pulled at his dark red hair. "Jeez, guys! This is another fine mess you two have gotten me into."

Jerri silently looked from one man to the other, wondering at her next move.

"*Us?*" Paco returned, dramatically flailing his arms in the air. "Whadda ya mean *'us'? Yer* the one who caught her the first time!"

Benny joined in. "Yeah, Carl! If it wasn't for me and Paco, you'd've filleted her! Hell, if me and Paco hadn't raised a ruckus, you'd'a had you one *mother* of a fish-fry!" He laughed and swiped his arm across his nose. "Lucky for you, Boss-Man stopped you a'fore you could sharpen your knife."

"Are you two freakin' crazy?" Carl yelled. "We can't leave a *freakin' mermaid* on the boat! We can't take her back to the *freakin' dock* without attracting attention! *You know how important it is for us to lay low!* Hell! We might as well have a *freakin' pink elephant* on board! *How're we gonna freakin' EXPLAIN her?*"

Paco laughed. "Do you think you could work 'freakin' into a sentence just one more time? Get `hold of yourself, Carl!" Paco laughed again. The burly crewman slapped his frantic friend on the back and laughed once more. "Now, why don't you calm down before the Boss-Man hears you and comes up on deck to see who's kickin' your dog?"

"So, I'll bite," a deep voice came from the shadows. "Who's the wise guy kickin' Carl's dog?"

The men jumped as if all three were touched by the same hot wire.

"*Boss-Man!*" Benny crowed, trying his best to sound happy to welcome the mysterious man on deck. "*Hey,* Boss-Man! Did we disturb you with our little... *joking around?* Were we too loud?" Benny chuckled nervously as if the man standing in the shadows greatly frightened him. "I *told* the guys to quiet down or we'd wake you. Were... *were we too loud?*" The man dropped his eyes, not allowing his gaze to meet his employer's.

"Only if," the mystery man hissed, "you count a drunken pack of wild hyenas *as loud*." He motioned at the still unconscious mermaid. "Back like a bad penny," he growled. "How'd she get free?"

The man stepped out of the shadows, and Jerri gasped in shocked surprise. "*You?*" she yelped. "*What are YOU doing here?*"

~o0o~

Chapter 24

Arni Sims spoke softly into the phone, "Are you sure?" He nodded, momentarily forgetting the person he spoke to couldn't see his silent gestures. "Right, right." He agreed with the voice on the other end of the conversation. "We'll do that. Not a word to anyone. Right. I understand." Sims nodded again and answered the faceless voice. "Yes, I *do* understand the gravity of this situation. Meet you at the pier. Right."

After the doctor hung up the phone, the old lady whispered, "Arni? What did they say?" Watching him silently shake his head, she scolded, "Don't keep me waiting, young man! Tell me what the D.E.A. said about Daniel! Tell me before Daniel gets back from bringing the Rolls Royce around. I want to know *NOW!* And what's Daniel Striped Tiger got to do with the D.E.A. *anyhow?*"

Sims removed his glasses, closed his eyes, pinched the small of his nose, and sighed, "You're *not* gonna believe this...."

"Young man — *I've already warned you!!*"

"Okay, okay," he smiled, holding up his hands to ward off his irritated elderly friend. "I contacted the Agency. At first, they were giving me the run-around. Then, I mentioned the password, and they changed their tune. It turns out, our Daniel is very well known in certain circles."

Miss Marty's hands flew to her face in shock. She whispered through her fingers, "Oh-My-Lord!! Daniel Striped Tiger's a hood!"

~o0o~

The silence was deafening on the deck of the boat. Dressed in cutoff jeans and white tee-shirt, the man the crew feared, boldly stepped into the glow of the deck light.

As he left the shadows, Jerri's eyes never strayed from the man's face. She hissed, "*Answer me!*"

When he smirked, but held his silence, she raised her voice and repeated, "*I said,* answer me!"

Finally, frustration caused her to scream, "*What are you doing here?*"

Dolf Grüber laughed; his harsh laughter sending chills down Jerri's spine. "I have every right to *captain my own boat.* I assure you that — "

"Don't bother trying to assure *me!*" she growled in interruption. "I'm not your everyday clueless idiot! I think I can put two and two together. You're responsible for this... this... *mess.*"

She motioned toward the unconscious mermaid. "*And furthermore,* I have a sneaking suspicion something illegal is behind this. I'd bet dollars to donuts you've got your dirty fingers in some slimy pie. And I'll bet, if we dig deep enough, we could add smuggling or drug running to attempted murder."

Grüber shook his head, laughing again. "Jerri, dear Jer — "

Jerri cut his words short. "That's *Ms.* Delaney to you."

"As you like it, *Ms.* Delaney." The green-eyed man sarcastically saluted, smiled, shook his head sorrowfully, and said, "Pity. And here we were on a first name basis. Awww... tsk-tsk. Well, it's time you met the real Dolf Grüber."

He grinned at his crew, then turned to Jerri, gifting her with a wide smile showing a full set of gleaming, needle-sharp teeth fit for a shark.

Jerri's heart leaped to her throat.

"See why we don't like to wake the Big-Dog?" Carl nodded toward Grüber. "He can rip out'cher heart an' eat it for breakfast."

"V...v...vampire?" Jerri whispered a stutter. "But... vampires aren't real!"

"Vampire? Eh... not quite." Carl scratched his head. "`e's more like a — "

Jerri interrupted the crewman's explanation, "This is *so* not happening! *Things like this just are'nt real!*"

Grüber laughed. "Need I remind you, Ms. Delaney — there's a lovely lady resting on the deck who'd just love to differ with you? But, no. No vampire here. I'm just a Dybbuk. And a mere half-Dybbuk at that."

She whispered, "Dybbuk?"

"Old German monster." He laughed. "Much like my old man. In fact, it's my one and only 'inheritance' from the old bastard. ...yes — he'll me see in Hell, indeed. I'm sure, some day, he will." Grüber shook his head on a sour-tasting memory. "Dybbuk's are rumored to be 'soul eaters'. But I like to think that we're... *evolving*. Myself, I'm into so much more than mere *souls*...."

Jerri shuddered.

Grüber laughed, his sharp teeth gleaming in the moonlight.

"So — you were planning to 'take my soul'?"

Grüber laughed again. "Oh, no, no, no, my dear. My plans for you were much more... *delicious*. Yes, perhaps in time I would have taken your soul. But for right now, I was satisfied with a tiny... *taste*." He reached out and traced his fingertips over Jerri's cheek.

The man with the gentle touch, the man she'd thought as gallant just the night before, now caused her to recoil. "What are you talking about, Grüber?" Jerri whispered.

"Don't tell me you've forgotten our perfect night, Jerri. The evening was magical, and when I left you at the door... *ahh, the kiss*. The kiss under the moon and stars. Your soul tastes... *silver*. Yes, that's the only way to describe it. It took everything in my being to resist more than a taste on the tongue. Just thinking of that magical moment makes me quiver. You?"

Jerri whispered, "Makes me quiver, too. And nauseous, now that you bring it up. I'm trying to tell you — you make me sick, Grüber."

"And here we had such a promising future together. Of all the shrimp boats in all the world, you had to climb onto *mine*. It's really a shame, you know. You and I, we had potential. We

194

could've been so good together. Psychic said so."

"Oh — don't even go there!!!"

He laughed. "Don't you remember? She said you should 'look to *all* your potential lovers'. Like the psychic said — I think we would have made a perfect couple."

She snorted, grumbled, and tossed her eyes at his impudence. "Yeah, right! A perfect couple. But a perfect couple'a *what?* The way I see it, you don't need me. You've got 'perfect' tied up all by yourself. You're a perfect *assh* — "

"My, my, my," Grüber interrupted, wagging his finger under Jerri's nose. "Such a foul mouth on such a lovely lady!" He lowered his voice to a sinister hiss. "Do you say your *prayers* with that mouth?"

"Is that a threat?"

He smiled. "I said it before!" He punctuated each word by tipping the gun at Jerri. "*As... you... like... it.*" His menacing words were rewarded with nervous giggles from one of the crewmen.

Grüber glared at the offending man, and the high-pitched laughter stopped. "Make yourselves useful, bozos!" He ended the order by growling, "*And water the damn mermaid!*"

The handsome man returned his attention to Jerri while his face returned to his male-model features. He smiled his megawatt, 'blond-demigod' smile, and reached out to trace a well-manicured finger down her cheek. "It really *is* too bad, you know... if only you hadn't gotten so... *nosy.*"

She batted his hand aside, glared at Grüber and took a step backward, moving closer to Marissa. Carl dumped a bucket of seawater over the two women, and Jerri sneered at the burly crewman. "Thank you *ever so much,*" she snarled. "I *was* feeling a little bit dry. I don't know why I didn't ask for a bucket of water sooner."

"Women," Grüber snorted sarcastically. "Can't live with 'em; can't water 'em down."

Wiping the water out of her own eyes, Jerri knelt beside the mermaid, and grabbed up her hands. Rubbing and patting the unresponsive woman's greenish fingers, she whispered close to

195

the mermaid's ear coaxing her to speak. "Come on, Mariss... I mean, come on, mermaid! The time has come to rejoin the conscious set. Wake up and be alert! Lord knows, we could use more 'lerts' on this boat."

The mermaid groaned, her hands leaving Jerri's and wandering to her closed eyes. A few more moans brought her eyes open, and Marissa gazed into the face of The Amazing Delaney. "Where...?" She murmured, "Who...?"

"Don't worry," Jerri assured her. "You're going to be okay, now." She winked at Marissa, sending a silent signal to the still groggy woman, hoping she'd not mention Mark Pendragon. "I'm Jerri Delaney. I found you while I was night diving." She hurriedly continued, sending her words out in a panicky rush. "I broke the locks and brought you to the surface."

The mermaid whispered in a faint voice, "My name's Marissa."

Good. Even if she doesn't yet know who I truly am... at least she caught the signal. Jerri noticed the gills behind Marissa's ears. She watched them flutter and settle into the line of the mermaid's neck, becoming hardly noticeable, like tiny worry lines. She glanced up at Grüber, "Do you think you could step back and give the mermaid room to breathe?"

The green-eyed man scoffed, "Like she *needs* air! She's not even human. She's more fish than woman."

"I can't believe I *ever* thought you gallant! And, now I've got to burn that jacket you gave me," Jerri hissed. "Marissa is more human than you and your goons could even claim to be. Her people are more — "

"*Her people?*" Grüber interrupted. "I thought she was the only one."

Jerri's eyes flew open. *Oh! So, he doesn't know Mark's secret! ...well, I'M sure not gonna be the one to enlighten Mr. Wonderful!* She looked from the mermaid to Grüber, back to Marissa, and shook her head, forcing a chuckle. "How the hell do *I* know if she's the only one? Do I look like some kind of metaphysical ichthyologist to you?"

Paco muttered, "What's that? Meta-whozit Icky-whatzits?"

Carl cuffed his crew mate upside the head and growled, "*She means* — she's not a freakin' fish doctor, moron. Don't you know nothin'? Jeez, Louise! Buy a clue!!"

Benny giggled. The burly crewman parroted his slightly more intelligent friend. "Yeah, Paco! Moron! Buy a clue!"

"Will you three stooges shut up?" Grüber ordered, stalking across the deck to stand over Marissa. "Sometimes, I can't even hear myself think." He shook his head and sighed dramatically. "You just can't find good help these days."

"Cut the crap, Grüber," Jerri growled. "This woman almost died, chained up on that coral head. Are you just going to stand there? Or are you going to get her the help she needs?"

Grüber chuckled and shook his head. "That would be a gross conflict of interest on my part. Seeing as how we were the ones who sent her down to Davy Jones' locker, in the first place. What makes you think I can let her go now?"

"He can't let me go, because I've seen too much." Marissa's voice was weak. "I... I know about the... the..."

"*Cocaine,*" Grüber finished for the trembling mermaid.

~o0o~

197

Driving east on US-1, Daniel took a right turn off the road, just as he crossed the drawbridge at the end of Plantation Key. He pulled the Rolls Royce onto a short, white-graveled drive that ended at an unassuming two-story white building.

Doctor Sims spoke up, offering, "The man on the phone said he'd meet us down on the dock." He looked out of the car's windows, and whispered, "Boy. It's sure spooky here at night."

"Arni?" Miss Marty hissed, "Scared of the dark? Come on. Get out of the car. I want to find out what's going on. I hate mysteries." She gently shoved her younger friend until he opened the car door and stepped out. "If anything's happened to Jerri...."

Arni Sims looked around himself. Across the channel, on the opposite bank, he spied a few late-night fishermen pulling up small pan-sized fish under the wary and watchful eyes of a half dozen semi-dozing pelicans perched atop the pilings in the boat basin of the well-lit motel. The sound of the traffic driving over the grated drawbridge reverberated in the darkness. The night was not silent. The bridge's red, white and blue lights threw ominous shadows. Out in the bay, past the drawbridge, the full moon tossed a dazzling blanket of light on the water. "Creepy" was Arni's one word assessment. He hurried to the dock, leaving Daniel to help Miss Marty from the car.

"Are you the doctor I spoke to on the phone?" The man waited beside a cutter anchored at Snake Creek bridge; the Coast Guard station on the gulf side of US-1 at the southwest end of Plantation Key. "Forgive me, but I must ask you to repeat those four special words."

Arni Sims stepped up and took the man's hand in greeting. "Welcome to the Neighborhood," the doctor said.

"I'm Special Agent Sloan Richardson." The man smiled, returning Sims' handshake. He motioned toward the lavender-dressed young man assisting the like-dressed elderly woman from a lavender luxury car. "I assume that's your patient, Daniel Tiger. But, who's the old woman with the toy dog? I told you to bring *Tiger;* I didn't say you could bring your *grandma!* This isn't going to be a Princess Cruise, you know."

Sims snorted. "Believe me." He said, "She's *not* my granny. And, she's nobody's fool. But, if you're a smart man, you'll help her board the boat and not give her any lip." The doctor turned and offered his hand to his elderly friend.

Carrying Basil and stepping carefully so as not to trip, the woman climbed the two steps to the dock. Sims made the introduction. "Miss Marty, this is Sloan Richardson. He's an agent with the D.E.A. Agent Richardson, this is Miss Margaret Sebastian, or as we call her: Miss Marty. She's Mr. Tiger's employer."

"I'm Mr. Tiger's *friend*," Miss Marty tersely corrected, "and I'll stand by him, no matter what he's done. I'll see that he has the best criminal lawyers and — "

Richardson snorted.

The old woman puffed up to her full height of five feet and hugged the tiny dog closer. "I'll have you know, Mr. Richardson," she hissed, "I fail to see the humor in a missing young lady or *surrendering* my *friend* to the D.E.A.! Sure, Daniel must have been a dastardly hoodlum at one time, but for the past two years he's been the best chauffeur I could've asked for." She angrily poked her finger in the agent's muscular chest, and continued his dressing-down. "Daniel's a dear boy, and you're not sending him away without a fight from me!!" Basil barked and growled as if he wanted a piece of the D.E.A. agent, himself.

"Whoa!" Richardson backed away, rubbing his chest at Miss Marty's not too gentle digital assault. "Doctor! Call off your pit bull! And call off her little dog, too! I surrender! I surrender!"

The man reached out to pet Basil. The dog snapped at Richardson; a tiny warrior valiantly defending his elderly maiden. Rubbing his hand, the agent mumbled, "That rabid puffball is a Doberman in disguise. A tiny Doberman with a butt rash."

Sims smiled and hugged Miss Marty close. "I believe an intelligent man would escort this lovely lady, and her dear pet, to her seat on the boat. Wouldn't you agree, Richardson?"

Seeming to weigh his options, Richardson glanced from Daniel Tiger, to Dr. Sims and finally to the old woman holding the tea-cup dog. He shook his head. "Well, what are we waiting for?" The agent grinned, though his expression was strained. "Miss Marty? Won't you let me take you on a... sea cruise?" He dramatically offered his arm to the lavender-dressed lady. "Refreshments will be served once we're underway. A five-piece string ensemble will present chamber music for your listening pleasure and there'll be ballroom dancing under the stars." Richardson muttered under his breath: "As if...."

Assisting Miss Marty up the gangplank, the government agent gallently slowed his steps in deference to his elderly guest. "Doctor? Would you and your patient, Mr. Tiger, kindly accompany my lovely date and I aboard the Coast Guard's big, pretty cutter? Oh... and the captain is waiting at the helm for Mr. Tiger's navigational instructions." He eye-motioned his orders to the men flanking Daniel.

Five stern-faced uniformed Coast Guard officers welcomed the group aboard the boat. Two gruff-looking Coast Guard officers grabbed each of the chauffeur's arms, hurrying Daniel off to the helm, while three of the crew remained to release the cutter from the dock. The D.E.A. agent waited until the two officers shepherding the chauffeur cleared the deck before escorting Miss Marty, a low-growling Basil and Dr. Sims into the boat's galley.

Richardson politely seated his elderly guest at the galley table. "Have you taken anything for seasickness?" he asked. "It wouldn't do for you not to enjoy our little... uh... adventure."

"Don't worry about Miss Marty," Sims chuckled, joining the two at the spacious table. "I believe she was born with sea-legs. Myself, I took a pill on the way over here."

"Good," the agent ruefully smiled at the doctor, and returned his attention to his elderly guest. "Ma'am? May I offer you some coffee?" Richardson motioned to a huge commercial coffee pot. "That's a crew-sized pot of brew. It's gonna be a long night. I suggest we all take advantage of it."

Miss Marty removed her lavender picture hat, turned it upside-down and made an impromptu bed for Basil. The little dog sniffed the lavender organza, deemed it adequate, turned circles inside the hat's brim and retired for a nap. Seeing her pet contented, she removed a small black and silver bag of amethyst crystals from her handbag, settled back into her seat and made herself comfortable on the padded galley bench. She closed her eyes, caressed the lavender stones, occasionally bringing one or two to her cheek and murmuring low as if in prayer. "If it'll help clear Daniel of this mess or find my friend Jerri — then bring it on."

"Jerri?" Richardson asked as he poured three mugs to the brim.

"That would be our friend Jerri Delaney. She's missing. I spoke with you about her over the phone." Dr. Sims spooned sugar into his steaming coffee. "Daniel seems to think she's in trouble — he doesn't seem to be that worried about *himself* — just her. Daniel's not *really* in that much trouble, himself, right? *Right*, Richardson? I can't for the life of me think what he could have done...."

"Uh-huh" was Richardson's only comment.

The ship's twin engines fired up, and the deep roar temporarily drowned out the conversation in the galley cabin. A sideways movement signaled the cutter's departure from the dock. The engines evened out to quarter speed and the boat slowly headed away from the dock going into the channel.

Their course pointed them toward the drawbridge, the boat steered hard to port and the cutter's captain gave two short blasts on the air-horn. The Bridgemaster, the watch on duty in the drawbridge's pilothouse, caught the cutter's signal and set the levers and gears in motion, causing the bridge to part in two and rise.

Arni Sims watched the choreographed 'marine dance' as the cutter headed under the bridge. He marveled at the twinkling lights defining the bridge, knowing their presence was more for safety than for show. Looking to his right, he spied the small marina and motel, likewise lit-up, its twinkling lights rivaling the drawbridge.

The motel's lights danced off the black water, and bathed the fishermen in red and blue hues, giving the scene a strange Jekyll/Hyde ambiance. At once, it seemed both romantic and sinister. Arni laughed out loud and Richardson turned to the young doctor.

The agent coughed into his hand and asked dryly, "See something green, Doc?"

"No... no... Well, yeah!" Arni chuckled, pointing out the starboard side window. "Doesn't it strike you as strange that the motel across from the Coast Guard station is named Smuggler's Cove? I mean... *who* do they think *they're* kidding?"

Richardson snorted. "Apparently not you," he said. "I'll have to inform the Head of Covert Ops you're on to our little games." His expression was stony.

Arni's grin widened momentarily, then his face fell. "I have a feeling you would, too."

The D.E.A. agent smiled, threateningly. "Fess up, Doc. What *other* government secrets do you know?" He moved a step closer to Sims. "Should I call you Deep-Throat?"

The doctor sheepishly raised his eyes to Richardson. "No... you can just call me Big-Mouth." The boat passed under the raised drawbridge, and the captain signaled the Bridgemaster with three blasts of the boat's horn. The Bridgemaster answered this signal, that the boat had cleared the drawbridge, with his own three horn blasts. The boat continued on into the dark water of the bay, and after it cleared the low-speed buoy, the cutter picked up speed.

Arni Sims glanced out the galley's window at the dock

lights, growing dimmer with the gradually mounting distance. He quipped, "I guess Daniel Striped Tiger must be singing like a nightingale. He's apparently charted our course for this moonlight cruise. I suppose, Daniel's got information that's vital to the D.E.A. He's very important to you, isn't he?"

"Well... let's say... he's interesting." Richardson hedged.

Miss Marty interrupted. "Oh, no!" she moaned, "I would've never imagined Daniel a criminal." She covered her eyes and dropped her head, "How could I be so wrong about a person? How could I have been so wrong?" Again, she caressed her crystals.

"Your Mr. Tiger's got connections." Wrapping his hands around his tea-mug, Richardson smiled cryptically.

~o0o~

"*Cocaine?*" Jerri whispered. "So, *that's* what this is all about!"

Grüber sneered, and threw up his hands. "Ding! Ding! Ding! We have a winner! Give the little lady a Kewpie doll! Guys," he addressed his crew, " — have you ever seen anyone so slow on the uptake? ...oh, right. We *all* know Paco."

Benny and Carl dutifully laughed, pointing at their weak-minded companion. Paco, busy coiling a rope beside Marissa, glanced at his coworkers and dim-wittingly joined in the laughter with his marginally more intelligent friends.

Marissa pulled herself up to a sitting position, using Jerri's B.C. as a backrest. Turning to Jerri, she whispered, "I stumbled into their smuggling operation by accident." She continued her explanation, completely unselfconscious of her above-the-waist nudity. "I really wasn't looking for trouble." Her luxurious tail flipped and gently slapped the deck with nervous energy. She kept a close watch on Grüber, while she spoke. The fear was very evident in her eyes when she murmured, "I guess it wasn't a wise idea, traveling by night, alone."

"Traveling by night?" Jerri shook her head.

Marissa nodded. "Yeah. I've lived in Cancun for the last eight years. Usually I fly, but this time I took the scenic route and swam across the Gulf. A few years ago, I made the same trip. This time... big mistake!"

Overhearing the two women, Benny offered, "Yep. Big — *BIG* mistake. She got tangled in our nets." Emptying another bucket of saltwater over the mermaid, he chuckled and said, "When we pulled her up the first time, you should've seen Carl's face! He had a — "

"What a fascinating story," Grüber interrupted. "Remind me to ask you about it some other time. This tale sounds like it's filled with suspense, but I'd like to keep all my brain cells intact. Paco, you and Carl suit up." He motioned to the two deck-hands. "Since Greg and Larry haven't come back yet, you two are going on a little night dive. Guys, the time has come to help Ms. Delaney into her dive gear and get her — "

"Hold it!" Jerri interrupted the man and jumped to her feet. "I'm done diving for the night! I've logged more than enough downtime today. My dive computer will throw its memory chip if I go down again so soon! I don't want to risk getting the bends."

Grüber sarcastically clucked his concern. "Oh, *too bad!* Ms. Delaney? The way I see it, you owe me a couple of divers. Don't know what you did to 'em, but it appears as if they're gone. And they were the brain-trust of this operation, Heaven help me....

Think of it like a big game of chess. You took out my two knights, now I'm coming after your queen — *you*, Jerri. So, you see, I can't afford for you to die on the *surface*... at least, not from any kind of *trauma*. No guns; no knives, no — "

Again, Jerri interrupted. "Back up, Joy-Boy! No way!" Her arms crossed stubbornly in front of her chest, she suddenly seemed to lose her bravado, murmuring, "Did I hear you say something about somebody *dying*?"

~o0o~

He hit the bluetooth button on his earpiece and spoke. "What's our e.t.a.?" The response went unheard by the doctor and Miss Marty, but the agent seemed satisfied.

Richardson grunted, nodded his head and disengaged his phone. "The captain says we'll be in the general area in about five minutes. Once we penetrate the one-mile radius, he'll shut down the engines and we'll go into silent running. We'll search a mile wide grid using the coordinates your Daniel Tiger remembered."

Miss Marty gasped, quick tears springing to her eyes. "You mean, Daniel's... confessed?"

"I've said too much, already," Richardson enigmatically replied and shook his head. "Let me freshen your coffee. I'm sure it won't be too long now."

~o0o~

"I'm not diving, *and you can't make me*," Jerri stated adamantly. She set her stance for battle, her fists on her hips. "*Nothing* you can say will make me suit up," she growled, "and nothing you can *do* will send me down."

Grüber smiled, sadistic evil peeking through his expression. The viciousness twinkling in his green eyes glowed with a satanic light; he fought to contain his wicked humor, but his chuckles won out. "I *said* it wouldn't do for *you* to be found dead with bodily trauma. But, it doesn't matter about Fish-Lady, here." Pulling the pearl-handled pistol from his waistband, he cocked the small handgun, and touched the barrel to Marissa's temple. "Suit up, or the mermaid gets it. You'll go down, or we'll have fish

205

brains splattered *all over the deck...* and they say it's not wise to chum the waters before a dive. Sharks, you know. Gets the sweet little darlings in a frenzy."

Jerri glanced up at Grüber. *There's nothing left... no trace of the man I went out with the other night... no grace...no manners. No humanity.*

He noticed Jerri studying his face, and he smiled once more; touching the mermaid's temple with the gun. As he traced Marissa's cheek deliberately and slow, using the gun barrel, instead of his fingertips, terror showed in her eyes, and she trembled, a moan escaping her lips. Her beautiful iridescent tail quivered in fright. Silently beseeching Jerri, the mermaid cowered away from the gun, a tear trailing down her face. Grüber grinned, enjoying the effect of his sadistic and menacing tactics.

I've never meant harm to another person, Jerri thought, *but I truly believe, given the chance, and given the proper weapon, I'd see this man dead....*

He chuckled toward Jerri. "See? I believe Fish-Lady *really* wants you to suit up. Hey, Amazing? Whadda you say? Be a sport!" He wagged the gun held against Marissa's head, and reiterated his threat. "The clock is ticking... time is running out! Tick-Tock! *Does Fish-Lady live or die?* Oh, the suspense is killing us, isn't it guys?"

He giggled, and the grim realization came to Jerri — *the man was insane.*

Persistently, Grüber continued, "It's at *least* killing the Fish-Lady! What's it gonna be, Amazing? Come on! *I don't have all night!* It's all up to you, Ms. Delaney."

Her father's whispered warnings tickled her ear: *Don't let him see you're scared, Jerri-Bird! Give `im all you got! Razzle-Dazzle `im, Baby!!*

"Tell me, Grüber," Jerri hissed. "Does it make you feel proud to be a bigger bastard than your rotten father?" She waited for the venom behind her words to register in his mind, before she spoke again. "What kind of abuse did you endure at that monster's hands to turn you into such a creep?"

Sensing a victory close at hand, Jerri went in for the kill. "After all these years... to find out you're *just like the man*... how can you stand it? Please tell me.... *How* can you stand it? And your *worthless mother* just let the bastard do anything he wanted to you, right? *Any damned thing he wanted! Right? RIGHT?* Tell me, Grüber! I wanna know what went on in your childhood to turn you into such a... a... *son-of-a-bitch!*"

Ruthlessly, she drove the 'sword' home for its final taste of blood and forced herself to hold his gaze, whispering, "*What kind of mother* abandons her child to an *evil* like that?" Jerri knew, as soon as the words left her mouth, she'd hit her target.

Swift-hot anger flashed in Grüber's eyes.

Jerri's heart clutched as she watched his face. The gold flecks scattered among the Gaelic-green of his eyes — eyes she once thought mesmerizing — swirled and seemed to halo, encircling the model-handsome man's emerald orbs. Jerri looked into the monster's swirling eyes. *What the Hell???*

His gun hand trembled — so great was his rage — and his anger almost visibly traveled down his arm to the gun in his hand. He drew back the pistol as if to slash it across Jerri's face, then seemed to think better of it. Fierce hatred battled between his eyes and his lips, but no sound came from the man.

This is no silly illusion, Jerri! Her father once again voiced a warning, *Take care! Don't let the Dragon win!*

"I never should've told you *anything* about...." He shook his head, visibly attempting to dislodge his hurtful past from his mind. Suddenly, the man left the mermaid's side, and in one swift move, grabbed Jerri around the waist, pulling her to him. "One kiss, before your dive." He hissed, "One *perfect* kiss." He bent Jerri at the waist, his gun hand at her back, his lips intent upon a soul-stealing lip-lock.

~o0o~

The darkness was all encompassing, even for him. His vision reduced, he hovered near motionless on the ocean's floor. Pendragon cursed his frustration. Even with his genetically enhanced low-light vision, he strained to see through the silt and sand kicked up from struggling with the two black-suited divers. With a flip of his tail, he headed toward the surface to get free of the dark and cloudy water.

He shuddered. No matter how harshly he scolded his inner thoughts, he couldn't get the horror of the carnage on the ocean floor out of his mind. It threatened to set up housekeeping in his head, deep-seated, disturbing and dark. *The gluttonous sharks feasted on those two divers... their knives and spears proved no match for the terrible white teeth and the black-gray eating machine's mindless feeding.*

Being the sole witness to the violent death of his attackers, left Mark stunned and wounded; not in body, but soul. He desperately fought to clear his mind from the terrified men screaming — *though underwater* — while being eaten alive.

His heart ached with fear for the woman he'd left chained to the coral head; and it throbbed with a deeper dread for the tiny magician, threatening to tear itself from his chest. In the scant few moments he'd spent by her side, Pendragon could tell from Marissa's greenish skin tone, the mermaid was close to death. And the last time he'd seen Jerri, she was busy working her magic with her professional lock-picks, struggling to free the mermaid. The gills beneath his ears flared wildly from the adrenaline rushing throughout his body, and his mind fought for control in an onslaught of imagined disasters.

Jerri was only packing a fifty for an air tank, he thought. *What if I don't get back to her in time? What if she stays with Marissa too long? What if she runs out of air? What if...? Oh, God! I can't lose them both!* He hurried his ascent, not wanting to spend even one extra moment in the black water; fresh blood accounting for the blackness as much as the lack of light.

Breaking the surface with a mighty crest of water spray, Mark resembled a graceful dolphin erupting triumphantly from the sea, though his tortured screams of anguish couldn't lay claim to the voice of such a delicate creature. Fists clenched in anger, he cried for the fear that consumed him. He roared for the hopelessness that gnawed at his heart. He raged at the smirking full moon for its selfish impudent sailing across the black sky, a lone sailor riding an inky star-filled cosmic sea.

Lightning flashed, and thunder rumbled far in the distance, as if God had taken notice of the injustice unfolding below the water's surface. Reflected quicksilver moonlight frolicked on the gentle swells, skipping a fairy dance in a straight line, worshiping the golden orb that gave it life. Mark closed his eyes and searched the innermost quiet of his mind, listening for the slightest hint of Marissa's voice. All was silent; his internal senses crying out for contact with the mermaid, but receiving no reply. Frustrated, he ripped his hand through his still wet hair.

From this distance, the shrimper he figured for the base of the two unfortunate divers resembled a toy boat on the western horizon; he'd dragged his attackers quite a span before the cruel interruption of the ravenous sharks. As Pendragon floated on the surface, his neck gills flared erratically. The full moon targeted his eyes causing them to sparkle as if they were filled with Saint Elmo's Fire; he raked his wet black hair out of his eyes and swore under his breath. "Jerri's on that boat," he hissed. "She's in danger... *I can feel it!* I've got to get to her! I've got to help her *and* Marissa, *before it's too late!*"

He leaped into the air, clearing the water, and dove gracefully into the black depth, the report of his tail slapping the surface mimicking the distant thunder.

~o0o~

The Coast Guard cutter powered down and idled at a leisurely speed. "We're getting close," Richardson breathed, a hint of excitement in his voice. "Let's shut down the lights, now. Everything except this little flashlight."

He switched on a small battery-powered fluorescent table light. "We're going into silent running." He smiled patronizingly at Miss Marty. "That means we're trying to sneak up on the bad guys," the D.E.A. agent said.

"*Really*," the old woman huffed, "what kind of a simple dolt to you take me for? I'll have you know, young man, I know bad men when I see them...."

209

Her voice trailed off as she remembered her chauffeur. Her mind provided her with troublesome images of her young friend held prisoner at the helm, in handcuffs, on the wrong end of a gun. "Oh, Daniel... Daniel Striped Tiger. *What have you done?*" She turned to the doctor, grabbing his hand across the table. "Arni, how could I have been so *wrong* about Daniel? I mean, we've both known him for two years, now. How could he have hidden his true self from the people closest to him? Tell me, how?" Tears streamed down her cheeks. "*Please?* Can you tell me?"

The doctor scooted across the bench seat and took his elderly patient in his arms, giving his shoulder up to the weeping woman's sobs. As he soothed Miss Marty's tears, Arni Sims glared across the table at Sloan Richardson, his expression conveying scorn for the other man's silence.

"Shhh... quiet," Sims cooed. "Everything's gonna be all right. No matter what Daniel's done, I promise, everything's gonna be okay. Isn't that right, Richardson? *Richardson?*"

Checking out his manicure suddenly seemed to take on a great importance to the shamed D.E.A. agent, and he frowned while he mumbled to his hands. "We'll be at the site soon. I'm sorry." He raised his eyes to the mismatched couple huddled together across the galley table, and simply said: "I wish I could say more."

~o0o~

Jerri saw the man aiming his lips toward their target, and she froze.

Grüber, his eyes closed in anticipation, pressed his deadly lips to Jerri's, passionately caressing her mouth. Briefly breaking the kiss, he moaned, "Silver. Jerri, sweet Jerri...your soul is simply *delicious*." Again, he bent to her lips, intent upon the theft.

Jerri's eyes widened. *What's he doing??? His kiss... his lips are so... cold....* She felt his icy tongue probing, parting her lips in its quest for her soul. She heard Grüber groan in climatic ecstasy, while a silver taste bathed her mouth. She stiffened.

Listen to me, Daughter! Her father's voice shot through her

210

mind. *This is the Dragon! The Dragon is here, now! You can't let him win! Never let the Dragon win!!!*

With a low growl — which Grüber mistook as a passionate surrender — Jerri found his murderous tongue, captured it, and bit down hard; simultaneously kneeing the Dybbuk in the groin.

He screamed and roughly pushed Jerri from him, sending her to the deck. He spat a mouthful of blood next to her legs.

"*No soul for you!*" Jerri cried in her best 'Seinfeld Soup-Nazi' imitation. She rubbed the remnants of the monster's kiss from her mouth and spat.

Wiping his bloody mouth, Grüber pointed at Jerri, crumpled on the deck. "Get... her... down... under... guys," he growled, his battle controlling his quivering anger obvious. "Get her down under... before I do something I'll... *regret in the morning.*"

Jerri sneered at the blond gunman. "Death in the deep is preferable to one more moment in *your* company. So, okay...." she snarled as she grabbed up her weight belt. "*Let's get wet!*"

~oOo~

Chapter 27

She threaded her arms through the B.C. jacket while Benny held the weight of the fresh tank. Snagging the jacket closed and snapping the clasps tight, Jerri purposely stayed her hands from her B.C., not wanting to risk drawing attention to her pockets. *A good illusionist keeps the mystery hidden until the end of the trick,* Jerri heard her father's voice. *You can do it, Jerri. Baby Girl... You're my little piece of magic in a mundane world. You're my Magic Star. Razzle-Dazzle 'em, Jerri-Bird!!*

She whispered, "I will, Daddy. *I will.*"

"What's that?" Benny asked as he handed her the mask and snorkel. "Were you talkin' to me?"

Pulling the strap over her head, she allowed the mask to hang down onto her chest. "I was just noticing your unique aftershave. That's quite an unusual fragrance."

He snorted. "Ain't wearin' any... *hey?* You sayin' *I stink?*"

"Like Eu de Shrimp Boat," Jerri sneered.

"I don't know any Odie Shrimp Boat," Benny growled. "An' if I did, I sure as hell wouldn't go around smellin' like 'im."

"Good one, Benny," Grüber grinned. "You *are* the master of the clever retort. After you've gotten the lady all tricked out for her last dive, would you be so kind as to fit this lovely bracelet on her wrists?" He shoved a shiny pair of handcuffs at his henchman and chuckled, turning his attention to Jerri. "Ms. Delaney? The other evening, on our most memorable date, didn't you share with me the fact you wear only silver? This matching set of delicate silver wristbands comes to you courtesy of Pressman's Locks and Security. Please be so kind as to model them for our enjoyment."

Grüber smirked at Jerri, an evilness glowing in his eyes.

Jerri held her hands out before her, wrists touching, fists clenched tight. She looked into the stocky crewman's unshaven face as he roughly grabbed her wrists. His eyes shone with an repulsive gleam and she thought: *He's enjoying this, almost as much as his slimy boss.*

Watching expressionless as Benny clamped the cuffs on, one wrist after the other, snugging each tight, she steeled herself against the discomforting, skin-biting handcuffs. "You realize," she hissed at Grüber, "*this* could be behind the problem you have meeting women? You'd have to pay me to get this kinky... wait a minute — *that's* how you score a *second* date!! *So* like your bastard father!"

Grüber glared at her. When he spoke, his voice cracked. "You're having just too much fun for a woman who's about to die," he snarled.

She smiled, watching the man's face betray his emotions, knowing she'd hit another nerve with her taunting. "What did your father teach *you,* Grüber? *My* daddy always said: 'Never leave an audience bored. Leave `em wanting more. *Razzle-Dazzle `em, Baby!*'" She boldly quoted her own father, a hint of rebellion behind her words. "And I'll fill you in on a little secret. I can 'Razzle-Dazzle' like *nobody* can!" Jerri hoped she could hold her bluff; her insides quivered with anger and fear.

This time, he laughed out loud, and still holding the pearl-handled gun, he clapped his hands in sarcastic applause. Grüber gleefully chortled. "Ms. Delaney! Thank you for a *stellar* performance! One would almost think you held the cards on this high-stakes poker game. But, alas! Your luck has run its course. Benny, help our little Magic Girl over the side. Paco? Carl? Are you guys ready to go down? Good!"

Benny, suited up and ready to dive, guided Jerri to the side of the boat. While encumbered by the cuffs, she adjusted her mask as well as she could. Carl and Paco stepped out over the water in their giant strides; the reports of the two men entering the ocean were thunderclap loud in the dark silence. Jerri drug her feet, buying a few precious seconds as she turned to Marissa, cowering at Grüber's feet.

"Don't worry," Jerri whispered to the frightened mermaid. "Mark will come. *I know he will.* He'll come for — "

"Pendragon?" Grüber scoffed in rude interruption. "He's nothing but a joke. If you're waiting for that wimp to save you, you'll be shark bait before he gets his hair blown dry. That lunatic Miss Marty only keeps him around because she's a horny old broad. She's so horn — "

"*Shut up!*" Jerri screamed, cutting off his hurtful words. She pulled away from Benny's grip, and threw herself against Grüber, knocking him back against the large, coffin-sized deck cooler. She had a great satisfaction that she'd knocked the wind out of the monstrous man.

Grüber hissed his fierce anger: "Benny — *do your damned job!*"

With an impatient growl, Benny roughly grabbed her again, wrenching Jerri away from his angry boss. The burly deckhand then pushed her against the railing, and she could see the dark water waiting at the bottom of an eight-foot drop.

Jerri held tight to the metal bar, knowing her struggle was futile, but resisting just the same. "Grüber!! *Just shut up!*" she yelled, her voice muffled by the dive mask. "Don't say another word about that sweet old lady! She's been like a grandmother to me! She's my friend and *I LOVE HER!* You may make me go down, but I swear... 'Eines Tages verbinden Sie mich in der Hölle.' — *I'll see you in Hell* — you black-hearted bastard!!"

"Benny... *What* are you waiting for?" Grüber hissed through clenched teeth, as he rubbed his stomach — the target of Jerri's attack. "Are you going to let her sing the death aria from Carmen? *Please, man! Do your job!!* Put her out of *our* misery!"

Benny looked at his frustrated employer and frowned, then shrugged his shoulders as if to say: *Whadda you expect me to do, here? Pick her up and throw her in?* Suddenly, as if a dim light bulb went off in the crewman's head, he grinned. In a pantomime of Laurel and Hardy proportions, he pointed his right index finger to the night sky, checking the breeze direction. Grasping the bottom of Jerri's air tank, Benny effortlessly flipped the slight woman up and over the boat's railing. "Uppsy-Daisy!" he quipped, watching her sail through the air. "Have a nice trip! See you in the fall!"

Grüber hung his head in disgust. Catching Marissa's eye, he groaned, "Boobs and morons. See what I have to work with here?"

~o0o~

In the dimmed lighting of the black boat, peering through the galley port, Miss Marty could make out little, save moonlight shining on a large-sized boat with netted-wings, making it appear to be a ridiculously outsized night bird or bat. She whispered, "Is *that* our destination? That boat decked out with fishing nets?"

"Yeah." Richardson nodded his head and returned her whisper, "That's a shrimper *supposedly* working the site."

Dr. Sims joined the couple at the boat's window. He asked, "Since when is shrimping illegal? There's hundreds of boats running the Keys, making an honest living from the ocean."

Richardson snorted. "The keyword, Doctor, is *honest.* We've had our eye on this particular shrimping operation for quite awhile. That boat hasn't left a mile radius of this area in over five years. Now, call me stupid, but I don't think an honest shrimper would dip in the same minnow bucket for all that time. Do you?"

"Frankly, Richardson, I don't know *what* to think. I brought Daniel to you on good faith — and you've told me zip. Nada. Zilch." Sims hissed, "I don't know if my patient is a *criminal* or *Man of the Year*. I don't know if I'll ever see my other patient — Jerri Delaney — again. I gotta tell ya, I'm gettin' kinda pissed off by all the stuff I'm not knowin' — know what I mean?"

"Sorry. I can't say any more. Security. Just one more reason you and the lady should've skipped this cruise. This is a need to know situation."

"Need to *know* situation???" Sims ripped his hand through his red hair. "Are you freakin' *kidding* me??? We're five miles out in the middle of the Gulf of Mexico — they're both my patients

— and I *damn well need to know!*"

Seeing the tension between the two men, Miss Marty again gathered her crystals, closed her eyes and folded her hands.

The bluetooth chirped. The agent listened and spoke, "Copy that." He looked to the doctor and Miss Marty. "It's a go," he murmured.

Richardson slapped the doctor on the back, hard enough to rock the slight man away from the table. "Ready, Jethro? We're closing in on our target. *Let's rock and roll!*" He hurried from the galley.

Coughing from the D.E.A. Agent's rough jostling, the doctor whispered to Richardson's back, "The name's Arni."

~o0o~

Jerri descended into the dark water as Carl pulled her down at his side, yanking on the handcuffs, causing the metal to bite into her wrists. Air bubbles danced a fairy dance in a sparkling explosion of expelled air, back lighted by the men's feeble dive lights.

Carl leered at her through his dive mask, his silent message clear. If she could have grabbed the determined flunky, she would have gladly punched him out, but being shackled allowed her little leeway in her movements.

The pain of being forced deeper, descending too swiftly, attacked her ears. She frantically cleared her eardrums by swallowing every few feet she was dragged toward the sandy floor.

She scolded herself, *Well, Delaney... isn't this is another fine mess you've gotten yourself into! There's always something to be said for being dragged away by a caveman afflicted by testosterone-overload... and every single word is R-rated.* She tugged ineffectually at Carl's grip on the handcuffs.

Gradually, the coral head emerged from the darkness, and Jerri knew their swift journey to the bottom was at an end. Carl signaled Paco, indicating the other man should untangle the chains Jerri dropped to the sand when she'd released the locks trapping Marissa.

216

Paco passed the chains over the handcuffs before lacing them in a figure eight around Jerri's arms. Next, he looped the heavy links around her ankles, causing her to fall to her side beside the hill of coral, trussed up like a rodeo steer. Frustration burst from Jerri's regulator in a rush of bubbles as she vehemently cursed Grüber's henchmen.

Carl laughed underwater, the sound muffled by his regulator's bubble-explosion, his dive light bobbing erratically, sending a thin spear of light careening over the rainbow-hued coral. He signaled, with a few deft hand movements, that the more Jerri struggled, the more air she'd lose. Ending his underwater overacting, holding his regulator from his mouth, he stuck his tongue out, mimicking the death throes she'd soon suffer.

The other man finished his work with the old chains by reaching into his B.C. pocket, and showing Jerri a shiny new combination lock, which he used to fasten the links snug around her ankles.

For a brief moment, she panicked, knowing combination locks could prove stubborn and unyielding. *At least I'll have the dive lights,* she thought as the two men prepared to return to the surface, leaving her to die alone beside the coral.

Paco pointed toward the surface in the diver's signal to rise. Carl nodded his head in agreement, then reached out, grabbing his partner by the arm, pointing at Jerri with his other hand. Paco made a motion indicating confusion.

Cuffing the other man's head, Carl returned his attention to Jerri. He grabbed her by the B.C. jacket and rummaged through both pockets in turn. Suddenly he paused, grinned around his regulator mouthpiece, and pulled Jerri's lock pick packet from its hiding place. He held them up, wagging the set of picks in front of her dive mask.

Laughing into his mouthpiece again, Carl waited for Paco to kick off for the surface, then sarcastically saluted Jerri. Lastly, the man gathered the dive-lights Jerri used earlier in her bid to free Marissa. Pointing upward, he joined his partner, taking the last dive light with him.

As the glow of Paco and Carl's underwater lights faded upward into a gradual growing darkness, Jerri's heart sank. She searched her mind for a quip to boost her courage, but for once, her smart-aleck inner voice was silent.

~o0o~

He moved through the water soundlessly, the full silver moon being the only witness to his silent surveillance. The two men moving about the deck of the shrimp boat said little, at least nothing Mark could pick up even with his super sensitive hearing. The merman watched the pair from a safe distance of a dozen yards, his shoulders barely above the water, the gills under his ears flaring with every beat of his fearful heart. He silently wondered, *Are they the only people on deck? I'll have to get closer to hear what they're saying.*

A flick of his tail brought him to the dark side of the shrimper, and he floated on his back, his iridescent scales breaking the dark water's cover, barely shimmering in the sparse moonlight that peeked around the hulking boat. His tail gently slapped the surface of the bobbing waves, much like a person would nervously, and unconsciously, tap their foot in frustration. The feathery tail's report on the water matched the wave's lapping on the side of the shrimp boat.

When one of the men lowered a bucket over the side, filled it, and dumped a load of water on the deck, Mark was taken by surprise. The merman pondered, *Boy! That was too close! Don't think he saw me, though... he'd have 'yipped' and raised the alarm if he had. Hmmm... salt water on the deck? You use FRESH water to swab the decks... Marissa? Marissa must be on there! That's got to be the reason I couldn't sense her under the water! She's still alive — but OUT of the water!! ...now... what about Jerri?*

The last thought brought renewed apprehension for the woman he'd long since thought of as just a client. He drug his fingers through his glistening black hair, subconsciously trying to wipe the fear from his mind. Reverting to his people's old beliefs, he whispered, "Poseidon — keep her safe!! Please protect her as

218

You would any of Your Water Children!"

Much like a trained dolphin, he dove beneath the surface without leaving a wake, silently closing in on the shrimp boat.

~o0o~

In the total darkness, she found the sandy bottom's silence unnerving. For a few minutes, the only sound Jerri picked up was her own breathing; which for the moment, she concentrated on solely, to keep her rhythm slow and even.

She realized, if she allowed panic to set in, she'd die alone in the darkness. At first, she could see nothing, complete and total blackness being all that greeted her searching eyes. Her vision adjusted, and gradually, a faint glow from the full moon reached her; enough to see vague shadows. All the coral's bright colors were gone, replaced by grays and blacks.

At this depth, the coral colors washed out even in dimmed light. With just moonlight as a light source, Jerri could only make out the outline of the coral head and the vague dark shapes she took for the shrimp boat and The Little Lavender.

Lying on her side in a fetal position, her cheek pressed against the sand, she wriggled her feet and hands, taking stock of her situation. The chains were bound tightly around her ankles, biting into her skin above her dive shoes.

My hand restraints are looser, she thought, *but not for lack of trying on Paco and Carl's part. It woulda been a bad scene if they'd known I was bunching up my wrist muscles, making them bigger so the handcuffs would be looser. Boy, that big jerk thought he put a hurt on me when he took my lock picks. What did he think I'd do with picks, anyway? Scratch my name in the sand? Pick my nose? I mean... that's a shiny new COMBINATION lock holding the chains tight around my feet. Right now, I need my picks like a fish needs a bicycle. Yeah. I need lock picks as much as I need a man... Actually... I really NEED Mark right about now.*

She listened to the sound of the water around her head, and concentrated on breathing in and out. Feeling the air bubbles tickle past her right cheek, she wondered how much air was left in the tank. The men who'd thrown her over the railing hadn't let her check the gauges before dragging her down into the water, and her dive computer wasn't in view now. *Guess I'll have to go by feel and intuition.* She pondered the problem. *I'll try not to worry about running out of air until the regulator gets sluggish. Besides, first things first. It's Razzle-Dazzle time!*

~o0o~

Mark raised his head from the water on the port side of the Little Lavender. Miss Marty's boat was anchored between Pendragon and the shrimp boat, and the merman used the small boat as cover from the sight of the shrimpers. He was deathly quiet as he pulled himself halfway out of the water.

Leaning over the railing enough to peer into the toolbox sitting behind the back bench, Mark grabbed a large wrench and a length of nylon rope, before again disappearing beneath the water. Swimming under The Little Lavender toward the shrimper, he kept his depth at eight to ten feet to avoid a surface wake. Passing under the net-laden water craft, Pendragon made his way to the stern of the shrimp boat. A few flips of his tail left him hovering in the water, level with the steel-bottomed craft's twin props.

A gentle glow from the full moon reached into the water, giving Mark more than enough light for his intended task. First, he wound the rope from prop to prop, pausing in mid-wind long enough to tie the wrench into the figure eight nylon tangle that immobilized the twenty-four inch props. Then, he finished his handiwork by snugly tying off the sabotage-intended Gordian Knot. *Let `em try an' get outta this one,* he thought, patting the ensnared steel blades. Pendragon left the back of the boat, swimming silently, circling the large craft. On his second pass swimming slowly around the shrimp boat, Mark sent out physic signals to Marissa, hoping she was indeed on the deck as he'd surmised.

Come on, Marissa, he silently called out. *Answer me. Answer me!! Let me know you're okay. Tell me where Jerri is. Say something, so I can find you. Say something so I can help you!*

220

Mark... Mark... came a plaintive plea, *Mark, where are you?*

Marissa? He answered the thought/voice, in the manner of their kind, *Where are you? Marissa, tell me where you are!!*

Boat.... She sounded weak, her thoughts a mere whisper. *Be careful, Mark. Two men — armed....*

Hang on, he thought, trying to sound comforting. *Just hang on, Marissa. I'm working on a plan.*

Hurry... She sounded weaker with each word, as if the mental telepathy between her and Pendragon was draining. *Please, hurry!! Hurry, Mark! I don't know how much longer I can hold on.*

He soothed. *I know you're weak. But, hold on just a little bit longer. Where's Jerri?*

...Jerri?

He nearly spat out his thoughts in frustration, *Jerri!! The woman who freed you from the chains! JERRI!!*

Her... they... they took the girl down below.

Down below? He sounded confused. *Down below deck?*

Nooo.... By the raspy quality of her thoughts, it was apparent each word was strained and the mermaid grew weary. *No... two men took... took her underwater. She's been down... a long time. The two men are... back on deck now. Be careful... they're... dangerous.*

Save your strength, he thought/whispered. *I know. They're armed. Don't worry about me. I'm going after Jerri. I've got to bring her back. I'm the one who brought her out here. I'm the one who put her life in danger. Hold on. Be safe; I'll be back for you. Neptune's Blessings, Marissa.* Not waiting for the frightened mermaid's reply, Pendragon tipped his tail to the moon and disappeared beneath the water.

~o0o~

221

Chapter 28

"Okay, you two stay in the galley, stay away from the bow,"
Richardson told Miss Marty and Sims. "You never know how
things will go. This could get nasty. All kidding aside — I'm
being completely serious, here. I don't want you two, or one of
my men to get hurt. So, stay out of the way." His finger sternly in
the air, and nodding silently, he left the cabin to join other agents
on the deck.

Miss Marty looked at Sims, sighed, and shook her head.
"Arni, you realize," she said, "I can't just sit back and do nothing.
I'm too old to be too careful. I've got to go out on deck to see if I
can catch sight of Daniel!" Not waiting for her doctor's opinion,
she rushed past him and headed for the cabin door.

"Wait!" Sims hissed. "Stay back! Richardson said not to get
in the way!" The galley door closed behind Miss Marty. "*I said* —
hold up! Wait for me!" He looked to Basil lounging in the
lavender picture hat, and threw up his hands in frustration. "Well,
you know how she is," he addressed the tiny dog. "She'll be
stubborn until the day she dies... and probably two or three days
after that." He shook his head. "Basil, my man... I believe we
should *both* go keep her out of trouble." Snatching up the toy-
sized pooch, he hurried out the door after the old lady.

Sims caught up with Miss Marty as she hugged the outside
cabin wall, and peered around the corner, trying to stay out of
sight of the agents gathered on the bow as the cutter closed in on a
darkened boat. The doctor recognized the craft by it signature
wing-like nets. Its nets idle; it looked like a huge bat floating in
the silvery moonlight. At this distance, only vague shadowy

shapes could be seen moving about on deck, but Sims couldn't make out enough distinguishing traits to tell whether the people were male or female.

He hissed at his elderly patient, "What are you doing out here? Richardson said you should stay out of — "

"Richardson told me to stay out of the way," Miss Marty interrupted, hissing back. "Well, *I'm out of the way.* And if *you'll* pipe down," she shook an admonishing finger at her doctor, "he'll never know we're here. *Don't you understand?* I've *got* to see about Daniel! He's — " A sudden rush of footsteps down the pilothouse ladder cut her words short. Miss Marty held up a quieting index finger, shushing the doctor, while plastering her other hand over his mouth, ensuring his silence. Daniel was flanked, both front and aft, by armed officers leading him to the bow to join Richardson.

"Oh, Arni!!" Miss Marty gasped. "*Daniel?* What are they going to do to Daniel?" She dropped her muffling hand from Sims' mouth.

Once free of his elderly friend's suffocating hand, Sims took a dragging breath. "Jeez-O-Pete, woman! At least let me breathe!" Noting how close they were to the officers, and hoping not to be overheard, he added an extra hiss: "Quiet!! This is against my better judgment; I oughta force you back to the cabin. *What am I saying?* Force you? Force *you?* Fat chance. Easier to pet a rattlesnake. Here, take Basil. At least, keep him still. If you want to watch the action, then you better keep him quiet. We're closing in on that boat! I think things'll happen fast, now!"

From his position on the bow, Richardson hand-signaled the pilothouse and three powerful searchlights hit the mysterious boat, illuminating the deck like a theater stage. Speaking into a microphone, the agent's voice boomed out from the cutter into the darkness. "Ahoy there! This is the U.S.S. Coast Guard Cutter Champion. You are advised to prepare for boarding."

~o0o~

The air bubbles fled from Jerri's regulator like tiny round pixies racing for the surface. Knowing her air supply might be low, she purposely slowed her breathing, centering her thoughts on comforting images. She concentrated — imagining herself sprawled lazily on her back in a fragrant field of wildflowers — which brought visions of Pendragon languishing beside her. She shook the images from her mind, causing a contagion of bubbles to make their escape.

Again, she concentrated — finding herself on a warm tropical beach, palm tree fronds rustling in the warm breeze. As she gazed out at the endless azure horizon, Pendragon lifted her hand to his lips, while wrapping his other arm around her waist, causing her to sink back into his strong arms. Another shake of her head lost more air to the sea.

Come on, Jerri, she scolded herself. *What will it take for you to listen to me? You can do this! Look... I'll make you a deal. Pull the rabbit out of the hat on this one, and I'll let you... I'll let you... I'll let you have whatever you want!* Her eyes opened wide on this thought and she shrewdly haggled with her inner-bully. *Let me have WHATEVER I want? Really? And what if I want Pendragon?* Her eyes darted back and forth, bantering with herself in the darkness. *Well... if that's what you REALLY want.... But — are you COMPLETELY sure?* She shook her head again at the self-asked question. *Completely sure? I DON'T KNOW!! All I know is... if I don't try... I'll never find out! And I don't want to lose him before I get the answer!*

She smiled to herself around the regulator's mouthpiece; the short self-searching debate easing her mind and giving a boost to her resolve. *I've got to try,* Jerri thought. *I'll begin with the relaxation exercises Mark showed me.* She knew if she failed at the techniques Pendragon taught her, death would be the only reply she received.

With a fierceness she didn't know she possessed, Jerri queued up for the physical therapy trick about which she'd earlier mocked Pendragon. *Mark's anal-retentive methodological training might come in handy after all!* The memory of bantering with the sexy physical therapist brought a smile to her face, assuaging some of the panicky fear.

Systematically relaxing the muscles of her body was much tougher than usual, but she realized the vital necessity of the Zen-like exercise. Moving her imaginary muscle-relaxer from the top of her head, down her neck to her shoulders, down from her shoulders to her arms, she finally arrived at her wrists. Twisting her left wrist counterclockwise, she tested which handcuff was tighter. *Here's hoping I tensed my wrists hard enough when Benny slapped on the cuffs! I won't get a second chance at this!*

One of Jerri's magical illusion tricks was to tense her wrists before her assistant bound her in handcuffs. The 'bunched' wrist muscles would be smaller when relaxed, giving her room to slide the cuffs from her arms.

She could almost, but not quite, slip the left cuff over her thumb. *Fine... okay, I'll try the other hand,* she assured herself. *If it's no better, I'll dislocate my thumb if I have to.* She could almost see her right wrist in the darkness. Placing the image of freedom in her mind, she visualized the Little Lavender floating unmanned in the moonlight. The thought of Mark awaiting her on the surface fueled her resolve. *All I've gotta do is get to the surface. When I get to the Little Lavender, Mark will be there, and I'll be safe.*

She slowly twisted her right wrist, sliding the handcuff toward her fingers until the metal pinched her skin. *Gotta...* she sighed, *I've just gotta...* Jerri pushed it farther, ignoring the pain in her wrist as hard metal warred against delicate tissue. Again, she pushed, ignoring the pain as hard edges bit into her wrist.

Taking a few cleansing breaths, Jerri made herself ignore the pain as she forcibly dragged her hand from the cold metal ringlet. Even in darkness, she knew she'd broken the skin and was bleeding out into the water. She reasoned, *At least there's no need to worry about sharks! I mean, why worry about something you can't see? I mean, what me worr —*

Something large bumped her shoulder, pulling her thoughts from her halfhearted humor attempts. Her eyes darted around the darkness, searching for the unseen monster hunting on the coral head. A chill ran down her spine, and suddenly Jerri was very,

very cold.

~o0o~

"Repeating! I'm Special Agent Sloan Richardson. This is the United States Coast Guard Cutter Champion. You are ordered to stand down and prepare for boarding. Any resistance will be taken as a hostile action and — "

The shrimp boat engine's roar drowned out Richardson's amplified voice. The D.E.A. agent covered the microphone with his hand and barked, "He's making a run for it! *Let's go!!*"

Suddenly, a deafening canticle of noise split the night, sounding like metal eating metal. Black smoke rolled from the back of the shrimp boat as the clanking racket ended abruptly. The next few seconds held an eerie silence.

Miss Marty whispered to Sims, "*What happened?*"

The doctor shushed her, pulling her backwards toward the galley. He shook his head in confusion. "I don't know," he said, "I think... something's wrong... somewhere."

"Will *somebody* please tell me what the hell *that* was?" Richardson glanced at each of the officers standing on the cutter's deck, not waiting for an answer. "Belay that pursuit order," he chuckled. "I've got a little hunch... something's telling me he's not going anywhere."

Grinning, Richardson returned the microphone to his mouth. "Naughty, naughty," he said. "Mustn't try to run out on your own little surprise party!" He motioned for his men to board the shrimper the second the cutter came alongside.

Keeping up his easy banter, he amplified his voice into the night, all the while signaling the armed men in the order they were to board the disabled boat. "*That* would make you a party pooper," he joked, although the expression on his face was stony-serious, "and you *know* how much your Uncle Sam hates party poopers."

The cutter sidled up against the shrimper and Richardson dropped the microphone. "Sic `em, boys," he mumbled. The ready and waiting Coast Guard officers leaped the rails from boat to boat, weapons in hand, already trained on the shrimper's

226

deckhands.. Richardson and Daniel Tiger followed close on their heels.

"Stop right there!! Back off!!" a man's voice roared from out of the shrimper's shadows. The cutter's searchlights centered on the murky threat, its blinding glare falling on an armed man looming over a nude woman. Cascading dark red curls tumbled over the woman's nakedness, barely providing a modest covering. Her legs quivered, her skin pale with fright.

"You again... It seems we meet again," the man addressed Daniel. "At one time, I thought we left you dead on the beach. Imagine my surprise, when you survived and managed to get yourself adopted by that loony old broad. I've watched you for these two years... watched you for any sign of recognition. Your amnesia *literally* saved your life."

"*Grüber....*" Daniel hissed his displeasure.

The man laughed, and said, "Oh, looky-looky. Daniel's back from the Land of the Lost." He returned his attention to the Coast Guard officers warily hanging back beside the railing and spoke his words dispassionately: "We're taking over your craft, gentlemen."

He chuckled in good humor, and continued, "Unfortunate circumstances warrant a necessary change in midstream, so to speak. Benny? Please take up a collection. These fine gentlemen would like to make a 'love offering'."

A stupid grin mashed over his face, the jovial crewman opened a storage compartment, reached inside and removed a cloth bag. "Hand over your hardware," the dim-witted crewman ordered the officers. "Drop `em in the bag."

Noting the gun held to the trembling woman's head, Richardson locked eyes with the gunman. "Do it guys," he ordered.

Benny held out the open gunnysack, collecting weapons all around.

Grüber smiled as the government men reluctantly dropped their guns into Benny's offered bag. Watching as the last gun fell into the gunnysack, he allowed a slow smile to spread across his face. "It's good to see there's not a plastic superman among you. At least, I hope none of you want to *die* a hero... nor do you wish to take responsibility for *this* beautiful lady's death."

Marissa screamed. "*He'll kill us all!* He's a dybb — " Her interrupted warning brought a rough cuffing from Grüber.

The evil man laughed again, and nudged the gun at the nude woman's head. "Hold on, darlin'. There's no need for superstitious talk like that. People who live in... *aquariums* shouldn't throw stones, wouldn't you say? Richardson? While you call the rest of your crew down from the pilothouse, we'll just be settling into our new digs. Benny? Again, it appears I'm imposing upon your generous nature. Will *you* be so kind as to tell Captain Dave to rip out the radio before joining us on the cutter?" Grüber looked to his crewman with a silent order, and watched as Benny rushed to the pilothouse, intent on relaying his boss' desire.

The handsome man then smiled as he again addressed Richardson. "Tell me... what good would it do to leave you guys on a crippled ship with a working communication system? Now, I ask you," he snickered, "where's the fun in that?"

Scowling, Richardson signaled the cutter's pilothouse, calling down the last two officers. The captain and the first mate climbed down the upper deck's ladder. Crossing over to the shrimper, the pair stepped onto the deck, joining Richardson, the other officers and Daniel Tiger.

"Captain Dave eighty-sixed our radio," Benny quipped, running back to Grüber's side. "Wires ripped and cut. He'll be here in a sec and we'll all be good to go."

Snickering like a school boy, Grüber gathered Marissa into an upright standing position. His arm tight around her waist, the blond man held the frightened woman forcefully against his body, the gun snug to her head.

The evil accountant motioned with the gun barrel, moving it less than an inch from the mermaid's head. He smiled wickedly. "Benny," he said. "Show our gallant guests to their quarters down below deck, in the catch-hold."

"No. No — " Daniel murmured. "Not... catch-hold."

228

Grüber effortlessly lifted Marissa until her toes barely brushed the deck. Dragging the frightened woman backwards toward the Coast Guard cutter, Grüber hissed at the government agents. "Don't even *think* about being heroes," he warned. "I don't need *much* reason to waste this lovely lady." Sarcastically kissing the struggling woman's cheek, he chuckled at the transformed mermaid's repulsed reaction, and crooned, "Don't be that way, darlin'. I *hate* it when we fight." He forced her to follow him over the rail to the cutter, all the while feigning affection for the terrified woman.

Kissing his hostage once more, he quipped, "Sweetheart, you're going to give these fine, fine officers the wrong idea!" Addressing Richardson, Grüber grinned. "I swear," he said. "Her absence of garments is none of my doing. My crew and I — *we've* been perfect gentlemen. Really. Believe me, we *found* her this way; but if I told you the whole story... let's just say, you'd think I was telling you *an outrageous fish tale.*" He laughed at his own wit.

"Come on, Benny," Grüber wagged the gun for emphasis. "Time to shut down this little shindig." He caressed Marissa's cheek with the gun barrel, and continued, "I want them to be *comfortable* after you open the seacock in the engine room. Let's scuttle this bucket of bolts so it can do its Titanic impersonation." Snorting as an afterthought, he added, "Oh... and by the way, Benny. Before you leave... be so kind as to bolt the hold's hatch."

~o0o~

Jerri wanted to scream, wanted to struggle, wanted to flee, but even though her right wrist had escaped from the handcuffs, the combination-locked chains still held her ankles tight, and now, she was certain she felt/heard the low-air warning bells which accompanied her breathing. The telltale sound was unmistakable.

Once again, a large shadowed object bumped her shoulder, and she fought hard not to cry out, knowing every breath of air was precious. *I'm not going to let it end like this!* She told herself,

229

If I give up now, how can I call myself worthy of the Delaney name? How can I face myself in the mirror tomorrow? Another mysterious nudge in the darkness stressed her fear. *God help me! I hope I still HAVE a face in the mirror tomorrow!!*

As best as she could, she struggled to sit upright. Reaching down, she ran her hands over the chains binding her feet, her fingers searching out the combination padlock. Finding the tumbler knob, she gingerly tested the dial, twisting the cylinder three complete clockwise turns. Pulling the casehardened steel shackle taut, with just the right pressure, she felt for the subtle telltale 'hiccups' from under the dial. She knew, if she could only manage to place her ear to the padlock, the microscopic sounds would be easier to pick up.

All I've got to do is get my ear to my ankles. But, if I could do THAT, I'd have a boffo career in the circus! I'll just have to settle for my fingers.

Trying to reassure herself, she thought, *This oughta be a piece of cake!* Her trained fingers 'listened' for the faint but inaudible clicks signaling the key to solving the secret combination number. *I can do this. Daddy and I used to play 'Safecracker' like other people played Charades!*

In the shadowed darkness, Jerri sent all of her tactile senses to her hands, drawing forth the tumbler's nearly negligible 'bumps' transferred to her sensitive fingertips. Slowly, she twirled the dial counterclockwise. Each time she felt the tumblers give, she carefully reversed the dial's direction. *Easy — easy.* The first two attempts ended in failure, and she took her hands away from the lock, flexing her tense fingers. Frustration threatened her concentration.

Overhead, the muffled sound of a large boat motor caught her attention. She looked toward the surface, barely making out the dark shape of a boat's hull meeting the shrimper. Jerri wondered, *What's going on?* She absentmindedly rubbed her fingers. *Another boat? What's--*

The growl of the shrimper's motor turning over, interrupted her inquisitive thoughts, and she momentarily stilled. Suddenly, a

230

great wrenching sound filled her ears, and Jerri instinctively covered her head, cowering from the noise. Seconds passed, and all was quiet once more. *What in the name of Harry Houdini was THAT?*

Another bump to the shoulder startled her from her shock. The darkness held unseen monsters, and the ringing of the air tank ticked off Jerri's remaining minutes of breathable air. She tried not to think what the growing difficulty drawing breath from the regulator meant.

Easy, Jerri, she whispered to herself, *easy does it. Slow and steady wins the race. Okay. Enough of a break. Come on, get busy! Let's get this show on the road! Holy Mary... full of grace. Help me win this stock-car race!*

Again, her fingers found the lock in the darkness. In a small way, the absence of light and not being able to see the numbers on the dial aided Jerri. Instead of thinking of the lock's combination by number designation, her mind formed the answer to the confining riddle in clicks and bumps.

Taking the knob between her fingers, she twisted it to the right, until she felt the first tumbler give way. Then a left turn took her to the release of the second tumbler. Knowing this might be her last chance, she forced herself to take the third revolution carefully, almost reaching out — *straining* — for the last tumbler's opening.

The combination lock's hasp sprang open and Jerri fell still, not moving, nearly paralyzed from disbelief. Never before had she conquered a strange lock so quickly.

Perhaps, it's not my day to die, after all!!

She pushed the chains from around her feet just as she realized she was *completely out of air.* Her attempts to pull air from the mouthpiece were only met with a hollow dinging and a dry emptiness. Jerri berated herself, *Outta air! OUTTA TIME!! Wish I'd practiced my emergency ascents more. Who am I kidding? I practiced as much as the rest of the class. It's just not one of my favorite things to do... shoot for the surface like a bat outta hell WITH NO AIR!!*

Calm yourself. Reach in your pocket, Jerri. Her grandmother's voice came to her as if she whispered in her granddaughter's ear. *All the love you'll ever need is in your pocket, my love.*

Jerri dug in her B.C's pocket and removed a stone. It was hard and heart-shaped. In the darkness, she *knew* it was an amethyst. *Miss Marty's Lavender Magic. How'd this get here?*

She squeezed her fingers around the stony heart and brought it to her useless regulator in a symbolic blessed kiss. Then, dropping her weight belt, Jerri remembered to keep her mouthpiece in place, making sure a thin stream of air bubbles escaped her lips.

Wearing only dive boots and no fins, Jerri kicked off the sandy bottom, feeling as if this would be the longest ascent she'd ever made. Knowing her lungs would literally explode unless she slowly released air from her mouth at a regular pace until she reached the surface, she once again squeezed the Lavender Magic and concentrated on 'humming a monotonous one note', as she'd been taught. Leaving her watery prison, she ascended through the dark water.

~o0o~

"That's right, guys," Benny growled. "Jump down into the hole. It's just a twelve-foot drop. Nothing for you big strong boys. Like the Boss-Man said: 'All G-Men down below or the woman gets an air-conditioned brain.' Go on." He held Richardson's gun, taken from the bag, and he used it to nudge the men toward the large built-in live well. "Whew!! I don't envy you guys!"

Benny held his nose. "That hole don't get used much, but I think the last time we threw fish down there, I believe we *might* have forgotten to rinse it out. Sorry." He sarcastically shook his head. "Didn't know we'd be having company. Jump in! *Go on!*" He poked Richardson with the weapon.

Richardson sneered. "Men? Do like he says. We can't endanger civilians," the agent said. He jumped into the darkness of the dank, insulated catch-hold; followed closely by the other officers.

232

Daniel Tiger held back, waiting until he was the last man standing beside Benny. Tense seconds passed. Finally, the still lavender-uniformed man snarled and haltingly said, "*Benny...* I remember... *you.* I remember what... you did to... me... on the beach. See... you... in Hell, you slime... bucket."

The crewman laughed. "Ebba-Dee-Ebba-Dee — save it for Satan." Benny laughed again. The burly thug slapped the butt of the pistol across Daniel's face, knocking the chauffeur into the huge live-well, where Tiger landed on top of the others who'd fallen before him.

Slamming the double hatch cover over the catch-hold, Benny then passed a steel bar through the latches.

"Now for a little creative repair down in the engine room," he chuckled, heading for the round hatch at the back of the shrimper. Two minutes later found him twisting the seacock valve to the full-open position. Just as if Benny had opened a medium-sized fire hose, seawater poured from the opened valve spilling into the engine compartment.

"This oughta take less than ten minutes," he snickered, looking around the small room, playing the flashlight across the salty water filling the back of the boat. "This rust-bucket oughta go down faster than I can spit." He shook his head, grinned at what he thought of as his quick wit, and left the engine compartment to the spewing seawater. Having carried out Grüber's orders, the crewman wasted no time boarding the pirated Coast Guard's cutter.

~o0o~

Chapter 29

Slicing through the water like a dolphin, Mark searched frantically for any hint of Jerri, but because she was completely human, the psychic communication from *her* was weak. Frustratingly, he found only glimmers of Jerri's thoughts — fear dispersed in the water — not a very useful tool for pinpointing her position.

I'll make a diminishing concentric search, he thought as he calculated the most effective method. *After all, I can't go off in every direction at once.* Not wasting a moment, Mark made a wide counterclockwise sweep off the west side of the shrimper just as he watched a cutter close in on the rogue boat. *At least, it appears help's arrived,* he reasoned. Preparing to dive in a swirling vortex movement, he embarked on a search for the woman he loved. *I have to believe Marissa will be rescued. Jerri needs me!*

Mark employed all of his senses on his descent into the dark water. Seconds counted. He feared what he'd discover if he found her too late. And that fear caused his heart to pound with a dread he'd never known before. He swam deeper.

~o0o~

Now, she could see the surface. The water's flat plane was in reach, although she feared she was only halfway to her goal. From the second she'd kicked off from the sea floor, she'd let her breath out as evenly as she could. Jerri hummed one monotone note into the regulator's mouthpiece, feeling the breath leave her in a tiny stream, all the while fighting the urge to drag in nonexistent air. Looking skyward, she noticed the shrimper's keel

234

sat at an odd angle; the stern hung low in the water.

How odd — it's sinking, she thought, just as her one note ran its course. Her burning lungs empty; completely out of air, she felt panic's icy fingers. Again, fear gripped her heart causing her to squeeze the Lavender Magic. *Heaven help me... got to make it to the top!* She pleaded, bargaining with God — *literally* — for her next breath. Her goal tantalizingly in sight, she kicked, once more, with all her might.

Reaching a hand toward the surface, flecks of light exploded in her vision. Quick-silver sensations coursed through her chest, and her conscious mind faded away. Suddenly, a bright light appeared just above Jerri, and she was touched by an easy — and *extremely* peaceful — feeling. Incongruously, though her body was suspended in warm Gulf water, she took a hesitant step toward the brightly lit tunnel.

Though the words left her lips, and she felt their leaving, her mind formed them as the sound of tiny bells. *I feel absolute... acceptance.* Now, as she *stepped closer,* she realized the peaceful sensations emanated from the tunnel's apex. A faceless being, seemingly formed from nothing but emotions, held out welcoming hands, reaching for Jerri, extending the promise of peace and eternal life. She thought/heard a bell-clear, silvery voice calling from a near distance. *Jerri! Come into the Light,* it echoed, *Light... Light... Light.... Join us in completeness... join us... fill your soul with never ending Love!*

Jerri reached out to the enticing white radiance and in slow motion, moved nearer the mouth of the tunnel. *Love,* she thought. *Love... the love I've missed for so long....* Joyful tears streamed down her cheeks.

The loving voice spoke again, so near, so near. "*We know you're weary... tell us... are you ready, child?*" The words caressed her in a soothing embrace. The warm light drew closer, extending its bright glow out of the tunnel, and she felt a compelling desire to surrender to it.

"*Are you ready, child?*" As the silvery voice repeated the question, a swift surge of nostalgic memories filled her mind. She *felt* her grandmother's loving presence moments before she realized the familiar voice *was* her grandmother's; and when she did, she perceived the warm words as if from a fuzzy and faraway dream.

Ahead in the tunnel, her grandmother stepped further from her concealment, leaving a blinding circle of white light. Slowly, dreamily, the light-bathed vision floated toward Jerri. The luminous figure's outstretched arms welcomed. Her soft smile soothed. Her voice still gentle, but stronger now, not muffled-soft, as if a gap had closed between a great distance. She called her granddaughter to the promise of eternal peace.

"Jerri, dear! You're home!"

Her breath caught in her throat, and even with a fragile hope, Jerri's heart thrilled. She cried out, *Grandmother? Granny Tyler — Is that you?*

"Yes, child."

You've come for me, Granny?

"No... *I've* not come for you, my dear. I couldn't come for you, because I've never really left you." The silver-haired woman smiled and traced her granddaughter's hair with sparkling lights.

I don't... don't understand.... You never left me? But... that night.... Confused, Jerri's words trailed off.

"Do you remember what I told you that last night?"

Told me? I remember... I remember you came to me. You woke me up. You told me to call my father. You kissed me. And then I remember... you left me. That past memory brought fresh tears to Jerri's eyes, as if it'd happened minutes ago. *Granny — you left me.*

"No, child. I never left you. Think back. Think.... Which came first? My leaving? Or the last kiss?"

...your last kiss.

"Are you sure? Really sure?"

You left my bedroom. I followed. And... In shocked awareness, Jerri's eyes flew open as she remembered the sequence of the final meeting, and realized with an adult's understanding, her grandmother had died sometime before she'd awoken her with a final good-bye.

"That's right, child. You found my earthly shell. But — that's all right — I've been with you every minute since. Haven't you heard my voice?"

Like a sudden breeze, memories of the Key West date filled Jerri's mind — came in a rush — came to her ears in Madame Serena's musical voice: '*Idle hands, idle hands*'. In a whisper, Jerri mimicked the psychic, speaking Granny Tyler's cleaning day mantra.

"Yes." Her grandmother smiled and fairy lights danced around her upswept, silvery hair. "Yes. You *WERE* listening that evening in Key West."

You... were there?

Granny Tyler smiled once more, and whispered close, tickling the tiny hairs in Jerri's ear, "Dear child... how many times must I tell you — I never left you — I'm with you always! You're never alone. In fact, your father is waiting, and your mother... and so many more people who have gone before. We're all waiting for you... waiting to bring you home. Are you ready, child?"

Yes. I'm ready, she returned the whisper.

"Then it's time, dear," Granny Tyler smiled, nodded, and beckoned her nearer. "Time to lay down your head and leave the world behind. Nothing binds you here. Come away, child. Come with me. It's easy. Come!"

Jerri reached out needy fingers toward her grandmother's offered embrace, hungry — *starved* — for the family love she'd missed for years. Again, an incredible peace filled Jerri's heart, and she sighed, *Granny? I'm so lonely. Please, let me climb up into your lap; I want you to hold me and rock me to sleep like you did when I was small... Please!*

As gentle as an ocean breeze, the older woman caressed her granddaughter's cheek. Suddenly, the woman's expression changed, ever-so-slightly. Granny Tyler laughed, her gentle chuckles decorated with the peal of tiny silver bells. "Oh, my dear child! I was mistaken. Now that I touch your cheek, look upon your sweet face," she said, "I don't think you're ready after all!

Your time is not now. All you really need is for someone to love you. An Earthly someone. Look around yourself, dear. Sometimes, we don't *SEE* the love in our life because we can't let go of the loneliness in our heart. Don't search for the love you long for... on *THIS* side."

Confused, Jerri again looked to her grandmother's smiling face.

"Remember." Granny Tyler whispered, "Jerri... your heart. Remember...."

With a flash of recollection, Jerri thought of Mark and the others, newly a part of her life. *Daniel Striped Tiger... Conchita... Cory... Miss Marty...* The thought of leaving these people behind was incomprehensible.

Abruptly, Mark's voice captured her thoughts, as if he were speaking telepathically, as if he were speaking *directly* to her heart: *Don't leave me. Please. I need you, Jerri. I need you.*

Mere steps away from her grandmother's arms, Jerri hesitated. *How can I leave Mark? God — don't even ASK me to leave Mark!!!*

Her grandmother smiled. "See? It's not your time, Jerri. You only had to look to your heart, my dove. Let your heart rule you... and listen... just listen." The genteel lady continued, "Don't worry. Our love will always be here. It's waiting for you, my dear... when the time is right. Open your eyes now, Jerri. Open your eyes to the love within your grasp."

But... my eyes ARE open.

"No, sweet child. They're not. Open your eyes, then open your hand. See the love you hold in your hand. ...and remember."

Jerri thought of the magic stone she still grasped. *All the love I need, here in my hand....*

"*Jerri!!!*" She heard her name screamed from a great distance. "*Jerri! Breathe for me!*"

Looking once more to her grandmother, Jerri saw the older woman's lips moving, but couldn't make out her words. Shaking her head in confusion, she reached out to the woman who'd raised her from a toddler, but her grandmother merely smiled, and gently pushed her away. A bittersweet expression formed on the elderly woman's lips and Jerri watched her kiss her fingertips and blow the 'last kiss' her way.

Tears sprang to Jerri's eyes as her own fingers brushed her grandmother's outstretched kiss-sending fingertips. Invisible hands pulled at her, wrenching her from Granny Tyler's side. Jerri fought being dragged away from the comforting light, as if she were ripping her soul away from its only desire. With what felt like her last breath, she screamed: *Granny! Granny — don't! DON'T LEAVE ME AGAIN!*

All at once, a great wave crested over her head, tumbling her over and over, end over end. A tumultuous sea-sick sensation gripped Jerri, torturing her until finally she relented, giving herself over to forces greater than her own. Struggling and coughing, she opened her eyes to see gentle waves rolling on the water's dark surface. The light from the swollen moon and the unnumbered stars replaced the warm and loving glow from the memory of the still beckoning tunnel.

Disoriented, Jerri focused on the first thing her eyes found in the darkness: Mark's face. Her dive gear, gone — pulled from her lifeless body — his arms around her, holding her face out of the water. ...but... *once more,* she felt unconditional love.

Raising her shaking right hand, Jerri brushed tears from his eyes. "I.. I heard your voice," she murmured. "You called me from the light. You brought me back. *You* saved me... *again.*" Opening her other hand, she wondered at her empty palm. The lavender stone, long gone, had left a heart-shaped imprint with its absence. "Love saved me. *You* saved me."

He touched his lips to her forehead, whispering, "And I'll *always* be there for you."

~o0o~

"Let's get this tub fired up!!" Grüber barked the orders to his henchmen, all the while roughly dragging Marissa across the cutter's deck. "Captain Dave? You and Paco get us away from your old deathtrap before she takes her final swan dive. Carl, you and Benny get on the radio and monitor it. We're making a run for freedom, boys! We'll run this barge into shore and get to the airport," he ginned. "With a little luck, we'll be in Jamaica by tomorrow afternoon."

Miss Marty and Arni Sims huddled out of sight behind a huge freezer. Miss Marty cuffed the doctor's shoulder and hissed. "*Jamaica?* We *can't* let him get away!"

Sims hissed back. "And, just *what* do you expect *me* to do about it? If you haven't noticed, the man *has a gun!!!*" He shook his head, returning his attention to the drama unfolding before them.

The crewmen went about the task of pirating the cutter, each man going to his station, leaving Dolf Grüber alone on the deck with his naked hostage.

Grüber jostled Marissa and growled menacingly, "Would you like to come to Jamaica with me, Fish-Lady? We'll sit on the beach, drink champagne, and eat the catch of the day. No. Wait a minute," he chuckled. "Strike that. We might accidentally eat one of your relatives."

In response, Marissa's scathing glare earned her a rough shove.

"Sit still and keep your mouth shut." Grüber pushed her down onto a deck bench. "Don't give me any trouble, and you *might* stay out of a tuna can."

"You are a *very* rude man," the mermaid murmured, still weak from her underwater imprisonment. "I wouldn't sit on a beach with you if you were the last man on Earth."

He gripped his chest, feigning pain. "Aurrggh! That hurts! 'Rude man' — you're a kick — that's what *you* are. You really cut me deep, Fish-Lady."

"Well, *someone* needs to cut you!" Miss Marty stepped from the freezer's shadow, still holding an excited and quivering Basil. "*Someone* needs to cut out your black heart, you *demon!*"

As the last word left the old lady's lips, Grüber's eyes flew open wide.

Miss Marty continued her tirade. "I'm *so* ashamed of you. You... you... *you dirty hoodlum!*" Basil emphasized his mistress' anger with two shrill barks.

Grüber's laughter was harsh and caustic. "*Good-gawd, woman!* Is your whole fam-damily in cahoots with the D.E.A.?" He laughed again, threw up his hands and shook his head. "Just my luck. First the Fish-Lady, here — then that little magician, then Daniel Tiger and the Coast Guard. And now, *you...* Senility's poster child. Who's next? Did you, by any chance, bring your precious Mr. Rogers along on this ship of fools?"

Miss Marty hushed her tiny dog. She whispered, "*What* did you say about the magician? *Jerri?* Is Jerri all right? What did you do to her? *You son-of-a —* "

"Now, now, now!" he scolded, mockingly. "Keep that up, and I might have to wash out your mouth. *Mustn't use potty words, Miss Marty.*"

The elderly woman hissed venom. "That's *Miss Sebastian* to you — *Bastard!!*"

Still stunning in his island-beach-bum attire, the man with the good-looks to rival a male-model's turned his gun on the woman who for years had treated him like a son. "How dramatic, *Miss* Sebastian. I suppose a man who'd shoot an old sweetheart like you might reasonably be called a bastard." He chuckled again. "But before you go to your long overdue heavenly reward, just let me say: Thanks. I *really* appreciated the money."

She huffed. "I paid you fairly, just as I've always paid my accountants..."

Grinning, he said, "Yes, I'd have to agree. The pay *was* good. But, I was talking about my five-finger bonus."

"I... I don't understand." She absentmindedly touched her amethyst necklace.

"I was robbing you *blind,* you old bat!"

Tears came to Miss Marty's eyes and she seemed to shrink in stature. "Oh, Eddie," she murmured, "*Eddie... why?*"

"See?" Grüber sneered, "I *said* you were senile! My name's not 'Eddie'. I'm Dolf. Remember?"

"Oh, Eddie... *my heart!!*" Miss Marty gasped, grabbed her chest, and stumbled to her left, dropping Basil into Marissa's arms. "Oh, dear!! *Eddie — help me!*" Trembling and shaking, the elderly woman fell to her knees, tightly gripping her purple-jeweled necklace as she folded in on herself, her head pointed toward the deck.

"Miss Marty!!!" Arni Sims screamed. He broke from his hiding place behind the freezer, rushing for his friend; but before the doctor could reach her, Grüber pushed him aside. Sims stumbled and fell at the feet of the nude woman. The two exchanged swift and silent glances while Marissa clutched Miss Marty's tiny dog in her arms, trying to keep a frantic Basil from running to his troubled mistress' side.

Taken by surprise, the accountant momentarily forgot himself and crouched over the stricken woman. "Is it your heart?" He demanded, "*Are you in pain?* What can I do?"

"Come close... closer," she whispered, drawing him in nearer to hear her faint words.

Concern etched Grüber's face as he hovered nearer the woman, who now was on her hands and knees, clutching both hands to her chest while nearly writhing on the cutter's deck. The old lady mumbled something incomprehensible causing the worried man to drape himself even lower over her back, his ear shoved nearer her lips.

"Tell me what's wrong," he urged, sounding much like his former persona of 'Dolf Grüber: Accountant'. He asked again, "Do you have any pain?"

"I got yer pain! *Right here!!*" She suddenly brought the heel of her left shoe up in a powerful jab to his crotch. "And, here's some more, for good measure!" she trilled as she double-kicked the same target. Then, the elderly lady swung both elbows back toward his face and trumpeted her victory, shouting: "*And here's one for my Eddie!*"

Marty Sebastian once more connected with her target, slamming Grüber's right temple and his left jaw, surprising and knocking the man backwards. His legs went out from under him and he fell hard to the deck, the impact so great, the air flew out of his lungs with a loud whoosh. Miss Marty's unexpected and

242

shocking chicanery caused Grüber to drop his gun, and the weapon skittered across the deck coming to rest beside Dr. Sims.

Coming up from her battle position to her knees, Miss Marty cried, "Don't just lie there, Arni!! Grab the gun! *Grab the gun!*" The words were barely out of her mouth when Grüber spun her around and reached for her neck.

Arni, being used to obeying his elderly friend, automatically leaped to action and practically threw himself on top of the weapon. But, hidden from the frantic doctor's view, Grüber got to his knees and opened his mouth wide. The charming accountant bared his shark-like teeth, his hands snaking out to encircle the elderly woman's neck.

Grüber moved closer, intent upon a soul-stealing kiss, his gold-green eyes swirling with fury.

Likewise on her knees, fearlessly staring evil in the eye, Miss Marty shoved her lavender pendant against the monster's cheek. For a mere moment, it glowed and sizzled upon his flawless skin. The old woman hissed, "I've eaten meaner things for breakfast than you, *Dybbuk!*" She shoved her steepled fingertips between Grüber's clinched hands, like a wedge, breaking his death grip on her throat. The old lady ended this battle move by simultaneously slamming her palms hard over both the man's ears. He quickly released her, once again falling back to the deck.

Grabbing his ears, Grüber shook his head, as if something in his skull had been knocked loose and now rattled around like a stray marble. He raised a hand, first to the heart-shaped mark left by Miss Marty's Lavender Magic — his fingertips seemingly reluctant to touch the spot — to a bump already swelling on the side of his head and he hissed venomously at the old woman. "How did you *know*, you old bat? How can you *see?*"

Miss Marty appeared none the worse for wear, in spite of her unaccustomed aerobics. She got to her feet and smoothed invisible wrinkles from her lavender dress. "Since the light was stolen from my life," she murmured, "I vowed to never... *never...* be blind to evil again. And a dybbuk is a dybbuk is a dybbuk."

"You old battle-ax...." he spat. "Where'd you learn *those* moves?"

Miss Marty giggled. "Don't you remember? *You* arranged for me to take that senior citizen's defense class... said you were worried for my safety."

"Just you wait, you vicious little witch," he snarled, *"that's* gonna earn you the first bullet. But not before your soul belongs to me."

"Be a mighty hard trick," Arni Sims chuckled, holding the gun in both shaking hands. "I may not know much about guns, but I *do* know which end to point at you."

Grüber grinned. *"You* wouldn't shoot me. Not such a *good* doctor dedicated to healing."

"Dedicated, my left foot." Sims wagged the gun at the man sprawled on the deck. "I'd shoot *anybody* trying to harm Miss Marty. Sure, I'd do my best to patch you up after... but, not being such a 'hot' shot, I can't promise I'd miss your vital organs. And, with my luck, you'd bleed out before we reached the marina." He shook his head. "No — I wouldn't risk it. You better stay right where you are — me being twitchy an' all." The doctor affected a tic and grinned at the man still rubbing the bruised knot on his temple.

"I want you to call your men out here," Sims ordered, "and tell them there's been a change of plans. Tell them there's been a mutiny, and you've been replaced." With his free hand, the doctor motioned to Miss Marty. "Help me remove my jacket," he asked. "Carefully. I don't want to take my eyes off this guy."

While Grüber glared up at the pair standing in front of him, the elderly woman eased Sims' arms from his jacket, and handed it back to the doctor. She asked, "You've chosen an odd moment to undress, don't you think, Arni? What do you want with this?"

"There's a lady here, who looks a little chilly," Sims grinned and offered his jacket to Marissa. "Cover up, before you catch your death."

She smiled shyly. "Thank you," she said, sliding her arms into the jacket. It swallowed her up, the doctor being taller and broader across the shoulders. "I'm sure I won't catch a cold. In fact, I feel safe now... now that you're here. I'm Marissa."

Still holding the gun on Grüber, Arni Sims blushed and stammered, "Sims... Arni. Doctor." His blush reddened, playing connect the dots with his freckles.

"Pleased to meet you, Sims Arni, Doctor." Marissa smiled again. Her jewel-blue eyes sparkled in the moonlight. "I'm Pendragon. Marissa. Artist."

Miss Marty gasped. "*Pendragon?* You must be Mark's — "

"Sister," the mermaid finished for the older woman. "Mark's my big brother." She focused her full attention on the man who'd loaned her his jacket. Marissa smiled and asked, "Do *you* know Mark?"

Sims returned the beautiful woman's smile. "He's one of my closest friends," he said.

"Oh, for cripes sake!" Grüber grumbled, resting his elbows on his knees as he sat on the deck. "Isn't *this* a sickening development? *What a pair!* Fish-Lady and Doctor Dweeb."

Miss Marty reached over and swatted the disgruntled man hard on the back of the head. "Hush, Grüber," she commanded. "I think it's *magical!*" She smiled at her young doctor and the pretty woman huddled inside his jacket.

"You would, wouldn't you?" Grüber groused. "It's just like you with your stupid Lavender Magic, and all. Wait a moment.... If Fish-Lady is Pendragon's *little sister* — "

Suddenly, the old woman shocked everyone on the deck by interrupting Grüber. "Hush, you!" Again, she swatted the grumbling man hard up side the head, and added a hissed warning to her 'love pat': "*Didn't I just tell you to hush?* No one wants to hear secrets — *yours included,* if you get my drift! If you don't want the world to know what you *REALLY* are — track you down and stake you like a vampire — then keep your mouth shut, *Demon!*" All at once, Miss Marty seemed to realize the words she nearly used and slapped both hands to her mouth in shock. "Oh... my... my *word!*" Shamed, she looked to her young doctor friend.

"Couldn't have said it better, myself, Miss Marty. Though, I might have called him something other than *demon*. This scum deserves every foul word that comes to mind. In fact, I think I'll add a few of my — " Sims paused, pointed and suddenly cried out, "*Look!* The shrimp boat's sinking!"

Grüber laughed sardonically. "Good! Perhaps," he growled, "at least *one* thing will go as planned tonight. It seems, for once, Benny actually carried out my orders and opened the seacock on that smelly deathtrap. Looks like it's 'Taps' for the Feds." The shrimper made little noise as it backed into the water; soon to be claimed by the night's blackness.

Miss Marty moaned, "Oh, Daniel!" Her trembling fingers found her lips as if trying to hold in her fear for her chauffeur and friend. She watched while the shrimper's front section raised out of the water, the bow almost pointing toward the night sky, suggesting a great amount of water filled the stern. The elderly woman and Doctor Sims both held their breath while the water closed over the tip of the bow.

Grüber grinned.

"I'll see that you pay for this, Grüber," Sims said quietly. "One of my best friends was on that boat."

Miss Marty openly wept, as she cried, "My dear, dear Daniel! You never hurt anybody! *I can't believe I'll never see you again!*"

"I wouldn't say... that," came a newly familiar voice from the back of the cutter. "You can't get rid... of me that... easily." Daniel Tiger climbed up from the dive platform, water dripping from his lavender uniform. One by one, the other men climbed from the water. Three saltwater-soggy Coast Guard officers hurried to take control of Grüber and his henchmen from a still shaken Arni Sims.

Richardson, the last man up the ladder, patted Arni Sims' cheek. "Good job, Doogie." He wearily winked, and added, "Seriously. You da' man, Doc."

Miss Marty hurried to the back of the cutter. "Daniel!" she chortled. "Daniel, my dear boy!" The elderly woman took the wet chauffeur into her arms for a long, grandmotherly, embrace.

"Thank God you're safe!" She sobbed into his shoulder, "What would I do without you? *What would I do* if you'd *drowned* on that horrible man's boat? It doesn't matter what you've done in the past! *It simply doesn't matter!* I'll get you the best lawyers money can buy." In her excitement, her words tumbled all over each other. "You'll have the best — "

Richardson slapped Tiger on the shoulder, interrupting the lavender-dressed man's reunion with Miss Marty. "We owe you our lives, man." Richardson coughed out the seawater he'd swallowed on his swim back to the cutter, and continued breathlessly. "If you hadn't known to kick out the panel into the engine room, we'd never have escaped that fish hole. We owe you big time. And don't think we'll forget it."

"Does that mean," Miss Marty disengaged herself from Daniel's embrace, "you'll let him go — you'll pardon him?" She looked hopefully to the D.E.A. agent and then to her chauffeur, both men dripping water all around. Gripping Richardson's wet arm, she roughly shook him. "Tell me! *Tell me* Daniel isn't going to prison!" She moaned, her eyes pleaded with the man, *"Please."*

Richardson laughed, shook his head, and grabbed Miss Marty in a rousing hug. "Miss Marty? I can assure you — *you kooky — you wonderful — you lavender lady* — your precious Daniel Tiger will *never* spend the night in prison." He grinned sheepishly, and continued, "I'm sorry I kept you two in the dark. I couldn't be sure you weren't connected, in some way, with Grüber and his smuggling." The agent shook his head again. "I know that sounds crazy, but I had the safety of one of my men to think of. Miss Sebastian, allow me to introduce you to Special Agent Rogers." He indicated a smiling Daniel. "Rogers. *Fred* Rogers. You know? Like that man on television?"

The elderly woman laughed in incredulous relief. She patted her handsome chauffeur's cheek, and trilled, "Oh, Daniel! I should have known. *I've always liked you just the way you are!"*

"So have I!" Jerri cried, pulling herself up the ladder. "Besides being a snappy dresser, he's a *fine* judge of character." She wicked the errant seawater from her eyes, all the while trilling a drumroll. "Lad*ieeees* and gentlemen!" She announced, "Fresh from her boffo-escape from a watery grave — allow me to present... for your entertainment... the Ama-*zing* Delaney!!!" Jerri bowed low.

Except for Grüber and his sullen henchmen, everyone on deck erupted in cheers and applause. Benny showed his displeasure by spitting in front of his officer-guard, who in turn offered the slovenly crewman a quick seat on the deck — by way of slamming his gun barrel into Benny's chest.

"Hey! Jerk! I just mopped that this morning! Have some couth, man!"

Miss Marty crowed her excitement, and clapped her hands. "*Jerri!!* You're safe!! Thank goodness!! Dolf wouldn't tell me where you were!" She crossed the deck in three steps, grabbed Jerri in a bear hug, and wept with relief. Finally, she released the girl she'd come to think of as a granddaughter, ran her hand over the girl's cheek and whispered her next question, "What happened?"

"*That* man!" Jerri pointed at Grüber still sprawled on the deck. "*That man tried to kill me!* Daniel warned me about him. Told me he was up to no good. Sorry, Daniel. I should have listened to you." Gently disengaging herself from Miss Marty, she hurried across the deck and enveloped the soggy chauffeur in her arms. "Daniel! You're my hero!"

"Right." Daniel grinned. "Sometimes even... a shy Striped Tiger can... catch a slimy snake in the grass."

Grüber hung his head and dramatically sighed.

"But... how did you know? How did you *really* know? What told you I was in danger tonight?"

Daniel murmured, "I found your... note. You... said you were diving... about six miles out."

"But — Daniel — the Gulf is so big!"

"Played a hunch," he explained. "Grüber always anchored around these... co... co... coordinates. Nightmares woke me — ran... ran... your room... to warn you about... him — found your note — "

" — and Daniel Striped Tiger saved the day!" Once again, Jerri hugged her friend. Abruptly, she pushed him away, then grabbed him again and cried out, "Daniel! *Daniel!!!* You talk! You *talk!!!*" As she practically danced on the balls of her feet, she was taken by surprise, being snatched from her friend's embrace.

This stranger swung her around, her feet clearing the deck by five inches, finally planting her steady again, he sealed the 'fun ride' with a full-on-the-mouth kiss. Grinning widely, he finally spoke. "Special Agent Sloan Richardson. Very pleased to meet ya, Ma'am. You don't know how pleased we all are. Rogers told me so much about you — "

"Whoa, cowboy!" Jerri interrupted. "First off — while I *do* appreciate the warm welcome... in fact, I'm thinking you must be my number one fan — hands off the goodies, `kay?" She freed herself from the grabby man in the still-dripping D.E.A. jacket. "Secondly — who's this *Rogers* guy who's so chatty about me?" Richardson laughed deep, his men joining in on his relieved humor.

He looked to Daniel, gave a silent nod to the lavender-dressed chauffeur, stood back, and watched as his missing — but newly found — agent again grabbed his magician friend. This time, the shy striped tiger gently bent the purple bikini-dressed girl backward, kissing her lips long and hard.

"The name's Rogers. Special Agent Fred Rogers, Ma'am. Welcome to the neighborhood. ...eh — Pilgrim."

Recovering from the kiss worthy of a romance novel cover, Jerri staggered in place and murmured a single word: "Wow." Grinning broadly, Daniel took her in his arms once again, rocking her from side to side. He chuckled. "Jerri — looks like... you're the one who's... dumbstruck, now."

Laughter erupted around the cutter's deck.

Noting this, Grüber and his crew scowled. "Shoulda' shut you up good," the accountant pointed at Daniel and snarled. "For good — *the first time* — Benny shoulda' finished the job before those bratty kids found you on the beach." He nodded at his crew, now cuffed, sitting in a huddled circle, guarded by two damp and burly officers. "Benny? *You hear me?* You shoulda' finished the job. You shoulda' finished the job on Tiger and Delaney, *both.* And don't forget the mer — don't forget Fish-Lady, here. Should have wasted her, too, while you were at it. Hell... if *I'd* have been even *half* smart, I'd've filleted *her* myself. You know? We had a good thing goin' with this gig. Brought in hundreds of thousands... month after month. *You* — " he again pointed at Daniel. "You had to go get nosey. We woulda' gotten away with it too — if it wasn't for you and them troublemakin' kids."

Daniel laughed, grinning at Richardson. "Sloan?" He said, "Doesn't that sound... like Scooby-Do just made a full... confession... in front of a whole... *boatload*... of government agents?"

"Sure does, Shaggy. Rruby-Rruby-*Rrrruuuu!!!*"

~o0o~

Chapter 30

Sitting on a bench beside the cutter's ladder, Jerri glanced around the deck at all the people she'd come to care about in the last two months. Miss Marty restrained a wiggling Basil. Still dressed in wet lavender, undercover D.E.A. agent Fred Rogers — Jerri *knew* she'd always think of the man as Daniel Striped Tiger — held a gun on Dolf Grüber and his crew. Dr. Arni Sims snugged his jacket around Marissa, trying his best to warm the naked lady. Jerri smiled to herself with the new knowledge of the mermaid's true identity.

Before my most fortunate accident, Jerri mused, *who'd have thought I'd be part of this extended family. And who'd have thought I'd care for them all like I do. ...and Mark. What about him?* Hoping no one noticed, she peered over the boat's rail, her eyes searching for the dark-haired merman hiding in the water's darkness.

Mark Pendragon floated at the side of the boat, keeping low in the water, taking care not to reveal himself to the Coast Guard and D.E.A. agents onboard the cutter. He caught Jerri looking his way and grinned. *Join me, Jerri,* he mouthed.

She nodded, smiled and held up her index finger. *Give me one moment,* Jerri signaled. *I'll be back!* She mimed throwing a quick kiss.

"Miss Marty!" she called. "I'm returning to the Little Lavender. Mark Pendragon's waiting there. I'm sure he's worried about me," she moved to the cutter's ladder. "Besides... between you and me," she turned to wink at the mermaid, "Pendragon isn't known for his seafaring skills. *Someone's* got to keep him from hitting an iceberg. As usual, The Amazing Delaney has the 'titanic' job of *rescuing a mere-man*." Again, she winked at Mark's sister, secretly relieved at the beautiful woman's revealed connection to the man she loved.

Miss Marty cried out: "Wait!" She hurried to Jerri's side. The feisty senior whispered, "You *really* don't want to leave the boat, do you?"

Jerri patted her friend's hand. "Don't worry about me, I'll be fine. I'd feel better knowing Pendragon isn't floating out here without me... eh... lost... *lost in the darkness*."

"You *can't* swim over to the Little Lavender," the elderly woman fretted. "You shouldn't. It's got to be over 500 yards away...." Her voice trailed off as she peered over the cutter's side. Pregnant seconds passed. Finally, she grinned, and nodded, "Of course. You know best, dear. We've all got our little secrets, don't we? Wave when you reach the Lavender?"

~oOo~

Hand in hand in the moonlight; they swam up to the Little Lavender. Jerri climbed the platform ladder and waved toward the cutter. The merman levered himself over the side of the boat until his hips rested in the pilot's seat. To assure he'd not transform, Mark allowed the tip of his tail to dangle in the water. Pulling the anchor up, he set the yellow deadweight on the floor behind him.

"Let's get back to shore," she said. "Daniel... I mean — *Fred Rogers* — will need our testimony about Grüber, and Arni's watching after your sister — *she's wonderful* — *by the way!* And Miss Marty is... is..."

"Is Miss Marty," he finished for her. He grinned that maddening grin she'd come to expect. "Don't worry about it," Mark said. "She knows you're safe with me. She knows I won't let anything happen to you. In fact, I wonder that she doesn't know *everything....*" They watched the cutter fire up its powerful engines and leave the area.

Jerri removed two sodas from the cooler, handed the merman one and shook her head. "That's not what I meant," she said, "I know I'm safe with you. But, I have a feeling I owe Miss

252

Marty an apology."

"An apology?" Mark asked. "Why? Did you sit on Basil?" He popped the top on the can and took a long drag from his soda.

She chuckled. "No. No, I didn't sit on her bratty dog. But, I feel I owe her an apology. Let's just leave it at that. Can we go back to shore, now?"

He turned the key and the boat's engine roared to life. Shoving the throttle forward, he yelled over the engine noise. "Your wish, my lady, is my command!" The boat reared up and shot through the water leaving a rooster-tail sparkling in the moonlight.

She stood behind the merman, her hands on his shoulders. The wind buffeted her hair and she grinned, feeling a lightness, a happiness, she'd lacked since the death of her father. Looking to the star-speckled sky, she sent her happy thoughts Heavenward: *Daddy, I fought the Dragon — and won!*

Mark tipped his head upward and looked back, seeing the joy in Jerri's face. Placing his hand over hers, he yelled, "Happy?"

She answered at the top of her lungs, "Yes... *oh, yes!* Much more than you could know!" She squeezed his hand and smiled down into his blue eyes, made more intense by the silver moonlight.

Suddenly, the engine choked, coughed and sputtered. Finally dying, the boat settled down onto the waves. Mark turned the key and was rewarded with the stuttered chug-chug growl of an unyielding starter. After fruitlessly trying the key three times, he slammed his fist down on the dashboard. Frustration showed visibly on his face.

Jerri asked, "What's wrong? Is it broke?"

"Broke?" he parroted. "*Is it broke?* What a mechanical question. *No.* I don't think it's *broke.*"

She sat down across from the merman, and threw up her hands. "You don't have to bite my head off! *I* didn't break it!"

Mark laughed. "I'm sorry. Of course, you didn't break it. In fact, it's *not* broken. I'm afraid I'll have to take the responsibility for this." He shook his head, sheepishly meeting her gaze as he murmured, "We've run out of gas."

"*Outta gas?*" She snapped. "*How* can we be outta *gas?* Pendragon, I don't believe you! What a cliché! Only *you* would be brazen enough to pull something so blatant and sophomoric as claiming to run outta gas in the *middle of the ocean!*"

He laughed again. "It may be blatant and sophomoric, or any other fifty-cent word you'd like to drag out of your Funk and Wagnalls." He sighed, and continued, "But, the sad truth is, I was so worried about Marissa, I forgot to check the tank. No big problem. Give me a minute... I'll radio on the ship-to-shore — " he picked up the microphone, pushed the buttons waiting for the familiar hissing static signaling an open line, and finished his meant-to-be-assuring-statement, " — and they'll come pick us up...."

The silence of the radiophone was deafening in the moonlight. Searching under the dashboard, Mark soon found the problem, and he held up a mishmash of jumbled wires, many bearing the tale-tell signs of sabotage. "Grüber's goons cut the wires," he groaned, "it'll take me hours or days to rewire this... I dunno what we're — "

"*What* are we gonna do *now?*" she wailed her interruption. "*Walk back?*"

He chuckled. "Lighten up! Or calm down! Up or down, one direction or the other. Delaney, this is so much *not* a disaster."

She looked at the merman with an incredulous expression on her face. "Not a disaster? *Not... a... disaster?* If being stranded in the dark in the middle of the Gulf of Mexico is *not* a disaster, then I'd like to know what a disaster *is* in your book!"

"Ahh, Delaney, Delaney." He shook his head in mock sorrow and reached out, touching the tip of Jerri's nose. "Oh, ye of little — *tiny* — faith." He grinned and said, "Have you forgotten whom you're stranded *with?* I may not be able to *walk* on water, but I don't have any problem *swimming* through it. We'll leave the Little Lavender out here; I can come back for it later." Mark dropped the anchor over the side, and said, "I'll take you home. But, just promise me one thing."

"And what would that one thing be?"

"Promise you'll leave all your sharp weapons here in the boat before I offer you a ride back to shore." He grinned.

"Ex*cuse* me? Are you suggesting we *swim* back to shore?" She scoffed, "*Are you for real?*"

Grinning his most wicked grin, the merman laughed again. "As you've so wisely pointed out... no. I'm *not* real. I am the stuff mythology is made of. My people have existed for hundreds of generations; and yet, Land-Walkers insist upon denying our existence."

"Land-Walkers?" She shook her head.

He touched the tip of her nose again. "*Yes, Delaney.* Land-Walkers. Like *you.* Like every other person you know. Your kind walked the Earth a few years before my people even discovered what all the fuss was about... having legs, that is."

Again, she shook her head. "*Your* kind? *My* people? You make it sound like you and I are worlds apart. I disagree. Just because my people originated from Europe, and your ancestors *swam* alongside the Mayflower; don't you get to thinking we're so very different from each other. Sure, you're able to survive underwater because of a unique hereditary trait. But, because of science and technology I can survive underwater for extended periods of time, myself. Thinking of you as less than human would be tantamount to thinking of myself as superhuman because I can convince an audience they've seen me chop a man's head off with a sharp guillotine." She shook her head again, and continued, "I learned a long time ago, things are not *always* what they seem to be."

He whispered so softly she nearly failed to hear him, "Are you trying to say you accept my idiosyncrasies?"

Jerri smiled. "*Now* who's using fifty-cent words?"

Mark grew serious, taking Jerri's hand in his. "Tell me. *Can* you accept me... will you accept all *this?*" He indicated his glistening tail. "Can you accept me, knowing my secret?"

"Yes."

He smiled and shook his head. "Just a yes? Are you sure

you don't want to save your answer for after you've awakened?"

Jerri giggled, playfully punching the merman in the chest. "No, my eyes are open... *now*. I'm sure I'm not dreaming." Catching a wicked gleam in his eyes, she quipped, "And don't even *think* about pinching me!"

He threw his head back and laughed with relief. "Jerri... You've made me *so* happy." Mark breathed out his happiness with his words. "You can't know how I've agonized these past few weeks. I knew if I told you, I'd never see you again."

"No such luck, Happy-Boy," she whispered, tracing his jawline. "You can't get rid of *me* so easily." The silence of the next few moments found the two gazing into each other's eyes. Jerri lost herself in the depths of his sparkling cobalt orbs. By the time he broke the spell by bringing her hand to his lips, she felt she'd lived a lifetime in his bottomless blue pools, and she feared she'd never want to leave. She cleared her throat and tried to keep her voice light, as she said, "Did I hear someone offer to give me a ride back to shore?"

"That depends."

She narrowed her eyes playfully. "On what?"

He smiled. "Ya got yer ticket punched?"

Jerri leaned in and kissed him full on the lips. Reluctantly pulling away, she whispered, "Hey — Happy-Boy! I've got your punched ticket *right here.*"

~o0o~

"Don't worry," he grinned. "I've not lost a passenger yet."

"So," she asked, swimming up beside the merman as he floated alongside the anchored boat, "how many Land-Walkers have you transported through the water?"

He rubbed his chin as if in deep thought. "Hhhhuummmm," he mused, "counting you? Well... I believe you'll be my first."

She crowed, "Oh! May I take that to mean, you're a virgin?"

"*Delaney!!*" He feigned indignation. "I'm shocked! And, quite frankly, I'm speechless! That you would have the *audacity* to inquire about my sexual status? *Why, I never!!*"

She leaned in, touching her nose to his and whispered,

256

"Well, aren't *we* just a little bit *TOUCHY?* I think you've got a lot of repressed rage!"

"Repress this," he growled. The merman pulled her closer, kissing Jerri slowly and deeply. Ending the kiss by whispering her name, Pendragon reclined into the warm water, taking her into his strong arms. She stretched out along the length of his body, her head and shoulders held above the water. With one flex of his wide tail, he swam effortlessly toward land; his body cutting a slim wake.

Jerri laughed, exhilarated by the swift ride in the pre-dawn air. She giggled, and said, "I've never felt so free!" Resting her elbows on his chest, she playfully traced his lips with a fingertip.

He raised his head, kissing her, the wake sending a fine spray around them both. She ended the long kiss reluctantly, lingering long and close to his face. The waning moonlight sparkled in his cobalt eyes, making it appear tiny sapphires frolicked there.

Mark's words were breathy. "You finally know my secret." He shook his head and accented his words with another kiss. "I've wanted to tell you for days, but — "

She interrupted with a quip, teasingly kissing the merman's nose. "But, you didn't know how to tell me, you had a little damsel fish on a string?"

Pendragon raised an eyebrow. "Is that some kind of Land-Walker humor? *A little damsel fish on a string?* Delaney," he frowned, "I'll have you know you're treading mighty close to an ethnic joke."

"Ethnic joke?" She shook her head. "What's ethnic jokes got to do with you... with your... *condition?* I believe if — "

"*You believe,*" he interrupted, wagging an admonishing finger under her nose, "just because I appear to be 'unreal', that I don't have an ethnic heritage. I'll have you know, Delaney, I'm descended from a very *old* family. I trace my ancestry back *many* centuries." He softened his stern expression with yet another kiss.

She grinned wickedly. "I was gonna say — before I was so rudely interrupted — that you, Sir, are to be celebrated, not mocked." She roughly pinched his forearm.

"Owww! What the — "

Jerri grinned. "I'm giving you notice, Mer-Boy. I'm the one who sees through your smoke and mirrors. Your... *illusions* won't work their magic on me. Don't even try to tell me you're related to the Arthurian Pendragons," she scoffed. "King Arthur was your great-grandfather. Yeah, right."

"Not quite," he grinned, the effortless undulations of his tail moving them through the water at a fast clip. "You know? As I recall, I don't think he was one of my *grandfathers*. No, I believe he was some kinda distant cousin."

The merman watched his passenger's face, searching her eyes for any hint of disbelief. When Jerri failed to react, he continued. "Actually, my family has a theory about the Lady of the Lake — the woman who gave King Arthur his Excalibur, and Morgan Le Fay. In some legends, mermaids are also referred to as "the Morgan" and Morgan Le Fay figures heavily in Arthurian Legend and perhaps — I'm reaching here — the Lady of the Lake and Morgan Le Fay are one and the same.

Anyhow, that whole branch of my family exclusively became Land-Walkers when the clan split and we lost track of each other." The faint cries of seabirds drifted through the darkness, providing a dreamy echo to his words.

"Interesting theory. A little *fishy*, but interesting." She grinned and laced her hands behind his head, pulling herself farther up his body until they were nose to nose. "Let's leave that fascinating discussion for a night when a Key West snowstorm knocks out HBO." She kissed the tip of his nose. "You're a fast swimmer," she whispered, enjoying his body writhing beneath her own. "Aren't you breaking some kind of law? Can't you get a ticket for operating a speeding water craft without a boat?"

He grinned. "Your job's to keep an eye out for the cops."

The water grew shallow, and Jerri said, "Look! I think I see shadowy palm trees on a white sand beach. We're getting close to land." She looked into his face, and offered, "Think you should slow down?"

He grinned again and gave her a quick kiss. "Take a deep breath, hold it and hold on tight."

Suddenly, he flipped Jerri over until she was fully underwater while he swam toward the beach. As they crested the backwash of his wake, Mark flipped over again onto his back, still holding her tightly in his arms. He effortlessly slid himself up on the beach, a surprised Jerri reclining on his body. The gentle surf bathed his tail and hips, keeping his lower body wet; while his shoulders rested on the soft white sand.

"Where are we?" she asked. "Look! There's somebody's house! *We're on someone's private beach! We can't stay here!*"

He held her closer and chuckled, smoothing her wet hair from her eyes. "Calm down, Delaney," Mark whispered. "It's *my* beach. That's *my* house. I've got a pretty good internal guidance system. *I said* I'd take you home, and I did. *My* home."

She looked around the little beach and smiled. "It's lovely," she murmured. "I... I didn't know if you lived on land or — "

He smirked and interrupted. "Or whether I lived in an underwater castle? That's *so Disney*. For your information, I don't pal-around with any singing and dancing crabs, either."

"Point taken," she said. "Believe me, I'd never mistake *you* for the Little Mermaid."

"Just to let you know, if it isn't obvious, yet, I don't have to get wet to survive," he grinned, playfully twirling an errant curl away from her eyes. "So, you don't have to worry about me drying out and blowing away. That's one of the old wives' tales about my people. That cartoon is about as accurate on my people as their version of Pocahontas was in regards to Native Americans. Colors of the wind, indeed."

"But, you've got to admit, the music *is* catchy," she teased. "To hell with accuracy when we can have music!"

"Grrrrr," Mark growled from deep in his throat, ending his non-threatening comment with a smile. He rolled his passenger off her perch on top of his scaly lower body onto the beach. Carefully moving over Jerri, he pressed her body into the wet sand. "*I'll* give you music," he whispered.

Their lips met, and she was shocked at her own eager response to the taste of his kiss. Her needy moans signaled Jerri's mounting pleasure; prompting Mark to shower kisses around her lips and along her jaw. As he kissed her neck, she gasped at his use of his lips as a greedy vehicle to carry him down her chest to the front clasp of her lavender bikini.

She closed her eyes and sighed deeply, her senses heightened by the sounds and scents all around her.

Pendragon slowly unfastened the simple clasp. Both of the swim top's bikini cups fell to her sides, and his wonder and appreciation of Jerri's near-nakedness came out in a rush. "So lovely... so beautiful," he breathed. His hand trembled as he brushed his fingertips over her skin. Shyly, Mark outlined the circle of her breast. A deep rumbling satisfaction rose up from his chest as he watched her nipple harden like a tiny pink marble.

Jerri closed her eyes and imagined being caressed by butterfly wings; his touch was so gentle and soft. Her breaths became sighs; her sigh quickly turned to moans as his lips took over for his quivering fingers.

Suckling reverently at her breasts; first one, then the other, his fingers caressed her waist.

Her needy fingers found their way into his damp long dark locks cascading around his shoulders. Pulling him closer, and closer still, she drifted into a warm ecstasy. *Oh, God!* The thoughts and feelings rushed together and jumbled in her mind, *I never knew such wonderful sensations existed! I feel like... I want this to last forever!*

Reluctantly leaving the sensuous thickness of his hair, her thirsty fingers caressed the length of his back. Jerri's soft tickling touch continued down to his scale-covered hips, and her hands lingered, wondering at the slick silkiness she found there. She clutched his hips, running her fingers over his merman skin.

His scales feel like fine silk! Jerri smiled at the tactile sensations her fingertips reported. *Oh, his body's glorious!*

Pausing but for a moment, he gently tugged on her bikini bottoms, and whispered in her ear, "Please... *please.*" He gazed into her eyes with a desperate pleading. "Let me show you my love..." he whispered. "Jerri, *please....*"

Her heart melted as she lost herself in his smoldering eyes. Jerri's wordless answer, a moan, fueled his passion. Slightly raising her hips, she allowed him to slowly slide the last piece of her swimsuit down her legs. Smiling shyly, she watched the dark-haired merman toss the tiny garment up on the beach. Likewise, the lavender swim pants landed beneath a palm tree.

Starting at her ankles, his fingers traced a returning path up her silky legs. Shivers of delight followed his touch, his hands traveling up her thighs, leaving tingles and chills in their wake.

The dark-haired man's gentle caress of her legs brought back memories of the first day she'd met Pendragon and his magical therapeutic massage technique that had left her breathless. *Yes,* she thought, *his hands ARE magical! The Magician's Guild should make him an honorary member. Ohhhhh! Yessss!!!*

The merman's satin touch found its destination; his eager questing fingers converged upon her most tender core and Jerri drew her breath in — *sharply.* Closing her eyes, she floated on wispy clouds of desire. Hypnotized by his touch, she tingled under his caressing fingertips. Lacing her fingers behind his head, she pulled Mark toward her; the better to meet his hungry lips.

Breathing her name, Pendragon took her hands, shepherded them, encouraging them to explore his body. Gently gripping her hand, he guided it to his hardness; his building passion bursting through the scales beneath his abdomen. This time, he was the one sharply drawing a breath in, as Jerri caressed his length.

"Too rough?" she whispered.

He moaned, "Nooo. Your touch... your touch is heavenly. I wish you would touch me forever."

Forever! she thought. *He said FOREVER. Yes! Oh, yes! Forever!! Please! Let it be, forever!* She marveled not only at her complete acceptance of the merman's love, but also the power and urgent need throbbing under her trembling fingers. She heard Mark moan again, felt his hands move downward, skimming either side of her body. And she suddenly realized that his maddening pause, when his fingers reached her thighs, meant a point of no return.

She wondered, *Am I truly ready to give myself completely? Ready to give up my life? Lose my freedom? Give myself to this magical man? ...oh, yes!! I simply can't deny it any longer... I want him! I need him!* And with these thoughts, her vow not to become involved with a man completely shattered. Her thoughts fragmented as his hands and lips continued their hungry search of her body.

His body imprisoned hers in a web of growing arousal. Tenderly parting her thighs, he lowered himself over her, guiding his engorged length to her welcoming body. His first tentative, but gentle, prods were greeted by her body's instinctive arch toward him. A low and lusty growl rumbled up from deep inside him as his thrusts became more urgent. His hard demanding passion battered against her tender moistness, and with one last urgent thrust, he gained entrance. In a bittersweet and fleetingly-fiery moment, he buried his length deep within her, and Jerri gasped in sweet agony. As swiftly as he'd invaded her tender body; he paused, not moving.

"Jerri — I... forgive me, Love," Mark whispered, tenderly tracing his finger over her lips. "I didn't realize you... I thought with all your bravado and teasing that you... that it wasn't your...."

"First time?" Jerri finished her lover's thought. "Yes...."

He caught a small tear before it could trail down her cheek. "I'm sorry. I've hurt you. I've been too rough," he groaned. "I'd never hurt you for the world. You know that, don't you?"

She smiled. "I know... I'm okay. Now. I love — "

" — love *you,*" Mark joined Jerri in her last words.

Enveloping her in his warm arms, he captured her lips in a deep, searching, kiss. Not pausing to break the kiss, he rose to his scaly knees; one hand supported her hips, the other, her back. Bringing her body up with him, still connected, skin-to-skin, they were one.

He gracefully scooted them both up farther on the beach, his glorious blue-green tail now out of the salty water. His tongue still greedily devouring her soft mouth, he gently lay her down, and slowly resumed his thrusting, while subtle changes overtook his lower body.

The iridescent colors of the merman's magnificent tail faded, the scales becoming less defined. Mere seconds brought the metamorphosis full circle, and Pendragon again possessed legs, long and tan.

She snuggled against his warm body as their legs intertwined. Another kiss greeted their new-found tempo, binding their bodies together.

Her body melted against his and her world was filled with him. Suddenly, she shattered into a million glowing stars, feeling drowned in a flood tide of her mind and body's liberation. In the seconds before dawn, the real world spun and careened on its axis. The waves of her soul-awakening ecstasy had not yet ebbed, when the morning sun finally crested through the palm trees, chasing the darkness from Pendragon's tiny island with its renewing light.

Jerri marveled silently as she gazed into his remarkable eyes, their blue-murky depths glittering in the early morning sunlight. *This man... this man who I once thought brash and crude. This gorgeous man loves me — Loves ME! And I believe I could stay in his arms forever. ...forever. Forever? ...like the psychic said? 'Look to ALL my potential lovers?' Mark? Ohhh... it was all in the cards...* She whispered her satisfaction in a breathless rush, "Mark... oh, Mark! I've never been so happy! You've given me — "

" — all my love," he whispered his hot breath into her ear, completing her thoughts with a shower of kisses down her neck. Gathering Jerri into his arms once more, he once again resumed his gentle rocking inside of her. Suddenly, his movements became urgent; and she was once more caught up in his passion, her own desire chasing and finally keeping tempo with his. For one singular moment, their bodies were in exquisite harmony with one another, and their mutual pleasure was pure and explosive.

They both breathed in deep soul-drenching drafts of dawn-kissed air, and his mouth once more sought hers. His chest crushed her breasts closer until their heartbeats sounded like a drum duet, beating to the count of the same drummer. "I love you, Jerri Delaney," he whispered between kisses, "don't even *think* of a life without me."

"Unthinkable," she answered him, reaching up to trace his perfect mouth. "I believe, without you, the sun would refuse to rise; the moon would hide its face in sorrow. I love you more than I thought possible. More than I ever thought — no — more than I ever *dreamed* I could *ever* love anybody! Once upon a time, I wholeheartedly believed the words my dear father used to tell me: 'Daughter, you need a man like a fish needs a bicycle'. But, Mark — I *need* you! Much more than any stupid fish needs any stupid bicycle. *I love you with every drop of magic within me, and with every morsel of my soul.*"

~o0o~

Chapter 31

Knocking on the door of the Southwestern decorated suite, Jerri waited for an answer. Moments later, masculine utterances emanated from inside the room.

"Come... Come in."

The voice was still unfamiliar to her, but she entered and closed the door. She found the man busying himself at the lighted curio cabinet. Miss Marty's chauffeur carefully packed marbles into a cardboard box, one by one, giving each one a close examination before wrapping them in tissue paper.

"Moving is... never easy." Daniel smiled, indicating the boxes containing his belongings.

Jerri crossed the room to his side. "Wow. I can't believe you're leaving Miss Marty."

"Not... not leaving," Daniel shook his head. "Just moving into my... own apartment. I'll always stay close to... Miss Marty... and my family." He removed a particularly stunning two-inch marble from the cabinet and handed it to Jerri. "This is a cobalt-blue, six-banded... onionskin Lutz. It's called a Lutz because of the gold... glitter embedded... with... with the color bands."

"It's lovely," Jerri commented. "Such vibrant colors." She held the large marble up to the light and marveled at the sparkling Lutz banding.

Daniel nodded his head. "Yes. It's doubly special to... me. This was the very first marble Miss Marty gave me. She started my collection." He smiled. "She is one *very special lady*. No way I could *really*... leave her. For as long as she'll have me, I'll be in her life and no matter what, she'll always and forever... *be in my heart.*"

"Why, Daniel Striped Tiger...." Jerri grinned and placed the special marble back in the agent's hand. "I didn't realize you were such a poet."

He smiled, kissed the marble, wrapped it and gently placed it in the packing box. "Chalk that bit of poetry up to Miss Marty Sebastian. She inspires... men... to reach beyond themselves."

Jerri reverently chose another marble from the cabinet. "Yeah... how true. Except for Grüber. The only thing that inspired Grüber about Miss Marty, was her money." Like the Lutz before, she inspected the smaller marble, holding it to the light. This one was a red, white and purple peppermint swirl with a three-banded 'cage' of yellow.

Daniel handed Jerri a lighted magnifying glass, so she could inspect the marble closer. "Yes, Grüber," he shook his head. "I *knew* he was... sc... scum. But to stoop so low as to embezzle from that sweet old lady. So many attempted murder charges on top of the smuggling business. You *do* know the attempted murder charges that'll put him away for good, right? When he locked our guys in the fish hold. You just don't *do* that to the DEA." He packed the peppermint swirl away and handed Jerri another marble. "Here's a very collectible contemporary marble." He shook his head and grinned. "Grüber's lucky I didn't recover my memory sooner. I'd have... *collected* him."

"What utter slime," Jerri said as she passed the magnifying glass over the large many colored swirl marble with a lattice encased dark core. She noticed a look of confusion cross the former chauffeur's face. Giggling, she held up the bright marble, and said, "No... I meant *Grüber* was slime. Not the marble. It's gorgeous! I can see why you collected them." She wrapped the marble herself, reverently placing it in the box.

Daniel chuckled and nodded his head. "Miss Marty is one savvy old woman. She realized from day one how frustrating... it would be to suddenly be mute. And between her and Dr. Sims, I immediately had a hobby. There were days and... nights where I thought I'd explode if I couldn't get the words out. After I started collecting... well... I had an outlet to express myself. And let me tell you, it was a life-saver."

"No," Jerri took another marble from the case. "Daniel, *you're* the life-saver. Finding my note and bringing help. I can never thank you enough. You saved my life... you saved *so* many lives that night."

"Mah pleasure, Pilgrim," he drawled. "Just doin' mah... job." He ended his spot-on John Wayne impression with a wide grin.

Standing on tiptoes, Jerri reached up and kissed the cheek of the shy Striped Tiger. "Well, I for one, feel safer having you on the job. Daniel? You're as special as any one of your pretty marbles, and I hope you stay close to me... and Mark while you're staying close to Miss Marty."

"You... got it, Amazing."

~o0o~

"Now, don't peek through that blindfold!" Miss Marty scolded. Basil yapped happily around his owner's ankles, as if the little dog picked up on the festive atmosphere of the small group of people gathered on the back patio. Conchita, Phyllis and Cory joined in on Jerri's farewell party.

After Miss Marty tied a black scarf around Jerri's head, covering her eyes, Fred Rogers led Jerri by the elbow. "Peek... not..." the recovering D.E.A. agent stammered, then chuckled and paused, concentrating on the words he reached for, because excitement still caused him to jumble his words. "No... no peeking."

Rogers, his former employer, and Mark Pendragon navigated the magician through the open pool-gate. Miss Marty laced her arm though Jerri's new fiancé's arm. She smiled pixie-like up at the much taller dark-haired man, her finger to her lips silencing him to keep her secret.

Rogers chuckled, tugging playfully on Jerri's elbow. He repeated, not stammering this time, "No peeking!"

"Okay, okay." Jerri patted his hand. "I get the picture! You don't have to hit me over the head with a two-by-four. I promise.

I'll not peek, even if you're leading me to the gallows. Hey! you're *not* leading me to my death or anything, are you?"

Miss Marty twittered her amusement. "Oh, you dear, sweet, crazy child! What a perverse sense of humor you have! We've brought you out here to praise you, not to bury you!" She grinned up at Pendragon, watching him enjoy the festivities.

"Jerri, we wouldn't harm *our little magician*," Mark smirked, clearly expecting a scathing rebuff from the blindfolded woman.

"Wait a minute, Happy-Boy!" Jerri pulled Rogers to a halt, sputtering, "I'm not anybody's... I'm not..." Her heated retort died down like a spent hurricane, and she grinned under her blindfold.

"What happened?" Mark teased, "Your anger fizzled out before you could even work up a good hissy-fit!"

Still blindfolded, Jerri groped the air for Pendragon's hand. "It just occurred to me," she smiled. "I can't say I'm nobody's little magician anymore. I'll be yours forever."

He leaned down and gently kissed her forehead. "If you'll have me," he whispered.

If I'll have you? As she silently mused, she stood on tiptoes, lips pursed, waiting for a lip kiss in her darkness. *IF I'll have you? When the cards practically screamed you — YOU are my destiny!* The awaited kiss came to her lips and she sighed. "I'll have you and no other," Jerri whispered.

"You two dears make a delightful couple." Miss Marty winked at the sexy physical therapist as she quipped at Jerri. "Sweetie, just humor us for another minute. Are we ready, Daniel? I mean — *Fred.*"

"Call... me Daniel, Miss... Marty. I'll always... be *Daniel* for you," he offered, leading his blindfolded magician friend around the pool, out the back gate to the tennis courts. "Jerri, care... careful. Okay. Blindfold off."

Jerri eagerly removed the black scarf and blinked her eyes against the bright tropical sunlight. There before her on the tennis court sat a massive box wrapped in bright purple paper, a two-foot-wide lavender ribbon encasing the baby elephant-sized carton. Stepping over to the box, Jerri touched the huge bow as if in awe. She murmured, "What?" A smile of childlike joy spread across her face. "What?" she repeated. "What?"

Rogers laughed heartily and said, "Jerri... you... you sound like... *a light bulb!* Watt-Watt-Watt!"

Running her hand over the lavender bow, Jerri grinned back at the man she'd always remember as Daniel Striped Tiger, the namesake of the genial little puppet on her now favorite television show. "Daniel, you know, it's good to hear your lovely voice. But, take care you don't become a smart aleck... *like me.*" She winked at her friend to show him she was teasing.

"Oh, I can't wait any longer!" Miss Marty clapped her hands together in anticipation. Basil took his mistress' excitement to mean she desired a command performance; the little dog stood on his hind legs and pirouetted a tiny canine ballet, all the while accompanying himself with vigorous yaps and barks.

The elderly woman giggled at the sight of her dancing pet. "It appears," she said, "Basil can't wait either! Open it, Jerri! Open it! The suspense is killing us! Daniel, cut the ribbon for her!"

The delighted D.E.A. agent used his pocketknife to slit the ribbon snugly holding the sides of the purple-papered box. Pulling the lavender ribbon from the top of the carton, Rogers smiled and placed Jerri's hand on the side of the box. "You... you should do... the honors." He helped her lower the side of the box to the ground, then he flipped the top of the heavy wooden box to the other side of the ground. The end sections of the big carton followed suit, leaving the surprise totally revealed.

"*Baby!!!*" Jerri yelped. "It's Baby! It's *my* Baby! *It's my Baby!!!*"

Pendragon leaned down and stage whispered into Miss Marty's ear: "She *was* checked for head injuries, right?"

The pixie-like senior laughed and lightly cuffed Mark's shoulder. "Oh, go on, Good-Lookin'. Jerri's as sane as you or I... at least, she's as sane as *me.* I've heard tell some people say some mighty *fishy* things about you. But, don't worry your pretty head over it. Your secret's safe with me." Miss Marty winked.

269

Pendragon glanced warily at his feisty friend, as if something told him perhaps he should pursue the old woman's hints of his aquatic secrets, when Jerri suddenly cried out.

"*It's lavender!!!*"

Miss Marty released Mark's arm and stepped up to Jerri as the younger woman caressed the Bug-eye's hood. The elderly philanthropist whispered, "Is there a problem, dear?"

"It's lavender!" Jerri repeated, with a shout, "Baby's *lavender!!!*"

"Of course, dear girl. Baby's lavender." The older woman suddenly appeared contrite. "Oh, my! I'm sorry if you don't like Baby's new color. Phyllis had a devil of a time keeping my secret, but I had your precious car completely repaired and then I had it painted lavender so you would always have fond memories of me."

Jerri twirled around and grabbed up Miss Marty in a hug. "Don't be silly! Forget you? Never in a million years!" Before she released her elderly benefactress, she kissed the older woman on her grandmother-soft cheek and babbled her glee. "I love it! I'll treasure it forever! Baby's never looked so good! Thank-You!"

The old woman suddenly burst into tears.

"What's wrong?" Jerri took her friend into her arms again. "Were you so afraid I'd not like the color?"

Miss Marty daubed at her eyes with a lacy hanky and shook her head. "No...." She whimpered. "No, that's not it *at all.* Cars can *always* be repainted. I was just dreading this time. I was dreading this *day,* because I knew when I handed Baby back to you, you'd leave... you'd leave your *fam-i-ly!!*" By her last words, her whimpers had grown into full-fledged sobs.

This time, Jerri burst into tears. She took the old woman into her arms and sobbed the words, "Do you *really* consider me a member of your family?"

"Good Gravy, Pendragon," Rogers whispered to the physical therapist. "We better... break... break... out the life jackets. It's get... getting deep here." The handsome D.E.A. Agent surreptitiously caught an errant tear from his own eye.

Mark nodded his head in agreement, all the while wondering if Miss Marty had shared her rumors and suspicions with her chauffeur. He watched Jerri and the old woman dry each other's tears, and smiled. "I'm sure *my* secret's safe... for now," he murmured.

Pleading with the tiny magician, Miss Marty lightly shook the girl she'd come to think of a granddaughter. "Promise me you'll never leave Marathon?"

Jerri smiled. "Just try and run me off. If I have my way, The Amazing Delaney's home base will always be here in Miss Marty's Purple Plantation. You're one class-act I *don't* want to escape!"

~o0o~

Miss Marty hesitated as she opened the door to the Victorian suite. Most every flat surface held art-glass filled with the dowager's 'Lavender Magic' and lavender scent filled the air. "I keep my most precious memories in this room."

She led Jerri into the elegant sitting parlor and both women paused under the large painting. "Sometime's it's hard to look at this painting without feeling pain. Mind numbing pain. But, sometimes... I come into this room, just to feel his presence."

Gazing up at the loving couple captured on the canvas, Jerri kept her silence, as if she knew she stood in a sacred place. Miss Marty broke the reverence by removing a Mother-Of-Pearl inlaid box from its honored place on the mantle in front of the portrait. She opened it to reveal the jeweled pendant Jerri had seen her benefactress wear many times. The purple heart hung on an elaborate chain, the same necklace she wore in the portrait, when her hair was long and golden.

Jerri smiled and secretly squeezed her left hand where the pendant had rested when she'd made her frantic ascent. *Yes... It's back where it belongs. Truly magic in that little lavender heart.*

Miss Marty removed the exquisite necklace from its nesting place. It was a large amethyst caught in a woven cage of silver wire. "Jerri, this treasure is all I have left of my Eddie. He called it our '*Lavender Magic*'." She chuckled softly, and murmured, "He

271

said... if we were ever parted, I should wear lavender — *his favorite color* — hold the necklace and know I was holding his heart. I swear... even after all these years, when I'm feeling all alone, all I have to do is lock myself in this room, hold the Lavender Magic, and talk to my Eddie." She gazed lovingly up at his image. "When I do, it's as if he's right here at my side."

She draped the necklace around her neck, twirling to catch her reflection in the massive mirror. "Though you've seen me wear it, I don't wear it very often, nor visit it every day. To do so would somehow diminish its power... *its magic.*"

"That's so beautiful! *Magical!*" She looked over her friend's shoulder into the mirror. "To know a man loved me so completely," her voice a whisper.

"Yes... we *were* so much in love." The old lady reached up to the canvas, her fingers lightly touching the portrait. She continued, her voice a whisper, "So very *much* in love. He was the light in my life. Eddie was my lifelong soul-mate. Eddie was... Eddie was my fiancé."

Silent moments filled the room, until Jerri thought she could almost feel Miss Marty's pain. Finally, she reached out and took the old lady's hand in hers. She spoke quietly. "Fiancé?"

Miss Marty nodded sadly. "It was in the early thirties," she said. "As unlikely a couple as we were, Eddie and I were so much in love. Eddie was on the force, months away from getting his detective's badge...." She paused, as if momentarily losing herself to the past.

Suddenly, the old woman took a deep breath and continued her narrative. "I lost my Eddie on our wedding day." Her voice quivered, a tear fell and she paused again. "I'm sorry, Jerri," Miss Marty whispered, "I *still* find it hard to speak of that horrible day."

"You don't have to tell me if you don't want to."

The white-haired senior shook her head. "No... I *want* to. It's important that you know. It's difficult, but I *must* tell you. Bear with me, dear."

Jerri squeezed her hand, "Take your time."

The elderly woman's gaze fell on the mantle portrait. Minutes passed. "Our wedding day...." Miss Marty began again. "New York. A beautiful autumn day. Not a cloud in the sky. I carried a huge bouquet of violets and babies' breath. I was in my white tatted-lace wedding gown. The gown I'm wearing in the portrait. It seemed the train trailed a mile behind me." She paused and smiled. "*Huge* wedding." She shook her head. "My father... my *wonderful* father... spared no expense. It was the happiest day of my life." She took another deep breath.

"Father and I waited with the priest," she continued, "ready to walk down the aisle. I looked out the church window and saw my Eddie coming up the front steps. He'd been delayed, as usual; but I wasn't worried. ...I wasn't worried. ...stupid me. Coming up the church steps, he looked *so* handsome in his black tuxedo. Eddie paused before opening the church doors, glanced toward the window and saw me."

She chuckled, without a trace of humor. "You know the old superstition? The groom isn't supposed to see the bride before the ceremony?" She sadly smiled. "Well... when my eyes met Eddie's... an ominous premonition screamed at me — *it screamed at me, Jerri* — sending a chill up my spine like ice water being poured over my grave. A big black 'Studie' — that's an old Studebaker — already well on its way to being an antique at that time, by the way — anyhow... this huge ugly car rounded the corner and I knew in that microsecond...."

She balled her fists in impotent frustration, and continued, "*I just knew* — Eddie and I were *never* to be married. I opened my mouth to give Eddie warning when the shots rang out." Miss Marty whispered, nearly spitting her words, as if she truly hated to even give them voice: "They gunned down my fiancé on the steps of St. Luke's Cathedral."

"How horrible!" Jerri interjected, her hands flying to her face.

"What I remember from that day...." Miss Marty fingered the Lavender Magic, her voice catching as if she relived the most horrendous moments of her life. "What I *really* remember — my three most *vivid* memories — were the sound of someone screaming and screaming — " a strange smile crossed her face and she shook her head, " — *must have been me.* And I remember Eddie's red, red blood gushing from his body... I remember Eddie's last words — Simply 'Lavender Magic' and nothing more... and finally... the self-satisfied smile on my father's face." She choked back tears, looked at Jerri, then turned her face back to the portrait. Whispering, barely loud enough to be heard, she said, "I fear... I fear... I never forgave Father."

"Your father? What did your *father* have to do with it?"

"Remember I told you Eddie was a cop." Miss Marty spoke the words as a statement and waited for Jerri to nod before continuing. "Yes, he was a cop. A good cop. The best. And I should have known when my father gave Eddie his blessing, he had a hidden plan."

"Are you saying your father had your fiancé *murdered?*"

"*Yes,*" Miss Marty emphatically stated. "*Father ordered my Eddie's death.* You see, Father was the head of the local organized crime family."

Jerri sympathetically moaned, "Oh, no!"

Miss Marty looked at Jerri and nodded her head. "Yes," she whispered. "To look at him, you never would have known Father was such a dangerous man. He was *very* handsome, with dancing eyes. He looked a little bit like Cary Grant. But behind those dancing eyes lived a monster. A cold-blooded killer."

"What did you do?"

"Well... first thing I did was to go insane for about a year," the old lady chuckled sardonically. "Then, after my release from the sanitarium, I got my revenge."

"You *killed* your father?"

Miss Marty placed her fingertips to her lips in shock. "Oh, no!! *Dear girl, no!* That would have been a sin! I got my revenge, but it took me years and years. *Long* after my father died."

"I'm afraid you've lost me. I don't understand, what — "

"Don't you see?" the old woman interrupted. "*Everything* my father stood for was evil. Everything the man touched was dirty. So I dedicated my life to being the best daughter I could be. For years, I stood by that awful man's side. I was the dutiful child. Whatever Father said, I did. Except for one thing. I never married. I refused all the suitors my father chose for me. His fondest wish was for me to marry into the 'family' before his death. But, I held out, and my reward was the disappointment in his eyes on the night that evil man died in bed. Can you believe I held that monster's hand on the night he died?"

"Of course you did," she patted the old lady's hand, "after all, he was *still* your father. I'm sure you'll — "

"Oh, *I'm* sure I'll burn in Hell someday," Miss Marty interrupted again. "I'm sure that's my final destination — because mere moments before his final breath, I whispered my hate for him in his ear and I *smiled* when the light went out in his evil eyes. I swear, I relished every second of his final pain and suffering. Every moan, every tear, every indignity... I *relished* it, Jerri."

"And that was your revenge?"

Miss Marty smiled. "No. That, my dear, was just the icing on the cake." She chuckled. "Can you imagine, being sent to Hell for a little icing on the cake? But, I'd be lying if I told you I was in the least sad when my father died. If I could've, I'd have danced on his grave. But, since I couldn't do that in a polite society, I did the next best thing."

Jerri shook her head. "And what could that have been?"

"I hit him, figuratively, where it would hurt him most." The old lady smiled and took a sip of her orange juice. "Since I was my father's only child, I inherited everything. Not bragging in the least, but the inheritance was — *even in today's numbers* — far more than *you,* my dear girl, can possibly imagine. And, to think... *every red penny blood-stained....* But within a few years, I doubled, tripled and quadrupled Father's filthy fortune."

"You've lost me, again," Jerri sighed. "Just *how* did expanding your father's money get back at him?"

"*Think,* Jerri," the old lady coaxed. "Just *think* about it. I've told you, my father was pure evil; everything he touched was dirty. So, after I snowballed his dirty treasure, I moved down here to Florida and tried everything in my power to give Mother Teresa a run for her money."

The twinkle returned to her eyes, and she again caressed the necklace. "For the last fifty years or so," Miss Marty said, "Father's money has made a lot of people *very* happy and with any luck, the old bastard is spinning in his grave. So, Amazing Jerri Delaney — *that's* why Miss Marty Sebastian is a devoted follower of the Tao of Fred. Any questions?"

Jerri glanced over Miss Marty's shoulder for one final look at her benefactress' handsome fiancée, represented in the wedding portrait as eternally young — eternally Marty Sebastian's hero. For one brief moment, tiny fairy lights danced around his black hair and Jerri blinked. *Did I see that? Naw....*

"Jerri, dear — questions?"

"Only one."

"And that is?"

Jerri smiled. She murmured as if she were ashamed, "Can you forgive me? I had you pegged for a lunatic."

"Ahh, yes...." the pixieish elder chortled. "A lavender loony," Miss Marty said. "I believe *those* were your words?"

"Allow me a second question?"

"Yes, dear?"

Jerri grinned sheepishly. "Does Cook serve crow?"

Peals of jolly laughter fell from the old lady's lips, and she grabbed Jerri up in her arms. "Jerri, Jerri, oh, Jerri! What a delight you are to this old Lavender Loony! You get on to bed, now. You've got a big day tomorrow," Miss Marty said. "We all do!"

Jerri kissed her grandmotherly benefactress' cheek and turned to leave the room, pulling the door closed. Suddenly, one more question came to her mind and she silently reopened the door.

Opening her mouth to address Miss Marty, Jerri automatically made to close it when she witnessed the old woman dancing a slow waltz in the arms of a handsome man. It was as if Miss Marty's fiancé had stepped down from the portrait over the fireplace. It appeared so... but he wasn't as *solid-looking* as the man in the portrait.

Miss Marty's back was to the door and for a split second Jerri locked eyes with Eddie. His wispy arms were around his lady love. He winked at Jerri and smiled, causing her eyes to fly open in alarm. She quietly shut the door on the two lovers.

"Ghosts?" Jerri murmured. "*Ghosts?*" She still gripped the doorknob. "Oh, right! Crystal magic, tunnels of pure light, dybbuks, mermaids and mermen. I think it's a little late to get my panties in a knot about a *ghost*...." She shook her head, smiled and quietly made her way to her room.

~o0o~

A good hour before sunset, Mallory Square was already crowded. Every day, nearly two hours before the sun took its nightly plunge into the Gulf of Mexico, at the southern-most point of continental American shore, the vendors and street performers took up their stations on the decorative stone-tiled dockside promenade.

There would be performing housecats, tightrope walking dogs, people who painted themselves completely silver or white to stand dead still as if they were statues, jugglers, small time magicians, amateur musicians and other talented, but eccentric, Mallory Square performers. Before the evening was over, people would be feted, fed, thrilled and entertained, simply for the price of parting with a dollar bill or spare change tossed into an overturned waiting hat or open coffee can.

Standing at the bed and breakfast's second floor window, overlooking the center of the Square, Jerri pulled back the filmy white curtain and gazed down on what was arguably the most famous gathering of sun worshipers in the world. "There's over five hundred people down there, easy," she murmured.

People of all races and nationalities milled around the Square, enjoying margaritas topped with real Key Limes and other colorful 'Boat-drinks'. The festive crowd gave the Square an ambiance of Carnival.

The bedroom door opened and a lavender dressed Sandy Kersey bustled into the room, her arms overflowing with wedding dress. "*Jerrrrrrrrri!*" came the Maid-of-Honor's brassy cry. "Come away from that window! You know it's bad luck for the bride to be seen in her underwear!"

Jerri laughed, but stepped away from the window. "I think you've got your bad omens bass-ackwards, Sandy," she giggled. "Doesn't that old superstition have something to do with the bridegroom?"

Sandy hung the long elegant dress in the corner. She put her finger to her chin as if pondering the problem. "Okay... how's this? Before the ceremony, it's bad luck to see the bridegroom in the *bride's* underwear. In fact, I'd say that's very bad luck. *Very* bad luck, indeed."

"Sandy...." Jerri grinned. "You are *such* a nut. You know? I'm beginning to understand this *thing* you have with Mongo. Both of you are certifiable. Right?" She crossed the room to stand in front of her still-hanging wedding gown.

"Oh, Sandy," she whispered, "*have you ever seen anything so beautiful?*" Jerri reached out and brushed her fingertips over the white antique lace. A strand of diamonds and amethyst stones were fastened over the bodice, like a fine necklace draping the low-cut neckline. A Juliet-crown of matching diamonds and amethysts rested on a table beside the dress, a long veil trailed to the floor. The gown was fashioned entirely of old Irish lace. Almost as if speaking to herself, Jerri murmured, "This dress looks strangely familiar...."

A polite knocking on the door caught Jerri's attention. "Come in," she offered, "if you're not Mark, Mongo or *any other man.*"

"Mark or Mongo?" Miss Marty's familiar giggles announced her arrival. "Now, Jerri — *dear girl!* Why would Mark or Mongo — either one — interrupt the dressing of the bride?" The old lady hurried through the bedroom door, a lavender-ribbon-adorned Basil snug in her arms. "Sandy? Are we going to have this blushing bride dressed in time to walk down the aisle?"

"I don't see why not," Sandy chuckled. "Now that *you're* here, Phyllis, Conchita, Marissa and I will have this girl put together in no time!" As if hearing their names, the secretary, the maid and Mark's sister came out of the spacious bathroom wearing matching sleeveless sarong-style lavender gauze bridesmaid's gowns.

Her long blond hair pulled up into a relaxed formal twist with tiny ringlets falling around her face, Phyllis sweetly smiled and her usual professional demeanor disappeared. "We're ready to get this show on the road!" she cried. "Come on, Conchita! Let's show these people how it's done." Between the two ladies, they removed the jewel-encrusted gown from its hanger and helped Jerri step into the back of the dress.

Fastening the wedding gown closed, Conchita patted Jerri's cheek. "Ah, chaquita... mí muchacha. Tú tenga muy bonita. You look very lovely. Qué una novia hermosa que usted es! Te quiero quiera que usted fuera mi propia hija."

Jerri smiled and lightly brush-kissed the Cuban woman on the cheek. "How sweet. You think of me like a daughter — mi madre latina. And I think of you like a mother. You and Miss Marty will *always* be close to my heart.

The formal-dressed maid intercepted a tear before it could make its way down her own cheek. "Mi nena rubia pequeña," she whispered, daubing a lavender handkerchief under her eye. Purposely brightening, Conchita suddenly smiled and announced: "Now we need the things of the four!"

"The things of the four?" Jerri asked, "What *things?*"

Sandy lifted the Juliet cap and placed it on Jerri's short blonde hair. "I believe she must mean 'something old, something new, et cetera, et cetera'. Right, Conchita?" Sandy smiled at the middle-aged maid as she smoothed out the veil hanging down Jerri's back.

"Sí," Conchita beamed. "I have something new." She handed Jerri a delicately embroidered lavender silk handkerchief. "Put inside bra, on left side. So will always bring a remember... *remembrance* — us — us keep close to heart."

Again, Jerri kissed the air beside the maid's cheek, careful not to muss each other's makeup, then she stuck the tiny kerchief inside her clothing. She smiled, and whispered, "How could I forget any *one* of you dear people?"

Phyllis chimed in next. "I've got you something old!" She held up a tiny silver hat-pin, which she used to snugly fasten the Juliet cap to Jerri's head. "I collect antique hat-pins. This one is over a hundred and fifty-years old. I think *that* qualifies it to be in this wedding."

Next, Sandy came forward with a blue garter belt, two tiny pair of fuzzy pink and blue booties dangled from it, strung together with a yellow ribbon. "It's obvious what *these* are for," she teased as she lifted the front of Jerri's gown and slipped it over her foot, sliding it up to her thigh. "For luck and good times. Plus — something blue... *and pink.*" She grinned as she teased her friend. "Knowing you, Jerri, you'll put them on a yappy poodle-dog."

"Got that right!" Jerri quipped. "The only baby I want right now is my car."

Marissa stepped up and carefully hugged her soon-to-be sister-in-law. "I don't have anything old or new, borrowed, or blue. But, I do have this." She handed Jerri a tiny heart-shaped box, wrapped in white paper, adorned with a silver bow. "It's to celebrate your new life and to welcome you to our family. I'll be proud to call you my sister."

Jerri opened the box and found a tiny silver merman, a faceted amethyst in his clasped hands. "It's lovely," she said. "Is it a pin? Necklace?" She removed it from the box.

"It's an ear wrap," Marissa smiled, taking the earpiece from Jerri. She fastened the ear drape over Jerri's right ear. "Mark asked me to give this to you. Wear this and remember your new family, Jerri. Wear this, and never forget the heritage you're marrying into, *forevermore.*"

"Then I'll think of you... and Mark... and my new family every day." Jerri vowed, "*I'll wear it always.*"

"Now it's my turn," Miss Marty crowed. "Now for something borrowed. How's this?" The tiny senior sat Basil on the floor and removed the lavender necklace from around her own neck. "This is my most precious keepsake... *the real thing.* It doesn't have much value monetarily, it's just a simple amethyst stone on a silver chain, but it's worth more to me than all my diamonds put together. I'd be honored if you'd wear it when you become Mrs. Mark Pendragon. It was meant to dwell among love. This wonderful evening, will you wear it for me, Jerri-Dear? For me... *For me and my Eddie?*" She closed the necklace's clasp around Jerri's neck.

Jerri reverently held the lavender bauble in her hand, feeling the warmth transferred from Miss Marty's body to her own. "I don't have the words to tell you how honored I feel that you would trust me with this precious treasure, Miss Marty. I... I love you. I love you very much." The two women hugged gently, mindful of the delicate clothes they both wore.

"Now, now, now!" Sandy scolded, "If you two keep up that talk, we'll all be blubbering all over these fancy wedding duds." She discretely daubed a tear from her own eye.

"Miss Marty," Jerri whispered. "This dress is *so* familiar." She indicated the gown she wore. "Where did you find it?"

Miss Marty teared up and reached for her own lavender hanky. "I had that dress made special for *you,* Jerri. It's an exact copy of my own wedding gown. Just like the one I wore so many, many years ago. I couldn't give you the original. It was ruined when... when...."

"Yes. I remember," Jerri patted her friend's hand. "Isn't my wearing this gown going to bring back hurtful memories?" She waited for her grandmotherly benefactress to compose herself.

After a few seconds, Miss Marty smiled sadly. "Sure, there's painful memories. But, my Eddie helped me design that dress. He wanted more than anything for me to be wearing it and waiting at the altar for him. That never happened. But, today, in a tiny way, I can change history. Love can win, after all. In a few moments, when you say your vows to your own true love, remember two other people... who were *so* much in love... *so* many years ago."

Folding the precious necklace into her hand, Jerri clutched it to her chest and vowed, "I will. *I promise,* I will."

~o0o~

Chapter 33

At the sound of the Jamaican steel-drum and trumpet band striking up 'The Wedding March', the bed and breakfast's double doors opened and Sandy Kersey stepped out on the arm of a lavender tuxedo-wearing, smartly-dressed Mongo. Phyllis and Cory followed the engaged pair, walking arm in arm. Then came Conchita and Sloan Richardson, and Marissa with Arni Sims.

The women of the wedding party each sported the same sarong-style lavender gauze gown, a long lavender scarf trailed from each lady's neck, while the men complemented the ladies in their lavender tuxedos. The couples proceeded across the walkway to the stone tile-decorated dock, where they took their positions in front of the minister, standing with his back to the Gulf of Mexico. Mark Pendragon waited for his bride on the right side of the altar, his eyes searching the still open doors of the bed and breakfast.

Two sections of lavender ribbon-decorated folding chairs adorned the dock, leaving an aisle down the middle, covered by a lavender carpet-runner. Miss Marty was seated as the mother-of-the-bride. Basil, decked out in his doggy-finery, squirmed in the old lady's arms.

Suddenly, the trumpets blared a salute; all eyes turned to the open doors of the bed and breakfast and a very nervous Jerri stepped across the threshold on the arm of Fred Rogers, a.k.a. Daniel Striped Tiger. The wedding gown's diamonds and amethysts caught the glow of the setting sun and a rainbow enveloped the bride and the man who would give her away.

Jerri searched out Mark's face and she watched him exhale,

an expression of pure love settling over him. Though she remained nervous, her heart melted and she touched the tiny silver merman who rested over her right ear. Across the dock, Mark caught the signal and winked. Jerri smiled again, and squeezed Fred Roger's arm.

"Nervous, Jerri?" Fred asked. "You can... *still* back out. It's not too late."

"Not on your life, Daniel," Jerri whispered, adjusting her white roses and lavender sprigs bridal bouquet. "*Not... on... your... life.* But, I *am* nervous. I'm shaking like a leaf."

The former chauffeur laid his hand on her arm in a comforting gesture. "You'll do fine," he said. "From looking at you, I'd never know you were heading toward the... guillotine."

"Oh, great," Jerri groused. "So, I get an official D.E.A. *comedian* to give me away...." She smiled at her friend. They stepped onto a long lavender carpet that led all the way to the altar.

Put one foot in front of the other, Jerri reminded herself as they continued the bridal march to the altar. *You want to do this — you REALLY want to do this. Daddy? I know you always told me I didn't need a man. You always said a woman was complete in herself. But... just look at that man over there. He loves me! It's written all over his face. S*he smiled at her fiancé waiting for her beside the altar. *Daddy — he loves me. He truly loves me. And I truly love him. Everything would be perfect... if only you were here with me.*

She glanced at her surrogate grandmother, Miss Marty, and wondered at the significance of the empty chair on the old woman's left. Catching the briefest glimpse of Eddie sitting in the empty chair, Jerri remembered the Key West psychic's life-affirming words. All at once, she realized Miss Marty's Eddie *truly* occupied that particular seat. Then just as suddenly, the sure notion came to her — her father was *just as much* in attendance as Eddie. A new smile blossomed on her lips and she again sent a thought to the father she missed every single day: *So glad you could make it, Daddy!*

Reaching the altar, Jerri handed her wedding bouquet to Sandy and turned to clasp hands with Mark. "Here I am... for better or worse," she whispered.

"You're beautiful," he whispered in return. "So lovely. Nervous?"

"No," she nodded, a smile on her face, vowing to herself this would be the *last* time she lied to this man.

"Yeah. Me too — you little liar." He grinned and touched the tip of her nose. "It's not too late to back out, you know...."

Jerri tugged on her right ear, jostling the silver merman who rested there. "Have you been talking to Daniel? Not on your life, Happy-Boy. You're all mine from here on out. Let's get this show on the road!" She winked at the love of her life and whispered, "*It's Razzle-Dazzle Time!!*"

Arm in arm, they turned to face the minister who would link their lives together for eternity. Jerri blew a kiss to Sandy, her maid of honor, while a very elegantly dressed Mongo stood beside Mark, in his role of best man.

"Dearly Beloved," the minister intoned. "We are gathered here on Mallory Square to join *this* woman and *this* man into the gentle bonds of matrimony. If there is anyone present who objects to this union, let them speak now or forever hold their peace."

Mark and Jerri both turned to the people seated behind them with a mock expectant expression on their faces, which brought forth giggles from their audience.

Again the minister addressed the small crowd. He asked, "Who gives this woman to be married?"

Fred Rogers spoke up, before gently kissing Jerri on the cheek, "I — Daniel — and her--" he turned and indicated Miss Marty, "--*grandmother* — give... this woman." He then brushed a gentle kiss from Jerri's cheek, turned again, and took his seat next to Eddie's empty chair, close to his former employer.

"Life is," the minister began, "...*strange*. Can anyone contest that? I think not. But, while life is strange, it is also beautiful. And, if we look for it, we can find beauty in almost everything. Look around yourself, today. Mallory Square is host to some of the most beautiful people in the world. It is also host to some of the *strangest* people you'll ever see. But, one thing these vastly different people share when they visit Mallory Square at this time of the evening is *a smile...* a smile when they experience the glory and the splendor of God's art gallery." He paused, and took Jerri and Mark's hands in his.

"Now, these two young people come before you," he said, "declaring their love for each other. And they've chosen this special place to bind their lives together. Don't think for a moment, their choice is frivolous or silly. What better place to start a new life together and to commune with the vast love of God. A God who loves us *so* much, He wanted to give us a nighttime *kiss* of a beautiful sunset. And Jerri and Mark wanted to share this loving kiss with each and every one of you."

As the minister spoke, Jerri looked out to the horizon. The sun was falling to the water, back-lighting the colorful ketches, cruisers and sailboats that swept the bay every evening in celebration of the sunset. Beams of light shot out in every direction the moment the tip of the blazing sun touched the ocean.

For one brief second, a kaleidoscope of color danced across the water, and Jerri lightly touched Miss Marty's magical amethyst necklace, invoking the remembrance of Eddie and his beloved. She turned to Mark and lovingly smiled.

"A kiss for you," Mark whispered.

Jerri returned his whisper, "From this moment on... every evening — *every single time* I watch the sunset — I'll be kissing *you!*"

Jerri and Mark exchanged rings while the minister segued into a short sermon, but his nearly sing-song words were lost to Jerri as she gazed into the dark blue eyes of the man she loved. *This man... I once thought this man to be the brashest, rudest man to draw breath....* She fought to hold back tears of happiness. *And now I'm going to spend the rest of my life in his arms. The cards were right — and the psychic was very wise. And If I'm lucky — really, really lucky — we'll grow old together — he and I.*

" — now pronounce them man and wife."

A thrill ran through her heart as she heard the minister end his miniature sermon.

"Mark? You may kiss your bride. Of course, to remain politically correct... Jerri... *you*," the minister grinned, "may kiss your husband." He raised his hands over both their heads and proclaimed: "*I give you, Mr. Mark Pendragon and Mrs. Jerri Delaney-Pendragon!*" The crowd burst into applause as Jerri lost herself to their first kiss as man and wife.

Reluctantly ending the kiss, Mark bent to her ear and whispered, "*Wow!* What a kiss... from an old married lady."

Jerri grinned. "And here I was just thinking," she said, "what a neat old married man *you'll* be some day." Her teasing gained her another lingering kiss from her new husband.

"No fair!" Mongo scolded. "I *distinctly* heard the minister say *one* kiss! Besides, we gotta set this party *swingin'!* Jerri? You and Mark go take the floor for the first dance."

The lavender-dressed clown signaled the band and, by Jerri's request, they struck up a Calypso version of Jimmy Buffett's humorous ballad 'Mermaid in the Night'.

Jerri smiled as she thought of the song, a saga about a fisherman relaxing on a 'sandy beach' who snags the 'catch of the day'. *So true,* she smiled to herself. *So... so true.* Glancing up into her new husband's eyes, she smiled again. *What a catch!* She melted into his arms for a greedy third kiss.

"Pendragon!" The lavender tuxedo-wearing clown lowered his voice into a conspiratorial tone. "I gotta warn ya — I'm cuttin' in after this dance. I've been waitin' for this day a long time comin'." He wiggled his eyebrows and tapped an imaginary cigar, in a dead-on Groucho Marx impersonation.

Mark laughed and led Jerri out into the middle of the Square, under a canopy of lavender and white lights, which twinkled in the gathering darkness. There, he once more took her into his arms and they fell into the rhythm of the pleasant tune. They swayed in time to the soft exotic music, while half way through the song, their guests paired off to join them on the dance floor.

Jerri glanced over at Mongo and Sandy, happy in each other's arms, while Daniel danced with Miss Marty. Mark's sister Marissa danced with the very smitten doctor, and Cory danced with the motherly Conchita.

"Look over there," Mark mused. "What do you make of that?" A blushing Sloan Richardson bowed and offered his arm to Phyllis.

Jerri giggled. "Looks like a certain D.E.A. agent is straying into dangerous waters." She quipped. "Fins to the left, fins to the right — and he's the *only bait in town....*"

"*What?*"

She giggled again. "Never mind," she smiled, shook her head and gave Mark a quick kiss. "I'll have to give you some long overdue Parrothead lessons." They swirled with the music, stepping over the patterned stone pavement.

"I'm game for any class *you're* teaching," he whispered and returned the kiss.

As they danced their first dance as man and wife, Jerri sighed and dropped her head to Mark's chest, listening to the strong beating of his heart, knowing it beat only for her. The song ended — their first song as a married couple — and the happy pair indulged themselves in another kiss.

A tapping on his shoulder turned Mark around to find Mongo fiddling with his own lavender bow tie, preening like a peacock. "I *gave* you fair warning, Pendragon," growled the Moe Howard clone. "Now give up the girly."

Mark grinned. "Mongo, my man. Yes, you *did* give me warning." Mark nodded, passing Jerri's hand to the clownish magician. "I'll entrust my beautiful bride to you and only you — while I have a word or two with *your* lovely intended." He kissed Jerri, briefly, before joining Sandy across the dance floor.

Watching her new husband and her best friend begin the next dance, as the band played a steel-drum version of 'My Heart Will Go On', Jerri turned her attention to the man standing before her. "Wanna dance, Clown? Do ya feel lucky? Well, do ya, huh?"

She groused the words, trying her best to sound offended, but feeling her traitorous mouth pull up into a smile.

"Oh, Jerri, sweet-sweet-sweet Jerri," Mongo moaned and gently took her into his arms for a romantic waltz. "This is the happiest day of my life — so far. That is, until I marry my own darlin'. I've completed my mission. Your father would be proud."

"What's my *father* have to do with your '*mission*'?" Jerri demanded, stiffening in Mongo's embrace. "For that matter, why would *my* wedding be the happiest day of *your* life?" She stopped dancing and crossed her arms across her chest, tapping her foot to a different tune than the band was playing. Her words were sub-zero as they left her lips. "*You've got two minutes to explain yourself, Mongo.*"

"Wha... but... when...." Mongo stuttered, waving his hands animatedly in the air. "So... I... you see...."

"Are you gonna spill the beans or are you signaling a safe landing for incoming flights?"

"Okay." The clown-magician hung his head. "Okay, I'll come clean. My mission was to keep an eye on you. Before his death... in fact, the very week before he died... your father asked me to watch over you — *keep you from harm* — if anything should happen to him. When I heard of his death, I honored his wishes, and I — "

" — *booked after me any time you could,*" Jerri interrupted and finished Mongo's confession.

"Guilty as charged." Mongo hung his head again.

The tapping foot accelerated. Her nostrils flared and Jerri snorted steam. Mongo cringed. Dancing couples paused mid-step, watching the mini-drama unfolding next to them. Even the band took notice and the music died down to one anemic note. Everyone held their breath, wondering what the bride would do, though not knowing the reason for her apparent anger.

Suddenly, Jerri lunged at the clown, gaining a number of gasps from among the guests. Mark and Sandy exchanged horror-stricken glances, but exhaled along with the other guests, as they witnessed Jerri wrapping the big, blustery, lavender-dressed

Mongo in her arms.

"Oh, you beautiful... sweet... lovable... silly... soft-hearted... *clown!*" Jerri gushed, kissing him full on the mouth, while Mongo stiffened like a mannequin in her arms. She continued, "You're not a psycho-stalker after all!! *You're just my Fairy Godmother!!*"

Mongo's eyes flew open wide and he squealed: "*Sssssssssssandy!!! Help!* Save me from the crazy lady!!! *Sandy!!! Sssssssssssandy!!!*"

Shaking her head at the sight of her nearly six feet tall fiancé being terrorized by her petite friend, Sandy disengaged herself from Mark's arms. "Tsk, tsk, tsk," she scolded as she rescued Mongo from the arms of his attacker. "I can't take you anywhere! That's okay. Sandy will protect Mongo from the big-bad bride. Do you think you can stay outta trouble if I get you some punch?" She led the whimpering magician-comedian away toward the refreshment table.

Mark came up behind Jerri and placed both hands on her shoulders. "So," he huffed. "I leave my wife alone for just a moment, and she's Frenching clowns." He whispered in her ear, "Now, what am I supposed to make of *that?*"

"I'm a woman who craves adventure? And you should," she smiled and leaned back against his chest, "consider changing professions and *becoming* a clown? Not the right answer? How 'bout — *never again leave me alone for a moment?*"

His breath hot on her neck, Mark nibbled her ear and whispered, "I like that *last* suggestion...."

~oOo~

Epilogue

"And now, Ladies and Gentlemen — The Outlander Lounge is proud to present, in her premier comeback performance — *The Ah — Maze — Zing De-lan-eeeey!!!*" The emcee practically screamed the name.

Recorded rock music blasted from every corner of the lounge. A controlled center-stage pyrotechnic explosion preceded a lavender cloud of smoke, and Jerri stepped from the concealing purple-tinged mist, dressed in her custom designed shorty skirt. The specially made costume featured skin-toned illusion fabric with strategically placed lavender rhinestones. Jerri's eyes sparkled, rivaling the glitter of her new costume. Her hands held triumphantly above her head, she beamed a dazzling smile out at the audience; her eyes secretly searching the crowd for the faces of her loved ones.

Dressed in her trademark lavender chiffon, her precious amethyst amulet adorning the flattering filmy gown, Miss Marty reigned over her front row center table. She rested her right hand on the lavender necklace, and Jerri realized her friend was communing with her beloved Eddie. It was also apparent to Jerri, her 'adopted' grandmother had gathered three of her favorite men for her 'dates'.

Wearing lavender boutonnieres on their stylish tuxedo lapels, Sloan Richardson and Fred Rogers sat on either side of the jovial white-haired senior. Miss Marty's third date, wearing the third lavender boutonniere, was Jerri's own husband.

Mark's eyes spoke volumes to her, even at this distance, and she thought back to her wedding day... and of the fine-crafted

291

silver and amethyst merman ear-drape Marissa had given her on Mark's behalf. Almost as if Jerri could hear her words when Marissa had handed over the tiny heart-shaped box, her sister-in-law's voice came to her ears: *Mark asked me to give this to you. Wear this and remember your new family, Jerri. Wear this, and never forget the heritage you're marrying into, forevermore.*

I've got my own Lavender Magic, now, she told herself. Her heart soared, her eyes met Mark's again, and she tugged on her merman-adorned ear, 'Carol Burnett style'.

Conchita and Phyllis shared a table on the left-side wall. *They must've borrowed their gowns from Miss Marty,* Jerri mused. *I'll wager every woman wearing lavender in this room is a member of my new family.*

At a table to Jerri's right, Doctor Sims and Marissa Pendragon sat at a table for four. Sandy and Mongo held hands across the table, mirroring the happiness in their later-in-life engagement that their table mates, the young doctor and his secret mermaid, also very obviously enjoyed. From the stage, Jerri noticed how the two couples chattered with each other as if they'd been lifelong friends. The tall yellow drinks adorned with pineapple spears, orange slices and stemmed cherries sat virtually untouched, ignored in the excitement of Jerri's opening night.

Jerri smiled to herself with the knowledge that Miss Marty's Lavender Magic had worked its special miracle with the shy physician and the physical therapist's sister. Secret word from Mark was: his sister and the young doctor had grown so close, no one would be surprised if they announced their engagement soon. Jerri thought Marissa made a welcome addition to her new family.

This is the first time I've performed for my whole family, Jerri smiled to herself as the audience welcomed her to the stage with a thunderous applause. She bowed deeply and swept her hands stage right, indicating a tanned young man dressed in a rhinestone-sparkled lavender tuxedo costume. "Please welcome my handsome assistant — *Cory Sebastian!*" Jerri clapped her hands, leading the audience into drawing Miss Marty's adopted son onto the stage.

Cory stepped into the act as if he'd been performing all of his life, instead of mere weeks. The Purple Plantation's pool-boy had proven himself to be a natural, learning Jerri's complete act on the weekends and holidays from school.

Jerri and her teen-aged assistant began a hyper-kinetic performance. They started off with the simplest illusions, saving the most difficult for the finale. First, Jerri suspended a melon-sized silver ball in midair above her hands, causing it to dance and swirl around the stage, while Cory occasionally stepped in, taking control of the shiny orb. The simple illusion trick brought forth 'oohs' and 'ahhs' from the crowd. The lavender-costumed pair performed many smaller sleight of hand tricks, pleasing the audience with their graceful expertise.

The next elaborate trick involved a Chinese enameled box, a foot square. Jerri released the front panel, revealing the interior to be empty, a circular opening at the bottom of the intricately painted black and red prop. "Cory has bravely volunteered to test this next illusion." Jerri turned to a couple sitting near the stage and confided, "Did I mention Cory is the *third* assistant I've had this year? Yeah... I have the worst luck with assistants. *I keep losing them.*"

Cory shot Jerri a concerned glance.

"Problem, Cory?" she asked. He whispered into her ear. "What's that? What *became* of my previous assistants?" He whispered into her ear again. "Oh, don't give it another thought!" Jerri brushed him off and said, "No need to worry your pretty little head about it. When I *said* I *lost* my last three assistants, I simply meant I *misplaced* them... yeah — yeah, that's my story! That's my story and I'm sticking to it!" Cory reacted with broad animated skepticism, and the crowd roared their laughter.

With an exaggerated flourish, Jerri settled the wooden illusion box over Cory's head. She closed the decorated cover over her young assistant's face. The tempo of the background music picked up, as Jerri held a long flaming torch aloft over her own head. Suddenly, the music reached a dramatic crescendo, and she plunged the fiery rod through the box, the still burning tip exiting the other side of Cory's small, head-sized prison.

Apparently sure the illusionist had cruelly skewered her young assistant, the gasps and cries of astonishment from the audience delighted her. She knew she had the crowd on the edge of their seats.

Yanking the flaming torch from the box, she flung open the head-chest's tiny door, revealing the magic prop's empty interior. Cory's head had disappeared from his shoulders! Jerri feigned shock and surprise, while Cory, using his hands and body, mimed horror, finding himself headless. The pleased audience exploded in thunderous applause.

"Thank you, Ladies and Gentlemen," she took a deep bow, "and *that* concludes this night's performance — "

Cory interrupted Jerri by frantically tapping her shoulder, gaining her attention, then crossing his arms in irritation while tapping his foot impatiently.

"Yes, Cory?" Jerri asked sweetly. "Is there a problem?"

He silently indicated his headless state.

Jerri slapped her forehead. "Of course! How forgetful of me! I'd forget my head if it wasn't attached...." She mugged for the audience. "Fortunately for me — " she ran her fingers over her neck, " — *it is!*" The crowd erupted in laughter. Cory threw up his hands in exasperation and made to walk off the stage.

Jerri grabbed his shoulder and stopped him. She said, "Don't go away mad! No need to lose your head!" Cory threw up his hands again.

She addressed the crowd, "Whadda ya say, Ladies and Gentlemen? Shall I give him back his head?" The audience applauded. "Yes..." she teased. "*Perhaps* I should return his head. After all, it's getting harder and harder to come up with *alibis* — I mean, it's getting harder to come up with *new assistants.*"

Again, Jerri closed the tiny door on the head-chest. She made a big production of grabbing up a cheap glitter-covered star-topped wand, whacking the top of the magic prop and loudly exclaiming: "Abra-Cadabra-Bibbity-Bobbity-Boo!" The audience laughed at her absurd antics.

Throwing open the Chinese enameled box, Jerri revealed a triumphant Cory, his head safely returned to his shoulders. She removed the shiny wooden container from Cory's shoulders and carefully placed it on a side table before joining her assistant in a deep and well-received bow.

Daddy? How's THAT for Razzle-Dazzle? She smiled to herself, triumphantly clutching Cory's hand. *I believe I'm finally The Amazing Delaney. Thank you, Daddy. Thank you for giving me my wings. Thank you for giving me the magic.*

The crowd's wild applause carried the pair into the next illusion. Cory presented her with leg shackles, much like the handcuffs that weeks before had bound her underwater. For good measure, before locking the cuffs around her ankles, Cory helped her into a snow white straightjacket. After strapping all the jacket's latches, and snapping the cuffs and chains around Jerri's feet, Cory pulled a white linen bag over her head.

Assuring the audience the magician was secure in her restraints, he carried Jerri to a dark antique wooden trunk. Placing her inside the trunk, Cory closed the lid and fastened chains from the bottom over the top, like he was tying a bow around a massive square present. Holding a large padlock over his head, he demonstrated the solidity of the metal lock before latching the four chains together, securely trapping Jerri in the trunk. He called for a plush curtain to be raised from the floor, surrounding the trunk. Seconds after the rising curtain reached the ceiling, an explosion sounded, bringing down the shield to reveal a billowing lavender cloud, an open trunk, and Jerri holding the straight-jacket aloft for all to see. The audience cheered wildly.

Jerri cried, "Thank you, Ladies and Gentlemen! Now for our final illusion, I need a volunteer from the audience. I need a big strong man. A big strong man who's not afraid of danger. Do I have any takers?" Eager hands went up in the audience, it appeared many men hoped for a chance to join Jerri on stage.

She laughed. "Unfortunately, I need only *one* volunteer." She stepped to the center of the stage, and pointed to Miss Marty's table. "Sir?" She indicated agent Fred Rogers.

"You're not scared of a little danger, are you?" The formerly silent D.E.A. agent smiled and shook his head. "Please join me for the final illusion." She reached out her hands to welcome him onto the stage. "What beautiful *blond* hair you have. *Remember that*, Ladies and Gentlemen. There'll be a pop-quiz later," she teased.

"Well — aren't you gorgeous!" She greeted her friend as if she'd never met him before. "Would you tell us your name?" Jerri asked. "It makes it *so* much easier to contact the next of kin."

Fred laughed along with the audience. "Daniel," he smiled, "my name is Daniel." He winked toward a beaming Miss Marty. His speech nearly flawless now, he'd recently returned to part-time government duties.

"Daniel," Jerri grinned, as she led her blond friend to a tall black enameled box that Cory pushed center-stage. "Please be so good as to step into this empty cabinet." She helped the young agent into the six foot tall magical illusion prop, then turned to the lighting booth and asked, "And, may we please have the lights turned down low? For the more fainthearted members of our audience — the dim lights hide the... *blood*."

Cory helped Jerri fasten Daniel inside the tall bamboo-side-paneled rectangle. After Cory secured the third lock across the front, Jerri knocked on the shiny black enameled door and said, "Oh, yeah! Daniel? I forgot to tell you something. The name of this last illusion is the *Dance of the Seven Deadly Swords*." Almost immediately, loud banging noises came from inside the box.

"Let me out!!" Daniel's frantic screams came from the locked cabinet. "Let me out! Not swords! No, no, no! *No — not swords!!*"

"What's that?" Jerri put her ear to the door and feigned concern. "Are you trying to tell me something? Speak up, man! I can't hear you!" The banging grew louder. "Cory? Bring me my swords. We've got a dance to perform!" The pyrotechnic explosions erupted on either side of the stage and the rock music provided a revved-up tempo for Jerri and Cory's carefully choreographed presentation.

First, Cory handed the petite magician a black-handled sword and Jerri dramatically sliced a cucumber with the long weapon to prove its sharpness. Then, without missing a beat, she stabbed the sword through the side of the cabinet. Just as the sword tip exited the opposite side of the bamboo-paneled box, a gut-wrenching scream emanated from inside the locked container.

"Did you hear something?" Jerri asked Cory. Her young assistant shook his head and threw his hands up in confusion. "No matter," she chuckled. "I have six more swords. I hate to waste them."

Jerri and Cory danced from one side of the tall box to the other, spinning the illusion prop around between them. At one point, they staged a mock sword fight; a fluid ballet of slashing swords.

Swords number two through six pierced the cabinet without further comment from Daniel. As the final sword found its mark, lavender explosions again clouded the stage. "And, now," Jerri announced, "for the *messy* — I mean — *hard* part of the *Dance of the Seven Deadly Swords*. I must remove them. Cory? Do we have the paramedics standing by?"

Cory nodded.

"Good!" she cried. "Let's do it! *Razzle-Dazzle!!*" She pulled the swords out one at a time, each one stained blood-red. The final sword literally dripped blood. As Jerri held the gruesome weapon aloft, the audience gasped. Cory unlocked the triple locks of the cabinet to allow Jerri's access.

She opened the cabinet's door to the audience's expectation of the mortally wounded, golden-haired, Daniel. But, instead of finding a bloody corpse sagging against the back of the box, a man knelt on one knee. Dark wavy locks cascaded to his shoulders, his head bowed as if in reverent meditation. The appreciative 'oohs' and 'ahhs' of the crowd mingled with Jerri's own sigh of satisfaction.

The man with the obsidian hair, black as onyx, raised eyes

so blue they rivaled the most colorful coral. His dark-shrouded gaze met Jerri's and held her eyes for century-long seconds. *Daddy, I've come full circle,* she thought. *You always taught me to know my own mind... to not believe I needed a man to complete me, because I'm a whole person unto myself. But, Daddy... because I AM my own person, I now know my heart. And, I know now I want to give myself completely and eternally to this man... this wonderful... magical... man.*

"Ladies and Gentlemen," Jerri announced. "I'm thrilled to introduce my new husband. Mark Pendragon. A man who is amazing in his own way." She reached out a hand to bring Mark to his feet. He stood beside her, outside the opened illusion prop. Jerri gazed into his eyes again as she continued her introduction. "A special man, who taught me that true love doesn't have to be confining or stifling. And, above all, with the help of some wonderful new friends...."

She turned to Miss Marty sitting beside Daniel, who'd returned to his seat under the cover of darkness. Jerri winked and pulled on her ear, again. "He taught me that true love is truly eternal. And truly *magical.*"

-End-

ABOUT THE AUTHOR:

Daughter of a Sunday School teacher and a prankster, Ginny grew up in the best of both worlds. The jokes flowed from her father, but were tempered by weekly Bible lessons (bi-weekly, daily or whenever the Holy-Muse struck her mother). She's written various screenplays (optioned), short stories and novels. In her life, she's peddled Hallmark cards, hawked books, sold craft supplies and worked at a pot factory (Louisville Stoneware). While she didn't inhale the wares, she did paint them. A long-time member of the Southern Indiana Writers Group, Ginny's work appears in their anthologies:

http://southernindianawriters.com/

"Keys of Illusion" reflects Ginny's love of the Florida Keys, scuba diving, eccentric billionaires, magical illusion, the color lavender and All-Things-Mermaid. Find Ginny's blog "Mermaid Muses" here:

http://themermaidmuses.wordpress.com/

"The Florida Keys — A gift you give your soul."